D0381989

IMPRUDENCE
THE CUSTARD PROTOCOL: BOOK TWO

By GAIL CARRIGER

The Parasol Protectorate
Soulless
Changeless
Blameless
Heartless
Timeless

The Custard Protocol
Prudence
Imprudence

The Parasol Protectorate Manga
Soulless: The Manga, Vol. 1
Soulless: The Manga, Vol. 2
Soulless: The Manga, Vol. 3

The Finishing School
Etiquette and Espionage
Curtsies and Conspiracies
Waistcoats and Weaponry
Manners and Muting

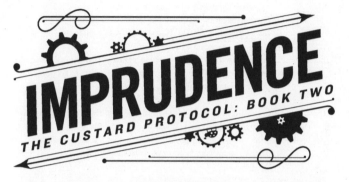

IMPRUDENCE

THE CUSTARD PROTOCOL: BOOK TWO

GAIL CARRIGER

orbit

www.orbitbooks.net

Copyright © 2016 by Tofa Borregard

Cover design by Lauren Panepinto
Type design by Chad Roberts
Cover illustration by Don Sipley/Michael Roberts
Cover copyright © 2016 by Hachette Book Group, Inc.

Orbit
Hachette Book Group
1290 Avenue of the Americas
New York, NY 10104
orbitbooks.net

Simultaneously published in Great Britain and in the U.S. by Orbit in 2016
First Edition: July 2016

Orbit is an imprint of Hachette Book Group.
The Orbit name and logo are trademarks of Little, Brown Book Group Limited.

The publisher is not responsible for websites (or their content)
that are not owned by the publisher.

The Hachette Speakers Bureau provides a wide range of authors for speaking events. To find out more, go to www.hachettespeakersbureau.com or call (866) 376-6591.

Library of Congress Control Number: 2016936829

ISBNs: 978-0-316-21221-2 (hardcover), 978-0-316-54644-7 (Barnes and Noble signed edition), 978-0-316-21219-9 (ebook)

Printed in the United States of America

RRD-C

10 9 8 7 6 5 4 3 2 1

CHAPTER
ONE

In Which Queen Victoria Is Not Amused

"We are not pleased, young lady. Not pleased at all."

Despite the acute sensation of being crushed under a hot fruitcake of embarrassment, Rue was impressed by Queen Victoria's ability to eviscerate in so few words. The Empress of India was short in stature, wide in girth, and wore a black silk dress positively drowning in ball fringe. She looked like an extraordinarily angry hassock. To the best of her knowledge, Rue had never before been scolded by a footstool.

"Imagine circumventing the Crown's authority in such a manner. Did we grant you any kind of diplomatic autonomy? No, we most certainly did not!"

Rue hadn't enough self-preservation to keep her mouth shut at that. "But you conferred sundowner status upon me. If a lady can kill supernaturals under legal sanction, isn't that a kind of diplomatic autonomy?"

Primrose, had she been present, would have fainted at the very idea of arguing with the Queen of England. But Rue was accustomed to quarrelling with powerful people. To be fair, when the most powerful woman on the planet looked like a hassock, it made quarrelling easier.

Said hassock, however, was having none of it. "Which was

intended for you to clean up a supernatural mess, not cause more of one."

Rue thought that unfair. After all, she had prevented a major military action and saved a number of lives. Admittedly, she had sacrificed a great deal of tea. Unfortunately, if past record was anything to go on, Queen Victoria was a bloodthirsty little thing. She probably wouldn't have cared about the lives and was more upset over the tea.

The queen settled into her scolding. "So you establish an illegal concordance between the Shadow Council and a group of vagrant weremonkeys without any kind of by-your-leave? What sort of precedent does that set? A clandestine agreement between disparate groups of supernatural creatures – no government sanction, no proper treaty, no taxation! Young lady, may we remind you, we have *ambassadors* for this kind of thing, not" – Queen Victoria sputtered to a pause, taking in Rue's outfit with a critical eye – "round velveteen schoolgirls!"

Rue had thought her brown velvet and gold striped visiting dress most proper for a royal summons. It was sombre in coloration and striped. Queen Victoria was reputed to be fond of stripes. Or was that plaid?

But the "round" stung. Rue thought that insult quite ripe when coming from the queen, who was very round indeed. By comparison, Rue felt she was only *moderately* round.

"We are most seriously displeased," ranted her high-and-mighty roundness.

"I beg your pardon, Your Majesty." Rue resorted to placations.

Fortunately for Rue, Queen Victoria elected not to clap her in irons. Instead she took a more direct course. "We hereby strip you of sundowner status."

Rue swallowed her objection. *I didn't even get to use it properly!* "Yes, Your Majesty."

"*And* all other legal protections and rights previously granted unto you."

Rue frowned. What other protections had she enjoyed? And

why had she needed them? She opened her mouth to ask and then shut it at a glare from her most royal of majesties.

"Now remove yourself from our presence, and if you know what's good for you, avoid royal notice for the foreseeable future."

Rue backed away a few steps, dropped a deep curtsey, and scuttled to the door.

She heard the queen say to one of her hovering advisers, "I did hope she would turn out more stable than her parents."

To which the gentleman answered, "A girl who can change into any supernatural creature she touches? Stability was never likely a companion personality trait."

"Well, she's no longer our concern." The queen sounded almost smug.

Rue straightened her back, standing as tall as her – round! – frame would allow and bit the inside of her cheek so as not to cry. It was one thing to be told off by a queen, quite another when some court nobody took against her.

Rue strode out of the palace in high dudgeon. Her long skirts swished. There was a shocking amount of leg outline visible with each step because she eschewed the requisite number of underskirts – even when visiting the queen. Society condemned this as a modern affectation brought about by her travels abroad, but Rue simply found it easier to change shape when she hadn't an overabundance of underthings.

She paused outside the gates, breathing the night air in angry pants like a perturbed bellows. It was a crisp evening, the gibbous moon illuminating a busy street. London was awake and bustling, for while the season was over, the supernatural set still carried the torch.

Dama's carriage was waiting for her. Her father had insisted she travel to the palace in style, although his aesthetic – one of gilt and ribbons and plush velvets – was not to Rue's particular taste. Dama was peeved with her over the loss of his tea but refused to let that affect standards in conveyance arrangements.

"Don't trouble yourself, Winkle." Rue waved off the drone on the driving box when he made to hop down and help her inside. She swung herself up easily; fewer skirts and a lack of corset improved one's mobility in a marked manner.

Winkle made an affronted noise but it was too late to insist. He whipped the horses up and they set forth at a brisk clip.

Inside the cab, Rue slouched into her lace collar, feeling sorry for herself.

Sooner than they ought, Winkle drew the carriage to a halt. There was no way they had traversed all of Mayfair. Rue leaned dangerously far out the window and craned her neck to see the box. There was some kind of commotion going on in the middle of Oxford Circus near the recently reopened Claret's.

"Turn back and go around, Winkle, do."

"Everyone seems to have the same idea, miss."

There was quite the ruckus surrounding them. Conveyances of all types were circling and trapping each other at odd angles as they jockeyed for position.

"Has there been an accident? Should I get out and see?"

Winkle had a much superior vantage point. "I don't think that particularly wise, miss."

Which, naturally, caused Rue to pop open the carriage door and swing down.

The first thing she noticed was that there was a great deal of yipping and some growling. Someone was also singing a bawdy song, off-key, at the top of his not-inconsiderable lungs.

"What the devil?"

Rue pushed through the confused mess of carriages, steam-powered Coccinellidae, monowheels, and assorted bicycles. She then forced her way to the front of a jeering crowd. It surrounded the dramatically carved marble entryway of Claret's Gentleman's Club, out the mahogany door from which oozed a stumbling mass of masculine rabble composed of several officers of Her Royal Majesty's service, a handful of tight-trouser-wearing thespians, and one or two large dogs in top hats and cravats.

Ah, not dogs, wolves.

There were only eleven members of Paw's werewolf pack, but as they tended to be rather large dramatic specimens, there always *seemed* to be more of them than there actually were.

Most of them were now in front of her and, much to Rue's horror, at their cups. Now, far be it for Rue to object on principle to the consumption of the divine pip: even werewolves should be allowed a snootful on occasion. No, it was the fact that, ordinarily, werewolves did not get soused in the way of mortal men. They required a great deal of formaldehyde, of the type used to embalm human remains, not surprising since they were technically undead. Yet the pack before her was so very juicy that they had taken to, and there was no nicer way of putting it – *troubling* a group of beautiful and beautifully dressed ladies and gentlemen.

The beautiful group was not amused by this attention. There was something to their quick movements and very high collars that spoke of training and the covering of neck bites.

Vampire drones.

These were not the highly dressed pinks of the type her dear Dama collected. These drones must belong to one of the London hive queens.

One of the werewolves was harrying them, darting in and out like a sheepdog, only bigger and meaner. It had to be Channing; none of the others had a pure white coat. He was a beautiful wolf, if not very friendly with teeth bared and tail lashing.

"What in heaven's name is going on?" Rue demanded of no one in particular.

Channing ignored her.

One of the other uncles, Rafe, still in human form, looked up. "Infant! What are you doing here? No place for a chit."

Rue planted her hands on her hips. "You are no longer *inside* your club, you do realise? This is a respectable thoroughfare and I'm perfectly within my rights to be— Wait a moment. Stop distracting me. What is wrong with the pack? *Corned beef, the lot of you.* Oh, do stop it, Uncle Channing! You can't go around growling at someone's drones in public. It's not done."

They ignored her. Although Hemming, who made for a handsome wolf with his black and gold markings on creamy white, lurched in her direction – possibly operating under some latent need to protect.

Rue took that as permission and pulled off her gloves.

From behind her, Winkle said, "Miss, I don't think—" but it was too late.

Rue buried her hand in Hemming's thick coat, seeking his skin. That was all it took. There she went, bones breaking and re-forming, eyesight and hearing shifting, sense of smell increasing. Rue the brindled wolf stood among the tatters of a lovely striped gold and brown velvet visiting dress. And Hemming lay quite naked and somewhat less handsome as a confused man.

Winkle scooped up Rue's dress and draped it over the now-mortal werewolf. The drone was quite brainy enough to know, at this juncture, there was no way he could safely interfere.

Rue leapt to protect the frightened huddle of drones. In actuality, they weren't *that* pathetic, but she liked to think of herself as coming to the heroic defence of the innocent.

Hackles up, she bared her teeth at Uncle Channing, backing him away, challenging him.

Channing was not the kind of wolf to resist a challenge. As a major in the British Army, there had even been several duels, much more messy than a wolf brawl. Duels were illegal and had to be stuffed under carpets at great expense to avoid scandal. Channing had a vast collection of lumpy carpets. Rue usually allowed him some leeway because he was obviously a wounded soul of some sullen Shakespearian ilk, plus he wore angry petulance so beautifully. But tonight he was drunk, and she wasn't going to put up with any of his nonsense.

Uncle Channing, unfortunately, was so far gone into the pickle that he either didn't care or didn't recognise that Rue was Rue and not some male werewolf *actually* challenging him.

He growled and crouched to leap.

Rue was loosely aware that the drones had taken Uncle

Channing's distraction as an opportunity to get away but that other pack members were corralling them. It wasn't only Uncle Channing acting irrationally; it was the entire pack. Even Uncle Bluebutton who was *practically* civilised – he owned a smoking jacket and everything – was participating.

What had gotten into them? Certainly Rue noticed that the pack was generally more rowdy since she returned from India, but she hadn't thought it would come to brawling in the street. Where was their restraint? Where was Paw? Paw was Alpha and he was supposed to have them under control. This was outrageous! They should all be disciplined. Paw was always one for a good fight. He was positively cheerful about it. When Dama and Mother weren't looking, he even encouraged Rue to train with the pack.

Which is how Rue knew to fluff up her ruff in an attempt to look bigger. If someone had to fight for their sobriety, she would do what must be done.

Look at me, she thought. *I'm joining the Teatotal Abstinence Society.*

Uncle Channing tensed.

Rue, never one to back down from a challenge either, reared up. She was under no delusion as to her chances. Uncle Channing was the pack Gamma, not to mention a professional soldier. He was a tall rangy fellow who made for a big rangy wolf, but any leanness was deceptive, as in both forms he was composed mainly of muscle. Rue, on the other hand, made a tough-looking scrappy sort of wolf, but she wasn't big, vicious, or muscly. This was not going to be a fair fight. But she might distract the pack long enough for the drones to get away.

Uncle Channing leapt, teeth bared.

And was knocked out of the way by another wolf, slighter than Channing, with dark brown colouring and blood-red chest fur.

Uncle Rabiffano!

Uncle Rabiffano was – technically – pack Beta, although he

never much acted like it physically. He ran a very well-regarded hat shop not too far down the street from Claret's.

Rue had never seen Rabiffano fight. In fact, if anyone asked, she would have said he couldn't. He was more the type to shame a fellow into doing what he wanted. A few slow blinks of disapproval from those sad eyes and perhaps a cutting remark, and nearly any werewolf would do as Uncle Rabiffano suggested, even Paw.

However, it turned out he *could* fight.

He might be smaller than Uncle Channing, but he was also sober, and quick. Really, *very* quick!

Rue sat back on her haunches in shock, watching as the most urbane and sweet-natured of her uncles turned into a whirling dervish of teeth and claws.

Channing, surprised by the attack and by its ferocity, whined and whimpered as his tender nose and ears were savaged. He wobbled to his side and then flopped on his back, presenting his stomach as quickly as possible.

Rabiffano took this as his due with one final nip of reproach.

Channing subdued, the oxblood wolf turned his angry yellow glare on the rest of the pack.

The ones sober enough to have realised what had just happened were already backing away from the drones. Hemming, whose form Rue had stolen, was sitting at Winkle's feet, wrapped in her striped dress like a bathing towel and looking thoroughly ashamed. Channing remained lying on his back. Which, given Rabiffano's expression of annoyance, was a good decision.

Two of the pack, Ulric and Quinn, in human form, were too far gone on the formaldehyde. Oblivious to the fight, they were actually pushing at the drones – male ones, thank heavens; at least they weren't so stupid as to shove a lady. But still . . . pushing . . . in public!

Rabiffano attacked them. He leapt against Ulric, teeth going for his neck and fortunately getting only shoulder. He took a bite out of the meaty part of the man's upper arm, ruining Ulric's coat and leaving him surprised and bloody, lying in the street.

Then Rabiffano went for Quinn. The simpleton met him head-on, without bothering to shift. Rabiffano sliced for the man's face. When Quinn flinched away, showing his neck in sudden realisation of who had attacked, Rabiffano veered off, only to chomp Quinn's thigh. Again he was gnawing at a meaty part that wouldn't cause any real damage.

It must hurt Rabiffano terribly to have to enact justice. Not only because he liked his fellow pack members, but also because he disliked the wanton destruction of perfectly good clothing. It was Uncle Rabiffano, after all, who took most of the pack shopping.

He's disciplining them, Rue realised. *But that's Paw's job!* Except Paw wasn't there. She looked around, hoping to see her father's massive brindled form barrelling through the crowd, but nothing disturbed the fascinated onlookers.

The whole uncouth business had taken only a few minutes, but it was a scandal so outrageous it could not possibly be kept secret. The entire London Pack had just behaved very badly indeed, and their Alpha was missing. The morning papers were going to make mincemeat out of progressive integration policies.

On the bright side, Rue thought, *my transgressions will be forgotten while the three parentals deal with this mess. That's something.*

Nevertheless, she couldn't suppress her fear. This was the London Pack, the tamest werewolves in the country. They didn't drink, certainly not in public! Something must be very wrong for them to be so out of control. Rue had the horrible feeling it was to do with Paw. All those rumours she had tried not to hear, to deny. All those pitying looks.

She shook herself like a wet dog. *No! He's fine, simply getting a little absentminded in his old age.*

It was only a matter of time before BUR appeared with the Staking Constabulary in tow. Rue would rather not be in wolf form when they did so. Supernatural creatures may be out in society but they weren't permitted to be untidy about it. Reports would need to be filed. Uncle Rabiffano would have to explain everything. The others were clearly not capable of coherent speech. Rue thought it best – given Queen Victoria's oh-so-recent admonition to stay out of trouble – that she make herself scarce.

She nodded to Rabiffano, who was circulating, keeping a careful eye on the remaining pack. He inclined his head in response. Then, tail high, decorum paramount, Rue relieved Uncle Hemming of her gown, leaving him bare. His dignity didn't concern her. With a toss of her head, she flicked the dress to drape over her back so as to drag as little as possible. Holding it carefully with her teeth, she trotted towards Dama's carriage.

Winkle, shaking his head, followed.

Ten minutes of manoeuvring later, Winkle managed to extract them from the crush, by which point BUR had arrived and hustled all those involved back inside Claret's for questioning. The spectacle was over.

Once they were far enough out, Rue's tether to Uncle Hemming snapped and her human form returned. She pulled the striped dress back on. It was a little worse for its werewolf encounter, but then wasn't everyone?

She bit her lip and fretted. Paw hadn't turned up at all, not even with BUR. Was he sick? Missing? Dead? Well, more dead than normal? She would not let herself think that he was losing control. Missing or sick would be preferable.

"Winkle, please hurry," she yelled out of the window. "I do believe something awful may have happened to one of my parents."

Rue lived with her adoptive father, Lord Akeldama. Dama was many things: vampire, rove, potentate, fashion icon, and nobbiest of the nobs. He ruled over a house of impeccable taste and harmonious design replete with assorted stunning works of art, scintillating conversation, and beautiful young men. Rue appreciated his skill, and mostly bowed to his authority, although as he was no longer her legal guardian so she did not technically have to.

Her blood parents, Lord and Lady Maccon, and their werewolf pack lived in the townhouse adjacent. It was only as tasteful as Uncle Rabiffano could impose, otherwise being characterised by dark wood, practical accoutrements, and the general aura of a bachelor residence over which Lady Maccon wafted like a hen in full squawk.

The two residences were connected via a walkway hidden behind a large holly tree. Rue had found it a fun, if wildly erratic upbringing, for three more different parents one could never find than Dama, Paw, and Mother. Nothing was ever agreed upon, except teatime. Rue adored her Paw, who was a big softy and always let her have her way with only token protestations. She respected her Dama, in whom love was tempered by razor wit and a strict adherence to etiquette. But she was in awe of her mother. Given Rue's metanatural abilities, one might have expected this. For while Rue could steal werewolf form from Paw and vampire form from Dama, Alexia Maccon could cancel both out. Only Rue's soulless mother could put a stopper in all her fun. And usually did.

Lady Maccon was *difficult*. She couldn't be managed or charmed. She wouldn't be moved once she made up her mind. She was as tough as old boot leather and as inevitable as clotted cream when scones were in the offing.

So it was with real fear that Rue overheard her indomitable mother in conversation with Dama sounding *upset*.

"He won't listen to me. That in and of itself isn't unusual, but this has gone on far too long. I'm worried he may be beyond saving. It's past time the plan was enacted. We need to leave. Soon. Have you heard from India at all? Is he coming home?"

"Really, my dove, why would you think I know anything about *him*? Why don't you ask your husband's Beta?"

Rue paused in the hallway, ears perked. *Uncle Rabiffano?
What has he to do with anything? He seems the only one able to control
himself these days.*

"My dear Akeldama. This is serious." Her mother sounded
almost cross with the vampire, yet he was one of her favourite
people.

"My darlingest of Alexias, I am *never* serious. I resent the
implication that I should be."

"Not even about love?"

"What do you take me for – *sentimental*? Wait, before you
continue on at me, I do believe we have an audience." Dama
opened the door and tilted his head at his daughter. "Good
evening, Puggle. What have you been up to? Your gown looks
as if it has been dragged through the streets by a dog."

"You aren't far off, actually. Is that Mother? May I speak to
her?"

Dama quirked an eyebrow over the edge of his monocle. His
movements were always precise – calculated. "Mmmm, you
know I'd rather not be involved in one of those *conversations*. But
if you insist, come in. You're sure you won't change first?"

"It is rather urgent."

Lord Akeldama waved her in. Tonight he was dressed
sombrely, for him, in teal and cream with a gold monocle and
gold rings on all of his fingers. His hands sparkled as he gestured
for her to sit.

Lady Alexia Maccon was taking tea, nose up and commanding in one of the wingback chairs. She didn't rise as her daughter
entered the room, as it was, after all, for Rue to go to her.

Rue did so, delivering a polite peck on the cheek and then
sitting opposite on the settee.

Dama remained standing, leaning with a studied casualness
on the back of one of the other chairs.

Rue's mother did not demure. "Infant, please tell me you
didn't look like this when you saw the queen? Your hair is down.
And the state of your gown defies comment."

"Apparently not, as both you and Dama have now commented."

Lady Maccon narrowed her eyes.

"Mother, really. What do you take me for – a harridan? No, don't answer that. I assure you, I was perfectly respectable during my audience with the queen. You may ask Winkle for confirmation. Where is Winkle anyway?" But Winkle had squeaked off the moment he heard Lady Maccon's voice. He, like all the drones and most of the pack, knew never to come between Lady Maccon and her daughter when there were *incidents to explain.* The ladies tended to engage in verbal skirmishing that became semantic battles in which bystanders were skewered.

Dama's expression said he wished to vanish as well. But this was his house, and he was host, and twenty years of intimacy and shared familial responsibility were not enough to cause him to abandon a guest in his drawing room, not even when his daughter was there to entertain. Standards *must* be upheld.

"Tea, Puggle?" He came around to pour her a cup. It was a rhetorical question. As far as Rue was concerned, the answer to the great question of life, "Tea?" was always "Yes." And Dama was perfectly well aware of this character trait.

Rue sipped the tea gratefully, mustering her courage and attempting to frame her worries about the pack in a manner that would offend her mother least. Meanwhile, she withstood Lady Maccon's opening tactics: a series of sharp, fast questions on her visit with Queen Victoria. *If Mother has the wherewithal to be concerned about that, then there can't possibly be anything seriously wrong with Paw. Can there?*

"Oh, Mother, you should be perfectly pleased with everything. Queen Victoria was utterly beastly, took me to task for all the things both you and Dama already reprimanded me for. Said something about rescinding my legal protections and rights."

Mother and Dama exchanged a look.

"Majority?" queried her mother. "The government *and* the vampires?"

"Just so." Dama did not look as surprised.

Rue only just stopped herself from foot stamping. "I *hate* it when you two do that!"

Lady Maccon ignored her daughter and added, to the vampire, "We have to assume we've done enough training. It's more than I had."

"Mmmm," was all the vampire said, and then to Rue, "Go on, precious dove, what else?"

Rue glared at them but said, since they would find out at the Shadow Council meeting later that week anyway, "She also took away my sundowner status, which I call most unfair. I never even got to kill anybody, not really."

"Sometimes you remind me so much of your father." Lady Maccon sniffed. "Violent leanings. Can't have been my doing." She chose to ignore the fact that she had, in her younger days, a well-deserved reputation for biffing people with her parasol.

Rue chose to ignore this in turn, jumping on the opening her mother had inadvertently given her. "Speaking of Paw, where is he this evening?"

Lady Maccon was taken aback. Rue generally showed little interest in the nightly duties of her parents. All three of them were heavily involved in secret government work, so they preferred it this way.

"With BUR, I suppose. I didn't ask. Why do you want to know?"

"He's not with BUR, or I would have seen him."

"Oh? Was BUR called in to your meeting with the queen?" Lady Maccon's voice went dangerous.

"No. I was no threat. Do give me some credit. They were called to deal with the pack. There was an incident at Claret's. You haven't heard?"

Lady Maccon looked very tired. "What did they do now?"

Lord Akeldama removed his monocle and began to clean it carefully with a silk handkerchief. This was, Rue knew from experience, him trying to hide how interested he was in the conversation.

Fascinating that neither of them had yet heard of the were-wolves attacking the drones. Lord Akeldama, at least, had a fast network of informants. Rue had come directly home, but still, she wasn't accustomed to being the only one who knew what was really going on . . . except with her own private business.

She took a moment to relish the sensation but then realised that Mother and Dama *should* know. It was their *business* to know what went on in London, especially with the supernatural. She became worried, which made her less diplomatic than she ought to be. "They were sloshed. In public. The entire pack. And they were *shoving* drones. It was most decidedly *not on!*"

Lady Maccon's face fell, her large dark eyes troubled. Rue had her father's eyes, a weird yellow colour, and she'd always envied her mother for the soulfulness her brown eyes could impart. Now, however, Mother looked as if she might cry. It was more sobering than anything else that had happened that evening. Rue instantly regretted her harshness.

Dama gave Rue a reproving look. He bent over Lady Maccon, taking her bare hand in one of his. The action turned him human, as Mother's preternatural power stole away his soul. It wasn't like Rue's abilities: Lady Maccon did not turn into a vampire herself. She simply made Dama mortal while he touched her. It was a mark of concern that he would take the risk; Dama was usually so careful about such things.

Mortal, Dama was less ethereal – less like some woodland sprite and more like a warn attic-bound artist with a taste for laudanum. There were lines on his face and smudges under his eyes. His hair was dulled to an ashy tone, and his movements became weighted.

"Don't worry, Alexia, my *dearest posy*. We shall get you both moving soon. You're right. It's past time. We must merely find the right *chivvy*."

Lady Maccon stood and reached for her trusty parasol. "I should go and find him. He'll need my touch. Would you—?" She hesitated, unsure.

Another frisson of fear spun up Rue's spine. *Paw is ill; there's no other explanation.*

Lady Maccon closed her eyes and took a short breath. "Would you consider talking to Rabiffano? He might listen to you. Quite frankly, I've run out of options."

Dama let go of her hand. His features and manners snapped back into smooth immortality. "I don't know that it should come from me."

"You're right. I shouldn't have asked. I apologise. I shall send an aetherogram to India. Perhaps it's not too late."

Dama smiled without showing fang, a sympathetic smile. "Now *there*, my dear dandelion, I *can* help you. I have already alerted them to the situation."

Lady Maccon relaxed. "Good. Good. Thank you."

"Mother, what is it? You're looking quite green round the gears."

"Infant, I do wish you wouldn't use such ghastly modern vernacular. It's nothing for you to worry about. Just . . . I should find that errant husband of mine."

She whisked out of the house. She didn't stride, not like Rue strode, although she was a good deal taller and more stride-worthy. No, Lady Maccon kept to the current fashions, her movements hindered by underskirts, but she still managed an air of purpose and authority which Rue envied. She'd never have her mother's presence, curse it.

Rue turned back to her vampire father. "Dama, what on earth is going on? What is wrong with everyone? And why do we need the Kingair Pack? I assume that's who you sent for in India."

"Ah, my *dearest* Puggle, if your other parents haven't told you, it's not my place at all."

Rue frowned. Someone else had said something exactly similar to her recently. Who was it? "You sound like Uncle Lyall," she remembered out loud.

Lord Akeldama started. His mouth twisted a tiny bit. Which surprised Rue. Uncle Lyall, London Pack Beta before Uncle

Rabiffano took over and now stationed with Kingair in India, was a sublimely *good egg*. Why should Dama not like him? Everyone liked him.

Dama would not allow her to question him further. "Enough, Puggle. This is *not* your problem to solve, *especially* when a solution is already in place. It simply needs to be acted upon."

He was annoyed enough for Rue to hear some long-forgotten accent slip into his words. Everyone was fracturing this evening.

"I hate it when you are cryptic. I'm all grown up now, remember? I assure you I am equipped to handle truths."

Dama tilted his head at her and raised his monocle. "No, I don't think you are if it means too much change. But you'll have to be soon. You were a little tough on your mother just now, dear. Not to put too fine a point on it."

"Oh, really! That is unfair. I had no idea she would be sensitive. This *is* my mother we're talking about. She's *never* sensitive."

Dama puffed out a suppressed laugh. "You must begin to think through the consequences of your actions. *Sweetling*, you've already caused an international incident and risked your own safety. You can't go around mucking up London politics as well. They're quite *absurd* enough already."

"Are we still talking about Mother or have we moved back to the weremonkeys again? I am sorry I had to bargain away your tea, Dama. Really, I *am*. But I couldn't think of another solution. I was trying to save lives."

"Oh, *lives*." The vampire flopped one hand dismissively. "I'm concerned about *you*, Puggle. You gave the queen her opening and she's removed Crown protection. Plus you've achieved your majority, so you no longer have me as a guardian."

"Freedom!" crowed Rue. "I shall shop wherever I please." Rue had always known her majority had all kinds of legal repercussions, but she'd never bothered with the details except the part where she no longer had to do what any of her parents told her to do.

"Exactly, you take on *great responsibility* and danger now, my *reckless* little poppet. The proper shoes alone . . ."

Rue knew he was being flippant to cover genuine concern. "I know it doesn't seem so to you, my darling Dama, but I've got old. Twenty-one and no one's ward. But you needn't worry. I've got my own dirigible and friends and everything. You and Mother and Paw have given me all the advantages of a" – she paused, struggling for the right words – "peculiar upbringing."

Dama looked modestly pleased. "We have done our best. But, my dearest child, we have all trained you, in our way, to compensate for the mistakes of our own pasts. We cannot predict your future. I worry that you are no longer quite safe."

"Isn't that part of being an adult?"

"Yes, but you're not the same type of adult. You're unique, not exactly human, and there is some question as to your right to legally exist. I don't think any of us fully understand the implications. Without government protection, or we vampires looking out for you, there are people who may want you dead."

Rue rolled her eyes. Really, this was too far. "*Everyone* wants me dead. That's nothing new. Dama, I love you, but you are overreacting. I can take care of myself."

"Like you tried to take care of a drunken pack? You cannot expect me to believe that you stayed out of *that*, puglet. Your mother may be distracted, but I am *not*."

Rue pursed her lips, suppressing the urge to frown furiously. All right, so she shouldn't have challenged Channing, but someone had to do something! However, there was no way to justify the action to Dama when she was already fighting from an inferior position. She didn't want to admit to any wrongdoing.

So she finished her tea and stood, radiating smugness. "You'll have to ask Winkle for a full report now, won't you, Dama dear? I'm certain he'll be most forthcoming."

With which she was about to whisk dramatically out of the room, except that at that precise moment the front doorbell rang. Dama had recently had the latest style installed, which tolled deeply rather than a proper ringing. It sounded a bit like a death dirge. But Rue supposed that even Dama needed the occasional undead wallow.

She paused and cocked her head; a familiar voice was chatting with the drone at the door.

Moments later, Primrose Tunstell came trotting into the drawing room trailing Virgil in her wake.

"Oh, Rue, were you heading out?"

"Only in a huff. What is it, Prim? You look positively overcome. And what are you doing with your brother's valet? Much as I respect you, Virgil, you're hardly an ideal chaperone for someone in Miss Tunstell's position."

Virgil didn't take offence. Despite being a jaunty lower-class stripling, he was well versed in proper etiquette. He knew he was the worst possible escort for a lady of Prim's rank. Since he was also an inveterate snob, he would have been the first to tell her so.

Primrose is usually good about such things.

Rue examined her friend.

Despite her odd companion, everything else seemed in order. She was perfectly dressed in an elegant cherry gown patterned in cream mignonette with ribbon detail exactly on point, right down to the wide sash at her enviably small waist. Her rich brown hair was swirled atop her head and crowned in the latest gentleman's inspired boater hats. She wore a not-too-ostentatious brooch at her throat, below which fell a quantity of not-too-ostentatious lace. She held leather gloves in one hand and a decorative fur purse in the other. *Decorative* because Primrose would *never* be so crass as to actually carry money on her person. The only thing even remotely out of character was the fact that she was trailing her brother's valet. However, Rue was confident that a perfectly sensible explanation would be forthcoming.

The net over Prim's face did nothing to disguise her worried expression. Primrose was an even-tempered little thing. On those few occasions when sentimentality overwhelmed her, Prim was ever willing to share her feelings with her dearest friend. In fact, it was practically a requirement of their relationship.

"Prim, my sweet, what is it?" Rue rallied round. This was *exactly* what she needed right now. Prim's worry was something Rue could manage. Prim would tell her what was wrong, with no attempt at redirection or miscommunication, and Rue would find a way to fix it. Whatever it was.

"It's Percy. Virgil says that he stormed off in a temper several hours ago. You know I wouldn't ordinarily trouble you, but he left his club, unaccompanied, at night. I understand that he dashed out of the reading room leaving behind an *unfinished manuscript*!"

"Oh dear."

"Oh yes! You know my brother. He is not equipped to handle London, even during the off-season. I'm certain he forgot his hat. Virgil, did he?"

Virgil nodded.

"You see? There he goes, outside, into society, without a hat. Did he at least have a cravat on?"

Virgil shook his head.

Primrose went white. "Oh. Oh no. No."

Dama, until that moment lurking quietly in the background, could not repress a gasp. "I must *apologise*, darling ladies, but I simply *cannot* listen any further. It's *too* bad."

Primrose looked at him, eyes shining with tears. "No, of course not. Nor should you. I do apologise, dear Lord Akeldama. And if you could try to keep the shame of this from getting out? For as long as supernaturally possible. Perhaps Rue and I can find him and convince him to return indoors before anyone of any importance *sees* him."

Dama came over all severe behind his monocle. "Yes, I think you had better. But surely your mother will have her drones posted to follow him?"

"Oh, dear me. Imagine what Queen Mums would say if she heard Percy was gallivanting about without a hat in public? This is a *catastrophe*; hats are all she loves best in the world. Rue, we really must go *now*."

"But he was staying at his club. Where would he go? Any ideas?"

Prim shook her head so violently she nearly dislodged her own hat from its position, exactly where it ought to be.

Rue looked into the forlorn face of Percy's young valet. "Virgil, we don't blame you, of course we don't. But can you recall anything that might help us track your master?"

He felt this keenly, naturally he did. Virgil was a gem. He took more care of his master's reputation than the Honourable Percival Tunstell warranted. But even a fully grown valet could only control his master so much, and Percy at the best of times was eccentric in both his manners and his dress. Still, Rue could hardly have supposed even Percy to be so rash as to head out at night . . . hatless.

"He read an article, Lady Captain. Got quite steamed up about it. I've never seen him so pipped."

"He does have red hair. You know those rumours about the temper." Rue tried to console him.

"Yes, Lady Captain, I do. But this was more serious than red hair."

Rue frowned. "What was the paper about?"

"It was a recent publication from the Royal Society. You know, the type that announces the latest discoveries. I didn't see the particulars."

Rue didn't press the matter. It was Virgil's job to take care of Percy's person, not his mental stability – questionable as that may be.

"Well, if I were Percy and *very* upset, I should head to my library. We should try there first."

Prim brightened. "Oh yes! What a good idea. Naturally, he would go there."

Rue was pleased to have come up with a plan. "To *The Spotted Custard*, then. And, Dama, I shall be careful, I promise."

Lord Akeldama looked slightly nonplussed.

As they closed the door to the townhouse behind them, Rue

said to Primrose, "Out with it. What else is there that you didn't want Dama to overhear?"

Prim looked at her sideways, cheekily. "You guessed?"

Rue only gave her a look. A look that reminded her that they had spent almost twenty years in each other's company.

They climbed into Prim's carriage. Fortunately, it wasn't nearly as ostentatious as Lord Akeldama's. It did belong to another vampire, the Baroness Tunstell, Primrose's mother. But Queen Ivy's outrageous taste ran to fashion more than transport, since she never left the hive. Thus her carriage was pretty and proudly crested – a rampant hedgehog wearing an old-fashioned feathered bonnet – but built for speed and manoeuvrability, not first impressions. Rue suspected Aunt Ivy's Egyptian vampires had a hand in its purchase. They were the type to think along more subtle lines.

The door closed behind Virgil, who'd given the driver instructions to the *Custard*'s mooring place.

Prim finally deemed it safe to talk openly. "Virgil says that *strange men* have been round asking after Percy. We're both worried my difficult brother has offended the wrong person at last. Someone with real power and not the usual cadre of academics. Apparently, they asked all sorts of questions and were quite the most suspicious-looking fellows."

Virgil nodded his agreement. "Most suspicious, Lady Captain. They even asked about the ship and the crew."

"Ah, I see your concern. Percy is always a bit of a problem, but this could be serious."

CHAPTER

TWO

In Which Percy Proves Difficult
and No One Is Surprised

The drive continued in companionable silence, until Primrose blurted out, "Oh, Rue, there's something else. I can't wait to tell you any longer. I'm to be engaged!"

"Again? This will be what, number three in the two weeks since we've been home? Aren't you laying it on a little thick?"

"Well, if someone hadn't played tiddlywinks with my reputation while we were in India, I wouldn't need to establish a solid air of respectability."

"I hardly see how three engagements in so short a time helps."

"They have all been *very* respectable men."

"Yes, you appear to be working your way slowly through the upper levels of Her Majesty's Airtight Puffed Doubloon, dirigible regiment extraordinaire."

Primrose appeared crestfallen at Rue's lack of enthusiasm.

Rue tried to buck up. "Oh very well, why don't you tell me all about him? Distract us from the problem of Percy."

Primrose did. Prattling on about strong lines and well-turned thighs and a full mane of brown hair in a manner that made her latest beau sound not unlike a very desirable racehorse. Rue would have been supportive if she sensed any real affection from her friend, but Primrose seemed to be in hot pursuit of a fiancé merely because she felt she *ought* to have one.

Rue was a romantic. Her parents were a love match. Had to be, for there was no other possible explanation for them tolerating one another. Thus Rue held the very peculiar opinion that love made for a most agreeable form of companionship.

Primrose, on the other hand, was trying to *arrange* a match for herself – affection be damned.

"Prim, are you sure it is a good idea? Do you love him?"

Prim gave a brittle laugh. "Oh, I'm not certain I'm capable of loving any man. I'm too sensible for that. This is easier. And he does have *very* nice legs."

Rue could think of no better reason, at the moment, for marrying. Quesnel, she mused, also had nice legs. And then she reminded herself she was annoyed with him. Her erstwhile beau had disappeared. He'd received an aetherogram while they were still in India and promptly floated off to Egypt. He was supposed to be educating her in the ways of the carnal flesh, or so she thought they'd agreed. But before anything got carnal or fleshy, he'd abandoned her for a *rented* dirigible berth with nothing more than a peck on the cheek and a cheery farewell. Rue felt rather rejected as a result. He ought to be teaching her French techniques and instead he and his nice legs were gallivanting about deserts and whatnot.

"I should be wary of a man with nice legs, if I were you." Rue considered stretched buckskin meditatively. "They use them rather too readily."

The Spotted Custard, Rue's pride and joy, was moored off Worple Road in Wimbledon, not far from Baroness Tunstell's hive house. Rue was paying a handsome sum to the All England Croquet, Lawn Tennis, and Airborne Polo Club for hovering rights and use of the green for outfitting and repairs. They'd lost their old mooring in Regent's Park to float squatters, and Rue wanted something with more security than Hyde Park afforded. The court was well lit, well guarded, and quite respectable, proving to be an ideal arrangement all around, so she tried not to resent the expense.

Although Rue adored her airship, she did have a tendency to push the chubby craft to its limits. This – plus a certain near aetheric attraction for sharp objects hurled by, for example, were-monkeys – had left *The Spotted Custard* more in need of repairs than outfitting upon their return to London. Thus, while the officers of *The Spotted Custard* – mostly comprised of Rue and her friends – kept supernatural hours, the rest of the crew switched to daylight for ease of visibility in order to conduct said repairs.

Outfitting had included restocking and refuelling and the addition of a sparkling new Gatling gun for the port side, much to Spoo's delight. Spoo, head deckling, was quite as bloodthirsty as any boy of her age was wont to be. Amusing when compared to her best friend, Virgil, who was as prissy as any girl of his age.

The gun was a gift from Dama, who, despite his tea-drenched grudge, refused to let Rue's twenty-first birthday slip by without acknowledgement. Rue had been in India on the actual date of the occurrence, likely acting the part of naked native goddess. Frankly, attaining her official majority had entirely slipped her mind. But no one could refute that she had indeed turned twenty-one, papers were filed, she was legally an adult, a free woman, and a ward of no one – vampire or otherwise. At her return home, Dama had presented Rue with a large shiny rapid-fire gun because, as he said, she was all grown up and a fully fledged independent now, and *knowing her family propensities, she'd need a ruddy big gun.*

It being well after dark, Rue, Prim, and Virgil were hailed from the *Custard*'s main deck by a solitary night guard and not by a teeming mass of decklings. Only one guard stood duty as only one was needed, as that guard was Tasherit Sekhmet.

Miss Sekhmet didn't seem like very effective protection. True

she was tall and imposing, but also very female, wearing some
sort of filmy tea-gown with her hair loose, and not a weapon in
sight.

Rue climbed out of the carriage and waved. "Only us!"

"Ah, good evening, Captain. I wasn't expecting you tonight.
And Miss Primrose? How are you this fine night?" Tasherit
turned her hunter's gaze onto Prim the moment she appeared.

Rue didn't have to look to know that Primrose was blushing.
Primrose was always blushing around Miss Sekhmet. She was in
awe of their resident werelioness, and despite Tasherit's easygoing
affection, Primrose refused to warm to her.

Tasherit, in classic cat fashion, thus found Primrose the most
fascinating thing on board.

"And young Virgil? A good evening to you."

Virgil nodded happily. All of the *Custard*'s youngsters were
fond of Miss Sekhmet. Partly because when she was in lioness
form, she let them ride her like a shipboard pony and partly
because she was one of the few adults on the dirigible who held
no immediate connection to, or official title within, the aristocracy. True she was a foreigner, but she was also a commoner, and
she was nice about both. As a result, Tasherit had turned most
of Rue's crew into her minions.

Rue might have minded, except that it was good for them
to have an adult to talk to in an informal manner. She herself
couldn't take on the role of mentor; as captain, she needed to
inspire discipline and awe. Being a round, cheerful young lady,
Rue was working on awe and discipline from a deficit. Also
Tasherit had taken on the duty of militia training. Back in
India, and now here, the werecat regularly put the deck crew
through their paces, to go up against not only daylight threats
but supernatural creatures as well. At her behest, Rue had seen
them outfitted with crossbows and everyone was feeling more
relaxed as a result. The decklings being, by and large, vicious
little scrappers had taken to the idea of being armed with disturbing enthusiasm.

Tasherit, being an immortal, was strong enough to operate the gangplank without assistance. She cranked it down manually and with enviable ease. The three came trotting up.

Even living together for weeks on end, Tasherit up close always took Rue's breath away. She was so beautiful it hurt, like breathing deep on an icy evening. She was all exotically strong features, tea-with-milk complexion, and long, thick dark hair. It was most upsetting, or would have been, if she hadn't been so nice about it. One couldn't really resent Tasherit for her beauty; that would be like resenting a sunset.

"Has Percy come aboard recently?"

"He has." Tasherit spoke English well, with only a touch of lilting vowels. Weeks spent talking regularly to Rue and Prim had coloured her vocabulary with the upper crust. "Off to his library in a funk."

Prim and Rue exchanged relieved looks.

"Well, thank goodness he's here." Prim's eyes were less worried.

"Has anyone been around asking after him?" Rue perused the decks by habit; everything seemed in order.

Tasherit was surprised. "No. Should there be? Does our dear professor have *friends?*"

"No, quite the opposite."

"Ah, no. But I'll bring up the gangplank and keep a careful watch, if you wish."

"Yes, I think that wise. And if you wouldn't mind, perhaps a lioness might be a bigger dissuader than a stunning diaphanous woman."

"Mmm. Quite right. I'll just go and change, then, shall I?" Tasherit winked at them both and disappeared below, only to return a moment later as a large silken-furred lioness. She blinked her slanted brown eyes at them and went to pace the railing.

Primrose let out a long breath.

Rue wasn't certain if it was relief at having Percy so well

protected or relief at being no longer under the scrutiny of the werecat.

They found Percy sulking in his library.

"Percy, there you are." Primrose bustled in.

Percy looked up. His expression suggested that his sister was akin to some kind of shoe fungus. "Would you care to make any more banal comments?"

"Percy! I was worried about you. So was Virgil."

"The answer is clearly yes, banal comments will continue." Percy was extra grumpy this evening.

Aren't we lucky? "What ho, Percy. I wasn't worried." Rue grinned at him.

"What happened to make you storm off so?" Primrose was nothing if not persistent.

Percy was rather fond of Rue, so it was startling to everyone when he rounded on her at this juncture. Rue had never seen such anger on his face and she'd known him since they were in nappies. She took a tiny step back.

"That French boy of yours! Have you *any* idea what he's gone and done?"

"Quesnel? Isn't he still overseas?"

"He can go to the devil for all I care! What has that to do with anything? Traitorous beast. I don't know why I'm surprised given his ancestry and inclinations. French *engineer* indeed!"

Rue and Primrose exchanged looks. All Percy seemed to be accusing Quesnel of was, frankly, being himself. True, Quesnel was theoretically French, but he'd been mostly educated in England. And there was nothing wrong with being an engineer. It's not like Percy would get his lily-white hands greasy; someone had to keep them floating while he navigated.

Rue shifted her stance. "Yes, yes, but what did he *do*, Percy?"

Percy went all broody. "If you don't know, I'm not going to tell you. I shall enjoy watching you find out exactly as I did. The shock of it. In the meantime, I'll have my revenge. Just you see if I don't."

He sounded like the villain in a gothic novel. Rue hid a grin. "Percy, darling, I realise, unlike some, that what I don't know could fill the Library of Alexandria. Hence the reason I keep you around, charming though you may be."

Percy puffed a bit at what he took as a compliment.

"Oh really, Percy!" Primrose did not find her brother funny. "Do try not to be so *ridiculous*. Have a nice cup of hot tea and you'll be more the tick in two shakes."

"I was thinking the same thing." Rue was slightly concerned about what Percy might do to get back at Quesnel for this perceived slight, but that was Quesnel's problem. If past experience was anything to go on, Quesnel could handle Percy. He could also rile Percy up like no one else. Since it was clearly some gentlemen thing, Rue refused to dignify it with her concern.

She pierced Percy with a glare. "So, why are these men looking for you?"

Percy stopped at that. "Men? What men?"

"Exactly what we wish to know."

Percy lost some of his pique in confusion. "I've no idea what you're on about, Prudence. Now, I will kindly ask you ladies to leave me in peace. I have some vital research to conduct and I need chatter-free quiet in which to conduct it. Is that my valet skulking in the background?"

Virgil moved further into the library. "Sir?"

"Oh good, I seem to have lost my hat. Find another one? There's a good lad."

Virgil said, "Yes, sir," in a tone that suggested he was humouring his master. He disappeared into the stacks towards a corner of the room that presumably housed Percy's wardrobe.

Rue and Primrose, summarily dismissed and knowing they would get nothing more out of the redhead, made their way out.

Spoo ran them down in the hallway, rubbing her eyes, short hair sticking up every which way. Spoo was rather a prize as far as capability was concerned. She was, as per usual, dressed as a boy and slightly smudged.

"Oye up, Lady Captain. I've been waiting for you to dock in."

"Good evening, Spoo. Everything shipshape and Bristol fashion while I was away?"

"Mostly." Spoo's tone indicated that she had gossip to impart. "*Something* is being installed in engineering. Old Aggie won't let me see, on account of her bitterness over me leaving off sootie for deckling. I think you might want to find out what it is."

Primrose wasn't interested in this conversation. She undertook the supervision of the ship's staff, ensuring that tea was served on time and other similar necessities vital to everyone's comfort were provided. She couldn't care less about the mechanics of *The Spotted Custard*'s crew.

"Rue dear, I think I might go and do something else." Strangely, Prim drifted back up on deck when there was nothing to occupy her attention, and the only one awake was Tasherit in lioness form.

Rue wished her a pleasant night. "Thank you, Spoo. I shall investigate at once." *I wonder if this is at Quesnel's behest? Is this what has Percy's dander up?*

Leaving Spoo to return to her bed, Rue climbed down the spiral staircase to the lowest level of her ship, where the two massive boilers were housed in all their teakettle glory.

Everything was quiet. *The Spotted Custard* was on low burn; only the main kettle was simmering. The other wasn't needed unless they were in full propeller mode.

A single sleepy-eyed sootie tended to the main. He gave Rue a nod as she passed.

Everything else was still and silent, except in a back corner, behind a coal pile where Aggie Phinkerlington was humming to herself and tinkering with a remarkable-looking gadget.

It was a large tank, not unlike one of those Wardian cases that the mad fern collectors used to display their obsession. This one was empty of ferns and in the process of construction and installation.

Rue cleared her throat delicately.

Aggie didn't jump, not really – she was too stoic for that – but she did reach to flip a horse blanket over the tank and turned around brandishing a wrench and a displeased expression.

Aggie was head greaser, second in command of the boiler room after Quesnel, which made her chief engineer while he was away. For some reason Rue did not understand, Aggie had never warmed to her. Which was a shame, because Rue thought that under more auspicious circumstances she would like the young battleaxe. Aggie reminded her a bit of Lady Kingair.

Aggie was a redhead with a vast sprinkling of freckles over porcelain skin under which blue veins were clearly visible. That skin spoke more to a life spent in engineering than ancestry. She was sublimely fit. Her arm muscles had arm muscles. Rue, who had grown up around werewolves, thought Aggie most impressive even by their standards. She was one of the few women Rue had ever met who actually *looked* like she might survive metamorphosis. Whether she was creative enough to have excess soul, Rue would never know. Aggie rarely let anyone see any part of her but the tetchy efficient bit.

"Oh, it's you." Aggie frowned. "What do you want?"

Not a promising start. "Good evening, Miss Phinkerlington. What is that, if I may ask?" Rue always found herself forced into politeness by the extremity of Aggie's dislike.

"You may not ask."

Rue gave a little sigh. "This is my ship, Miss Phinkerlington."

"And this is Himself's kit. Not for me to say if he hasn't deemed it necessary to tell."

Aggie was a pain but she was good at her job and she adored Quesnel in a bickering-elder-sister fashion. Which made her reliably loyal – to him if not the rest of the ship.

"Yet Mr Lefoux is not here, so perhaps you would be so kind as to enlighten me?"

"That I won't."

Impasse. Rue could order her to tell. But if pushed, Aggie was likely to chuck in the towel and storm off the ship, leaving Rue in a real lurch with no one supervising engineering at all.

That was the difficulty. Rue needed Aggie's skills more than Aggie needed Rue's respect. It put Rue in a chronically uncomfortable position.

"At least tell me if it is likely to explode or what have you."

Aggie raised one red eyebrow at her. "Isn't everything on this ship likely to explode?"

Rue bent to look under the blanket at the casement. It was difficult to tell anything in the flickering shadows of a single boiler's firebox.

Aggie interposed herself, crossed her arms over her chest, and leaned against the blanket, pinning it down.

Rue inhaled the musty scent of oil and soot. All in all, this was looking to be an extremely frustratingly evening. *Molasses over vinegar*, she reminded herself. This had been her tactic with Aggie from the beginning. The nicer she was, the more annoyed Aggie became. It was a minor sort of revenge, but it was all Rue had to fall back on.

"Very well, Miss Phinkerlington. But now I know of its existence, so you might as well carry on under more well-lit circumstances. Go to bed. There is no point ruining your eyesight over one of Quesnel's little toys."

Aggie began to sputter. Either out of disgust at the concern or out of the insult to Quesnel's inventing abilities.

Rue was already moving away.

"Quesnel," she muttered as she closed the hatch to engineering, "has a very great deal of explaining to do."

"What was that?" Primrose was coming down the main stairs.

"Only talking to myself."

Prim was flushed.

"Something wrong up top?"

"Only that Miss Sekhmet . . . she is" – Primrose paused, looking for the right words – "awfully playful when she is a lioness."

"Presenting you with her belly, was she?"

Prim looked down at her hands. "I simply" – she lowered

her voice to a whisper – "can't get over the fact that she is, you know, naked."

"She's a cat."

"Yes, but she's also *not* a cat."

Rue, being able to change shape herself, had an odd relationship with nudity. Some might even have called it Ancient Greek in its inclinations. Dama certainly did, regularly shaking his head at the goings-on of his neighbours. "Like a less oily gymnasium. One's imagination runs positively *rampant.*"

"The werewolf uncles never seem to bother you."

Primrose frowned. "They're men."

Rue didn't follow that reasoning at all. "Well, I'm sorry Tasherit has offended."

Prim blinked wide dark eyes, afraid she had brought Rue's ire down on the werelioness. "Oh no, it's not that. It's only . . ." She lost her train of thought. "Oh dear, I'm rather discombobulated."

"Yes, seems to happen to you quite a bit around Tasherit. Why is that?"

"She's so very foreign and . . ." Words failed Prim again.

"And?"

"Catty."

"Mmm. If you say so. Perhaps some tea? Shall we ring?"

Primrose grasped at the suggestion. "What a good idea. It has been a very trying night."

"Truth from the mouths of children," agreed Rue with feeling.

They turned towards the stateroom where they might ring for tea, when a most extraordinary noise coming from the squeak deck diverted their attention.

"What on earth?" said Primrose.

Rue was already running.

It was the sound of a lioness, shrieking.

Six men had boarded *The Spotted Custard* by means of grappling hooks. Four were already on deck; two of these were firing at Tasherit – understandable given that fact that the lioness had the other two down against the railings.

The guns they had must not be sundowner, for the werecat did not flinch at impact. Or their shots were going wild.

Still, shooting at a crew member was really not on, to Rue's way of thinking. Not at all. She dived towards the blighters with the guns.

Their shots conveniently woke up the slumbering decklings, who tumbled from their hammocks reaching for crossbows, as they'd been trained.

"To me!" shouted Rue rather grandly, she felt. She herself was entirely unarmed. With Tasherit already a lioness and doing a fabulous job of lionessing about, it made no sense to steal her shape. So Rue charged in without weapon or super-natural form.

Primrose, on the other hand, did not. Prim could defend herself if absolutely necessary but otherwise preferred to avoid physical confrontation. "I'm not a violent person, Rue. The very idea of killing someone. It's not in me. I'll leave it to the children. They do enjoy it so. Why spoil their fun?"

So Rue ordered her out of it. "Primrose, go to Percy and lock yourself in with him. Don't unlock it for anyone. We'll use the code word once this refuse has been rusticated."

Prim didn't answer. She was already dashing below, intent on protecting her twin from whatever it was that he had brought on himself.

Rue, for lack of anything better, grabbed up a sluicing mop and issued one of the bruisers shooting at Tasherit a full biff to the side of the head. He went down, dropping his gun. A deckling tumbled in, retrieving the gun in a somersault . . . Spoo.

Another deckling shot a bolt into a second gunman. Shoulder wound but effective, for the man cried out and clutched at his arm, falling to his knees. Two more decklings swooped in, screaming like banshees, swinging from the rigging – feet first at the still-standing man.

Rue closed in on her prey, flipping the mop about and pressing the wooden handle to the man's throat in case he had ideas on moving.

Meanwhile her two deckhands, Willard and Bork, pried off the grapples in case any more of the enemy tried to board.

Tasherit was handling her two invaders with bloody aplomb. To be fair, she was going easy on them. They were only mortal, and she could have killed them with one blow; instead she was batting at them like a house cat with field mice. One of them took his chances jumping back over the rails rather than continue to suffer those claws. The other huddled in a ball, his back a shredded mess. Occasionally, he would uncoil and skitter sideways. She'd yowl, charge, and swipe to stop him. He'd ball up again for a time and then skitter the other way. She'd let him think he could escape for a while, then pounce in a jolly manner.

Rue let her have her fun.

Out of the corner of her eye, Rue admired the decklings in action; like a small herd of lemurs, they swarmed their man and clung to every part of his body. Despite being a substantial fellow, he was slowly folding under their collective weight.

Rue turned her full attention back to the blighter lying below her. He was clearly not best pleased to have been felled by a gentlewoman with a mop.

He was a big man, almost as big as Paw, who was one of the biggest Rue knew. He grabbed the mop handle and yanked. Rue, who was no fool, let go rather than pit her strength against his. He rolled to his feet and swung. Rue darted back, out of reach, wary.

Spoo, having determined the small mess of decklings had the other gunman under control, came running over to Rue.

"This might work a bit more the treat, Lady Captain." Spoo was grinning in a decidedly evil manner as she handed over the man's revolver.

The man squinted at her in focused interest.

Rue wasn't overly fond of guns but they were awfully useful when facing a man twice her size with no respect in his eyes. Guns engendered respect and Rue did know how to shoot one – Dama had made certain of it. This one was a mite bigger than the muff pistols she'd learned on but seemed to function about the same in theory. It took both her thumbs to cock it, and she hoped not to have to actually shoot; it'd have a terrific kick.

Upon seeing her facing him with a revolver and not a mop, the man became wary.

"What do you want with this ship?" Rue demanded.

"It's not us. It's 'em as hired us."

Rue was annoyed enough to wiggle the pistol. "That is *not* an answer."

The man smiled. "That's all you're getting." He ran for the railing.

Rue was surprised enough not to shoot. They were about rooftop height above the ground. It wasn't a fall most daylight folk could survive. Except as he jumped, he shed his massive overcoat and had some kind of boxy device strapped to his back. She leaned over the railing to watch. It deployed into an articulated gliding apparatus which lifted off his shoulders with the pull of a strap.

Rue had never seen the like. He seemed to catch the breeze and sail about, directing himself with a tilt this way and a tilt that way, like a bat. It looked pretty darn fun and Rue instantly wanted a whole bunch of them for her crew. Parachutes were one thing, but this was much more mobile.

"Nifty," said Spoo. "Can we get us some of those, Lady Captain?"

"I was pondering along similar lines. I've not seen such a contraption before. Have you, Spoo?"

"No, I ain't."

"Well, then, new gadget, pretty advanced at that." Which made Rue think of Quesnel's mysterious fern tank down in the boiler room. Perhaps these men were after that? Exo-splorers, apparat-collectors, and cog-burglars weren't so uncommon these days, and if they heard of something new outside patent control, they might risk boarding her airship to steal it. Although, they didn't seem prepared to transport something as big.

As everything seemed to be controlled on deck, Rue ran below to find that Aggie had pulled an enormous metal carapace over the tank, which bolted to the floor through one of the securing rings meant for a boiler. Definitely Lefoux design. Rue had seen Quesnel in a steam roly-poly transport made with exactly the same kind of carapace.

If anyone was after that tech, they certainly weren't getting it. Rue was oddly reassured over its safety, especially given no one had asked her opinion on its presence.

Back on deck, Tasherit had her mouse supine and panting under one large paw. The decklings had their lemur tree felled and were sitting on every available part of him. They looked mighty pleased with themselves. Rue decided she would put on a very nice tea for them tomorrow as a thank-you. *I shall get some hot cross buns from Lottapiggle's.*

While they had been trained to repel invaders, it wasn't until that moment that Rue realised they were not at all equipped to take prisoners.

"Decklings, you're good with rope. Could you determine a way to tie these men up for questioning?"

"Yes, Lady Captain!"

They did their best, but the ropes they had were big, being intended for balloon work, so both men were rather wrapped about as if they were mooring posts. Still, they didn't look likely to escape and, being injured, were docile enough.

Tasherit, with a meaningful glance at Rue, disappeared below, emerging some time later in human form with two greasers in tow – big burly men with large fish knives at the ready.

"Ah, good, Miss Sekhmet, there you are."

They established early on that their werelioness did not want to be known as a werelioness. Her people had gone into hiding centuries ago and she wished to respect their secrecy. Whether this was preference or some sacred vow, Rue had never been so bold as to ask. It was clearly a private supernatural matter and the entire crew honoured the werecat's wishes. Just like a cat, to mould her environment to suit her whim. Thus, while Rue had told the Shadow Council – she had *had* to tell them – of her encounter with the weremonkeys, she'd left werecats out of her report.

Tasherit was invaluable muscle, being the first supernatural anyone had ever met who could travel through the aether. Although, truth be told, she slept like the dead the entire time. This, too, was intrinsically catlike.

Thus, in the face of their prisoners, everyone treated Tasherit as if she were different from the lioness. No reason for these thugs to know anything. Besides, it would only add to *The Spotted Custard*'s reputation as having a trained attack cat.

"Miss Sekhmet? If you could please assume control of the prisoners and begin questioning? See if you can find out who hired them and what they're after."

"It's not my area of expertise but I will do my best." Tasherit's beautiful face was impassive.

"If you can't get anything out of them, I'll pass them on to Dama. I'll wager he can."

The werecat nodded. "Agreed." Miss Sekhmet had yet to meet Rue's vampire father but she knew of him. At least, Rue assumed they'd never met – hard to tell with immortals.

"Still, I'd prefer to source this mess ourselves before we involve any of my parents. Things always get dramatic with them."

"And you're young enough to still hunger for your independence." Tasherit's tone didn't indicate whether she found this charming or annoying.

Rue had no idea how old the werecat was, but she would guess she was older than most werewolves if not as old as a vampire. Which meant three hundred at least. Under such circumstances, a little condescension was expected.

"You have the deck. I should go and tell the twins that everything is safe now."

Tasherit nodded. "Good idea. You sent the little flower down to her brother?"

"Yes. I find it best to keep Prim out of the way when things get rough. She's a delicate flower."

Tasherit laughed. "Or she likes to be thought a delicate flower."

Rue narrowed her eyes. "What are you doing to her anyway?"

The werecat's brown eyes went wide with assumed innocence. "Me? Nothing. Nothing at all."

"Mmm." Rue could almost see her licking her whiskers. "Try not to break her, please? She's my best friend and not your toy on a string."

Tasherit only looked smugger. "I assure you, I have no intention of harming one hair on that lovely head. And I am most assuredly not playing."

Rue issued her a measuring stare. "Cats."

Rue knocked on the library door.

"Yes?" said a tremulous voice from within. "Who is it?"

"Honeysuckle Isinglass." It was their agreed-upon code for all extenuating circumstances.

The door swung open to show the twins, wide-eyed and sobered after listening to the kerfuffle abovedecks.

Percival and Primrose Tunstell did not look like one another. Prim took after their dark-haired frippery of a mother and Percy their flamboyant father. Neither had inherited their respective parent's personality, thank heavens, aside from a certain flair for the dramatic.

"Has anyone died?" Primrose demonstrated her flair immediately.

"Possibly." Rue was thinking of the one man who had jumped overboard while not in possession of articulated bat wings.

At Prim's harried expression she added, "But no one we know or care about."

Primrose let out a whoosh. "And Tash – Miss Sekhmet?"

"She's perfectly topping. Been down, changed forms, and back up to take control of the interrogation. We have two prisoners."

"Rue, you never?"

At that juncture, Footnote made his appearance. Footnote was Percy's cat, as much as any cat belonged to any person. He mostly lived in the library, although he, ostensibly, had the run of the ship. Since Tasherit had boarded, he ceded most of the territory to her. They coexisted in a barely civil arrangement, with Footnote hissing up a storm whenever he happened to run across her and Tasherit threatening to eat him on a regular basis. In fact, she seemed the only thing able to ruffle the black and white tom's superior calm. At this moment, for example, he appeared to have slept through the battle. His impressive white whiskers arrowed forward as though sensing the oncoming yawn before it happened, pink mouth wide. He then stretched and wandered over to sit on Rue's foot.

"I did. I took my first prisoners. It's very exciting, not that I know correct prisoner acquisition etiquette." She bent over to scratch Footnote's head. "What does one do with prisoners?"

"Torture," said Percy with confidence.

"Yes, but what *kind* of torture?" Footnote lifted his chin commandingly so she scratched his neck.

Percy, true to his nature, had a ready answer to that. Same answer he always had. "I must have a book here somewhere on the subject. Excruciation, maybe. Would you like me to look?" He seemed to have lost the bulk of his distemper during the course of the attack.

"Oh, no thank you, Percy. What a nice gesture. But I think I can come up with something vile on my own." Footnote wandered over to Primrose to acquire a new set of scratches.

"Torture?" Primrose's tone was thoughtful. "Cold tea?"

"German poetry." Percy reached to a shelf and offered up an unpleasantly fat leather-bound volume.

Rue was arrested. "There's such a thing as German poetry?"

Primrose nodded seriously. "Yes. Save yourself."

Percy, in silent agreement, put the volume back.

Rue laughed. "Regardless, it's safe to come out now, if you care to."

CHAPTER

THREE

In Which German Poetry Is Entirely Irrelevant

They never did get around to the German poetry, or any other form of interrogation that evening. Someone, likely from the All England Croquet, Lawn Tennis, and Airborne Polo Club Annual Fiscal Reserves Ball below, had reported the invasion to the authorities. Shortly before dawn, the constabulary hailed them, along with a member of BUR, which meant supernaturals were involved. These authorities demanded they hand over their prisoners. *The Spotted Custard*, a law-abiding ship, floated down and allowed the silvers to board.

"It's not fair really." Rue crossed her arms and glared, trying to be as fierce as her unfortunately friendly visage would allow. "They're *my* prisoners. What business is it of yours?"

The bobby was not intimated one bit. He seemed to be trying not to smile, the chump. He flipped out a long writ of some irrepressibly official-looking variety and explained that these men were wanted on several counts of breaking and entering by various clubs, libraries, hive houses, and ministries of record all over London. Apparently, they were part of some kind of crime necklace, or ring, or what have you, which made Rue even more certain that they were after Quesnel's fancy tank.

"Besides, miss, even if they did board your ship without

permission, you can't simply keep free citizens imprisoned on a dirigible."

"I can't?"

"Not done, miss. Not done at all."

"Oh, very well."

Rue reluctantly handed over the two men.

The BUR operative was not one she knew from Paw's offices. He regarded the scratches all over the one man suspiciously but otherwise performed his duties with admirable aplomb. The Staking Constabulary disappeared once the prisoners were produced, and the crew of the *Custard* was left none the wiser as to the purpose of the attack.

They floated back up as high as they could while remaining moored to the croquet green, and Rue took to her bed, feeling rather the worse for a confusing night.

Rue awoke – it felt like five minutes after falling asleep, although the sun was high enough for it to have been five hours – to the dulcet sounds of Percy yelling.

Even as pipped as he'd been yesterday, and he was quite pipped, Percy rarely yelled. But somehow Rue knew it was him. She recognised the other voice, too. Both were loud enough to waft down to Rue's cabin from the poop deck directly overhead. The second voice was cooler, more calculating, lilting in a slightly French manner, as it tended to when overcome with emotion. He always lost some of his cloak of proper Britishness, did Quesnel, in times of stress.

I guess he's back, then. Rue stared up at the ceiling and tried to decide how she felt about this. *It's nice that he's safe but I'm still irritated with him. And so is Percy, which is not so different from normal.* She attempted to think of the right greeting for her erstwhile lover. It should be an irreverent quip, something casual and unruffled; she wouldn't want to look like she cared.

The crest of rising and falling tones above her suggested that the argument was likely to continue. It was, she realised, also occurring in public, in front of the decklings and the repair crew. *If we are really lucky, we will also have an audience of respectable croquet players witnessing my navigator and chief engineer's verbal fisticuffs.*

Rue bopped out of bed and – knowing it was shameful – spent an inordinate amount of time on her toilette. She even laced on a corset as tight as she was able without a maid, over a silk combination *and* petticoats, merely because of how small it made her waist look. Quesnel's presence provoked her into looking her best, anticipating the revenge of showing him a modicum of what he could *no longer* have.

Not until he adequately explained himself at least.

Rue's best day dress was white with black dots and black lace trim. It was a simple cut with decidedly old-fashioned sleeves, tight from shoulder to wrist, and a low square neckline over a muslin tuck. The muslin was filmy enough to show hints of her generous cleavage, which was about as much as one could show for daytime without being labelled a strumpet. Rue wasn't above using her assets for nefarious purposes.

She elected not to turn up her hair. It was one of her best features – thick and wavy like her mother's but with a few reddish honey tones in the full sun. She felt justified in leaving it down having been recently awoken from repose. This being her airship, and her home, she was in her right to appear in a relaxed state. Although, loose hair was pushing matters.

She might have taken a little too long. For when she paused at the top of the stairs to pinch some colour into her cheeks, the voices on deck had fallen silent.

She pushed open the hatch and climbed out, to find Percy with a tremendous frown on his face slumped over the helm consulting a greaser about repairs.

Quesnel was striding down the gangplank. Quesnel striding made for a lovely sight, but it was hardly fair of him to leave when she had put so much effort into looking good enough for him to regret having left before! It would not do to holler at him; that would ruin the dignity of her position. So Rue clattered down the gangplank after him. She moved as fast as her tightly laced stays would allow, instantly regretting having worn them.

She grabbed his arm just as he jumped to the ground.

Quesnel whirled to face her, hand up as if to strike, and she wondered if he thought her Percy. Had the animosity between them became so bad he would hit the man? Percy was a frightful bother, nobody denied that, but to strike another gentleman invited social retribution. Or was Quesnel on edge because he knew criminals were after his new kit in the boiler room?

Quesnel's violet eyes widened; then the lines on his face smoothed and he smiled.

"*Chérie!* How lovely."

"Leaving again so soon, Mr Lefoux? Is this to become a custom?"

"Most certainly not. How could I even contemplate abandoning such loveliness!"

"And yet you had no difficulty back in India."

"Duty and friendship called me away. Although, I must say, that dress would have made the move nigh on impossible. Is it new?" Quesnel Lefoux was one of the biggest flirts in London. He was also an inventor. Which confused people no end. Generally the academic set took after Percy, being prickly and not adept at grappling with the mundane intellect of the masses. Not Quesnel. Quesnel had a well-earned reputation with the ladies and a certain casual breeziness of manner he was only permitted because he was French and a commoner.

That said, he was certainly *not* the most agreeable man Rue knew. Lord Akeldama and at least four of his drones outpaced her blond engineer easily. Having been raised by such collective expert charmers, Rue would have been very wary of Quesnel if he *were* the most agreeable man she knew. She *liked* that his flirting had an honest bent to it. Quesnel flirted because he genuinely appreciated women, and Rue in particular. Rue had to give him credit for excellent taste.

"Don't you dare change the subject. Where *have* you been?" She lowered her voice. "I was promised ravishment. Do I *look* ravished to you?"

Quesnel positively baulked. Rue was being too blunt.

Pleased, she let him stew in embarrassed silence.

He opened his mouth a few times. It was a very nice mouth, good for kissing, but currently he did slightly resemble a kipper.

"You were saying?" Rue prodded.

"What are you doing here?" blurted Quesnel.

"Mr Lefoux, this is actually *my* airship, if you'll recall? Although that fact seems to have escaped your notice."

Quesnel collected himself. "I understood you to be staying with your parents while you were in town. Putting our arrangement, as it were, temporarily on hold. Don't you *have* to be with them right now?"

Rue narrowed her eyes. *Avoiding me, is he?* "Oh, did you think that? And how long have you been in town yourself, Mr Lefoux?"

He looked guilty. "A little while." Which meant he could have been around for days and been purposefully avoiding her. He may even have brought the tank to the *Custard* himself!

"Lovely." Rue pulled her shoulders back and applied her décolletage. "While I must say that this wasn't the education I asked for, I suppose you are giving me a good one. Nice to know where I stand."

"You stand very well."

Rue narrowed her eyes.

Quesnel's sweet boyish face fell. "Oh, now, Rue, it's not you I was avoiding. It's—"

"Percy?"

"—more complicated than that. Besides, I could hardly come calling while you're enfolded in an overabundance of parental concern."

"So now you're *ashamed* of me? Marvellous." Rue was feeling legitimately hurt. She had thought she and Quesnel had an *understanding.* But lo there he stood looking tanned and fit, his blond hair flopping over his forehead in that extremely annoying way that made her want to push it back and she didn't *understand* anything.

"Of course not, *chérie*! I'm terrified of your parents. I highly doubt they would approve of any lessons likely to take place between you and I." He gave her a winning smile.

Rue would wager good money that Quesnel and his mother, Madame Lefoux, were the only two people in London *not* terrified of her parents. Why did he feel he must lie? She had thought that their friendship was at least based on honesty. She wouldn't have been so frank with him about matters of the boudoir, otherwise.

"Oh, I don't think that's an accurate statement, Mr Lefoux." Quesnel didn't fill her pause with protestations, so Rue continued. "Fine, well, I guess that ended before it started."

Quesnel instantly protested. *"Chérie—"*

Rue rolled right over him and his moronic little pet names that she liked so much. "Never mind, let's get on to more important matters. What are you stashing in *my* boiler room? What does it do? And who is trying to steal it?"

Quesnel blinked. "Just something I picked up. It might come in useful."

"Oh yes? A Lefoux original design?"

"How did you—?"

"Give me some credit, Mr Lefoux. I'm not ignorant of the styles of different inventors. That carapace has your family signature all over it."

"I shall let my mother know we are becoming predictable."

"Did I authorise you to install new machinery in my boiler room? No, don't answer that. I know I did not. It doesn't match the aesthetic of the teakettles, quite apart from everything else."

"What if I crocheted a tea-cosy to go over the carapace?"

Rue's ire was briefly arrested. "You crochet?"

"Yes, as a matter of fact. Although that would be my largest endeavour."

Although Rue conceded that a tea-cosy cover would indeed go much better with the rest of engineering, she wasn't giving him any quarter. "If you won't tell me what that tank contraption does, you're going to have to make a case for keeping it."

Quesnel blinked at her. It was wildly unfair to have wasted such pretty violet eyes on a man.

Rue crossed her arms. This plumped up her breasts, straining the muslin of the neckline.

The violet eyes fairly goggled.

I do love this dress, thought Rue. *At least it's proving he's not completely indifferent.* "Go on, persuade me."

"I don't know what to say, *mon petite chou*, except that I really do think we may need it. It's for the preservation of specimens."

"You think we'll be collecting samples in the near future, do you?"

"Of a kind."

At least she'd rung *some* information out of him. "What makes you believe, Mr Lefoux, that you are still part of my crew?"

Quesnel frowned. "Now, *chérie*, I didn't take you for one of those kinds of girls."

"What kind?"

"Spiteful in response to rejection."

Rue bit down on a gasp of pain. *How dare he!* "So it *was* rejection. Thank you for making your position clear. You could have *said* before you went to Egypt that you'd rather not be the one in charge of my education. I'm not desperate!"

"Of course you're not! You're stunning, exasperating, and

occasionally overwhelming. *And* quite enthusiastic in twisting my meaning. When did I reject you? I thought this was you turning me out onto the streets. Did you not just roust me?"

"Mr Lefoux, you signed on to my crew knowing that it was for *one* mission. I assumed, given your disappearance and lack of communication since India, that our business arrangement had terminated. You must understand, under those circumstances, that you secretly installing a *specimen tank in my hold* comes as somewhat of a surprise!"

Rue's voice had steadily risen. However, it was only on that last line that she realised they had an audience. A croquet match was paused in play to watch a lady of the realm yell roundly at her apparent paramour. At which juncture "specimen tank in my hold" took on an entirely euphemistic meaning. Rue's face burned.

Quesnel stayed calm. "Oh, no, my darling girl, certainly not! I've no intention of abandoning my position as long as you wish me to stay. I love *The Spotted Custard*. She's a marvellous ship. Besides, if you're assuming I'm leaving, why not the Tunstells as well? They only agreed to one trip, but they aren't going anywhere."

He gestured behind her to where Percy, Primrose, and several decklings stood watching the show, rather as if they were Wimbledon spectators.

Rue was getting flustered. She wasn't certain what they were talking about any more: Quesnel's position under her as chief engineer ... or some other amorphous position the details of which – who was under whom – had yet to be determined.

He took her hand. Just like Quesnel to play to an audience. He knew she now couldn't do anything dramatic, like slap him. "I'm sorry I had to leave unexpectedly. I'm sorry about the tank in the hold but I assure you it's necessary and explainable. Just not right *now*. Later? Tonight even, in private? Please, Rue, trust me."

His hand was warm and strong – and shaking a little bit. His eyes were big compelling pansies of promise and Rue found it all exceedingly annoying. How dare he actually be upset about this, and how dare she worry about his feelings when her own were at risk. And she was in the right!

"I'm sure you can, but right now I'll settle for what you and Percy were arguing about."

Quesnel's winning smile faded.

Rue pursed her lips. "I will get the whole story from the decklings, you realise? You were arguing in public, loudly."

Quesnel sighed. "I might, just possibly, have published a paper with the Royal Society about the discovery of the weremonkeys."

"First?"

"Mmm-hmm."

"Without including Percy as co-author?"

"I shared with Mrs Featherstonehaugh. But, no, not with Professor Tunstell."

"No wonder he's angry with you. That's incalculably rude."

"I did think he had already published with the Board of Associated Supernatural Studies or I would have included him. Without a doubt I would."

"Whose name was first?" Rue raised a hand. "No, don't answer that. I do not want to get involved. Academics!"

Percy was livid because Quesnel had scooped his discovery. And it wasn't even Quesnel's field. He was an inventor. He was supposed to report on new things he had *created* not *found*. Frankly, the entirety of the Rights of Discovery and Reportage should have gone to Mrs Featherstonehaugh. Although it was difficult for a lady to be taken seriously in these matters. Nevertheless, if Quesnel was going to co-author any paper on weremonkeys, he ought to have included Percy.

"For a smart man, Mr Lefoux, you can be an insensitive blighter." Rue was not one for crass language unless the occasion warranted it.

Quesnel was taken aback.

Rue prodded him in the chest with two fingers. "You know what your character flaw is, Mr Lefoux?" The way she said his name made it sound like an insult. "You are not meant to be taken seriously, and yet you will go about seriously mucking about in everyone else's lives."

Quesnel's eyes narrowed. "That's rich coming from you."

Rue sucked in a breath. Her scalp prickled and her eyes stung. "You're absolutely right. Neither of us should be taken seriously. And how can we build any kind of relationship on that?"

"Are we still talking about my being your chief engineer?" A smile teased about his lips.

Rue decided that her only means of keeping herself from getting hurt by this man was *not* to take him at all seriously. She took a deep breath, leaned forward, and kissed him softly, right on those still-smiling lips. In front of half of London.

Quesnel blinked at her.

Ha, thought Rue, *mull that one over, you little traitor.* "You think you're so good with people, Quesnel, but you're better off with the machines. You owe Percy an apology."

Quesnel looked surprised and then petulant.

"We will figure out what you owe me later." Rue said that to see if she could get his expression to change.

It did, to one of wariness mixed with anticipation. Good. He didn't deserve to be in control.

Quesnel wasn't one to stay confused. Before she could turn and walk back up the gangplank, knowing that her dress looked even better from behind, he snaked out an arm and pulled her in.

This time he kissed her and it was not so sweet, instead quite scalding. Rue gasped a protest into his mouth. She supposed one ought to close one's eyes, but she kept hers open, yellow staring into violet. *A violet Cyclops, this close up.* It was a good kiss. She liked everything about it – the warm taste of him, the steady arm, the smell of machine oil and fresh lime. She would have melted against him except for that stupid corset.

She could feel the heat of his hand on her waist all the way through the layers.

There was a roaring in her ears, which did confuse her a little. After all, Quesnel had kissed her before. And while it was quite wonderful, for he was a superb kisser, it hadn't caused auditory hallucinations in the past. *Aha*, thought Rue. *That must be* actual *roaring. Who's roaring at us?*

Something large and hairy yanked Quesnel away and pushed him back. Quesnel looked dazed by their kiss. Although it could have been the fact that standing between them was Rue's very angry father. Her birth father, mind you, the werewolf, Lord Maccon.

Rue adored her Paw but he did operate mainly on emotion. Today, he was looking rough. He was an Alpha and old, thus one of the few werewolves who could withstand full sunlight. But under the soft afternoon glow, he did not look healthy. There were lines carved into his face and his salted dark hair was limp. He was scruffy, not uncommon since he slept the day through touching Mother, which meant he was mortal enough to grow a beard. But Lady Maccon usually stayed around so he could shave it off after. Rue's mother was not fond of beards.

"Good afternoon, Paw." Rue spoke calmly. "Where have you been?"

Lord Maccon watched her out of glassy yellow eyes, so like her own. *Well, except for the glassy bit.* He turned his head to glare at Quesnel, teeth bared.

The inventor was trying to look unruffled. But Lord Maccon was very large and, even in sunlight, very strong. Quesnel, while fit, was nowhere near his fighting weight. Rue wouldn't put it past her chief engineer to be armed with silver, possibly several iterations thereof, but she hoped he wasn't inclined to permanently damage her father.

It was an odd thought, that Paw might need protection. But he did look most unwell.

"Paw." Rue put a gentling hand to his arm. It was full daylight so she could touch him without hairy repercussions. For while her mother's power worked under sunlight, Rue's did not. As a little girl, she'd always loved it when Paw was awake during the day. He gave the best hugs. "What's wrong?"

He stayed distracted, growling at Quesnel.

Rue's beloved Paw was, as her mother often put it, only barely civilised. Yet this was a bit much, even for him. Not that it was odd for an aristocratic father to become agitated at finding his only daughter in a clinch with a commoner on a croquet green. But Lord Maccon was looking, and there was no politer way of putting it, *not in control*.

"Paw, I wasn't in danger. Mr Lefoux and I have an understanding." *Well*, she corrected the little lie in her head, *I understand that he is no longer to be taken seriously and that I should keep my heart out of it. And I also understand that I might as well keep trying to seduce him because a man who kisses that well has got to be good at more than kissing*. Rue's curiosity, it should be pointed out at this juncture, had got her into more scrapes than it ought. She should know better. But there was that kiss.

Lord Maccon didn't move. Just kept growling. Rue shifted into panic. This was different. He was already over the edge. Whatever cliff it was that tumbled werewolves into animal, he had fallen to the bottom of it.

Rue spoke carefully, trying to pull him back to her with the firmness of her voice. "Paw, are you able to speak?"

He didn't answer, simply stared at Quesnel. Had it been night, he would most certainly be a wolf. But the sun kept him human. Well, human-*looking*.

"Don't run," Rue advised her chief engineer. "He'll only chase."

"Mmm-hmm." Quesnel sounded as though he, too, might be losing the ability to speak.

"Are you tarnished?"

Quesnel inclined his head.

"Can you pull? Slowly?"

Quesnel moved with liquid grace, reaching with his right hand to scrunch back the cuff on his left arm. This revealed a dart emitter on his wrist. He made a tapping flick to load it, no doubt with silver. Not big enough to do serious damage, but if applied to the right area it could certainly slow a were-wolf down.

Rue let out a shaky breath and returned her focus to her father.

"Paw, look at me. Please."

He didn't move.

Instinct, this is all instinct. I have to play on that.

She gave Quesnel a wink to let him know she wasn't serious and then gave a small whimpering sigh. "Oh." She put a hand to her head in the manner of Aunt Ivy. "I feel faint. I feel dizzy." She stumbled slightly to one side.

And he was there, big arms scooping her up. So reassuring, usually, Paw carrying her like she was a child again, but his grip was too tight.

Rue tried a light touch to his bristled cheek. Finally, their eyes met. Yellow-to-yellow, grave and worried to glassy and . . . absent.

Rue could think of only one thing that might help this situa-tion – Lady Maccon. "Where's Mother, Paw? Where's your wife?"

Lord Maccon twitched, maybe hearing her, maybe not.

Rue tamped down on the realisation that the London Pack had been drunk and out of control last night, not for some bumbling adorable werewolf reason, but because their Alpha was out of control.

"Alexia, where is she?" *Instinct*, Rue instructed herself, *activate instinct.* "I'm fine, Paw. Everything is well. You need to find your wife. She needs you." *You need her.*

Alphas who lost their control went mad. They were put down like dogs, for the good of society. Her Paw was, more than ever before, a walking corpse.

Something Rue said went in and stuck.

Lord Maccon blinked and for one second he was back – her big gruff softy of a Paw. "Rue? What are you doing—?"

She took that moment of lucidity and ran with it. "Paw, find Mother. You *must* find Mother. Now."

He tilted his head at her. "But?"

"I'm safe." She did not mention Quesnel. He was standing as still as could be, dart pointed, barely breathing. No need to remind Paw of what he had interrupted; it may have sent him back to that place of the glassy eyes.

"I'm a modern woman, remember? Dama trained me."

Paw sneered automatically. "That vampire."

That was good. That was a normal reaction. "But, Paw, I think Mother needs you now. You should go to her."

He blinked again, like a small sleep-addled child. "Alexia? I should?"

"Yes, at once. Please?"

"If you think that necessary, little one. Is there trouble?" He set her down; huge hands still gripped her shoulders firmly.

"Yes, there's trouble." It was true enough, even if the trouble was him.

"Then I'll go." He whirled and ran.

Rue spared a moment to be grateful he was wearing clothing; the state he was in, it could have gone either way. She regretted that even in sunlight he could move faster than most humans. She should set a deckling to track him, but even if she was willing to risk the life of one of her crew, it was too late. He'd vanished.

The horror of it prickled her all over – sharp, painful spikes. Her Paw was going mad. She hadn't noticed. She'd been too caught up in leaving home, in exploring India, and angry queens, and her pretty ship, and her pathetic romance. And now she'd set him loose through London, where he could kill someone. Or himself.

Rue could only hope he found Mother soon. He wouldn't

harm Lady Maccon. Mother always said, "Your father's instincts are different with us, infant. It has to do with smell and family. Don't take advantage, but you should know when he's wolf he'll always try to protect you. Don't take it as an insult. He can't help it, poor dear." Mother would handle everything. She would make it all better. That was the awe and the grace of Lady Maccon.

Except that this didn't seem like a thing that could get better.

Rue had been raised with pack. Rue *was* pack. She knew what it was to be a werewolf. A little. She also did not understand in the slightest. She never hunted on instinct. Even at full moon she could stay in control. She never craved flesh. She simply liked to dash about hairy and on four legs once in a while. But she had *thought* she understood werewolves and their moods and forms. Yet she'd never realised a werewolf could be in human shape, yet still a wolf.

She let out a shaky breath and tried to find her equilibrium but her mind would not stop. *Paw will have to leave off Alpha. Will he be challenged? Will he be killed? Could I get him out of London first? Could I take him somewhere safe? Where could we go where Alpha's curse would not get him? It takes all Alphas in the end.*

Much to her own surprise and embarrassment, fat tears burned down her face.

Quesnel turned from where he'd tracked her father with his dart emitter and saw her crumble. Which was humiliating, because she had just decided not to trust him, and she really couldn't tolerate that loving sympathetic look in his eyes.

He took a step towards her, arms open to enfold her in a soothing embrace.

She couldn't suffer *that* either. She put both her hands up to ward him off.

Then there came a swirl of fabric and the scent of apple blossoms.

Primrose was there.

Primrose was making calm sweet noises, wrapping Rue in soft gentle arms and guiding her back aboard the *Custard* and away from all the staring. Away from Quesnel's hurt sympathy. Away from Paw's glassy wolf eyes. Up the gangplank and through a silent mass of sombre decklings and a strangely agonised-looking Percy, and down the stairs, and into the privacy of the captain's quarters.

There Rue could heave out the sobs of certain loss that come with change. For Paw was meant to be immortal, and for the first time Rue knew that he was not.

CHAPTER FOUR

In Which the Maccon Family Is Quite Imprudent

Primrose stayed, rubbing Rue's back and making sympathetic noises. Primrose was good like that. She didn't ask what was wrong.

Finally Rue said, "I" – sniff – "hate" – sniff – "stays."

"Let's get you out of that corset, then, shall we?" Which was a mark of how good a friend Primrose was, for she was normally the most proper young thing and tried not to know that Rue rarely wore underpinnings. Now she pretended delight at helping her strip and climb into a comfortable tea-gown.

Rue loved her for the pretence.

"Prim, something's wrong with Paw." Rue sat on the edge of the counterpane and looked at her hands, trying not to cry again.

Primrose perched next to her. "Yes. I do believe you might be right about that."

"It's Alpha's curse."

Prim did not mollify that horrible statement with platitudes. "Do you know how old he is, your father?"

"Old enough."

"Is that what it looks like, the curse?"

"It differs, depending on the Alpha. There are not many cases recorded, as most don't survive long enough. Prim, he looked right at me and yet did not see me. And in his eyes there was only the wolf. No Paw."

Primrose likely didn't follow but she nodded. "You might want to talk to someone who knows more about this situation."

"Dama?" Rue scrubbed at her face with her hand.

"No – your mother. I know it's not your favourite thing to do, but I believe you should confront her. They must have been hiding this from you. We weren't out of the country so long that he should have deteriorated this quickly."

"Unless I wilfully refused to notice."

"Rue, be kind to yourself. Even you aren't *that* obtuse."

"It takes a lot out of me, confronting my mother. I need a plan, in case she doesn't have one."

Prim gave her a look. "You mean if you disagree with hers? Your mother always has a plan."

"Fair point. Do you think Percy would look up Alpha's curse, see what he can find?"

"Of course. I'll ask him. You believe there's something we can do that hasn't been tried before?"

"To stop Alpha's curse? I doubt it. But we might isolate him for the safety of others."

"And stop him being challenged and killed by some whippersnapper? To what purpose? So he can die alone and insane? Be fair to him, Rue."

Rue closed her eyes and swallowed. Primrose was right. She couldn't decide her father's fate any more than he could dictate hers. "I have to try *something*!"

Primrose stood and went to the porthole. "A few hours until sunset. I'll put Percy on it."

"What happened to Quesnel?"

Primrose looked severe. "Mr Lefoux has gone about his business. He tried to follow us but Percy sent him on his way."

"Did he really? They didn't start yelling at each other again, did they?"

"No, thank goodness. My brother has been known to be capable in emergency situations."

"Is this an emergency situation?"

"Yes, I do believe it might be. Now I'll go and talk to him. Should I fetch tea?"

"Would you join me?"

"By all means. I'll stay as long as you need."

Rue found a small smile somewhere and pasted it on. "Would you read to me?"

It harkened back to their childhood days. Primrose was a quick study and had read earlier than Rue, who was frankly too lazy to bother with book learning overmuch. Primrose would read to Rue out loud in her halting child's treble. As they got older, Prim would do the voices and get all dramatic. Rue could read herself by then, but she liked being spoiled.

Primrose gave a tinkling laugh. "I'd be delighted. German poetry perhaps?"

"Something less painful, I think."

Primrose disappeared briefly. Tea arrived a quarter of an hour later, brought in by a worried-looking Virgil. He'd been sent by Percy, because tea detail wasn't ordinarily Virgil's responsibility. Footnote followed, or was pushed gently into the room by some redhead hovering out of view. The feline performed his catlike duty by jumping instantly onto Rue's lap and purring up a storm.

Primrose followed shortly. "I've brought you Byron – always makes things better."

Cook had included a few custard éclairs – Rue's favourite. She managed to inhale two while Prim sipped tea and read Byron in ridiculously sepulchral tones. Everyone was being so nice, Rue almost felt the urge to cry again. She put her tea down and buried her face in Footnote's fuzzy coat, which smelled faintly of cheese.

In the end, it did make her feel better. Byron was so ridiculously melodramatic it quite made her feel as if she were overdoing it herself. Tea, poetry, and cat duly applied, Rue girded her loins. The sun had set and it was time to approach her mother.

Percy appeared just as she was heading out. His hair was sticking up all over, as if he'd been tugging at it.

"Prudence? About your quandary?"

Rue was eager. "Do you have anything for me?"

"Aside from suggesting he stay in permanent contact with your mother? That might stave off Alpha's curse."

Rue shuddered. "I wouldn't wish that on anyone."

Percy shrugged. "Well, then, there's always Egypt."

"Oh? Oh! The God-Breaker Plague you mean?"

"Yes. There's very little written about it, and the more recent stuff is classified. But it does make immortals mortal, so it might counteract the curse. He'd go ahead and die, though. I mean, just like the rest of us."

Rue hugged him fiercely. "Thank you, Percy."

"Oh leave off." He brushed her away gruffly, but his eyes crinkled in pleasure.

Rue hailed a hackney. She considered herself a New Woman, thus she did not think it odd to travel alone in public hire, even if Primrose frowned upon it and Aunt Ivy thought it perfectly scandalous.

Nothing awful happened during the three-quarters-of-an-hour drive. She paid her fare, bidding the man on the box a pleasant evening, and took a deep breath to settle her nerves.

It was after dark so the werewolves were awake, and there were a number of clavigers also surging round. Many of them, duties discharged for the day, were heading off to their theatrical obligations or other pursuits. It was the pack equivalent of the changing of the guards.

"Evening, Lady Prudence. You're not in the wrong house, are

you?" A new claviger, whose name Rue did not know, let her in and gave her a small salute.

"You might well ask but I've come to call on Mother."

"Ah. My sympathies."

"Thank you. And where . . . ?"

"In the back parlour, miss, with himself. Last I checked they weren't admitting."

"I'm sure they will make an exception in my case."

The claviger looked doubtful, for the pack had strict instructions never to disturb Lord and Lady Maccon when they made it clear they did not wish to be disturbed.

"It's important."

"Your peril, my lady."

Rue gave him a nod and brushed by, heading for the back parlour. The dining room opposite was abuzz with humanity. The uncles sat at the table ripping into huge trenchers of raw meat, occasionally hurling bits at each other, boisterous as ever. Was it rougher than normal? Less controlled?

Rafe noticed her and said something. They all quieted. Most of them hung their heads and didn't look at her. Hemming gave Rue a cocky grin. She thought about reminding him how ridiculous he'd looked in her dress, but the pack would have to wait.

Except they apparently wouldn't. From a spot near the door, hidden from her hallway view, emerged a strapping blond gentleman.

Major Channing Channing of the Chesterfield Channings was both tall and broad, although not to Paw's scale. He was entirely comfortable with his size in a way that many large men of Rue's acquaintance were not. Few big men occupied space easily; most were constantly at war with it, trying to make room for themselves. Uncle Channing was elegant. He was also painfully good-looking, not a requirement for werewolves by any stretch of the imagination. In fact, Rue could never quite understand why he hadn't gone for vampire. His style was more suited to hive than pack. But pack he was. Gamma by station, which meant the only ones to outrank him were Paw and Uncle Rabiffano. In human form he had a petulant mouth and icy-blue eyes. Most of the time both were arranged into a sneer of such arrogance it kept everyone at a goodly distance. Rue had learned, over the years, that this was the point.

It never worked on Rue. She'd somehow understood from her littlest girl state that Uncle Channing wasn't intentionally mean; he was simply wounded in a way that made him scared of being prey. He hunted others as a great white wolf, vicious and bloody. And he hunted with words as a great blond man, equally vicious and bloody. Uncle Channing would do anything not to be vulnerable.

It almost hurt Rue to see him contort himself into shame before her.

"Lady Prudence?"

"Uncle Channing?"

He hung his head. "My behaviour last night. Please allow me to apologise. It was unconscionable. If I had known who you were, I would never . . . I can't possibly make amends."

"Pish-tosh." Rue sounded so like her mother it startled a few of the other werewolves into smiles. "You didn't hurt one hair on my pelt. There is nothing to apologise for. What's a little growling between family, hmm?"

Uncle Channing lifted his head, icy eyes hot with hope. "You aren't angry?"

"Of course I'm not angry. It's not your fault."

Uncle Channing looked like he wanted to protest. Only someone behind Rue said in a gravelly voice, "Channing, did you growl at my daughter?"

Rue spun to find her father looming in the parlour doorway with his wife, a slightly smaller loom, behind him. She was holding his hand. Keeping him mortal.

He seemed to be wholly Paw, tired but otherwise nothing like the creature she had encountered that afternoon.

"Paw, good, there you are."

He ignored her. "Channing?"

"It was all in good fun, wasn't it, Uncle Channing? And Uncle Rabiffano was there to keep the peace. Nice of him, actually," Rue prattled, squeezing past her father and into the back parlour. "Good evening, Mother."

"Infant."

Rue glared at her parents' joined hands. "Got your hands full this evening, have you?"

Lady Maccon was a mite taken aback by her daughter's tone. "I don't quite comprehend your meaning."

"How long, exactly, have you had your hands full, Mother? Since before I left for India or is this a new occurrence? Paw, would you please close the door and come in? Good night, Uncle Channing. Perhaps we will talk again a little later? No hard feelings, I promise."

Uncle Channing nodded at her, looking relieved, but he did not move. His Alpha had not yet dismissed him.

Paw gave him one more dominating glare. "Major." He slammed the door in his Gamma's face.

Lady Maccon focused on her daughter. "What's happened, infant?"

Rue examined her mother. Lady Maccon seemed more frustrated than was normal, even for her. *If she's been holding Paw back from insanity, she's had to stay touching him, flesh to flesh, whenever they were both awake.* Rue had never once doubted that her parents adored one another, but that kind of thing would strain any marriage.

"Had a little bit of a chat with Paw earlier. Although, I did most of the chatting. Paw was there but he also *wasn't* if you take my meaning?"

Mother's face blanched, as much as it could, for she was swarthy. She collected herself and tsked. "Oh for goodness' sake, you two, let's sit like a proper family."

They sat and stared at one another in awkward silence, which was quite familial.

Paw broke it. "Little one, did I drop by for a visit this after-noon? Or was that a dream?"

"I thought werewolves didn't dream." Rue didn't answer his question.

He continued musing. "I *did* stop by. I'm certain of it. Massive ladybug ship. And you were there and so was that blister Lefoux. And he was *kissing* you!" His voice rose.

Then he rose as well and marched back to the door, ripping it open. Luckily it was built for such abuse.

"Channing!"

Uncle Channing reappeared with more than supernatural speed, suggesting that he had been listening at keyholes, although with werewolf hearing a keyhole wasn't necessary.

Paw didn't care. "As a personal favour, I'd like you to go keep an eye on this Quesnel scrapper. You know him, Lefoux's spawn. He seems to be hunting rather the wrong prey."

"Oh, really, Paw!" Rue was moved to protest.

With a nod and an avaricious gleam in his eyes, Channing clapped his top hat to his head and headed out.

Lady Maccon took this all in stride and stayed focused on her daughter. "Kissing? In public? Is that wise?"

Lord Maccon slammed the door ... again ... and rounded on his wife. "How can you be so calm? He was *encroaching* on our daughter!"

"Husband," said Lady Maccon in *that* tone, "sit down! Our Rue has her majority. I should hope she has had more kissing than I at twenty-one. Young women need *some* experience. Rue, dear, remind me to discuss the precautionary arts with you at some point soon."

Rue looked nonplussed. She supposed she ought to have expected this from Mother. Lady Maccon always had a ready answer that was slightly more practical than anyone expected.

Lord Maccon sputtered. "But he was kissing her! And he is quite a bit older. And she was letting him. And people saw."

Lady Maccon raised her free hand in an awfully familiar

silencing gesture. "Now, now, let's take this one step at a time. Prudence Alessandra Maccon Akeldama—"

Uh-oh, full name. I may actually be in trouble. "Yes, Mother?"

"I will allow that kissing someone is indeed necessary for your education."

"Thank you, Mother."

"Although your father may not agree with me."

"He does not," Paw grumbled.

His wife continued as if he hadn't spoken. "But you really can't be seen to do so with a commoner in broad daylight, certainly not in front of your crew. And likely a few builders." Rue winced. "And perhaps some croquet players?" Rue winced again.

"He deserved it," said Rue petulantly. "He was being a rotter."

"Language!"

"Sorry, Mother."

"So you kissed him?"

Rue nodded.

Lady Maccon looked to her husband with a satisfied expression. "See there, revenge kissing, no harm done."

Rue couldn't help it; something about her mother always got her into trouble. It was that maddening calm. "Although, to be fair, when Paw arrived, Quesnel was kissing me back."

Paw came half off the couch on a growl.

Lady Maccon looked less pleased. "Was he indeed? Quesnel Lefoux? Interesting choice. You realise his mother and I are friendly?"

Lord Maccon made a funny huff noise. His wife tugged gently at their joined hands and he subsided back into the couch.

Mother added, with only a minor glare in his direction, "Although not quite as friendly as we might have been."

Rue didn't follow the byplay. "I like him well enough for a dalliance."

"Dalliance!" Lord Maccon positively roared.

His wife made a funny sputter noise that might have been outrage or amusement or outraged amusement. "Our girl is thoroughly modern, dear. Young people have a different perspective on such things. Will you be continuing this particular croquet match?"

Rue tilted her head, humouring her. "Not at the moment. I believe Mr Lefoux needs to stew. He thinks himself far too enticing. I won't be played with, croquet or no croquet."

"Good girl, very wise," approved her mother.

"Rejecting him because he kissed you back?" Lord Maccon perked up, not following but hopeful.

Rue finally sputtered to a halt. "It's no good. This is too bad. I can't be discussing this with you. You're my parents. Who I go about kissing, or not kissing as the case may be, really is none of your business."

At that, Lady Maccon became annoyed. "Of course it's our business! You're a proper lady, or as proper as we could turn out given the circumstances. You can't go around kissing coquettish Frenchmen willy-nilly. It's not done and the papers will positively float off the stands. Frankly, I'm not convinced Mr Lefoux is a top choice. I don't keep full accounts of your generation, but isn't he a terrible philanderer? Wasn't there something about an opera girl a few seasons ago?"

Rue was about to point out that what she meant was that she didn't want to discuss the specifics of the kissing, when a tremendous galumphing clatter in the hallway made further speech impossible and indicated that the pack was departing for the evening.

"Should you let them out?" Rue wondered aloud before she could stop herself.

Lady Maccon sucked in a breath.

Lord Maccon said, very deadly and quiet, "Are you questioning my authority?"

Rue dropped her gaze submissively, took a big breath, and leapt. "No, Paw. I'm questioning your control."

She wasn't certain what such a bald statement might do. Would he drop Mother's hand and shift, charge at her, roaring?

Would he crumble like a child into confessions and tears? But what *did* happen was almost worse. There was nothing but silence. Rue glanced up through her lashes.

Mother was grey under her olive skin, her eyes sad. Paw was hunched, small as he could get, which wasn't very. Her indomitable parents, Rue realised, looked defeated.

The silence stretched.

Desperate to see something of their normal dynamic, Rue sacrificed her own pride. "Look. I like Mr Lefoux. I think he's a prime piece, if you take my meaning. And it's good if one of us is well versed, don't you think? Paw, don't answer that. Regardless, I believe he is attracted to me, although I doubt he takes me very seriously."

"I canna be listening to this," said Lord Maccon. And then on a roar, "What do you mean he *doesn't take you seriously?*"

"Oh, Paw, be fair. I don't take me seriously most of the time. Why should anyone else? Besides, I'm not sure I want serious – it can be such a bother."

Lord Maccon looked exactly as if he wanted to bash heads, possibly hers and Quesnel's.

Rue soldiered on. "Besides, I don't think Mr Lefoux takes anything seriously except maybe inventions and boilers. He's charming, undoubtedly, but not a lot more than charming. I *was* hurt when he wandered off to Egypt and abandoned me, but I've learned my lesson. I believe he'll give me a good education, but keeping my heart out of it seems the best approach."

Lord Maccon looked pained, as if he wanted to stopper over his ears, but then he roared again. "He abandoned *you?*"

Mother, accustomed to the roar, was briefly distracted. "Did you say *Egypt?*"

Rue nodded, noting the emphasis with interest. "Then he returned to London without telling me and installed this tank in my boiler room without asking, so he's clearly not to be trusted."

Mother arrowed in on that like a pointer on a dead partridge. "What kind of tank?"

"I don't know! That's the annoying part."

Lady Maccon focused on her husband, ignoring Rue with an abrupt thoroughness that Rue had grown accustomed to over the years. "I need to talk to Genevieve."

"Must you?" grumbled her father.

She turned back to Rue. "Go on, infant. You were saying about the boy?"

Rue shrugged. "That was it. I only want a bit of fun. I think I've got it sorted so I don't get hurt. Neither of you need worry on that score."

Paw still looked upset. But Lady Maccon took Rue at her word. Mother was like that, mostly accepting of other people's assessments of themselves. She was eminently pragmatic, which came with being soulless. She also mistakenly assumed everyone else was equally practical. This ought to have gotten her into trouble, living with werewolves, but most of the pack accepted her at face value, too. They treated her not as another pack member as much as an anchor located well below the emotional aetheric currents upon which werewolves bobbed.

She was thoughtful. "I don't know the boy, not well. Young scamp of a thing running around blowing up contrivance chambers at the drop of a hat when I first met him. You'd have thought the same about his mother, though, flirty and inconsequential, had you known her when we were younger. Genevieve hides inside her inventions as a protection against affection. Perhaps her son is similar? Angelique, well, she was a different matter entirely."

"Angelique?"

"Quesnel's blood mother."

"What?"

"He never told you? He's adopted."

"Adopted?"

"Oh yes. Thought he got his looks from his father, did you? Oh, no, no. Angelique was this little blonde slip of a thing. Quite the beauty. Also French. Biggest pansy eyes you ever saw, dab hand with the curling iron as well. She was my lady's maid for a while there."

"*What?*"

"Nasty piece of work, in the end. Espionage. I rather think she might have broken Genevieve's heart. They were, you know, *together* for some time, back in the day."

Rue did know that Quesnel's mother preferred the company of ladies; he had admitted as much. And Rue was Lord Akeldama's daughter, too. Dama made certain her education included all possible options. He himself preferred the company of gentlemen. Rue had, in the end, decided that she did as well – prefer the company of gentlemen, that is. Boyish French ones with pansy eyes and, as it turned out, contorted views on family and love.

"That could explain a lot about him."

"Yes," said Lady Maccon, "I thought you should know. Could be hazardous should you relax your stance on not taking him seriously. From my own experience, I can assure you, it was very dangerous to care for Angelique. Who knows if that kind of thing can be inherited? You see, infant, he's not a great match in terms of the particulars of class and rank, but I also worry about other aspects."

Rue grinned. "Very thoughtful, Mother. I appreciate the information. And now if we are being perfectly honest with one another, may I ask what's wrong with Paw? Sorry, Paw, but I'm not perpetually blind to your faults."

Lady Maccon laughed. "Too many things to list, I should say."

Lord Maccon gave his wife a dour look. "Please don't try."

"It's Alpha's curse, isn't it?"

Mother's wide mouth twisted in a sad sort of grimace. "Yes, dear, it is."

Rue widened her eyes so as not to tear up. "Has he hurt anyone?"

"Not yet. Not as far as we know."

Paw stared down at his free hand as if it held the secrets of the world, thoroughly ashamed of himself.

"Paw, don't look so. It's not like you could help it. Doesn't it happen to every Alpha?"

Mother examined the ceiling. "He thinks he's superior to the others. Stronger. Better. Yes, Conall, I know, you always have been before. Except maybe the dewan. But you aren't perfect. Trust me. At least you're nowhere near as bad as Lord Woolsey got."

Paw looked horrified. In classic fashion, Rue's mother's attempt at consolation went wide of the mark.

"Lord Woolsey?" Rue prodded.

Lady Maccon was in a forthcoming mood. "Previous Alpha to your father, came over all violent and rotten to the core. Removing him proved to be quite the mess. Killed your grandfather, not to put too fine a point on it."

Rue was so horrified that even her notoriously obtuse mother noticed.

"Oh, don't worry, infant. All reports seem to suggest Lord Woolsey wasn't a very nice man even before he caught the Alpha's curse. Frankly, neither was your grandfather. You'll have to ask Professor Lyall if you want the details. Lord Woolsey was before my time. Although, I do know that he turned bad enough to almost cause a civil uprising. An insane Alpha is no small thing and can have wide-ranging political implications. Which I do keep reminding your father but he insists—"

"Enough, woman. Enough." Paw raised his free hand to the heavens as though petitioning for interference.

"He doesn't want you involved."

Rue nodded, understanding her father's feelings likely more than her mother did. Paw was embarrassed. He wanted to be her strong, solid comfort. She was his daughter and she wasn't allowed to see him weak.

She couldn't stop herself from asking in a small voice, "Are you going to die, Paw?"

"Och, sweetheart, no. Well, not immediately." Paw leaned forward across the tea table to put his hand over hers, where they were clasped together, white-knuckled in her lap. Her fingers ached, which meant she must have been clutching them together for a while, unnoticed.

Lady Maccon said, "Is that what you thought? Oh dear. I knew I should have told you sooner."

"Don't they all die, though?" Rue clarified, barely above a whisper. "Aren't they all killed, the cursed Alphas?"

"Well, yes, under ordinary circumstances. Sometimes by their Betas. Sometimes by a new Alpha challenging for the safety of all. Werewolves who go mad are put down by their own kind, for everyone's sake," Lady Maccon explained helpfully.

"Alexia!" snapped her husband at Rue's miserable expression. "Do shut up!"

He shifted over to Rue, gathering her into a one-armed hug. Still holding his wife's hand, he could touch Rue without any fear, for his daughter couldn't steal wolf while her mother kept him mortal.

Lady Maccon realised she was making things worse. "Don't worry, infant, we have a plan."

"Taking Paw to Egypt?"

"How on earth did you know?"

Rue looked at her in exasperation. *When will Mother stop seeing me as a child?* "I had Percy look into the matter. It's the most efficient and elegant solution. Which is your style. How do you plan to get Paw out of London alive?"

"Well, I had thought—"

"Alexia, enough. Little one, your mother has a big mouth. But we have figured it all out. We even have the Alpha transition in place. I wanted to wait for Kingair to return. I don't like to leave my pack with an inexperienced Alpha and no Beta. But they are still in India and I seem to have run out of time. I didn't mean to frighten you. Your mother has been a godsend. No Alpha could have held on as long as I did without a preternatural spouse. She'll not mind my saying, we are both wearing a little thin."

"Too true," said Lady Maccon with feeling. "I thought you were impossible when we only saw each other a few times a night. This" – she raised their joined hands – "is *torture!*"

Rue frowned, remembering something Quesnel had said. She'd been annoyed with him so it hadn't struck her at the time. *"I thought you were staying with your parents. Don't you have to right now?"* She'd thought he'd meant for propriety's sake, but had he meant because of Paw's illness? Because she could certainly help her parents in this particular arena.

"Oh, for goodness' sake, you two." She allowed her annoyance to show. "You should have told me from the start and this could have been avoided."

They blinked at her, confused.

"Just use me instead!"

"Oh!" said Lady Maccon. "What a fabulous idea."

Paw frowned. "If you're sure? You won't be able to accomplish much of an evening."

"I enjoy being a wolf."

Which was really all it took.

Lady Maccon, with an expression of profound relief, let go of her husband's hand.

Rue felt the snap back of the tether as it hit her own flesh like a physical wave of tingling. Then she was shifting and changing. And there she was, brindled wolf wearing her father's power in her skin and the remnants of a rather nice tea-gown. It didn't feel unusual; whatever it was that made Paw Alpha and insane didn't transmit to her. She felt like her normal wolf self. No different from the night before when she'd filched from Hemming. She wasn't surprised. While Rue's wolf form looked like a smaller version of her father's, she wasn't *actually* him. She never felt Alpha, either. No Anubis form, no urge to dominate, although as a female werewolf she should automatically be Alpha. It wasn't worth puzzling over, for even with her limited wolf eyes, Rue could see the profound relief on both her parents' faces. That was what mattered.

"You'll have to stay within tether distance of your father, infant. Please don't forget. He can't be allowed wolf form at night, unless he absolutely must fight."

Rue nodded her big shaggy head.

They were interrupted by someone knocking – loudly and persistently – on the parlour door.

Lady Maccon, freed up from her hand-holding obligations, went to open it.

Winkle stood there, looking sheepish. He was, as only to be expected from one of Dama's drones, perfectly turned out for the evening. His dark glossy hair, a true glorious blue black, shone under the hallway lights and his up-tilted eyes gleamed.

He took in the family dynamic without comment. "Lady Maccon, Lady Prudence." A small bow to both the woman and the wolf. "Lord Maccon."

Lady Maccon smiled. "Good evening. Winkle, isn't it?"

"Yes, my lady. I apologise for interrupting but it's a matter of some delicacy. It's Lord Akeldama."

Rue felt her stomach lurch. *Not Dama as well!*

"Is he unwell?" Even Mother was worried.

Winkle grinned. "Him? Never. He has sent me with a message. I'm afraid it's not the best news. But there seems to be – oh dear me, I don't quite know how to put it – a *brawl* occurring down off Worple Road. Some species of croquet green or what have you is playing host."

Rue's ears perked. *My airship!*

Lord Maccon grumbled, "What's that to do with us? Mobs are constabulary business. What is that vampire about? Disturbing us with gossip of brawls and—"

Lady Maccon looked to her wolf daughter. "Isn't that where *The Spotted Custard* is parked?"

Moored, Rue wanted to correct her but couldn't. She nodded.

"I'm sorry to say," Winkle continued, "this brawl looks to be taking place between your pack, my lord, and Baroness Tunstell's drones."

"Wonderful. Just wonderful," said Lady Maccon while Rue and her father both pushed past Winkle and ran out of the front door into the street.

Rue kept pace with her father easily; after all, she was the one in wolf form. He was fit as a mortal human but was big enough to be built for taking a stand rather than moving fast. In fact, Lord Maccon running was more an act of falling at speed. So really, Rue only had to trot.

It came as no surprise to her when Lady Maccon drew along-side driving a shapely little bounder. The dogcart was of the sporting style, where the driver sits facing and the passenger at his back in a reverse position – plenty of room inside the box for hunting dogs. Or, as was its use in the Maccon household, prematurely shifted werewolves.

"Get in," Lady Maccon ordered her husband.

"I'll drive."

"Don't be absurd, Conall. I'm a much better whip."

Rue sat on her haunches in the alcove of a delicious-smelling butcher's shop and waited for them to hash it out.

With a look of disgust, Paw swung himself up behind his wife in the transverse seat.

"Infant, keep pace but don't startle the prancer."

Rue resented being instructed by her mother to do something that she was going to do anyway. Being in the company of Lady Maccon without being able to speak might well drive Rue more bonkers than Paw. She was already regretting her offer. She bared her teeth.

Lady Maccon took off at a dangerous speed.

Rue ran after, wishing she could remind Mother that Paw was currently mortal, and perhaps a little care was warranted.

The dogcart careened around a corner, practically on one wheel.

Rue shook her head and put on a burst of speed to close the widening gap. Werewolves could outpace horses, especially one pulling Lord and Lady Maccon's weight. She caught up and jogged behind, nostrils flaring to keep track of the cityscape around her. That had been one of the hardest things to learn as a werewolf pup, how her map of the world changed to one of scents.

They made good time across town. Fortunately, traffic was light, as it was early yet. Balls and shows were hours off starting so no one was trying to get anywhere important. Given that Lady Maccon was all over the road, this was a good thing. *If Mother is the superior whip, Paw must be a sight.*

By the time they drew up outside the All England Croquet, Lawn Tennis, and Airborne Polo Club, Rue's senses already told her that things were in a bad state. The noise was absurd, a mix of yells, yips, growls, and foul language. The smells were those of sweat, fear, and blood.

Rue's attention went to her ship.

The Spotted Custard floated in chubby majesty under the moonlight, well out of a werewolf's leaping range. Decklings lined the railing of the main deck, armed to the teeth but not doing anything, simply watching the broiling mass below. Occasionally, one of them would point, shaking his head, and another would nod and spit in disgust. By deckling standards the fight was inferior entertainment.

There was a large, beautifully decorated hat among the spectators, which meant Primrose was there. *Good, Prim is safe. No doubt Percy is in his library, uninterested in such a plebeian thing as a werewolf brawl.*

It was quite the scrapper. All of the pack seemed to be there in wolf form. They were up against four vampires and a dozen drones, all male and all armed for battle with silver knives and grim expressions. None of them seemed to be packing *serious* firepower, but nevertheless an encounter between silver blade and werewolf flesh rarely worked out in the werewolf's favour.

As a rule, werewolves didn't fight vampires. Vampires were faster and better armed. Werewolves were stronger with both teeth and claws but couldn't exactly carry wooden stakes or anything useful like that. There were, however, usually more werewolves in a pack than vampires in a hive. All things taken together, hives and packs were evenly matched, so why bother fighting?

In this case, it didn't seem like the vampires were intent on serious damage. Their drones, on the other hand, were fighting with the white-eyed desperation of mortal against immortal and weren't doing well.

Baroness Ivy Tunstell's hive was, much to the general disgust of society, made up of mostly older Egyptian vampires, transported with her during her minting swarm all the way from Alexandria. They fought beautifully with swirling movements and lightning-fast flicks of the wrist. Over the past two decades, they'd learned not to kick – it wasn't done in British society – but against werewolves they seemed to believe this rule did not apply.

Rue swung her head, ears swivelling, nose aquiver, eyes searching the fray. There was Tasherit, in cat form, sitting atop the official's chair, whiskers twitching. She looked to be rendering amused judgement upon the mêlée, but she was a cat, and cats always looked to be rendering amused judgement.

Rue barked at her, sharply, once.

Brown cat eyes, so incongruous in the face of a lioness, swung regally in her direction.

Tasherit inclined her head.

Rue barked at her again.

Tasherit leaned over, whiskers arrowing in, eyes dilating to focus on the centre of the brawl, the swirling eye of the cyclone.

Rue stood on her hind legs like a circus dog and tried to see what it was.

Too many men and wolves were in between. The noise was too fearsome and the smells too potent for her to distinguish anything significant. She galloped over to the official's chair and leapt to stand next to Tasherit.

The lioness hissed at her, but only in a "this is my post, stupid wolf" kind of way.

Rue muscled her aside, trying to see what the cat had been pointing at.

Rue saw her father wade in, fists flailing, roaring at his pack to cool their blasted tempers or he'd do it for them. Mother was behind him, trying to touch vampires and werewolves alike, intent on sucking them into mortality. Preternatural touch itself wasn't deadly, but Rue knew from experience it was shocking, like having a chamber pot of humanity upended over one's head. Gave a soul pause, if nothing else. With her other hand, Lady Maccon flailed about with her parasol, the fifth or sixth in a long line of hideous accessories. It housed under its canopy more covert anti-supernatural technology than one might think possible. Despite this fact, Rue had most commonly seen it applied as a bludgeon.

Then Rue saw what Tasherit had been whiskering at.

There in the centre of the fight, grappling with one another, each trying to go for the other's throat, were the Right Honourable Professor Percival Tunstell and Chief Engineer Quesnel Lefoux.

CHAPTER

FIVE

In Which Rue Breaks Things

P ercy and Quesnel must have started the whole mess.
Aunt Ivy would have sent her darling baby boy some
drone guards and Paw had Channing tailing Quesnel. There
you have it, the perfect recipe for conflict. Paw, after all,
hadn't specified what Channing was to do with Quesnel. But
if Percy or his vampires made the appearance of wanting to
kill Quesnel? Well, Lord save anyone if a vampire tried to
steal a werewolf's prey, even if only to kill that prey himself.
Especially then.

Rue leapt off the post and wove through the mass of tussling
males. A vampire lurched in her direction. However, when she
drew her lip back from canines and growled at him, he recon-
sidered. He was diverted by Hemming, who crashed into his
side with a howl.

Fur was flying, flesh was scoured, slow old black blood leaked
everywhere.

They were all enjoying themselves immensely.

Rue ended her charge where Quesnel and Percy still grappled.
Percy was yelling something about publishing rights and discovery notification and respect for intellectual property. Quesnel
was yelling back about the public's right to information and
risk-aversion techniques and funding considerations.

Rue wormed her way between them and reared up. Rue the wolf on her hind legs was about as tall as Rue the human, which is to say still shorter than both Percy and Quesnel.

She did the only thing she could think of to distract them. She licked Quesnel across the face, a slobbering drenching wet slap. He smelled of lime and he tasted like meaty smoke. She rotated, put her paws on Percy's shoulder, and did the same to him, knocking his glasses off. He tasted of leather and dust.

Percy, with whom she had grown up playing games of "knight errant with his faithful werewolf companion," knew exactly what she looked like in wolf form even amid a brawl.

"Rue!" He slapped away the tongue. "Get off!"

Quesnel, thank heavens, had the grace to look ashamed and then the wherewithal to register the chaos around them.

"Good heavens," he said. "What on earth is going on?"

That made Percy pause too. "What are Queen Mum's drones doing fighting your pack, Rue? Is that *Lady Maccon*? Is that a *parasol*?"

He began shouting the names of his mother's vampires and drones, instructing them to "stop it this instant!"

Realising that their precious charge was no longer grappling for his life, the vampires slowed their attack. Although really, Rue thought, Percy had been grappling for his academic reputation not his life. She sneezed out the wolf equivalent of a laugh.

The pack slowed as well. After all, it was no fun to hunt something that didn't fight back. They weren't cats.

The drones stopped with relief on their faces and began to tend to each other's wounds, knowing the blood must be staunched before the vampires caught the scent and demanded second breakfast.

Percy marched up to one of the vampires and put his hands to his hips. "Gahiji, what in heaven's name do you lot think you're doing?"

"That man attacked you!"

The vampires all glared at Quesnel.

"Mr Lefoux," said Percy, "happens to be a *colleague* both aboard my ship and in academia. We were engaging in a gentleman's disagreement on a matter of grave import and no little delicacy. I should thank you, *and* my blasted mother, to keep your ruddy fangs out of it!"

Uh-oh, thought Rue, *Percy has resorted to swearing.*

Quesnel was annoyed at being defended by his rival but seemed to see the sense in it. After all, the vampires were most assuredly not going to listen to him. Besides, Channing, a great white wolf with cold eyes, was sitting uncomfortably close and staring at him.

Rue yipped at her uncle.

Channing twitched his fluffy white tail at her but did not move. Paw had ordered him to track Quesnel. Only Paw could call him off.

Rue rolled her eyes. *Bloody werewolves.*

Lady Maccon marched up looking horribly pleased with herself and swinging her ghastly parasol in a jaunty manner. "There you are, infant. My but I forgot how much *fun* adventuring was."

Rue sniffed.

"Quite right, quite right. I'm far too old for this nonsense."

Rue blew out air between her teeth in a canine raspberry.

Lady Maccon turned to Quesnel. "Good evening, Mr Lefoux. This mess is your fault, I take it?"

Quesnel was not afraid of Rue's mother. Which was an incredibly attractive trait, Rue had to admit. He tilted his head and dimpled winsomely. "Why, Lady Maccon, how do you do? My fault you say? But, dear lady, I am neither a hive queen nor a pack Alpha and yet I see a number of supernaturals milling about. What have I to do with them? Professor Tunstell and I were having a philosophical discussion. No one else ought to have involved himself."

Lady Maccon was taken aback. "Oh, well. Yes. I suppose I see your point."

Tasherit trotted up to weave in and around, getting underfoot and underhand and generally in everyone's way.

Lady Maccon was distracted. "Are you the lioness? Remarkable."

Rue barked.

But Lady Maccon knew how to keep a secret. She made no illusion to Tasherit's being a werebeast and only took great care not to touch the cat.

Tasherit reared away from Mother, realising the danger this statuesque woman represented. Rue could almost hear the were-cat's thoughts: *Soulless, stay back!*

Paw joined them. "So, young Mr Lefoux. Perhaps you and I should take a perambulation about this neighbourhood together?"

Rue placed herself between her father and her chief engineer. Things were confusing enough between her and Quesnel without Paw interfering.

Paw was not best pleased at being opposed by his own daughter.

When he tried to reach around her to grab at Quesnel, she growled.

"Don't you dare threaten me, young lady!"

"Leave it, dear," said his wife. "Remember back then, how you reacted to interference from *my* sainted mother?"

Paw looked shocked. "Are you comparing *me* to your *mother*?"

"If the hat fits."

Rue had never before seen Paw so quickly cowed.

Everyone was calming down. The vampires and drones beetled off to their nearby hive under Percy's annoyed instructions. Although, no doubt, one or two remained in the shadows to observe. The pack stayed, assembling in a loose circle of lupine curiosity. They seemed particularly fascinated by Tasherit. With regal cat superiority, she took the attention as her due and ignored them.

A touch at the top of Rue's head distracted her.

Quesnel had his hand buried there and was idly combing through her fur.

"You're so soft." He tugged a bit at her long silky ears and she flicked them at him.

He'd ridden her in the past. A fact she had carefully *not* told her parents; it seemed oddly intimate. But those had been necessarily hurried exploits. She had hoped to practise more, to give him some real training in wolfback riding. The twins were both skilled in the matter, and Quesnel had felt left out. But then he disappeared to Egypt.

"Get your greasy hands off my daughter," yelled Lord Maccon.

The petting stopped.

Rue instantly missed it.

"What is going on here?" Uncle Rabiffano strode onto the croquet green.

He was so very stylishly pulled together; everyone around him immediately became aware of how disreputable they looked. Lady Maccon's hands went to her hair, which was still up but full of flyaways. Lord Maccon reached self-consciously for his cravat knot. The other werewolves all looked guilty – cognisant of ruffled fur, scrapes, and the need to bathe.

Uncle Rabiffano's elegant dancer's stride ate up the distance until he came to a stop in front of Paw.

Lord Maccon tried to recover the conversational ground. "What are you doing here, Beta?"

Uncle Rabiffano shook his head in a short negation, eyebrows raised. "Delivering a hat to Baroness Tunstell, of course. The real question is, what are you" – one graceful hand took in the amassed pack – "*all* of you, doing *here?*"

Lady Maccon stepped in. "Biffy, darling, let me explain."

Uncle Rabiffano glanced briefly at her. "Oh, I can guess what is going on. Not the particulars, but I know why this is happening."

He turned his back on Rue's mother, pointedly, and she winced.

Rue's jaw dropped, and because she was a wolf, her tongue lolled out. No one, *no one* dismissed Lady Maccon. Certainly not Uncle Rabiffano. They were friends. Good friends, Rue had thought.

Uncle Rabiffano faced Lord Maccon, fighting stance now, not dancer's. "You've trained me up. I'm not going to be any more ready. It's time to let go."

Paw looked sad and militant at the same time.

Uncle Rabiffano tossed back a lock of hair. He had been made werewolf shortly before Rue was born. She wasn't familiar with the particulars – no one liked to talk about it – but there was some scandal surrounding his metamorphosis. But it still meant he must be at least forty years old. Yet, in that brief moment, he looked exceedingly young and frightened.

He confronted her Paw. Her mortal Paw, as if . . . what?

Rue struggled to understand. *As if he intends to challenge for leadership.*

Uncle Rabiffano took a breath to steady his tone, and spoke again – low and level, strong and clear. Stage training perhaps, or a singer? Rue didn't know what his art had been. She didn't know anything about Uncle Rabiffano before he became Uncle Rabiffano.

"I don't want to fight you, Conall."

First names. Equal footing.

Paw lifted his head. Anger slashed red across his cheeks.

What is going on? What is Uncle Rabiffano doing? It hummed as a litany through Rue's brain.

"You promised I wouldn't have to fight you." Uncle Rabiffano's words vibrated with both power and pleading. "You promised this would be a smooth transition. I don't know if I'm ready. You don't know. They don't know. But that is irrelevant to the fact that you *must* let us go now. You can't hold them any more. And you can't stop me from wanting. I can feel the tethers fraying. It's not only you who will go mad – it's all of us. Don't you see that? I'm compelled to stop it. I will fight you for it, because it's no longer an option. It's stupid, and it's brutish, but it's instinct. And you were the one who taught me to accept instinct."

Perhaps it was because Rue held his shape, but Paw didn't react in the way she thought he would. Uncle Rabiffano's words were a direct attack that no normal Alpha would tolerate. But Paw remained standing quietly before him. Yes, he looked angry but he also looked abashed.

I don't like this, wailed Rue to herself.

Sensing her distress, Quesnel's hand returned to her head. He didn't pet her this time, simply rested it there.

Paw didn't notice. He was focused on Uncle Rabiffano.

Mother didn't notice either. She was focused on Paw.

The pack sat, still as stone, waiting.

It was as though the world held its breath; even the sounds of London faded.

Then Uncle Rabiffano changed. Not to werewolf form, not completely. No, only his head shifted. Above his perfectly tied cravat and starched white collar, above the dapper grey suit with its smooth lapel, his sweet boyish face became a dark wolf's head.

Anubis form. Rue had seen her father do it. *But that means . . .*

Quesnel's gasp cut into the silence.

Only Alphas have Anubis form. Rue stared, riveted, dumbfounded. Anubis was for bite to breed; it was Alpha's gift to go with the curse. It was rare even so. Paw had Anubis. And Lady Kingair. And, Rue thought, mind drifting in shock, three other Alphas in England that she knew of but *not* Uncle Rabiffano. He was Paw's Beta. He was Beta by feeling too: calm and relaxed and easy-going. Always there to foil his Alpha, to balance the pack. Except, of course, that Uncle Rabiffano hadn't been. Not really. He'd simply been in the background and then off to his hat shop.

No, Rue realised, *Mother had done the calming and the balancing, as much as she was able.*

"You're an Alpha." Quesnel sounded as shocked as Rue felt.

Uncle Rabiffano inclined his wolf head slightly, so as not to disturb his collar points.

Out of the corner of one eye, Rue saw her mother do something awful. She stepped towards Uncle Rabiffano, establishing alliance.

"It's time, Conall. He's right. No more waiting. I can't handle it, literally. And it's too much to ask of our daughter."

Rue felt Quesnel's hand lift as everyone's attention focused on her. The top of her head, despite the fur, felt cold.

Uncle Rabiffano spoke again, through his lupine mouth. Rue supposed that with the rest of him still human, speech was possible. It was peculiar-sounding, though, echoing and deep, not like his normal voice at all. "Conall, look at what this is doing to your family. To your pack. I don't want to cry challenge, but I will if you can't leave on your own."

Paw seemed confused, indignant, and frustrated all at once. And betrayed, because his wife was standing against him. Rue had known her parents to argue – in fact, they seemed to enjoy it – but they had never in her life failed to present a unified front to the rest of the world.

Rue couldn't decide what to do. Should she rush her mother, make skin contact with a preternatural to break the tether? That would give her father his supernatural abilities back and a fighting chance, as erratic and dangerous as that would make him.

"Oh, for goodness' sake!" Uncle Rabiffano stepped in and, swinging from the shoulder with all his force, punched Paw in the jaw.

Paw fell back like a stone, senseless.

Everyone else remained motionless.

Uncle Rabiffano shifted back to normal. The fur of his face crawled up to the top of his head, chocolatey and thick, slightly less styled than before Anubis.

Rue growled and leapt at him, teeth going for the neck.

Only to find herself shifting back to human.

Her mother was gripping her hard. Preternatural forced change, exactly as if she were a misbehaving child.

"No, infant." Lady Maccon sounded brittle.

"But, Mother!" Rue, starkers and uncaring, could only protest.

"Go and sit with your father. We might need you to touch him once more."

"It's not fair. You can't use me as a weapon against my own Paw!"

"Prudence Alessandra Maccon Akeldama, I am not going to tell you again."

"You're asking me to choose between you," wailed Rue.

Quesnel pulled off his frock coat and helped Rue into it.

Lady Maccon glared at her daughter. "No, I am ordering you to take care of him. Child of mine, ponder what he has become. We've tried every which way to get him to Egypt. He agreed. Twenty-odd years ago this all looked to be so easy. But none of us knew how Alpha's curse would take him, or when. And the plan has failed."

Uncle Rabiffano's voice held no hostility. "We shouldn't have waited for Lyall."

Rue couldn't comprehend that. "The Kingair Pack Beta? Why on earth should he matter?"

Rabiffano gave the oddest huff of a laugh. "He's actually *my* Beta; they've had him on loan."

This was all too much. And Paw was stirring. Rue would have to choose and she couldn't face it. It felt like treason. If Uncle Rabiffano wanted the London Pack, if he was really meant to become its Alpha, shouldn't he challenge for it? Except that meant one of them would die. When Alphas fought for pack leadership, one of them *always* died.

"The God-Breaker Plague. You're going to take him into the plague zone?" Quesnel sounded oddly hopeful. Didn't he understand how awful all of this was?

"Yes. Exactly." Lady Maccon was pleased by his understanding.

"Where he'll *die*!" Rue did not care how bitter she sounded.

Lady Maccon hauled her off and slapped her, hard across the face. "Stop it."

It stung, but certainly didn't hurt as much as werewolf shift. Still it surprised her into shocked silence.

So did the fact that Quesnel turned and stepped up against her mother in an entirely ungentlemanly way. "I wouldn't do that again, Lady Maccon, if I were you."

Mother blinked at him. "Oh. That's the way of it? I didn't realise."

Rue clutched at her cheek and tried very hard not to cry.

"Prudence, little one." Uncle Rabiffano's voice was smooth as black treacle. He was so sure of himself. "This is not betrayal."

Rue nodded. How long had it been since she had heard that kind of confidence in Paw's voice? The slap seemed to have recharged her brain. They were right. The God-Breaker Plague would make her father an exiled mortal for the rest of his life, but he would *have* a rest of his life. Mother would surely go with him. Hadn't Rue already acknowledged to herself that Paw's time was running out?

It was a lot of realisations all at once.

"It's only that I love him. He's my Paw." Rue didn't know to whom she spoke, or why. Maybe it was for herself. She looked to Quesnel for reassurance. He was outside this. Outside her whole messy family with all its uncles and tethers and malingering life spans. "What do you think?"

"Oh, *mon petite chou*, it isn't my place."

"Please?"

"I think it's romantic, to live together in an ancient land."

"To die together there."

"Not many Alphas get a retirement, *chérie*. And the weather is reputed to be very nice in Egypt."

Rue gave a watery chuckle. Although she'd asked for his opinion, she did question his judgement. He'd no father and a dead birth mother. And, despite her indenture to a vampire hive, Madame Lefoux had never requested the bite. So his other mother would die too. He was accustomed to mortality.

"You do own one of the world's fastest dirigibles." Quesnel came to stand before her, not touching but there. And she adored – *oh dear* – the slight dimples when he smiled.

He was kind. "We could visit anytime you liked."

Rue took a breath and struggled for something she could do to help. "So, how do we get him to Egypt? Will *The Spotted Custard* do?"

"Werewolves can't float," said Mother sadly.

Quesnel frowned. "It's not the intent, but my tank might help there. The one Aggie's hovering over in engineering."

Lady Maccon looked thoughtful. "Prudence mentioned something about a tank."

Rue nodded, numb. "Let's give it a try? You'll have to supervise, Quesnel. I'll be indisposed."

Then Rue took off the frock coat and walked to Paw.

He was moving, sluggishly returning to consciousness. She placed a hand gently to his dear wrinkled forehead. Rue shifted back to wolf, bones breaking and reforming and hair crawling from her head to cover her entire body. For once, she relished the pain. It was a punishment she richly deserved for her treachery.

Paw, please forgive me.

She tried not to be grateful for the relief on Uncle Rabiffano's – and Mother's and even Quesnel's – faces.

Lord Maccon sat up, groggy.

And Uncle Rabiffano was hit full in his middle by a large vicious white wolf.

"Oh, for goodness' sake, Channing," Rue heard Uncle Rabiffano say just prior to shifting form. "I love this suit."

The suit was ripped beyond repair and among the tatters of perfectly lovely and very expensive grey cashmere and crisp white lawn, stood a dark chocolate wolf with an oxblood red chest.

The two wolves met on a leap and began fighting. This was not how the pack had been tussling earlier with vampires, but *really* fighting. Trying to kill and maim one another. It was sickening in its ferocity.

Rue wanted to look away.

Channing went straight for Rabiffano's neck. Rabiffano twisted so that Channing only got his shoulder. Blood dripped from deep puncture wounds as the white wolf bit down. They struggled with such force it was as though Channing were lifting and balancing the younger wolf on his nose. Rabiffano scrabbled at Channing's belly with his hind legs, claws out, decorating the white with red gashes. He chomped down on Channing's ear, fairly taking it off.

Rue came over queasy. She wasn't usually squeamish, but she had never before witnessed two men she adored trying to brutally murder one another.

The wolves reared up, biting and slashing with their front paws and generally turning themselves into a fur-flying fray of white, chocolate, and red in the moonlight. Channing yipped in pain. What looked to have been his battle to win suddenly wasn't any more. Rabiffano was braced in such a way as to give superior leverage against the white wolf, biting hard into the neck, applying a brutal pressure forwards and down. He was fighting smart, something very few werewolves could do, usually only the oldest or the most Alpha.

Rue leaned against her Paw, turned her wet nose into his leg, pressing her furred face against him helplessly.

There was no dramatic final moment; the fighters seemed likely to go on until dawn or exhaustion or death forced a separation. Except that, without apparent reason, they both stopped.

They backed away from each other, panting.

The pack leaned in, eyes gleaming.

So slowly that at first Rue wasn't sure it was happening, the white wolf stretched out his front legs and sank over them. Then he flipped to his back, stomach up.

The rest of the pack threw back their heads and howled in victory and acceptance.

Rue felt absolutely no urge to join in such vocal nonsense.

The chocolate wolf's tale swished once and then Rabiffano shifted back to human. For a dandy who wore his suits like armour against the world, Uncle Rabiffano was oddly comfortable wearing nothing but moonlight and the gaze of his pack.

His pack. Not Paw's.

Uncle Rabiffano addressed Rue's parents, uncompromising. "It is time for you to leave."

Lord Maccon twitched. Rue could feel it in the muscles of his leg against her cheek.

Mother hadn't watched the fight; her gaze stayed on her husband the entire time. Without acknowledging Uncle Rabiffano's order, she turned her indomitable focus onto Quesnel. "I assume it's a preservation tank you have, Mr Lefoux?"

Quesnel, slightly green about the gills from the battle, took a few seconds to react. "Modified from my mother's original design. It's not intended for werewolf transport, although the theory holds. If Rue thinks we should try, I'm game."

"Would he be in danger?"

Quesnel shrugged. "If it turns out the tank doesn't work on werewolves, he'll likely go mad with aether, break it, and jump overboard."

"Not an ideal outcome."

Quesnel arched an eyebrow in agreement and continued. "Otherwise he'll appear asleep or dead the whole time."

Lady Maccon paled considerably. "So how would we know it's working?"

Quesnel donned his delighted academic smile. Percy had the same smile. "Initially, if we stick him in and Rue here returns to normal, then we can presume the tank is at least preserving his tether."

"And after that?" Mother was a great deal more careful with Paw's well-being than she was with her own.

"We'd know when we arrive and he wakes up again." Quesnel would not sugarcoat the reality of science.

"*He* is standing right here!" Lord Maccon gave an aggrieved rumble. His voice sounded worn and shaken, as if he'd been recently crying.

"Quite right, your risk, Conall. Do we try?"

"I am at your disposal, Wife. I've no other duties now but to attend your whims."

"God help us all," said Lady Maccon with real feeling. She turned towards *The Spotted Custard*. It had floated down for a better view of the Alpha challenge.

Rue stayed behind and watched the pack.

One at a time, each werewolf was approaching Uncle Rabiffano. Each knelt low over his forelegs and then flipped to present the soft underside of throat and stomach. There seemed a prescribed order of rank, or was it age? Rue found herself trying to guess whose turn would be next. Somehow she always got it right. She wondered if she had some latent pack instinct after all.

Her parents and Quesnel were up the gangplank now, chatting almost companionably to one another.

"Infant," called Lady Maccon, "do come along."

But while her parents were apparently willing to lose everything, Rue was not.

The last wolf, Rafe, rolled to stand after his abeyance.

Rue approached the new Alpha. She slunk, chest low, neck cocked slightly to show her throat. She bowed over her forelegs. *Oh please, oh please, oh please, oh ...* And went to flip, to expose her belly to her pack.

Her *former* pack as it turned out.

Uncle Rabiffano's eyes were sad. But then, they were always a little sad. Yet he left – they left – without acknowledging her.

The London Pack ambled away in a group, heading for the outskirts of town. That group was cohesive and calm. They were off to chase some unsuspecting rabbits. Or perhaps they were going to celebrate at a local pub. Since they were all in wolf form, even Rabiffano, Rue had to assume they were after rabbits and not ale, or the London pubs had relaxed their dress requirements beyond imagining.

And Rue was not welcome among them any more.

CHAPTER SIX

In Which Our Heroine Defeats a Picnic Hamper

Rue didn't want to go with her parents. She didn't want to see Quesnel preserve her father in a tank in her boiler room. *As if Paw were an enormous gherkin.* But she followed up the gangplank because they needed her to keep the tether.

I've lost all my family in one night. Except Dama. Will he still want me around with Mother and Paw gone? Rue was wallowing. But there was no one to see, and being a wolf she couldn't cry.

She made her way down through the airship towards the oil and smoke of the boiler room. Had Quesnel predicted this eventuality and that's why there was a tank in engineering? Had he known all along what was going wrong with her pack – with her family – and not said anything?

The man in question, wearing a leather blacksmith's apron over his evening clothes, tinkered with the tank. Her parents watched, Mother with her head on Paw's shoulder and he with one arm about her waist. Rue had seen her parents intimate before, more's the pity, but this time they looked so relaxed. Just as the pack had walking away from her.

Rue wondered about their respective jobs. If they emigrated to Egypt, Lady Maccon must give over muhjah and Lord Maccon must pass on his position as head of BUR. Rue so rarely asked them about their professions, it was entirely possible they had already made arrangements.

Mother probably has, at least. If Paw's been running off the rails for a while now, BUR's likely already filled in an assumed vacancy. But muhjah has to be filled by a preternatural, and there's no other soulless in London. Well – an aura of satisfaction coloured Rue's thoughts – *Queen Victoria is in a pickle there.*

Quesnel popped the lid of his tank open. It was full of a bubbling orangeish liquid, not boiling but aerated with a colourless gas. Rue sniffed—odourless. too. Oxygen, perhaps? Or aether?

Tasherit appeared, still in lioness shape, and took a spectator's seat. Rue was relieved Primrose wasn't present; her father was, after all, still naked. No doubt Prim had skittered below the moment things went bare during the brawl. Primrose was not equipped to handle regular exposure to male nudity. Which would make her marriage bed quite interesting indeed.

Quesnel stepped back and gestured, with a little bow, like a butler.

Lord Maccon bowed in turn and then hoisted himself up into the tank. It was only just big enough for him, and it didn't look like a comfortable fit. He lowered himself gingerly with a funny look on his face like he was settling into a vat of pudding, squishy but not unpleasant. At the last, he sucked in a breath and sank under. Once completely submerged, he appeared to fall into a deep slumber.

Lady Maccon and Quesnel lurched forward, likely to check that he was asleep and not dead. Rue hadn't the attention to process, for she was shifting. Reverse shape change was no less painful, but it always felt nice, at the end, to be back in her own skin. Rue supposed this was because she spent less time as a supernatural than the real ones; being mortal felt comfortable. Although most of the time it was less interesting.

There were many things Rue could have done in a more dignified fashion at that juncture, but frankly it had been an upsetting night, so she sat on the floor. She pulled her legs up and wrapped her arms about them, cloaking herself in her own hair, for modesty's sake.

Quesnel and her mother ensured Paw's comfort. Apparently, he was still alive, or as alive as a werewolf got when in a preservation tank.

"This floor is filthy," said Rue to no one in particular.

The one sootie on duty heard her. The girl tended to her obligations with forced diligence, throwing glances at the corner of the room where naked aristocrats were doing suspicious things with tanks. Rue couldn't blame her for her curiosity.

"Sorry, Lady Captain, it's the boilers, see – full of soot."

The sootie's response drew Rue out of her funk. *What am I doing huddling here? I'm a fully grown, perfectly respectable young lady. So I've lost my pack and my parents are moving away, but I've the family I've built aboard this ship. Primrose won't abandon me. Primrose would never abandon me. Buck up!*

She took a breath and straightened. "Tasherit, would you be so kind as to fetch me a robe?"

The lioness considered this request and then, likely because she knew Rue couldn't do anything interesting if she had to stay huddled, and because the tank situation was proving dull, she trotted away.

She was soon back, clutching a robe in her mouth. It was one of hers, a voluminous silky thing that was too long for Rue but preserved her dignity.

Rue was standing with it on by the time Quesnel finished with his tank. She felt wan and worn but Quesnel looked at her as if she were the pudding course and he hadn't had any supper. Her hair was down and wildly tangled, and the silk of the robe was thin enough so that if she were not in the boiler room, she'd be cold.

Lady Maccon pinched him. "Stop looking at my daughter like that."

Quesnel rubbed him arm. "But . . ."

"Just because I disagree with my husband's mollycoddling doesn't mean I'm permissive."

Rue wondered if Tasherit might let her keep the robe. "Mother, do you still need me?"

Lady Maccon blinked, remembering Rue's purpose there. "No, dear, no. Clearly the tank works on tethers."

Rue turned to leave. She needed to see Dama. She needed to know he remained unchanged. The sunrise was not far off. She could ill afford to waste time, for she must dress properly for Dama.

A rustle of skirts heralded her mother's running to catch up. "Infant, do you require" – she paused as though unsure of the right word – "comfort?"

It was sweet of her to try.

Quesnel followed, his expression concerned.

"Now, Mother, you know you're horrid at that."

Lady Maccon was not offended by truth. Rue rather admired her for that.

"No, you're quite right. You'll be visiting your other father?"

Rue nodded. "Soon, before I lose the night."

Lady Maccon nibbled her lip and then, in a decisive move, folded Rue into a warm motherly embrace. It was a good hug because Mother was lovely and squishy, even corseted. Rue let herself enjoy it, even knowing that her poor old mother couldn't begin to understand why Rue was upset. Lady Maccon was thinking that everything was perfectly fine. Everyone was alive and mostly uninjured. Her plan to emigrate to Egypt was commencing. The pack had transitioned as smoothly as one could hope.

That was how Lady Maccon thought the world worked. She bent it to her will regardless of consequences. That was how Rue had come into existence. It was her mother's nature to be soulless. She couldn't be faulted for it.

Rue extracted herself from the hug. "Thank you, Mother. But I think . . ."

Lady Maccon waved her off. "Carry on. Your young man and I are going to engage in some nice civilised discourse."

"We are?" Quesnel was positively horrified by this statement.

"Perhaps I should stay, then," said Rue. "And he's *not* my young man."

Lady Maccon only waved at her again. "Oh, I think he might be. Go on, dear, you aren't necessary."

Rue, remembering how Quesnel and Percy and their ridiculous feud had started the whole messy brawl earlier, felt that he deserved some extended exposure to her mother. So she left them to it.

Dama was waiting for her, bless him.

"*Puggle*, darling!" His embrace smelled of lemon hair tonic and sweet lavender and only a little bit of old blood. He was bony where Mother was soft, and certainly too small to envelop her, but he did his parental best. And he understood, so it worked.

"Sit, my poor dear girl." Instead of insisting on ceremony, the vampire tugged her to the softest of his sofas, the one facing the fireplace with a little table for reading. He sat next to her, keeping her hand in his, for they both wore thick enough gloves. He was careful not to let any skin touch as he consoled her.

Rue was grateful. She didn't want to be a vampire right now.

"Tell me everything." His expression was all sympathy.

"Don't you already know?"

"I know the *facts*, my little pea blossom, but not the rest. Has my B—?" A slight mistake there, he collected himself. "Has the pack transitioned?"

Rue nodded. "New Alpha. Uncle Rabiffano, if you can believe that."

"I am the only one who was never surprised."

"No, you're good like that." Rue suspected there was something more than Dama's normal understanding of how the world worked but she didn't want to pry. The London Pack was no longer her business.

"He managed to do it without killing Lord Maccon?"

"Yes." Rue could see in Dama's eyes the miracle that this was.

"We truly live in a brave new world." The vampire shook his head. There was real awe in his tone, something Rue had never heard before.

"I suppose if anyone could manage it, it would be Rabiffano. He will be a *good* Alpha, my Puggle. You can trust me to know this."

Rue hadn't thought if it that way. "I suppose he will. Very cultured, exactly what a London Pack needs."

"And all those ties to that *horrible* Lord Woolsey will finally be purged."

"That was before my time, Dama." Sometimes he forgot how young she was, or maybe it was that he forgot on purpose, knowing how short her life-span would be. It must be horrible for him. How many pack transitions had he watched in his lifetime? How many friends had he seen die because of them?

He patted her hand. "*Of course* it was, periwinkle. But this must have come as *quite* a shock for you. I hope you understand, your father asked us not to say anything to you."

"I know. He wanted to be my strong solid mooring point for ever."

The vampire's blue eyes twinkled. "Forgive us immortals our sins of pride, child. We all age like cheese, growing strong and *tasty* but also covered in the mould of good intentions gone grey."

Rue gave a watery chuckle. "I didn't know I was going to lose him. Now he and Mother will go to Egypt and die."

"Ah, I see. You knew all along you would lose Alexia, but you had Conall and I stashed away in your heart, unchanging."

"Exactly."

"I'm still here."

"Yes. There's no vampire rove equivalent of Alpha's curse that you aren't telling me about, is there?"

"My *little jumping bean*, you are one of the brightest lights I've been blessed with in my very long time on this earth." Dama tugged her in to cuddle against him, careful that no flesh touched. "I never thought to have a daughter, not at my age."

Rue snuggled into him. Dama would fix everything.

"I shall tell you a little secret, shall I?"

"I don't know, Dama. I've had a lot of revelations in the past few hours."

"It's not shocking, I promise."

"Very well, then."

"I am two thousand two hundred and fifty-one years old. Did you know?"

"I calculated about that."

She'd managed to surprise him, not a frequent or comfortable sensation for a vampire. "You did?"

"Your accent slips sometimes. My guess is Ancient Greek, likely Macedonian. Plus you think like a military strategist even when it's only tea plantations." She paused and took her best guess. "Alexander, is it? Your given name, I mean."

He laughed. "I knew all those expensive tutors would come back to haunt me."

"What happened to your eyes?"

"Ah. Not everything stays the same with metamorphosis. I lost battle scars as well. Flaws are fixed."

"It was a flaw?"

"Apparently."

"Could we talk more, sometime, about your history and what's true and what isn't?"

Dama gave a sad smile, no fang, only memories peeking around the corners. "I think it's best left as it has been written down. Why mess with the past? It can't be altered."

Which explained a little of why he was so accepting of change. Lord Akeldama was the only vampire Rue knew not set in his ways. Even Aunt Ivy, who was very young for a vampire, was already fixed in her preferences and persuasive in her opinions on hats.

"I hate to send you out there, Puggle, alone. You will be careful?"

"Pish-tosh. I have my crew. And my new gun. And my metanatural abilities. I came back from India all right, didn't I? Mucked it up a bit, but survived. This is only Egypt."

"My dearest *girl*, even the *Romans* were changed by Egypt."

"You'll be here when I get back? Exactly like this, waiting."

"Exactly so. And your room will be there and more importantly your closet, but I'll have ordered you all new dresses for the season."

Rue grinned, feeling better about everything.

Rue returned to *The Spotted Custard* as the sun rose pink above the grey fog of the city. Primrose met her at the top of the gangplank looking tired and worried. They examined each other's faces.

Whatever Primrose saw seemed to make her feel better. "You're well?"

Rue nodded. "I'm well. You?"

"Topping. I put your mother in the best guest quarters. Knowing her, we might want to hire a lady's maid to dance attendance while she is in residence."

"We're headed to Egypt."

"Mr Lefoux said we might be. I assumed she is accompanying us?"

"Correct assumption."

Primrose was resigned. "I'll nip round to the agency this morning, see if they have a nice stable young French girl who doesn't understand much English and wants to travel. Best, I think, if your mother isn't entirely understood by her staff."

"Fantastic idea. We should try to keep regular hours while she is aboard, and formal meals. That way she has to dress. That will keep her at least partly occupied."

They moved together towards the centre of the quarterdeck where Spoo and the head deckhand stood in consultation with the lead builder.

Primrose checked the state of the sun. "I'll send to market as well. Egypt is quicker to get to than India, right?"

"I believe so, but only Percy knows the particulars."

"I'll have to wake him up." His sister did not look thrilled with the idea.

"We need to know the best current to catch anyway, put a departure time into place." Rue was not above batting her eyelashes so Primrose would awaken the beast.

"As long as you realise Quesnel is still up."

"Blast them, can't they sort this out like civilised gentlemen?"

"We *are* speaking of Percy."

"Point taken."

Prim deemed the matter settled and moved them efficiently on. "And the market, anything I should stock with Lady Maccon in mind?"

"Oh, Mother eats everything and likes it. I wouldn't worry about her. Horrible sweet tooth."

Primrose nodded. "Tea later? I'd like to know what happened last night."

"Later," agreed Rue. "I should be better able to discuss it then."

Primrose kissed her cheek softly. "I'll just go get my wrap, wake Percy, and be off. I'm sure I can borrow Mother's carriage."

"If you want to drive yourself, you can use the Maccon dog-cart. It's still sitting on the green."

Primrose looked horrified at the very idea. "No, thank you. Ladies don't drive bounders."

"Tell that to my mother. Send Percy up when he's decent, would you please?"

"By all means." Primrose whisked off, leaving Rue to the builders.

The builders were absolutely convinced it would be highly

dangerous to take *The Spotted Custard* up without a week's more repairs. Which, knowing builders, actually meant three weeks.

Rue said, "You have three hours," hoping Percy and the currents would concur.

The man in charge sputtered, not accustomed to ultimatums from young ladies. Mr Bapp had a face like a squished puffin which had eaten something sour a decade ago and never recovered.

Rue talked over his sputter. "Spoo, please raise as many decklings as we can spare. I want some left fresh and rested for float, but the rest we can loan to Mr Bapp here."

Spoo nodded and scampered off.

"Willard?"

The head deckhand looked at Rue expectantly. "Yes, Lady Captain?"

"Can engineering spare any muscle?"

He considered. "Two, perhaps. But if the *Custard* does turn out to be shaky, we'd best keep some in reserve."

"Agreed. Do what you can."

Quesnel appeared abovedecks, blinking in the sunlight.

"Three hours, gentlemen." Rue left the men to grumble about females with unreasonable expectations.

"*Chérie?*" Quesnel's face was contorted with concern. "Are you well?" His hand jerked forward and then fell to his side, empty.

Rue didn't want pity from him; besides, she had purpose now. She concentrated on the impending trip almost desperately. "How soon can we boil up for takeoff?"

Quesnel snapped into engineer mode. "Less than an hour. We only need basic maintenance down below. We've been running at full capacity for a week."

"And my father?"

"Very well preserved."

Rue winced, but stopped any other reaction. "Excellent. Soon as I've conferred with Percy, I'll call down with a time for float off. No need to stoke up until we know the specifics."

Quesnel nodded but didn't go anywhere.

Awkward silence descended.

Rue scanned her craft. The deck was crawling with people, all busy about repairs or preparations.

He shifted close, intimate, as if he wanted to grab her.

Then Primrose reappeared in her cloak and hat, bade them farewell, trotted down the gangplank, and headed in the direction of the hive house and her mother's carriage. Percy followed her as far as the deck, wearing a dressing gown draped over a shirt and trousers, and no hat. His hair was a wild spiky mess of ginger and his spectacles were askew. Virgil must not yet be awake.

Footnote trailed after. Tasherit having gone to sleep with the sunrise, he was free to roam the whole ship at will.

"Tiddles said you wanted me?" Percy was annoyed enough to employ his sister's hated pet name.

Rue looked him over. "We're headed to Egypt on the next available current. You'll need to plot a course."

"What? Now?"

"Yes. Now."

"But I haven't slept yet.".

"And whose fault is that?"

Percy stuck a thumb in Quesnel's direction. "His."

Rue was bound and determined to stopper *that* over before it could get started again. "Don't you dare. Charts, Percival. Now!"

Percy snorted and looked down at Footnote.

"You see what I put up with?" Footnote licked a paw. "No respect. You realise I am one of the most brilliant minds in all England and she orders me to *make charts*."

True Percy was smart, but since he seemed oh so aware of that fact, Rue wasn't in the mood to humour one of his snits. Of course, he might think he was being funny; difficult to tell with Percy.

Percy continued babbling at the cat. "How trying it is to be constantly catering to lesser intellects. Not you, obviously."

Footnote stopped washing and stared at his master as if he had never considered the matter and was now moved to deep contemplation.

"Percy," rumbled Rue in a threatening tone.

"I'd like to see you build, install and maintain a working preservation tank." Quesnel couldn't help but defend his own intellect.

"And I'd like to see you write a proper paper on a new species of supernatural examining all the theoretical implications and ramifications of the aetheric imprint on the vital humours. Rather than superficial waffle. Seems we're both doomed to disappointment." Percy left off the cat for more aggressive intercourse.

Uh-oh, thought Rue, *here we go again.* She was exhausted and really had, she felt, put up with a lot. Rue was like her Paw in that her default reaction when unhappy was rage.

She yelled, quite violently, and at the top of her lungs. "Enough!"

It was so loud it paused the workers on the main deck. Spoo's small face popped up from behind a pile of rope. Rue was a jolly commander, but not exactly awe-inspiring at the best of times. Clearly she had a pair of lungs on her and the fact that, until now, she had rarely used them seemed to make them all that more effective.

With a pointed gesture, Rue made it clear she was yelling at her compatriots and not her crew. The crew went back to work, although Spoo remained watching, wide-eyed. The thought of the young girl – who was really Rue's charge as much as her employee – acted as the discipline Rue needed.

Percy and Quesnel had both snapped their mouths shut and were staring at her.

Rue opted for a low fierce diatribe. "Enough, both of you. I don't care who is in the right or who is in the wrong and frankly neither does anyone else. Come to an agreement or stop talking to each other. At this point, either is acceptable. Percy, you are

behaving like a petulant child whose favourite toy has gone
missing. If you wanted credit for the discovery so badly you
ought to have written and sent the paper in for publication while
we were still in India. They had a perfectly decent aethographic
transmitter."

Percy was sputtering.

Quesnel was nodding smugly.

Rue rounded on the inventor. "Mr Lefoux, don't you dare
think you're not culpable. You know Percy well enough to predict how he might react. The fact that you didn't include him
in the authorship is an outright insult. I might even accuse you
of intentionally stirring up malcontent."

Quesnel started to protest.

Rue overrode him. "If it wasn't intentional, it was certainly
small-minded."

At which Percy started looking smug and Quesnel crestfallen.

So Rue switched again. "Don't you dare look pleased with
yourself, Percival Tunstell. The only reason you aren't a complete
disappointment is because I've never expected you to actually
rise to any given occasion."

Percy winced.

That might be taking things a bit too far, but it seemed once
her mouth started flapping it was not inclined to stop.

"And, Mr Lefoux, let's be perfectly clear on that other matter,
while we are at it."

Percy tried not to look interested.

Quesnel tried not to look apprehensive.

"Let us say, for the sake of argument, you didn't know how
your article would affect your colleague aboard *my* airship. In
that case you are not petty but thoughtless. Imagine how that
insight into your character affects my opinion of you? What
other relationships are you likely to be thoughtless about?
Especially considering you didn't see fit to tell me any of this.
Not your publication, not your travel plans, not even the fact
that you knew" – she took a breath to steady her voice, which

was inexplicably trembling – "*you knew* something was wrong with *my father* and you didn't tell me that *either*!"

Rue had no idea why she was unleashing upon poor Quesnel. Nor why the bulk of her ire had switched to the inventor when really both he and Percy were blameworthy. She was trembling with agitation. Quesnel was pale and miserable.

It was Percy who risked putting a hand to her arm. "Stop, Rue. Just stop."

Rue subsided like a hot air balloon deflating.

Quesnel said in a tight, rough voice, "I'll just go and make certain the boilers are in order. You'll let me know the course hops once they are charted, Mr Tunstell?"

"Certainly, Mr Lefoux," replied Percy quietly. And then to Rue, "I'll go and see what seems the best course."

"You do that." Rue sagged into one of the deck chairs, feeling thoroughly ashamed of herself. She had probably destroyed any possible French lessons with Quesnel; even his casual kisses would be gone now. She wished Primrose had been there because she would have smoothed it all over. *No*, thought Rue, *this is my mess.*

"Spoo?"

"Yes, Lady Captain?" Spoo bounced up to her with less enthusiasm than usual. She looked almost frightened.

Rue felt even guiltier.

"I'll be in my quarters. Will you muster me once Navigator Tunstell has the charts in order?"

Spoo looked relieved. "Certainly, Lady Captain."

Rue resurfaced at Spoo's knock a few hours later with spirits somewhat rallied. She'd always wanted to see Egypt. It was a matter of some intellectual debate as to how a metanatural would react to the God-Breaker Plague. Now she was going to find out. Of course, she had visited before, but she had been too

young to remember. Her mother said she handled the plague
fine, but everything had felt different when she was young.
Shifting into werewolf form hadn't hurt, among other things.

On deck, Rue found Primrose had returned and was in conference with her twin under the big parasol that stretched over
the navigation area.

"Oh, Rue, good, there you are."

"Everything go well with the supplies?"

"Yes. And I found a nice young French girl to handle that
other matter we discussed."

"Excellent. Percy?"

"You aren't going to yell at me again, are you?"

Primrose perked up. "Rue yelled at you? Spiffing. I'm sure
you richly deserved it."

"I probably did." Percy looked more than ordinarily morose.
"But she wasn't very nice. To me or poor Mr Lefoux."

"*Poor* Mr Lefoux, is it? Suddenly you're all over chummy?"
Primrose was not to be taken in by her twin being pathetic.

"More a solidarity in misery. I'm certain I shall return to
loathing him shortly."

Rue was feeling guilty. "While I stand by my opinion of your
behaviour, Percy, I might have couched it in somewhat kinder
terms. For that, I apologise."

Percy had many faults, but bitterness wasn't one of them.
"Apology accepted. Now here's our course." He laid out the
charts and pointed to the various swirling currents.

"Have you informed Quesnel?"

"I have."

"Without getting into a fight?"

"I suspect that he, too, is smarting from your ... uh ...
lecture."

Rue turned to Primrose. "Are the staff and supplies in order?"

"Just waiting on a few final necessities but we should be ready
by sundown."

"Are we missing anyone?"

"Virgil," said Percy promptly. "I sent him after the latest Royal Society Bulletin. I have a subscription but they cannot seem to find the ship to deliver it. I'm waiting on a very important article." He sounded suspiciously smug.

"Why on earth did you give them the address of a dirigible?" Prim rolled her eyes.

"This is where I keep my stuff. Books, beverages, boots, and so forth."

"It's a *dirigible,* you wiffin. It moves!" Primrose was ever exasperated by her brother's obtuse belief that the world ought to conform to his whims, rather than the other way around.

He sniffed. "Regardless, I sent Virgil off to collect a copy. I wish to have the latest in hand before float off. There have been several pamphlets warning of the hazards of reading during air travel. The evidence is sadly compelling. I'm quite distressed. I'm considering abstaining from partaking while we are in transit. So I want to read this pamphlet before we leave."

Rue and Primrose both stared at him, mouths agape.

Primrose put a hand to her cheek. "Not read while we travel? But you'll die!"

Percy always had a book open, even during mealtimes. The very idea of him abstaining for more than ten minutes was apocryphal.

Percy glared. "I assure you, I have plenty of self-restraint."

Rue had no more time for his eccentricities. "I shall believe it when I see it. I hope Virgil returns before we are scheduled to depart." Not only did she like the little chap, but he also seemed the only one able to tolerate Percy for any length of time. And if Percy wasn't going to read, well, all Virgil's resources would be required.

"We'll have to delay."

Primrose shook her head. "For your valet? Brother dear, that's hardly a good reason."

"No, for the *pamphlet.* Didn't I just tell you how important it was?"

"What's so important about it?"

"Never you mind."

This looked to be deteriorating into sibling bickering, so Rue interjected. "Now, Prim, should we have tea?"

Primrose left off the bicker with alacrity. "Jolly good notion. Shall we take it in the stateroom?"

"My quarters, I think."

"Ah, that bad, is it?"

"I'm afraid so."

Abandoning Percy abovedecks, the two young ladies went below together.

CHAPTER
SEVEN

In Which a Voyage Is Afloat

Rue filled Primrose in on everything, from her father's deteriorating condition, to her suspicion that Quesnel had known and her lashing out at him. She told Prim about her fear for her parents and about Dama's revelations.

Primrose listened patiently, making sympathetic murmurs in all the right places. She held Rue's hand, squeezing it during the dramatic bits.

"Oh, I say!" was her devout utterance when Rue finished. "And I thought my news was something exciting."

"Your news? And here I am babbling about my problems." Rue was arrested. "What news?"

Prim extracted her hand and drew off her gloves. A very expensive-looking ring graced her left hand.

"You're engaged!" squeaked Rue.

"To the finest gentleman I ever saw. Such nice legs." Primrose did seem sincere about it.

"Um, to which one, exactly?"

"Lieutenant Plonks."

"Oh."

"I know, but that is his only real drawback. Can you imagine me as a Mrs Norman Plonks? It hardly bears repeating. But he is handsome, and respectable, and Queen Mums will adore him.

She's been encouraging me to get married. I'm almost past my prime."

Rue tried not to let her disapproval show. Primrose was always so supportive. Rue owed her enthusiasm. But Prim had no real model of married life, since her father had died tragically when she was young. Rue had only heard it spoken of in hushed tones. A theatre actor of considerable repute, Mr Tunstell had taken a deep breath before Dionysus's famous soliloquy to the dancing Minotaurs, inhaled a pickled grape, and perished onstage to resounding applause for a most realistic portrayal. "It's how he would have wished to go," was all Lady Maccon ever said at Rue's prodding, "wearing a loincloth in front of a cheering crowd."

As a direct result, Primrose had never got over her fear of pickled grapes and she'd no practical example of what love was like. Aunt Ivy lamented her loss with no less a commitment than Queen Victoria did Albert, although Ivy returned to colour after the appropriate period of mourning. Nothing, not even the death of a beloved spouse, could make Ivy Tunstell eschew colourful hats for very long. But she refused to talk of her husband, enmeshed in the tragedy of his loss.

Rue was as sympathetic as she could be to the fact that Primrose was suckering herself for life to some minor officer because she thought that was the proper thing. This Plonks would have no idea what a prize he'd garnered and would likely squirrel Prim away with utter disregard for her organisational talents and interest in adventure. Besides which, Rue was tolerably certain that Primrose's real affections lay elsewhere.

She prodded. "And what about Tasherit?"

Prim went still. "What about her?"

"Have you told her of your engagement?"

"Not yet."

"Ah."

"What do you mean by 'ah'?"

"I'm thinking she might not be overly happy about it."

"Really, Rue, why should a werelioness care what I do with my future?"

If Primrose wanted to remain obtuse, Rue wasn't going to force reality upon her. Rue had been raised by Lord Akeldama and thus understood deviating taste. Primrose had been raised by Ivy Tunstell and thus understood hats. She would never accept being wholly outside society's purview.

Tasherit had a rough road ahead of her. *If she decides to take it.* She *was* a cat; she might simply settle for a less challenging sunbeam.

Rue demurred. "She holds you in high esteem is all. I should think she, like all of us, would like to meet the gentleman before you marry him."

Prim blanched. "She would eat him alive."

Rue pretended not to hear. "Have you told your brother?"

"Yes, silly blighter. He laughed at me and asked not to be in the wedding party."

Rue swallowed down a smile, surprising herself. *Amazing how a few minutes in Primrose's company makes everything that much better.*

By the time the young ladies resurfaced, the workers had gone and *The Spotted Custard* seemed as close to her original pristine state as possible. Decklings scurried about. Deckhands lumbered in their wake, issuing orders. Percy was in full navigator splendour, holding court over Footnote and Virgil.

Virgil had returned so recently from his errand that they were in time to watch him hand over the fated pamphlet. Percy bent over the manuscript, flipping through it rapidly, searching for a specific article.

"It isn't here!" He reached the end and discarded the now-insulting document petulantly.

His valet was appropriately sympathetic.

Footnote made a little *mur-rup* noise of enquiry.

"My point exactly! Where is it?"

Rue and Primrose trundled up.

"Where's what?" asked Rue.

Percy whirled. "Never you mind. It's a surprise. Should it ever happen."

Rue chose to be placating. "Very well, be like that. Everything ready for departure?"

Percy consulted his watch. "In about two hours and twenty-seven minutes." He looked pleadingly at his sister. "Nosh? I'm starving. Plus it feels as if I haven't slept in a million years. Oh wait, I haven't."

Primrose took pity on him. "I'll go and rustle up a picnic, shall I? Rue?"

"Yes, please." Rue perked up. "Hard-boiled eggs and pickled gherkins?"

"Sugarplums, if you're taking requests," added Percy.

"I'll see what Cook has lying about. I don't want to interfere with his system. You know how he gets just before a float."

"Of course!" said Rue and Percy in unison. Better never to upset a cook.

Primrose glided away.

Footnote, who knew very well what was what, followed.

They returned shortly. Primrose was in possession of a hamper of comestibles, including a wedge of Stilton, crusty bread, and the requested boiled eggs. Footnote was licking his chops.

After luncheon, Rue reviewed their course while Percy read. The last book before they floated, Rue supposed, wondering what tome could possibly be worthy of such an honour.

She peeked at the cover. *"On the Respiratory, Restorative, and Regenerative Applications of Aspic Jelly."*

Well, there you have it.

They should not have been faulted for being unprepared. After all, who would have thought a daytime attack at all likely?

It took Rue a few minutes to realise that *The Spotted Custard* was, once more, under siege. She had just re-emerged after an afternoon nap belowdecks via the captain's ladder.

Primrose was supervising the delivery of a cartload of kippers, dried apricots, raspberry jam, and other vital necessities. The gangplank was down as the last of the provisions were wheeled up.

Tea was laid out near navigation. Rue was contemplating whether she could manage a scone, when she suddenly had no options at all. The tea hamper was knocked up into the air and on top of her by a man apparently intent on throttling Percy.

Percy was understandably surprised to find himself under threat of strangulation.

Rue was not surprised at all. She often wanted to throttle Percy. But then, she *knew* him. Fortunately, he was not as easy a mark as he appeared. Aunt Ivy was quite silly – everyone knew this – and it's not like one became less silly because one turned into a vampire. However, she was not wilfully ignorant. She insisted both her children – yes, even the girl – be trained to protect themselves. Thus Primrose and Percival Tunstell knew the rudiments of self-defence against vampires specifically, but that translated pretty darn well to everyone else.

Percy twisted and elbowed his assailant in the throat.

Rue struggled to extract herself from a newly intimate relationship with the tea hamper.

Percy delivered a very nice punch to his opponent's eye. The man, who may or may not have been one of those who tried to board before, pulled a knife and turned his attention onto Rue.

Rue found a grip on the hamper and swung it in a wide arc, clipping him on the side of the head. Until that moment she had not realised how satisfying the sound of wicker crunching could be.

It didn't fell the ruffian, but it dazed him enough for Percy to get in another punch.

"Bloody hell," said Percy, shaking his hand, "that hurts."

"Imagine how he feels." Rue's attention drifted to assess the larger situation. She needed to establish command.

"Percy, can you manage this?"

"If I must."

Rue left the poop deck for the quarterdeck. Away from the helm and associated clutter, the quarterdeck afforded her a better vantage point on the battle taking place on the main deck below.

Several ruffian types had boarded once again. Decklings had one invader up against the forecastle break, four deadly crossbows pressing against his delicate parts. Other decklings had taken to the rigging and were poised for a clear shot, should any of the enemy try to escape. Deckhands engaged two others in fisticuffs.

The three remaining enemies seemed to be trying to make their way belowdecks via the main hatch to the staircase.

Behind her came a crash as Percy brought one of her potted sunflowers down on his assailant's head. The man fell, insensate.

"Oh, Percy, really, must you waste my disinfecting sunflowers?"

Percy look prim. "The evidence supporting the efficaciousness of sunflower use in aetherosphere transit is sketchy at best."

Rue turned back to the battle. *What are they after? Percy's research perhaps? Or Quesnel's preservation tank?* A tank that would allow vampires and werewolves to travel by air was a gold mine. No doubt Professor Lefoux was busy writing up petitions to modify the patent, now that they knew it worked on werewolves. *Quesnel will have told me everything. Or Mother will have.* Inventors did talk to each other. If someone knew what that tank could do and blabbed? It could be a target. And now her father was inside it.

Rue barked out orders, trying to cut through the yelling of excited decklings. "Threat headed belowdecks! Stop them! Willard, Spoo, marshal your troops. Don't forget your training."

Spoo gave a series of piercing whistles. "Decklings to the ground! Invaders at the main hatch!" Those who had been waiting high up to pick off stragglers leapt down.

Willard left off trading blows and, with a signal from his beefy arm, called one of his fellows to replace him. The deckhand stepped in and Willard followed Spoo's decklings towards the three men wrestling with the hatch.

The main hatch was big and heavy but not difficult to open. It operated on a hydraulic pump, with a foot lever on both sides, so someone carrying, for example, a large wicker tea hamper could make it down without need of hands. Fortunately, the concept of a foot-activated door seemed incomprehensible to the enemy. Two were scrabbling about looking for a hand lever and the third was trying to muscle the thing open with his fingertips. Since the hatch fitted seamlessly into the deck, there was no way to get a grip and the man was merely bloodying his nails.

There were two other ways to get below. One was the ladder which Rue had just used from the captain's quarters to the quarterdeck aft. It was a non-standard modification, so even had the enemy stolen schematics of *The Spotted Custard* they wouldn't know it was there. The other was the staff ladder near the forecastle, which no gentleman, not even one bent on criminal activities, would deign to use.

"He's staining my deck with his blood!" objected Rue.

"Don't you worry, Lady Captain, that's what swabbing is for," comforted Spoo as she nipped by to join the fray.

The invaders rather gave up at that juncture. No doubt they had not anticipated the ship to be so well defended and so populated, everyone being on shift in preparation for the imminent float off.

The leader, one of the three trying to go below, looked up and made eye contact with Rue. He was a darkly handsome man, or would have been had his visage not been marred by a fierce scowl that only deepened upon seeing Rue. Of course, when they attacked, she'd been out of sight. *Aha!* thought Rue, pleased. *Scared of me, are you? Quite right.*

Then Willard hit him broadside with one meaty fist. The man twisted away and yelled some fancy foreign word. With which all the invaders took off down the gangplank.

Two deckhands made to chase but Rue called, "No time. We've a current to catch."

Decklings took pot shots with their crossbows at the retreating men, but only in a desultory fashion.

Just like that, it was over.

"I want to know what they were after." Rue let frustration colour her voice. "Please report in with clues and theories. Nothing is too minor. Everyone understand?"

Her crew nodded.

"Now, is anyone injured?" No one seemed to be, except the tea hamper and one potted sunflower, which had taken the brunt of the battle. There were a few bumps and bruises, but nothing her crew might not garner during the ordinary course of work.

"Please see Miss Primrose for plaster and medicinals."

They hadn't a medic on board, but Primrose was capable in a pinch. She emerged from where she had taken refuge, behind the overturned cartload of kippers. She'd lost her hat and a smoked fish now draped over her lovely hair in a jaunty manner. Rue forbore to say, although she really wanted to, how this would only make Prim more intriguing to Tasherit. The werelioness was awfully fond of kippers.

Rue continued issuing instructions. "Cook will be authorised to distribute alcohol to soothe the nerves as needed." The decklings cheered, which made Rue rethink a little. "During off-duty shifts, obviously." There was a murmur of disappointment. "But you have all earned hazard pay for this action. It's not your job to fight for the honour of *The Spotted Custard*." Another cheer. "I want you all to know how much I appreciate the effort."

The decklings started up a raucous song at that.

> "We are *The Spotted Custard*!
> From the crow's nest to the tomb!
> *Spotted Custard* is your saviour,
> or *Spotted Custard* is your doom!"

Aren't they precious? We have a chant. Rue was utterly delighted. She wanted to march about in a drummer boy fashion, but that might be a smidgen undignified in a captain, so she only nodded to the beat with a pleased expression.

Rue raised a hand when everyone would have dispersed. "I know we are still an hour from float off, but let's get this basket up, shall we? London clearly isn't interested in doing us any favours. Decklings prepare the balloon, deckhands the propeller. I want those kippers cleaned up and loaded into storage. All non–crew members should be groundside in ten minutes and the gangplank tucked in. Navigation, prepare the helm for . . . Percy? Where the devil is Percy? Damnation, did they steal our navigator?"

Percy had not been kidnapped but had simply disappeared below via the captain's ladder to, as he explained when Rue found him, "Check on something."

Rue became even more suspicious that their attackers were after a Percy-related whatnot. Percy could hold the secrets of the universe against all comers, however, for he utterly refused to elaborate further.

"I understand we are floating early?"

"Yes, I thought we might take in the view, drift above London for a bit."

It being winter, London was a grey, gloomy thing. Percy was not impressed with this plan. "I did want to get in another chapter."

"Human life, I'm afraid, must take priority. I won't give our enemy time to regroup *again*. Whoever they are."

So *The Spotted Custard* let loose her moorings and drifted up. At a safe height, she bobbed, taking the opportunity to tune her motions. It had been a few weeks since she'd tackled serious floating, and while their plotted currents were not challenging, one could never be certain with the aetherosphere. Rue wanted her crew prepared for anything, especially now.

The sun set and they rose higher, waiting for Percy to call the mark for wind-up and puff.

Tasherit appeared on deck. She reached her long graceful arms above her head for a stretch, taking in the busy crew with interest.

"What's going on? Pleasure jaunt?"

Primrose stared at the werecat, eyes popping.

Rue explained. "Had to lift earlier than planned. We had visitors. Your troops, by the way, did marvellously. I'm impressed."

Tasherit lowered her arms. "They're charmingly enthusiastic. Early, you say? Are we off somewhere particular, then?"

"Oh goodness. I forgot you've been asleep. We're headed to Egypt. I do apologise. It must feel as if we catnapped you."

The werelioness only grinned. "Don't be silly, I'm thrilled. It's one of the reasons I joined up with you, Lady Prudence. Never a dull moment. It's been ages since I visited Egypt. Could get a little awkward for me, given the plague and all. Plus, in some circles, I'm not at all welcome. But we'll worry about that when we get there, shall we?"

She moved to join the twins in the navigation area. Her nose twitched and she narrowed her big brown eyes at Primrose. "Little flower, you smell positively delicious."

Prim blushed scarlet. "There was a kipper incident."

"Don't stop," begged the werecat.

Primrose rolled her eyes. "Would you like some?"

The lioness was not to be diverted. "Of you or the kipper?"

Primrose glared.

Tasherit would have twitched whiskers, had she sported them at the moment. "If we intend to break aether soon, then yes please. I should eat before I'm forced back to bed. Kippers would be lovely."

The aetherosphere reputedly made vampires insane and

werewolves ill. The werecat was affected as well, although not so badly. The moment they entered the grey, Tasherit fell into the deepest, most immovable sleep. Like a vampire during the daylight, she appeared dead, curled in a tight ball. Rue had asked her why she was different, able to travel in the aetherosphere where other supernaturals could not.

In classic fashion, Tasherit had answered with no answer. "I'm a lioness, darling. Heights are what cats *do*. We're good at being solitary, hence my lack of hive or pack . . . well, *pride* in my case. And we're good at being high up. And we're good at sleeping. I can't wake until we are out of aether, though. I doubt you can steal my form either, little skin-stalker." At Rue's expression, she added, "It might be dangerous to try. I am accustomed to the catnap-solid-state-flop. You are not."

Kippers arrived and Tasherit ate them with alacrity, accompanied by a large mug of heavy cream. She had horrible table manners, so the others left her to it, bustling about putting everything in order. Primrose retreated to wash her hair, given that while the kippers themselves had been removed, the stench had not.

Primrose still hadn't told the werecat about her engagement. Her gloves stayed very firmly on. *Little coward.*

Tasherit completed her meal and returned below to prepare for the journey.

Rue was looking one final time over the rail at the dim lights of her home city when she heard Percy having an annoyed one-sided conversation. He was on the blow horn to engineering.

Rue marched over and put out her hand.

Relieved, the navigator passed her the speaking tube.

The voice on the other end was mid-diatribe. "What the hell is going on up there? I thought we had another twenty minutes. What are we doing floating unnecessarily? You're wasting fuel, Mr Tunstell. I can't promise we'll make the beacon without risk. Stop larking about."

"It's me, Mr Lefoux."

"Rue, what the hell?"

Quesnel was calling her by her real name. He *must* be annoyed.

"We were attacked. I thought it prudent to float off before it could happen a third time."

Quesnel's tone altered. "Are you injured? Is anyone hurt? How's the ship? I'm coming up."

"No, you most certainly are not! We have only a few minutes before first puff and I want you in the boiler room. Everyone is perfectly fine. Tasherit's been training them, remember? There may be a sunflower that needs to be put out of its misery, though."

"She hasn't been training you."

"I'm fine, too. How's my father? Did he wake after sunset?"

"No. Nor should he, if my calculations are correct. The tank should hold him in an optimal non-degenerative sleep state for the entire trip. And keep him from aether illness once we enter the grey."

"Should?"

"It's not designed for werewolves, *chérie*."

"Oh? What is it designed for? Vampires?"

"It's designed for apologies and reparations. Or so my mother tells me."

"Lovely. Some day do you think you might reveal the particulars?"

"Some day. You sure you're unhurt?"

"I'm sure. I had an ignominious encounter with a tea hamper, which I roundly defeated, I'll have you know."

Quesnel laughed. "Of course you did. Very brave."

The tension was still there. Rue had apologised to Percy but not to Quesnel. The same truth held. He had deserved the reprimand, but she should have been less cruel about his shortcomings.

She only said, "Everything on track for float on your end?"

"*Naturellement.*"

"Then we will see you at supper once we've made our current."

"Yes, Captain." Quesnel sounded as tired as Rue felt.

"Carry on."

The puffing went smoothly and they achieved flotsam status with no trouble at all from any Charybdis currents. For all their bickering and dislike of one another, Percy and Quesnel made for a synergistic team. Primrose reappeared smelling of violets and kept Rue company while Percy manned the tiller and the puffer buttons with an aplomb one would not have thought possible a month ago. He was such a bookish boffin that to witness him acting like a sailor out of some piratical yarn was surprisingly charming. Percy could never look tough, not with his winsome face, but he could look dashing. Rue saw a glimpse, briefly, of what made him so deadly when allowed to roam free among impressionable young ladies.

They settled into the Gibraltar Loop with ease. The route to Egypt wasn't tricky to navigate – one of the reasons travel between London and Alexandria had grown so popular. A smooth current and a lower-level puffing made all the difference in the age of dirigibles. With the sail up, rudder down, and propeller off, they drifted through the grey nothingness of the aetherosphere. At first it had bothered Rue, the motionless gloomy quiet pressing against her, but now she enjoyed the peace. It felt like a physical blanket inside her skin.

Her mother still wasn't up. Rue decided to be happy about that. Should she check on Paw? No. Rue trusted Quesnel to tell her if anything was wrong and she felt that the sight of Paw's still body surrounded by that bubbling orange liquid might be too dismal.

After brief consultation, it was deemed safe enough for the officers to retire. Primrose had ordered in an interim feeding so they could hold off until later for supper with Lady Maccon. They tried to do it justice, but it was a silent group. Percy wasn't permitting himself a book, but that didn't mean he became loquacious. Quesnel's quick elegant movements were tempered by fatigue, although he was as neat with his manners and address as ever. He kept sending tiny glances in Rue's direction but she pretended not to notice. Primrose did her best to carry the conversation, but she was tired enough to allow it to lapse occasionally.

Finally, Percy was moved to exasperation. "For goodness' sake, Tiddles, you don't have to talk simply because it is mealtime. We are all friends here. Could we not eat in silence?"

Quesnel leapt to Prim's defence. "Now, Mr Tunstell, that's not fair. Societal conventions dictate—"

"Blow societal conventions. A little less chatter once in a while would be to everyone's benefit."

Primrose looked as if she might weep: a mark of exhaustion, for normally her twin's snide remarks rolled off her.

Rue could not tolerate having to mediate between Percy and Quesnel *again*. While the rabbit stew was delicious, she opted to leave the rest and escape. She stood abruptly.

Both men scrambled to stand as well.

"I'm for bed. Sleep well, everyone. I'll no doubt see you at supper. It's likely my mother will be joining us. Perhaps we could all try to follow Prim's example and behave in a polished manner for a change?"

"Thank you, Rue." Primrose sounded less like she wanted to cry.

Rue left them to it. She was at the door to her quarters, imagining the glory of soft sheets and a puffy coverlet, when her mother's voice stopped her.

Somewhere, somehow, Rue found the reserves needed to turn around.

"Mother."

"Infant. Report." Lady Maccon was not happy about finding herself in transit.

Rue took some satisfaction in that. Lady Maccon always

autocratically arranged things for her daughter, like a squishy benevolent cyclone. It was somewhat pleasing for Rue to find herself in the position of tyrant for a change.

"We've safely attained flotsam en route to Egypt. Quesnel says Paw is fine, in perfect preservation and seemingly untroubled by aetherosphere transition. I haven't checked on him myself. You are welcome to do so. Although, please do not distract my crew."

Lady Maccon looked relieved. "You decided to transport us immediately?"

"It seemed the best course of action given Paw's deteriorating condition. And you were both already aboard."

"I should have liked to say goodbye to some friends. And there's packing to consider."

"The clavigers sent over three massive trunks. Dama's drones sent eight hatboxes, three jewellery rolls, a cravat case, and a large Spanish sausage. Your butler sent one very old and battered portmanteau. All appear to be stuffed to the gills and are located in the storage hold. I'll have them brought to your quarters, if you like."

"It's not about the objects." Lady Maccon's voice cracked a little.

"Dama said to bid you farewell."

Her mother's eyes went wide and shiny. But she would not cry in front of her daughter. Rue knew this because she hated crying in front of her mother.

Rue felt a pang. Perhaps she had been too dictatorial. How would she like it if Lady Maccon unilaterally removed her from Primrose and Percy? But knowing Mother, she'd been prepared for this for months and already made her goodbyes.

"I will never see Ivy again."

"Oh phooey, Mother, don't be histrionic. Paw may be unable to leave Egypt for the rest of his life." Rue choked a little but soldiered on. "You, however, are not equally trapped. You can leave him alone once he's safely installed within the God-Breaker

Plague. Or that's the working theory. Nothing prevents *you* from returning to London for a visit."

Lady Maccon nodded. "Fair point."

"Speed is our priority, especially if Quesnel's tank fails. Let's concentrate on getting Paw to Egypt. Everything else can be sorted later."

"Quite right, quite right."

The fact that Mother was ceding ground to her floored Rue. She was determined to retire in possession of the field. Before Lady Maccon could find anything else to get annoyed about, she said, "There is food in the stateroom if you're hungry. Cook's laid on smelts, calf's heart, and stewed rabbit with cauliflower, and Norfolk dumplings."

Lady Maccon was preempted. "How divine! Now that you mention it, I'm fading away for the lack. You're napping?"

"Mmm," said Rue indistinctly.

Rue's mother didn't require an answer. She was already heading down the hallway. Very little diverted Lady Maccon from partaking of a decent meal.

EIGHT

In Which There May, or May Not, Be French Lessons

R ue dressed for supper with more care than normal. She told herself this was certainly nothing to do with her mother. She was quick about it, buttoning the appliqué front of her red travel dress with nimble fingers. The skirt was red, too, without embellishment except for three ruffles at the hem. Primrose had insisted Rue buy the dress. She felt like a tomato in it, but red was a commanding colour and she needed the confidence.

Primrose was the only one at the table when Rue arrived. Prim felt it her sacred trust to hold court the entirety of any given mealtime. Sometimes when duty, lugubriousness, and sleep schedules aligned, she could be in the stateroom, pouring tea and sympathy, for something on the order of three hours. Loving every minute of it.

Rue helped herself to a plate of kippers and eggs. Kippers were served at every meal, fish being Tasherit's favourite. The werecat required fresh raw meat at full moon but the rest of the time smoked haddock and the occasional pickled herring seemed to keep the beast pacified.

"Anyone else up?" Rue tucked in.

"Percy ate faster than you would believe. I think perhaps him reading at the table was not so bad; otherwise he positively devours his food. It's unseemly. Your mother has not been in, but she stayed awake longer than the rest of us."

"Was she horrible after I left?"

"Perfectly civil, but you know I've always muddled along well with your mother."

"You are the practical organised daughter she always wanted."

"That's not a very nice sentiment. Besides, you wouldn't want my mother in exchange."

Rue shuddered. "Heavens, the very idea. And Quesnel?"

"Are you asking because you want to see him, or don't want to see him?"

"Bit of both." Rue began to chew happily, if slowly, mindful of Prim's annoyance over Percy's inhaling.

"I'm worried about you two." Prim's eyes were grave.

"There's nothing serious between us."

"You're not like me. You aren't cold and indifferent."

"You're not cold and indifferent!"

"Yes, I am. But you're all bubbly and enthusiastic. When you go charging into something, Rue, you go all in and that could be dangerous." Prim sipped her tea and donned a concerned expression.

"Oh, Prim, how sweet! Are you worried that Quesnel will break my heart?"

Primrose looked into her teacup as though it held all the secrets of the universe. Which it might in some situations. "No. I'm worried that you'll break his."

Rue scoffed. "That man is in no danger. He's a horrible flirt and I'm a fluffy sort of person. He won't think to care for me. I'm not the type men fall in love with. You are."

"Poor chap! That's not—"

The man in question stalked into the room. He was smudged from engineering. *Just like Quesnel to check the boilers before seeking his repast.*

"Who's a poor chap? Aren't you two the jammiest bits of jam this evening?" Quesnel beamed at them before piling his plate with ham, eggs, and stewed tomato.

Technically it was suppertime but since the *Custard* kept
supernatural hours, the first meal after sunset was treated as
breakfast. In consequence, the officers were not waited upon at
table and did not stand on ceremony.

Primrose said, "You are, actually."

"Of course I am. Can you not see me suffering?" He nibbled
on a bit of toast while mixing together his eggs and tomatoes.
It was as though the events of the past few nights were now
nothing to him but mere boyish larks.

"You look positively miserable." Rue was deadpan.

Primrose looked back and forth between them with suspiciously bright eyes.

She wouldn't dare!

"I've just realised I must consult Cook about supplies. I
neglected to include Lady Maccon's enthusiasm for pudding in
my calculations. I should do it now, before next meal's preparations commence."

Apparently she *would* dare. Primrose pushed the tea tray in
Rue's direction. "You can play mother for a change. Pot's full,
milk is there, you pour like so." She made a pouring gesture
with her wrist. "Not too complicated for you?"

Rue gave her a dour look.

Quesnel stood to bow Prim out, still holding his toast.

Primrose, grinning, made a show of closing the door, leaving
Rue and Quesnel alone.

Quesnel sat back down. "Was it something I said?"

"You? Never. You seldom put a single word out of place. It's
exasperating."

"Here I thought you found me utterly charming."

"It would be nice if I could trust something charming you
said to *also* be honest."

"Don't talk gammon. You prefer frivolity."

No time like the present. Rue tried to stop her voice from trembling. "Quesnel."

Quesnel sliced off a bit of ham. "Mmm?"

"I must apologise. I didn't mean to call you thoughtless. I was annoyed with you for egging Percy on and I was upset about my father's condition. I took it out on you, which was wrong of me."

The inventor swallowed his ham. "Apology accepted. You had quite the shock."

Rue took a shaky breath. "How long have you known?"

"About your father's predicament?"

Rue nodded.   •

"Since before you recruited me. *Chérie*, I never realised that you didn't know. I assumed you simply didn't want to talk about a private family matter."

"And you going off to Egypt?"

"Had nothing to do with him. It was a favour to my mother. She asked me to visit an old friend."

Rue nodded. "It seemed suspicious, you must own, especially now we're are headed there ourselves."

"My dearest girl, I assure you, it's pure coincidence."

"And the tank?"

"Is not being used for its intended purpose. I did not build it for your father. Werewolf aetherosphere transport is an exciting new application for the technology, but innovative. Neither my mother nor I had that kind of forethought. We are inventors, not seers."

"Very well. I believe you." And Rue did. Partly because Quesnel would certainly take credit if it were due – he was no shrinking violet when praise of intellect was in the offing – and partly because she didn't have a choice.

"There's nothing else I should know about Egypt? No other *personal* connections?"

Quesnel stopped, arrested. "You think it was a woman? You think I flew leagues out of my way for a *dalliance*?"

Rue blinked at him. Actually, the thought hadn't occurred to her but it was possible. He was the type to dash across continents in pursuit of a soprano or opera dancer – or something else prone to humming and gyrating about.

"I assure you, my acquaintance in Egypt is quite grandfatherly."

"I wasn't . . . that is . . . I didn't . . ."

Quesnel grinned, showing his dimples. "I like to think you might be a little jealous."

Rue sighed. She was terrible at playing the coquette. That was supposed to be one of the things he taught her. "Have I reason to be jealous?"

"Certainly not."

"Is that because you've not had the will or the opportunity?"

Quesnel stopped smiling and put down his fork. He came around the table to kneel next to her chair.

"*Chérie*, I am not so much a rake as I have been painted. Every experience of mine has been my sole focus at the time, to the exclusion of all others. Do you take my meaning?"

Rue nodded. Thrilled a little by both his statement and his proximity. That meant she would get to keep him for herself, while it lasted.

He continued, still un-Quesnel-like in his seriousness. "But you are."

"I'm what?" Rue was suddenly interested in crumbling her toast.

"Innocent. You're bold and brash and very attractive, so I sometimes forget how innocent you are. I do not want to hurt you, *chérie*."

This was getting too earnest for Rue. "No danger there. I assure you, my heart is not available."

Was that disappointment she saw flicker in his eyes? If so, it quickly changed to avarice.

"But the rest of you is?"

Rue grinned. "Most assuredly. I believe I was promised French lessons. You accepted the position and I should like to learn the details and activities, not to mention vocabulary."

"Shall we start with some terms, then?"

Rue nearly choked in surprise. "Now? Over breakfast? Isn't that rather daring?"

"First lesson, *chérie* – nothing mixes better than food and French."

"Oh, dear."

"Oh, yes." He stood, trailing two fingers along her wrist, no doubt feeling exactly how her pulse fluttered.

Rue reminded herself not to be scared of Quesnel's lessons. Rather like breakfast, most of the population engaged in such things. Rue had confronted unknown beasts in Indian jungles and escaped airship battles. She wasn't scared of a little French!

He returned to his chair. "We should, perhaps, institute some rules of engagement?"

Rue considered. "Flirting is established. I should like to continue kissing as well."

"And we already know that language lessons are involved."

Rue thought that had been euphemistic. Now she realised there might be proper terms for actions and even anatomy. "I'm afraid that's part of the difficulty. I don't know how to establish rules because I don't know what to request. I won't know until you tell me." Rue took a big breath. "I think it likely that children would be an embarrassment for me and an inconvenience for you. We'd have to marry, you know, and I don't believe either of us wishes that outcome."

If Quesnel was surprised by her directness, he didn't show it. Although he did look ... what? Wistful?

"No, of course not. So I am safe in the assumption that you would like to experiment with the kinds of things that might cause children?"

Rue considered his kisses and his gentle hands. "Yes, I would." Her face felt hot.

"Capital. Now, I'm capable of protecting you up to a point. Once we reach that point, I will explain the risks. But there are many things that can be done that are of no danger whatsoever. And great fun, I might add." He finished his breakfast and pushed away the plate.

"I thought there might be, or people wouldn't make such a

fuss over it." Rue refilled his tea. "All those Roman poets." Rue's hand wasn't entirely steady but she managed to pour in a manner that Primrose would deem acceptable.

Quesnel took his cup with a chuckle. "Have you been reading Catullus?"

"A little. Kissing is awfully nice. Although we ought to stop doing it in public, especially with my mother around. And I don't want to corrupt decklings."

"If we allow ourselves regular kissing in private, we should be better able to resist traumatising the masses." His tone said he was humouring her.

"Is that so? You see, I'm learning already."

"Shall we try it and see?"

Quesnel set down his teacup, stood, and rounded the table towards her.

Rue pushed back her chair; luckily it didn't tip in her eagerness. He gave her a hand up, pulling her smoothly into his arms.

"Now, let us see. If I put my hands there, you could put yours there." He grabbed her shoulders, sliding one hand to her upper back while placing her fingers at his waist.

Rue was never daunted for long. She slid them immediately to the tight stretch of trousers over his posterior. "Not here?"

"That works, too."

She tried a squeeze.

He yipped.

Interesting reaction.

"Are you trying to skip ahead, Miss Prudence?"

Rue stopped squeezing and widened her eyes, attempting one of Prim's innocent expressions.

"How did I not know you would be trouble?" Quesnel asked, but did not let her answer, leaning in to press his mouth to hers.

He tasted of tea, which was no bad thing. Rue adored tea. His lips were warm and gentle at first. It was nice, but nothing new. They had done this before.

He drew back. "So, kissing."

Rue nodded. "I feel as if I have got the way of that particular lesson."

"Oh, do you?"

Rue went up on her toes and kissed him. She imitated his actions, nibbled a little, delighted by the way his breathing changed slightly.

"Well?"

He nodded, looking like a professor assessing exams. "Very good. But there is more than one kind of kissing."

"Show me," Rue commanded.

"This is the French variation."

It started the same but then there was a flick of tongue against the seam of her mouth. Rue found this, frankly, unseemly. *How am I expected to react?* His thumb came up to lightly press her chin down. Her mouth opened. His tongue took instant advantage, tasting her with a slow exploration.

He drew back. "Well?"

Was that a hint of nervousness?

Rue considered. She didn't want to hurt his feelings. Some parts of her body liked it, for she felt warm and languid, as if after a hot bath, but intellectually she wasn't convinced.

"The French really are centred on taste, aren't they?"

Quesnel laughed.

Rue was game. "May I try, or is it a thing that gentlemen do to ladies?"

Quesnel grinned. "I should have said at the start. Anything I do to you, you are more than welcome to do to me."

"*Anything* at all?"

"Yes. Anything."

Rue's mind raced. "Right, then, let's see."

She leaned forward and took over the kiss again. He opened his mouth willingly at the first hesitant touch of her tongue. She swept it in. She didn't want to be sloppy, but that appeared challenging when tongues were involved.

Halfway through, she decided she liked it, despite the

sloppiness. So, she thought, did he. He shifted against her, the whole length of his body in contact with hers. His seemed to be changing shape in a rather indelicate area.

Rue drew back. "What's . . . ?"

Quesnel blushed scarlet. If he was going to blush, surely he'd have done so before now?

Rue wasn't completely ignorant. Hoping to relieve his distress, she said, "Isn't that supposed to happen?"

Which made him laugh. "Perhaps not quite so quickly and at the breakfast table, but yes."

Rue grinned, rather proud. She herself was not unaffected. There was a curious tingling, and a sort of anxious sensation that, as far as she could tell, would require more kissing to allay.

She moved in for more. Clearly the French were on to some-thing. This time both their tongues were involved. *Utterly delightful.* Rue found herself squirming against him, enjoying the muscles she could feel through the fabric of her red dress, her own hands full of trouser-covered flesh and then . . .

He stopped.

Rue worried that she had done something wrong. She gath-ered her wits. He was breathing as roughly as she was.

"I must say, *chérie*, you're an awfully quick study."

"I've always been an enthusiastic student of new experiences."

Quesnel pulled himself together. "That's the problem with these kinds of lessons – you can use them against me."

"I see that now." Rue was delighted by this revelation. Quesnel had handed her a weapon. She did love to have leverage in any given situation.

"Just as I said, *trouble.*"

The door to the stateroom banged open and they sprang apart. Rue self-consciously smoothed the wrinkles out of the bodice of her dress. Quesnel smoothed the wrinkles out of the back of his trousers.

Oh, thought Rue, *did I do that? Oops.*

Lady Maccon marched into the room. She gave them a suspicious glance but did not say anything, merely piling a plate high with giblet pie, eggs, potted shrimp, stewed tomatoes, and kippered salmon. Lady Maccon had been accused of many things but being a feeble eater wasn't one of them.

Quesnel said, "Good evening, Lady Maccon."

"Mr Lefoux."

"Mother."

"Infant."

The salutations thus established, Quesnel retrieved his hat from a nearby stand and popped it on his head. "I'm off, Captain, unless you need me for anything further?"

Rue stifled a smile, realising that now nearly anything he said would sound euphemistic. Perhaps it always had and she simply hadn't known to realise.

"Nothing else, Mr Lefoux. Thank you. Perhaps we will discuss the matter in greater depth later tonight?"

Quesnel choked only slightly, recovered with aplomb, and flashed a dimpled smile at her before leaving the room.

Rue hoped that her mother wouldn't notice the rumpled state of his trousers. No doubt she would guess what they were up to if she did – or was that *down* to?

Lady Maccon made no trouser-based comment, only ate her breakfast.

Rue, conscious of the formalities, poured her mother tea and watched her shovel in the comestibles in awkward silence.

Breakfast eaten and a fourth cup of tea swilled, Lady Maccon cleared her throat, disturbing the now oppressive quiet.

"Precautionary arts," she began, slightly too loudly.

Then she commenced to lecture Rue in a voice curdled by acute embarrassment.

Afterwards, Rue could recall something about rinsing out the cavity with vinegar, French letters, and little hats made of sponge fitted inside one's delicate parts. It was mostly incomprehensible and quite possibly the most humiliating experience of Rue's entire life.

Floating the grey was largely uneventful. Once *The Spotted Custard* hooked into the right current, there wasn't much for anyone to do. Primrose bustled around, ensuring everyone's comfort. Spoo, Virgil, and the decklings played tiddlywinks. Percy mooched about abovedecks, avoiding the temptation of reading and not happy about it. Rue couldn't get over how amusing it was that he was refusing to *read* during float because he had *read* a pamphlet that warned of its dangers. It was so very circular. Lady Maccon marched about sticking her generous nose into anything in which it might be stuck. She wanted to know how the decklings operated, and navigation, and the Gatling gun, and the rigging, and the tea hamper. They humoured her, even the tea hamper. A replacement, mind you, the original one having died gloriously in battle.

Below them in her room, Tasherit slumbered. Below her in their lair, Quesnel, Aggie, and the engineering team tended the boilers, maintaining a steady heat.

At luncheon, Quesnel flirted with Rue, and she flirted happily back. Lady Maccon and Percy ignored them. Primrose made disapproving noises. Rue dragged her off for a private consultation in the stateroom. They left Lady Maccon in charge. Rue did wonder, horrified, if the gentlemen might be on the receiving end of another one of Mother's precautionary arts lectures.

Surely even Lady Maccon wouldn't go that far? *Well, if she wants to, she will. I can't stop her. Might as well get it over with.*

In the stateroom, Rue flopped into a chair dramatically so that Primrose would ask her what was wrong. Primrose, obligingly, asked.

"Quesnel and I have decided to proceed with our involvement."

Prim's eyes widened. "You have? Are you engaged?"

"Not *that* kind of involvement."

"Prudence Akeldama, you're a loose skirt!"

Rue didn't take offence. If the skirt fit, might as well loose it. "Maybe a little. Except that I'm not doing this for money. When all is said and done, as captain I pay Quesnel ... rather well."

Primrose fanned herself vigorously. "There is no call for the vulgar mention of pecuniary advancement."

"Quite right."

"I don't understand. If you aren't engaged and don't wish to be, what are you doing this for?"

Rue smiled. "I always wanted to learn French."

"Rue!"

"It's quite enjoyable, Prim. Haven't you ever been curious? Don't you want to know what all the fuss is about?"

"Not particularly."

"Haven't any of various beaux kissed you?"

"Several! I'm not *that* old-fashioned."

"And?"

Primrose was perturbed. Suddenly she was the one being questioned. "It was nice enough."

"Nice? *Nice* she says."

"What's wrong with *nice?*"

Rue leaned forward, eyes gleaming. "It was wonderful, Prim. Much better than nice. I adore kissing him. I should like to do it as often as possible."

Primrose was crestfallen. "Is that how one is meant to react?"

"I don't know, but it certainly feels right."

"Then I must be doing it wrong."

"Or Quesnel is particularly good at it."

"He certainly has experience."

Rue grinned. "I've decided that's not a bad thing. I should like to be worldly, and he has agreed to educate me. I've already learned a great deal about kissing. Did you know there is a tongue-in version?"

Primrose reared back. "How revolting."

"I thought so, too, at first, but it turned out to be quite lovely."
Prim was floored beyond speech.

Rue prattled on, hands flapping. "*And* I have discovered I enjoy a well-formed posterior. It's very nice to have something to grab on to, you know, when coping with tongues."

Primrose whispered, "Rue, that's a perfectly shocking thing to say!" Her voice was low and trembling.

"But it's true! And isn't that delicious fun? To be fully twenty-one years old and learning new things about one's preferences that one never even knew before?"

"No," squeaked Primrose, "that's awful. I prefer knowing my own mind and keeping it as it is! Thank you very much. I do not want to be surprised by bottoms!"

Rue couldn't stop. For some reason, the sheer depth of Prim's outrage only encouraged her. "Well, let me tell you, it's a *delightful* sensation. I recommend bottoms at every opportunity."

With which both girls dissolved into slightly hysterical giggles.

After catching their breath, they got themselves fresh tea.

"To be quite serious, Rue," said Prim, in an attempt to divert her friend from any more squeezing confessions, "you're toying with that man's emotions."

"I'm certainly toying with his bottom."

"Stop it." One of the reasons Primrose was Rue's best friend in the whole wide world was because she spoke her mind when called upon to do so.

"We've agreed that it's only for larks, Prim. I swear it. He'll stay loyal for the duration but that's all. It will end with both of us mighty bucked up. That's the plan."

"It's a stupid plan."

"That's rich, coming from you." Rue became defensive.

"Pardon me?"

Rue said, "You avoid Tasherit because you like her. And I don't mean in a friendship manner. I mean in a *French* manner."

Primrose gasped. "You've spent too much time with Lord Akeldama."

"Exactly."

Primrose pursed her lips. "I will confess to finding Miss Sekhmet unsettling. But that is because she persists in wooing me. I don't know how to react. She doesn't respect my engagement at all."

"Has she kissed you?"

Primrose sucked in her breath. "No."

Is that part of the problem? Rue wondered. *Do you want her to kiss you?* She didn't ask. Prim's character was nothing like Rue's. Primrose hadn't the same reckless curiosity and enthusiasm for the unknown.

"Rue, you cannot expect me to be as forthright with my secrets as you are with yours."

Rue put a hand to her friend's shoulder. "I respect that. But I am here if you wish to talk, no details required. And I won't judge preferences."

"No, not you. You never judge. It's both naïve and sweet. And likely to get you into trouble. If this dalliance gets out, others will judge you. Unmarried lady aristocrats aren't supposed to dally. Not with common engineers, even famous inventor-type common engineers. He's one step up from *an artist.*"

"That's part of the fun."

"Does your mother know?"

"Yes, curse it. Oh, Primrose, it was beastly. She gave me a *lecture* – on tiny sponge hats and vinegary measures a lady takes to prevent being inconvenienced."

Prim's face went pale and her mouth softened in sympathy. "Oh, Rue, how *awful* for you."

"It was quite the most unpleasant thing *ever.*"

After everyone else had gone to bed, Rue received Quesnel at the door to the captain's quarters wearing the pretty silk robe that she'd conveniently forgotten to return to Tasherit.

Quesnel was delighted. "You noticed how much I liked it?"

She nodded, nervous. "I thought that it would make things easier." *And give me a little control over the situation.*

Rue wasn't even aware she had linked her hands together until Quesnel placed his palm gently on top of them.

"*Chérie,* I wish to be very clear with you. This is not a rejection. I absolutely adore that robe. You are shaped in every way exactly as a woman ought to be shaped and someday soon I will strip it off you and convince you of this fact. But not now."

Rue felt the hot blush of shame. What was she doing, chucking herself at him like some wanton street hussy?

"No," he said, "stop it. What did I *just* say? This is nothing to do with you. It is my control I'm concerned about as you are inexperienced. This must be good for you. I have to make it good for you." He shook his head.

He is nervous, too? How adorable. Rue gave him a little nudge with her shoulder.

"I don't want to skip too far ahead. You cannot be expected to speak French in full sentences, having only learned a few words."

Rue took a shallow breath. "That does make sense. Nothing of an intrusive nature right away?" She gave his trousers a suggestive glance.

Quesnel chuckled, but not in a nasty way. "Shall we leave that for a week so you don't fret overmuch?"

Rue was both disappointed and profoundly relieved. "Oh, that would be nice. Not that I am rejecting you!" She wanted to take equal care of his feelings. "And I don't wish to restrict spontaneity, but I should like . . ."

"A reprieve from the unknown? Don't wind yourself up about it. And to that end, I have something for you."

"A book? How thoughtful." *How mundane.* It was something Percy would do, and so out of character. She glared at the volume in confusion. It was a plain cloth thing, dark green in colour, not very big. It was certainly something she could read quickly.

It looked to include a number of etchings – they darkened the edges of near half the leaves.

"That book is your first lesson. I would like you to read it, *chérie*. Mark the bits you like and the ones that confuse you, and we are going to talk about it. Really talk. Teasing talk, of course, that seems easiest for us, but I want you to read and ask questions. Please?"

She went to flip it open.

"Not in the hallway, *mon petite chou*. I bid you good night."

"Don't I even get a kiss?"

"Not in that robe you don't, far too dangerous."

Rue giggled. He really did like it. And her. He liked the way she looked, curves and odd tawny eyes, and all.

"Enjoy the book. Pleasant dreams."

Rue couldn't deny a pang as she closed the door. Primrose was right to accuse her of all too readily charging into the unknown. Even when heading into the aetherosphere, one charted currents and followed a course. Perhaps that's what this volume was meant to be – a travel guide.

She flipped it open.

"Oh dear me," said Rue into the silence of her empty quarters.

It was a very informative evening, as it turned out.

NINE

In Which Freckles Go on the Rampage

They arrived in Egypt before Quesnel's week's delay was over. Not that Quesnel avoided Rue. One morning, after days of increased teasing, he finally followed her into her quarters once everyone else was abed and declared it kisses time – no tongue, no hands.

Rue discovered she enjoyed having her neck kissed. And lower down. Quesnel clearly felt the same. They stopped at the waist but the book had reliably informed her that they could keep going. Since Quesnel had indicated he would welcome questions, she asked him about that.

He said he'd show her but that it would be necessary for the next lesson to be slightly delayed. He'd require twenty minutes in his own quarters first, and then they could proceed without, as he put it, containment problems. After the book, Rue had a tolerably good idea what he meant.

The next session, twenty minutes later than normal, they worked on kissing further.

It was about the best wheeze Rue had ever enjoyed, which she told Quesnel, because he ought to know these things, too. He was flustered by her praise.

He slid back from her. They were sitting on the bed. Not under the covers. He had declared that, unless they were cold, lessons were better conducted with the gas on low, grey light filtering in through the porthole, and everything out in the open – for the sake of a superior education.

Rue was still fully dressed, although she had opted for a tea-gown: better ease of access. Quesnel was stripped down to his trousers, because, as he explained, he was prepared for her to do most of the kissing this evening.

He jumped off the bed and removed the last of his clothing. He gritted his teeth and blushed, more self-conscious than the werewolves of Rue's acquaintance. Perhaps this was more an obligation rather than a pleasure?

"You don't have to." Rue didn't want him to feel forced.

"It's only a little embarrassment. You've seen pictures. It's time for you to do a little of that exploring you're so fond of."

"Goodie!" Rue clapped her hands only a tiny bit.

He grinned. "Standing or lying down?"

Rue pursed her lips and wandered over to him, letting her gaze and then her hands drift.

She wasn't taken with the idea of kneeling at his feet. The book was fond of depicting this dynamic but Rue had decided early on that it didn't appeal. She informed Quesnel of this.

He seemed oddly pleased. "Not that I don't think we can try it eventually – you shouldn't rule anything completely out – but I agree it's a little servile."

"Exactly!" replied Rue. "I'm a lady. We don't kneel." Since she had one hand on his posterior at the time in a completely unladylike manner, this comment came off as hilarious to the both of them.

"To the bed!" Quesnel lay back, utterly nude and looking only a little uncomfortable under Rue's interested gaze. He put both hands behind his head, as though they needed to be trapped there.

"Lady Prudence, I am at your disposal."

"Are we still on the only kissing part of the lesson plan?"

"For this, I think you should be allowed to do your worst. Hopefully matters won't get too ungovernable."

"Is that why?" Rue gestured, indicating that, unlike their previous encounters, not all of him was interested in these proceedings.

"Yes. Plus, I'm a little cold."

"A challenge." Rue was hesitant at first, using only a few fingers. She experimented with pressure, curious about the different textures of his skin. Unlike the werewolf uncles, Quesnel had very little hair on his chest, only a sprinkling that arrowed in and trailed lower down. Rue followed it, stopping when he sucked in his breath.

"Too rough?"

"Just ticklish."

All in all, it proved a most enjoyable evening.

Quesnel's prior preparations notwithstanding, Rue got to see about everything a girl could wish to see – a *most* instructive experience.

When he left her, it must have been almost noon, and they both were anticipating very little sleep.

It was entirely worth it.

"Tomorrow," Quesnel said, kissing her into slumber, "it's your turn." He let himself quietly out.

Rue didn't say, "Oh, goodie," this time. But she certainly thought it.

Rue convinced herself that this was her version of an airship captain's amusing dalliance – piratical in nature. When she was a retired adventuress, she would look back upon this as the romantic indiscretion of her pillaging youth. She was resolute in her commitment to avoiding deep sentiment, knowing that Quesnel was an irreverent butterfly apt to flit off to a new colourful flower at any shift in the breeze. For example, she was painfully cognisant of the fact that he left her after each encounter. When Rue finally slept, it was always alone.

While Rue and Quesnel occupied their time with each other, Primrose spent the grey in philanthropic pursuits, teaching the sooties and decklings to read. Spoo and Virgil took up gambling. Primrose put a stopper on that right quick, but not before Virgil owed Spoo most of his worldly goods. Lady Maccon discovered Percy's library and Footnote and took to both like a werewolf to venison. Percy mooched about the deck, displaced by Lady Maccon, or intent on avoiding literary temptation, or both. The destitute Virgil divided his time between assisting Primrose in her educational endeavours, running errands for Lady Maccon, and chasing after Percy with misplaced accessories.

They were near to leaving the aetherosphere when the idyllic journey became much less idyllic.

It was Rue's own fault. She went to engineering to consult Quesnel without ascertaining that he'd be there. When it turned out he wasn't, she was faced with Aggie. Rue couldn't very well turn around and leave without talking to anyone.

"Miss Phinkerlington?"

Aggie finished assisting one of the sooties with a boiler fill before brushing her hands down her shirtfront ostentatiously and approaching Rue.

"Captain?" The tone implied some level of incompetence on Rue's part.

"How are the coal bunkers? When we puff down, I've plans to refuel immediately, but I'd like to know we could get in and out on what we have if necessary."

"Expecting a less than enthusiastic reception, are we?"

"No. The troubles of the eighties are long settled. I simply wish to know if we're desperate."

Aggie chewed a fingernail, which – considering the state of her hands – revolted Rue. "We'll be fine to get down and back up, but we'd need a way station right quick after. Wouldn't be able to get to grey again without strain."

Rue nodded. "I appreciate your assessment."

"Hardly see as how you need come all the way down to ask. Could've used the tube."

Rue was ruffled. "It's only polite to come in person. I find the blow horn unfriendly, don't you?"

"No."

"Oh."

"Here I was thinking our little miss captain was chasing tail. Fraternising with the hired help and checking up on the peons." Aggie's freckles looked militant.

"I *beg* your pardon!" That was too far. "You don't like me much, do you, Miss Phinkerlington?"

"Not used to it, are you? High up-and-up miss toff-lofty who got herself a ship because her vampire daddy likes to give her big toys. You ain't earned one splinter of this beauty and everyone knows it."

That stung. Rue was afraid Aggie was right. She didn't deserve *The Spotted Custard*. She hadn't developed into much of a captain yet, but she was doing her best. It didn't help that Aggie kept undermining her authority.

Rue considered it quite an achievement that she did not flare into a temper, instead dousing her tongue with honey. "I *am* sorry you feel that way, Miss Phinkerlington. I assure you I'm well aware of the privilege of my position and I'm trying to do a good job. Did you have any constructive criticism or are you simply jealous?" She shouldn't have added that last bit. Of course she shouldn't. She should have been the better man . . . well, woman.

Aggie always had a rosy face because of the boiler heat, but at that she went bright red. "You" – she punctuated her words with a sharp puffs of angry breath – "are a spoiled little madam who no more belongs in charge of an airship than I belong as dance master to a dachshund."

Rue was so arrested by the idea of Aggie in a dancing costume, she almost laughed. But this was a serious matter of insubordination. Aggie was an invaluable member of Quesnel's team but should be dismissed for this kind of talk. Or would that be Rue behaving exactly like the spoiled girl Aggie accused her of being?

"Are you testing me, Miss Phinkerlington?" This was, in its way, an excellent challenge to her abilities as captain. Perhaps that was what Aggie was after.

"As if everything is about you."

Rue frowned. There had to be something more personal to this dislike. Was Aggie jealous of Rue's relationship with Quesnel? Rue didn't dare ask, because if Aggie weren't aware, the very question would expose Rue to further ridicule.

At that moment, the object of her thoughts rustled up. "Ladies?"

Rue gestured at him in a measuring way. "Miss Phinkerlington here was elucidating my innumerable deficiencies."

"Oh, Aggie." Quesnel's tone conveyed disappointment.

Aggie crossed her muscled arms over her chest. "She gets us in the soup all too often, charging in without any thought to the fact that we must go along with her."

Rue winced. She did have a propensity to enthusiastically drag her ship – and crew – off to goodness knows where. Egypt, for example. "Isn't that why you signed on, for the adventure?"

"No. I wanted a job. Just as all the greasers and sooties did."

"Do I not pay you well enough? Are you threatening a lock-out?" Rue pressed. *Am I ignoring my people, not being a proper caretaker?* "Mr Lefoux should have said something!"

Quesnel stepped in. "Nothing like that, Lady Captain. Aggie here is a rabid member of the Amalgamated Society of Engineers. She's fixated on you as the ideal representation of all that is wrong with the idle aristocracy."

Rue was further confused. "I'm an idle aristocrat? Oh dear."

Aggie was not mollified. "You and your mother. Frittering away your position in society without any attempt to effect change."

"I have a position that can effect change?" Rue supposed

Aggie's wrath didn't extend to Paw because his work with BUR was publicly known. Or perhaps it wasn't done to verbally abuse a man in a state of preservation. "What kind of change?"

"Useless, utterly useless." Aggie cast her hands up to the heavens and stormed away.

Rue turned to Quesnel. "Am I really that horrible?"

"Of course not. Perhaps I made a mistake in keeping Aggie on when she dislikes you so."

"It's most aggravating. I wouldn't mind if I'd done something to earn such ire, but I'm sure we never met before she came aboard. I've been perfectly civil to her since. I know I'm not the best captain, but I did think I was making some improvement."

"*Chérie*, you're doing fine. Don't take anything Aggie says seriously. She's still here after all. If she really hated it, she'd leave."

"Am I too enthusiastic and incautious?" Rue rubbed her gloved hands together as Quesnel steered her towards the spiral staircase with one hand to her elbow.

"I happen to adore your enthusiasm."

"But is it a valuable trait in a leader?"

"Stop worrying. Aggie's prejudiced. She doesn't like your mother either."

"I understand people not liking my mother. She's impossible. But I thought I was easier to suit."

"You're amiable, *chérie*. Aggie likely finds your charm suspicious."

"I have charm? She won't be mean to Primrose, will she? Prim couldn't take it. She's not equipped to accommodate verbal abuse from rampaging freckles."

"Fortunately, Primrose never visits the boiler room."

"I shall try to keep it that way. Aggie could destroy her with a single barb."

Quesnel sighed. "She resents your position in society."

"What *position*? Circus freak?"

"Pardon me?" Quesnel was actually shocked.

Rue shook her head. Despite her vaunted carefree nature,

Aggie's hostility stung. "You mean to say, you never wonder why I remain unmarried?"

Quesnel was taken aback. "No."

"Metanatural," Rue explained succinctly.

"What has that to do with it?"

"Good old Rue, fun for a laugh, but who would want to marry that? No idea what kind of creature she might birth, or become herself. Bad bet. Not even human."

"Don't be ridiculous. No one thinks . . ."

"Oh, yes, they do. It's fine. I've made my peace with it. And, yes, I have powerful parents, but most of the time that's a hindrance. Who'd want to marry into either household without ulterior motive? How do I trust any offer as genuine? I'm defined by my supernatural relationships."

"And me, where do I fit in?"

"It's not like you want to marry me. Oh, don't look so upset. I'm not fishing for an address. I'm only pointing out that who I am is tempered by *what I am* in the eyes of society. I'm liminal to the aristocracy, just as I'm liminal to the supernatural set. Not quite a member, not quite on the outside either."

Quesnel cocked his head. "Is that why you like captaining a dirigible so much? It's your place?"

"Although now it seems I'm not good at it."

"What did I say? Ignore Aggie. She's bitter. That's her personality flaw, not yours."

"You're sweet to comfort me." Rue patted Quesnel as they emerged into the hall of the midship level.

Quesnel lowered his voice. "I would, you know."

"Mmm?"

"Marry you."

Rue kissed his cheek absentmindedly. "Chivalrous, darling, but we both know you don't really mean it."

With which Rue drifted towards her private chambers.

She gasped when he caught her hand and pulled her into his arms. The mid-level hallway was empty, thank goodness. Rue smiled against the sweet insistence of his mouth. *Such a nice boy, trying to make me feel better.* It worked. His kisses were distracting — a soothing balm to her wounded feelings. There seemed a desperate intent behind them, as though he were trying to make her understand something. Her own worth, perhaps? His hands were firm against her waist. He also had learned much during their French lessons — what she liked, how she preferred to be touched.

He leaned back against the wall, pulled her against him, braced and eager.

Rue was contemplating inviting him to her room, although it was mid-shift and certainly not an ideal time for canoodling.

All of a sudden, he pushed her away to the other side of the hall — she was adrift, bereft.

Lady Maccon was coming out of the library. Fortunately, she had her nose in a book and hadn't witnessed their embrace.

By the time she looked up, they were a respectable distance apart, only a little rumpled.

"Infant. Mr Lefoux."

"Mother."

"Lady Maccon."

Rue said, "That book I was telling you about? I believe Percy has a copy. Would you like to . . . ?"

Quesnel followed her lead with the consummate skill of a natural charlatan. "Yes, indeed."

Lady Maccon gave only a slight rolling of her eyes to indicate her suspicions.

Rue suppressed a giggle as Quesnel guided her into the library.

A cursory glance about the stacks proved the room to be empty.

Quesnel had her back in his arms in a trice. "Where were we?"

"I believe your lips were here." Rue pointed. "And your hands here." She pointed again. "And mine were here." At the last, she suited her actions to her words.

"What a good memory you have, Lady Prudence." Quesnel was intent on covering her neck with kisses – what he could reach through the ruffles of her dress.

The library door banged open, interrupting them again. They sprang apart. Quesnel hurriedly buttoned his waistcoat. Rue patted at her ruffles to ensure they weren't in disarray.

"Oh, for goodness' sake." Percy glared. It was hard to tell whether he was annoyed at having discovered them in a compromising position or annoyed at encountering anyone at all.

"Come for a book, have you? Giving in to temptation at last?" Rue retorted quickly.

"Certainly not! In case you have forgotten, my desk is here. I wasn't going to *read* anything, only look something up."

He pointed to a corner where he'd pushed some books aside to make room for a tiny escritoire. Above it, he and Virgil had contrived a unique candelabra made up of hundreds of tiny books, on a pulley system that could twirl and raise and lower. The person seated at the desk could access any book he wanted.

"What on earth is that?" Quesnel was entranced.

"My information cloud." Percy was distracted into an explanation of his own brilliance. "It's an index of sorts. If I swing it like so . . ."

The door opened again. Primrose entered, followed by Tasherit.

"You most certainly are!" the werelioness was saying.

"I am not!" Prim responded, before noticing she had an audience. "Rue. Mr Lefoux. Percy."

"Miss Tunstell." Quesnel gave a slight bow. "Miss Sekhmet."

"Is *everyone* to invade my library?" Percy wanted to know.

"We were here first." Rue wasn't about to be bossed around by Percival Tunstell on her own ship.

"I very much noticed. But it's *my* library!"

"You haven't been using it."

"That doesn't mean you should be fornicating in here. This is a sacred space."

Primrose turned to Rue. "Fornicating? In a library! Oh, Rue."

Tasherit remained perturbed by something Primrose had said and didn't care about Rue's indiscretions. Well, to be fair, she wasn't British. She didn't think the same way.

"Wait a moment." Rue was struck with confusion. "Tasherit, what are you doing awake?"

"Oh, didn't you notice?" Percy was snide. "We've puffed out of the grey. Occupied with something else?" He gave Quesnel a nasty look.

Quesnel issued a smug smile at Percy.

Tasherit said, "Did you know Primrose was engaged?"

The question wasn't addressed to anyone in particular, so Rue, Percy, and Quesnel all nodded.

"Was I the only one not told?" The werecat did not look honoured by the exception. "Odd to be so singled out."

"I hadn't seen you to tell you." Never had Rue known Primrose to lie in such a barefaced manner.

"Fiddlesticks!" The word sounded exotic with Tasherit's accent. "You've been avoiding me this entire journey. When I haven't been asleep."

Rue's, Quesnel's, and Percy's focus bounced back and forth between the combatants as though watching a badminton match.

Prim went on the defensive. "If you wouldn't press me so!"

Tasherit's beautiful face came over all inscrutable. "I enjoy your company. I hardly think that pressure."

Footnote made an appearance at that juncture, ambling up in a welcoming manner until he spotted Tasherit, at which point his tail bristled up like a bottlebrush and he hissed.

The werecat sniffed. "Well, I know when I'm not wanted."

Despite Quesnel's and Rue's protestations, she exited the library with graceful finality.

Rue said to Footnote, although she was really addressing Primrose, "You're a bit tough on our stunning friend. She is a valuable member of my crew, you know."

Footnote subsided into a loaf position, looking like an upended Christmas pudding with interested ears.

Percy leapt to his cat's defence. "He's entitled to his own opinion."

Rue could hardly argue with that. "You'd best be wary, moggie. She is much bigger than you. Could easily turn you into an Endnote."

The little black and white tom twitched his whiskers.

Percy said staunchly, "He's tougher than he appears."

Rue looked at Primrose. Enough time had passed for her to calm down a bit. "What on earth is wrong, Prim?"

Primrose closed her eyes. "Arguing with that woman is like fighting a blancmange. Press too lightly and she only wobbles, press too hard and you get engulfed into her squishy mindset. It's disconcerting."

Rue muttered, "Blancmanges have squishy mindsets?"

Percy explained the situation to Footnote. "My dear sister doesn't like people she can't manage, organise, and categorise. I'm thinking our feline friend there defies all attempts."

Prim narrowed her eyes. "No one is interested in your opinion, Percy."

"Footnote is, aren't you, Footnote?" Her brother did not look up from the cat.

Footnote merped at him.

"Quite right," said Percy. "You *are* the only intelligent conversation to be found on this ship."

"Percy, be fair," remonstrated Rue. "He's the only one you condescend to talk to."

"And have certain persons steal my ideas again? I think not."

"For the last time," said Quesnel, "it wasn't your idea to have stolen."

Primrose raised both her hands. "Please don't start up again. It's already been a trying day."

"You don't know the half of it, sister dear. You'll never guess what I caught these two up to." Percy glared at Rue.

"Unfortunately, I think I can guess. Rue is my best friend, after all."

Quesnel blinked at Rue. "You told her?"

Rue didn't see what he had to complain about. "Naturally I told her. What good is an education if it is kept to oneself?"

"That sounds like one of my lines." Percy was, to be sure, ever eager to share his research into the world with the world.

Quesnel looked dubious. "You think she'll benefit?"

Rue followed this reasoning. "Well, yes, if she persists in this foolhardy notion of an engagement. It follows that there will eventually be marriage. To a man."

"You think she'll go through with it?" Quesnel was surprised.

Primrose interjected. "I am engaged – *of course* I intend to go through with it!"

"You see?" said Rue.

Quesnel raised his eyebrows. "Curious."

Primrose objected at any whiff of judgement. "No, it is not! I cannot believe you would take Tash ... Miss Sekhmet's side. Marriage is the correct course of action for any lady of quality. Just because she has odd notions about independence, and Percy is scared of women, and you two are playing out a protracted bout of scandal doesn't mean I am equally outrageous in my feelings on conjugational formality!"

"Independence, is that what Tasherit calls it?" Rue kept herself from smiling. Prim did seem in some distress. Poor thing, she genuinely felt that she should do what was expected of her. What a horrible way to go through life.

Quesnel turned to Rue. "Like to go somewhere more private and be scandalous some more?"

"Absolutely."

Without further ado, they made for the door, leaving the twins and Footnote in possession of the field.

Percy rounded on his sister. "You condone Rue's behaviour?"

"What did I *just say*, Percy? Certainly not. But when have I ever been able to dissuade Rue from action in any way?"

"Good point."

Quesnel and Rue made their way up the aft ladder to the captain's quarters – nowhere else on *The Spotted Custard* seemed safe from interruption.

Door closed behind them, Rue crowded in close but Quesnel didn't reach for her.

"You've been telling Primrose what we do together?"

"Some. She doesn't want to hear details. Keeps pretending to faint. I've nothing but nice things to say, don't worry."

Quesnel winced. "While that's kind of you, it's a little odd to know you are reporting on an affair that should be kept private."

Rue blinked. "Oh dear, have I broken some sacred code? You can't possibly believe that your previous lady friends keep your exploits to themselves?"

Quesnel was blond, so his humiliation was instantly evident above his cravat. "*Chérie*, you are a lady, much as you resent it. As such, we should keep up a pretence of discretion."

"Prim is nothing if not discreet."

"What have you told her so far?" Quesnel rubbed his face with one hand, as though to wipe away the blush.

Rue grinned. "That I like your posterior. That kissing can be extended to other parts of the body. That you are very well shaped in all places."

"Including . . ." Quesnel gestured to his trousers.

"Especially there." Rue couldn't help but enjoy his discomfort. All along he held the superior tactical position, being the more experienced partner; this was the first time she'd had the upper hand.

"Crikey."

"How else is poor Prim to learn anything about male anatomy?"

Quesnel was staring at Rue with an expression she'd never seen before – half bemusement, half frustrated affection.

Finally he said, "I wouldn't want to interfere in your intimate friendships, *mon petit chou*. However, I am – not to be blunt – your lover. Might my wishes be taken into account, just a little?"

Rue considered. "That's a fair request."

"Perhaps if you weren't to detail the specifics of my anatomy and instead focused on generalities of technique? Referencing the book I gave you, for example."

Rue blinked at him. "Would that make you feel better?"

"Most assuredly."

"Then consider it done."

Quesnel puffed out a breath. It fluffed up the lock of hair that always fell over his forehead.

"Although I don't see why. You have a very nice anatomy." Rue coupled her comment with an active form of appreciation.

Quesnel jerked against her with the cutest little moan. "Thank you, *chérie*, but I hope you understand that I only wish to share it with you."

Rue grinned. She couldn't exactly argue with that.

CHAPTER

TEN

Egypt

Egypt was stunning from the air – different from both England and India. With *The Spotted Custard*'s propeller running and a stiff southbound breeze, they made good time over the Nile Delta, a vast triangle of lushness. One long curved side nested against the variegated blue of the Mediterranean, with two shorter lengths stretching south, coming to a point where the Nile began her more solitary run. Egypt was greener than Rue expected, although the outside of the Delta was a seemingly endless expanse of inhospitable tan desert.

Lady Maccon stood on the forecastle, looking west at the long spear of Alexandria cutting into the green with white marbled humanity.

"It looks different from above." She made room for her daughter to stand beside her.

"We didn't approach by air when we visited last?"

"Sea. There weren't transcontinental dirigibles when I was your age. At least, not very good ones. You don't remember?"

"I was very young, Mother."

"Barely speaking. You had but one word to say to most things."

"I did? What word was that?"

"No."

Rue grinned. She had likely driven her mother to despair. "I was a difficult child?"

"Very. Still are."

"Thank you, Mother. I can always trust you to be frank with me."

"Don't be maudlin, infant. It doesn't suit."

"You mean it doesn't suit *you*." Lady Maccon had ever avoided sentimental talk. It made her uncomfortable at the best of times and irritable the rest of the time. "Feelings," Mother was prone to saying, "are meant to be felt and not discussed."

Lady Maccon changed the subject. "Should we awaken your father?"

"After we've gone to ground, I think." Rue twirled her parasol. It was burgundy with a thick fringe and a tassel. She thought it rather natty, more because it matched her cutwork leather bicycle boots than anything else. She also enjoyed the way the fringe moved. She'd chosen her dress with its white vest over a puff-sleeved shirtwaist and burgundy striped skirt because it matched the boots and not, as might ordinarily be the case, the other way around.

Rue explained. Her mother liked explanations. "It'll be several hours yet until we're able to de-puff over Cairo. Why wake him only to suffer a dodgy tummy?"

"As long as we do wake him during daylight. It's full moon tonight."

"Is it? I'd lost track. Best keep him tanked until tomorrow morning, then. Sorry, Mother, I know you miss him. But we have Miss Sekhmet to control already."

Lady Maccon raised her eyebrows. "Actually, I'm rather enjoying the peace and quiet."

Rue made a condescending noise, not fooled in the slightest.

Lady Maccon gave one of her wide smiles. "Very well, I *have* missed him. He leaves a large hole when he isn't around. Being a large sort of beastie, I suppose that's only to be expected."

Rue resumed enjoying the view. They were high enough up

and early enough in their approach so as not to be sharing the sky with many. A few other transcontinental dirigibles de-puffed out of the grey, flashing into being above them – a mail carrier here, a private pleasure craft there.

"Full moon's a bother. Delays matters." Rue turned back to her duties as captain. "Spoo? Warn Miss Tunstell, would you, please? Miss Sekhmet will need confinement tonight. I'm sure Primrose has the moon on calculation, but just in case. Best not let moons creep up on a girl. Miss Tunstell hates to be surprised by celestial bodies."

"Who doesn't?" Spoo had been lurking nearby in the guise of coiling rope. She made no attempt to hide the fact that she was eavesdropping on aristocrats. "Will do, Lady Captain."

Lady Maccon watched the deckling scamper off. "Cracking laddie, that Spoo."

Rue felt no need to inform her mother of Spoo's gender. Lady Maccon was at her best when not confused.

"Absurd name they've given you."

"Lady Captain? I rather like it. Better than Captain Infant, which would likely be your preference."

Her mother cackled. "She goes mad, like the wolves?"

"Tasherit? Yes, but in a crazy cat way. She runs about with her tail all fluffed up chasing invisible prey, stops suddenly, and claws violently at whatever is nearest. We've had to resurface her room several times. If there weren't weight to consider, I'd do the whole interior in metal. Prim came up with the notion of wrapping her bedposts and furniture in coiled rope and covering the walls in this rush matting we acquired in India. Not aesthetically the decoration I'd choose for myself, and Uncle Rabiffano would have fits if he saw it, but she hasn't destroyed anything since. Except the mats and the rope. And no matter where we travel, those seem easy to come by."

Lady Maccon was intrigued. "Fascinating."

"I've a theory that each shifter, as a matter of course, is true to their animal spirit on the full moon. It seems to be part of the curse."

"She doesn't think of it that way, does she? As a curse, I mean."

"No. Miss Sekhmet is proud of her state, for all she keeps it secret. I believe, when she metamorphosed, it was a noble calling. Or it's simply that cats are intrinsically snobbish."

Her mother nodded. "What happened to her pride?"

"Sensitive subject. I've not enquired closely. Perhaps she is a loner. Cats are like that, too."

The day crawled on. They drifted sedately towards the southern tip of the delta, where Cairo nested. The sun rose higher and beat down upon them with an unremitting disregard for the fact that it was autumn. Below, the green narrowed, that eerie edge, where the trees abruptly stopped and desert began, crept closer. It gave Rue a sense of impending doom, a sensation so alien to her nature she thought it likely due to a tea deficiency. *Or I'm hungry. The world always seems a worse place when I'm hungry.*

As if on cue, Primrose summoned them to an alfresco luncheon.

Tasherit declined to join. She was awake, but napping and not enamoured of abovedecks dining during daylight.

All the ladies sported parasols, not just Rue. Lady Maccon carried her brownish greenish one full of pockets and secrets. It was generally considered hideous by all, including Lady Maccon, and never matched anything she wore, possibly by design. Rue had once overheard a drone asking after its presence. Her mother replied, "I've made peace with its appearance, rather like my nose. Neither is fashionable, but both work as designed and haven't, to the best of my knowledge, frightened any children." Today she had paired it with an afternoon dress of a stiff wine-coloured-silk-embroidered with a paisley pattern and a grey velvet men's style jacket. The ensemble was the height of fashion and certainly new. The only possible explanation for her mother's wearing it being that Uncle Rabiffano had been shopping.

Rue wondered if he had known this trip was imminent and

ordered a new wardrobe for Mother full of practical travelling gowns suitable to a foreign climate. It made her feel bitter. How long had Uncle Rabiffano been planning to take Alpha? How long had he known Paw's time was up?

Primrose was standing under a large deck parasol at the head of the table, gesticulating at footmen with her parasol. She was embracing French fashion this afternoon in a fitted dark umber dress free of all decoration except brown velvet appliqué at the neck, cuffs, and hem. The dress covered her from throat to wrist to toe yet managed to be sublimely sexy and ought, by rights, not to appear on an unmarried lady. She was also still in a temper from confronting Tasherit earlier.

Thus Rue said only, "Daring dress, Prim. Is it new?"

"Yes. Now that I'm an old engaged woman, I thought I might cultivate sophistication."

"Don't strain anything."

Lady Maccon, never one to talk fashion when food was on offer, sat without comment and began loading up her plate. They ate informally aboard ship and rarely stood on ceremony. Rue had thought her mother would find this upsetting, but Lady Maccon embraced it readily when she realised it meant she never had to flag a footman down for a refill.

"Is everywhere we go likely to be more sunny than old Blighty?" Rue chose a safe subject as she took her seat.

"Very likely." Primrose forced a cheerful tone and poured the tea with a liberal hand for all comers. Even Lady Maccon was doled out a cup without comment. Fortunately she was not at all offended by the assumption that she would prefer tea to wine or water.

Percy left the navigation in Virgil's capable hands and gangled over to thump down across from her ladyship. "I say, it is rather too warm, isn't it?"

"Buck up, Percy." Quesnel took a chair next to Rue, looking damp and fresh. He'd splashed his face with water before coming to table.

Percy regarded the company glumly. "I detest nice weather. Everyone feels compelled to do things out of doors."

Quesnel's violet eyes twinkled. "Egypt is celebrated for her prevalence of outside activities."

"Frenchmen." Percy snorted.

They consumed a light meal of boiled whiting in parsley sauce and roast widgeon in orange gravy, with turnip and cauliflower for the corners, and baked codling pudding for afters. Rue's sensation of dread over the encroaching desert abated along with the gravy. Rue would drink gravy out of a teacup if it were proper.

They sat back, talking idly over the pudding. Quesnel was disposed to be at his most amicable, which helped lighten everyone's mood. Except Percy. Even Lady Maccon laughed at one of his off-colour puns and then got annoyed with herself for doing so.

"You're as bad as your mother," she told him.

"I shall take that as a compliment." He mock bowed at her.

"You jolly well should."

It was easy to linger in the oppressive heat, sipping tea while the crew rotated through their midday meal. They didn't move until a deckling on lookout gave a cry from the crow's nest.

Percy – uninterested if it didn't immediately contain threat of death, literary revelations, or academic standing – resumed his post at the helm.

Rue, Quesnel, Prim, and Lady Maccon took to the forecastle to squint into the haze and see what was causing the ruckus. The trees below them fell away in favour of a massive city, indistinct at this height from the colour of the desert but clearly a city by its angularity. The Nile was also fully exposed for the first time, where she ran along one side.

Cairo.

What had caught the deckling's attention wasn't Cairo, but beyond, to the starboard side where the famous pyramids rose up. Three brown angled shadows stood against the brightness of the desert sands – large and wide, tall and narrow, and a little one further away. How big they must be to stand out so when buildings and trees remained indistinct blurs!

"A true feat of engineering." Quesnel's voice was reverent.

The Spotted Custard did not drift any closer, for Percy was de-puffing them into Cairo and no nearer to the pyramids. Eventually they tore their eyes away to look at the city.

The vegetation around the river gave way reluctantly to a vast network of buildings both ancient and modern, mostly sandstone with some marble. Trees permeated throughout, particularly near the river and in prescribed city parks. There were several colossal yellow buildings with thick walls and forbidding auras – fortresses. Dotted about were graceful onion-shaped spires of mosques. The city was criss-crossed by tracks, black spidery lines over sand, dirt, and brick. Tracks in the sky, too, sliding up to unbelievably tall obelisks for dirigible shipping and receiving. Airships of various kinds were sunk over the Nile, taking on water, mixing with a river already crowded by boats and rafts. The closer they got, the more they could see of industry. A smattering of soot lay over everything and a haze lurked above the city – the dirty consequence of technological achievement.

The mooring obelisks were carved of exotic stone, black basalt, white marble, red rhyolite, and something green Rue couldn't identify. They were ringed and notched at the top with posts, serving dirigibles, hot air balloons, ornithopters, and other, weirder sky boats. Some were used by only one airship, while others were surrounded by clusters of patchwork and striped balloons, like enormous bouquets of fat painted hyacinth bulbs.

Lady Maccon pointed at a cluster. "Nomadic desert tribes. Twenty years ago they were called Drifters. They may still use the name. Cousins to the Bedouin, they took to the skies long ago."

"They're beautiful. For the first time, my darling *Custard* actually fits right in." Rue was delighted. *The Spotted Custard*'s cheerful red balloon with its big black spots was in good company in Cairo. In London, airships tended to be more sombre in appearance.

Percy, at the helm on the opposite end of the ship, had to yell to get Rue's attention. "How do we know where to tether?"

At which juncture, he came under attack from a native bird.

"Pigeon!" Rue ran from the forecastle, dashed across the main deck, hoisted her skirts, and leapt up to the quarterdeck, parasol swinging. "Get it!" Rue had a horror of pigeons.

But this particular bird behaved unlike any she had ever met. It landed without fear right next to Percy in the navigation pit. At rest, it was clearly not a pigeon at all, nor was it made of flesh. It was made of metal. And mechanical. And utterly forbidden.

Everyone on board stared at it with mouths agape.

Quesnel followed Rue, although without parasol brandishment, coming to stand next to her, looking up at the creature on their poop deck.

His face was white in shock. "Is that a . . . *mechanimal?*"

Lady Maccon came after.

"I thought they were prescribed." Primrose joined them.

"They are!" Rue and her mother spoke at the same time.

Percy was unperturbed. He looked at the bird as if a tropical bug or small child had approached him, which is to say, without much interest or intent to engage.

"Percival," said Lady Maccon in a low frightened voice, "come away from there this instant. Those things are explosive."

Rue panicked. "Get it off my ship!"

Prim clutched her hands together. "Oh dear oh dear oh dear. Didn't they destroy most of London half a century ago?"

Lady Maccon remained calm. "That's the rumour."

Quesnel's face stayed incandescently enthralled. "To think, in my lifetime! I got to see a mechanimal, in person."

The metal bird cocked its head at them and let out a peep noise. It burst the ear socket it was so high.

Percy objected. "Ouch. Stop that. What do you want?"

The mechanimal twitched and peeped again.

Then it threw its little beak back and its whole head rolled inside out and converted to a kind of morning glory flower shape, like a hearing trumpet. A human voice emerged, as if from one of those newfangled gramophones.

It spoke a short stream in some foreign tongue, then in French, and finally in English. "Unregistered airships report to the Ministries of Public Works Plus War, at the Customs and Tariff Obelisk." It then proceed on to various other languages before converting its head back to that of a bird and taking flight, returning the way it had come.

"Nasty piece of work." Rue felt it was one step removed from a pigeon.

Percy began twiddling dials. "Seemed pleasant enough. Now we know what to do."

"Oh yes? And where is this Ministries of Public Works Plus War?"

Primrose brightened. "Let me consult my *Baedeker's*." She trotted off to her room to retrieve the obligatory red leather travel guide.

Rue hated to do it but she shouted after her friend, "Prim, you might rouse Miss Sekhmet while you're there."

Primrose paused, turned, and gave Rue a nasty look.

Rue tried to look contrite. "We might need her interpretive skills."

Percy objected on principal. "I've studied several of the local dialects."

"Percy, my duck," said Rue, "there is a vast different between speaking and studying."

Percy grumbled, as did Prim continuing belowdecks.

Lady Maccon jumped on the matter of linguistic challenges. "You should hire a dragoman, infant. Although, hard to do so before we've visited the tariff office. As I recall, I had no little difficulty in Alexandria at customs when we visited last." She turned to Quesnel. "They objected to your mother's hatbox in particular."

"Oh?" The Frenchman encouraged all mentions of his mother's past. Rue had the feeling Madame Lefoux could be maddeningly close-mouthed as a rule.

"You don't happen to have any suspicious hatboxes with you, do you, young man? Could prove difficult."

Quesnel went deadpan. "Lady Maccon, I assure you all my hatboxes are perfectly respectable and contain hats, nothing more."

"That's what Genevieve always said." Lady Maccon was not reassured.

Primrose returned with her *Baedeker's*.

A convenient little map of the city showed that there was a Ministry of Public Works Plus War in the south-western part of the city. They made their way in that direction, eventually spotting what must surely be the Customs and Tariff Obelisk. It jutted up from the centre of a park in between the Ministry of Public Works Plus War and the British Consulate General. It was a particularly tall spire of black basalt. It must be the right obelisk because all manner of transcontinental airships were clustered around it. Each de-puffed and moored in, but not for long.

The Spotted Custard joined the general hubbub of air traffic around the spire. A severe-looking military dirigible of the kind favoured by Queen Victoria's colonial flotillahs appeared next to them, making the crew nervous. Likely its intent.

However, once they'd reached the obelisk and cast out their own mooring rope, the military craft drifted off to loom at some other newcomer.

A strange feeling of numbness overcame Rue's whole body as they sunk further down. It was like being submerged in a bathtub, only it wasn't wet. It felt a little like the moment when touching her mother cancelled out all metanatural abilities.

Rue sidled over to said mother. "Do you feel that?" She kept her tone low; no need for anyone else to be alarmed.

The crew was busy looking as respectable and efficient as possible. Not because *The Spotted Custard* was engaged in any nefarious activities – she was registered as a pleasure vessel with all the major regulatory bodies of the empire – but because the moment one entered the sphere of any bureaucratic body, one felt the need to put on a *jolly good show*. Nervous propriety was the natural consequence of proximity to an overabundance of paperwork. Even Quesnel popped off belowdecks to check with Aggie regarding the condition of the kettles and the general cleanliness of the boiler room.

Lady Maccon looked at her daughter. "The repulsion, you mean? Yes, a little. It's not as strong as it would be with a pre-ternatural skeleton nearby."

"Mother, don't be morbid. No, I'm getting a numbing sensation."

"I suppose it would be different for you. What exactly does it feel like? I mean, what would you compare the sensation to?"

"You."

Lady Maccon nodded. "Makes sense. It *is* me, in a grotesque way. Or, to be precise, a lot of dead mes. It's not as strong as it used to be. But I suppose they haven't been renewing or expanding it. One assumes over time, with exposure, even mummies decompose."

"Really, Mother, must you?"

Lady Maccon patted Rue in a condescending way. "Don't worry, dear. It's no longer important."

Rue fished about in her memories of family lore. "This is the God-Breaker Plague, isn't it?"

"Indeed."

"Well, then, I guess we can wake up Paw whenever you like, full moon notwithstanding."

"Oh, of course!" Lady Maccon slapped her head with her hand. "How silly of me." She immediately snapped her parasol shut and bustled below.

Rue didn't stop her. It would be much easier to have an awake

Lord Maccon when the customs officials boarded. Bureaucrats were likely to frown upon aristocratic Scotsmen preserved naked in tanks.

The three official representatives of the Ministry of Public Works, War, Customs, and Tariffs were exactly what one might expect. They were stiff and humourless. They sported, in varying degrees of vegetation, decidedly impressive moustaches. They kept a cottage, of sorts, at the top of the black obelisk. It was made of mud brick with slit openings instead of windows so that it looked quite grumpy. From under the cottage extended several articulated walkways. As soon as they were within reach, one of these clamped down to the railing of *The Spotted Custard* with the ease of frequent repetition. There were eight of these ramps, making the custom-house look like nothing so much as a brown spider waving long metal legs about and latching onto airships.

The wait was long enough for Rue and Primrose to don their frilliest dresses and most supercilious personas. Innocent young ladies with empty heads left officials feeling lost. There was something about the very rich, very young, very fashionable Englishwoman on a pleasure jaunt that defeated even the most hardened bureaucracy.

The man in charge was an agent of Queen Victoria by his dress if not his language, kitted out in something approaching a soldier's uniform – although not quite the correct colours. The other two wore long white robes and funny little hats that Prim's travel guide reliably informed her meant they were of Turkish extraction. The guide was very clear on how dress indicated social standing in Egyptian society. Primrose believed it wholeheartedly; Baedeker never led her astray. Rue was suspicious. What, for example, would Baedeker say of Primrose given only a few lines of dialogue and an encounter with her fluffiest hat?

While the customs officers conducted their investigation,

Rue and Prim trailed behind, chattering faster than a kettle at full boil about the most inconsequential things in a way that was not exactly distracting but certainly maddening and non-threatening. They tossed scones happily at one another in the galley, cooed over the crochet coverlets in the guest rooms, and giggled over a book in the library.

When Lord Maccon appeared, coming up the spiral staircase from engineering, entirely unclothed and covered in faintly orange slime, the customs officers were so worn down they only stopped and stared, mouths agape.

He examined the two Turkish officials with equal interest. "We're in Egypt, then?"

Lady Maccon came up behind her husband and dipped under one of his arms, supporting part of his weight with her shoulders. She was unperturbed by slime on her dress. No wonder Uncle Rabiffano despaired of her.

"Wife?"

"Yes, husband?"

"May I wear one of those relaxing-looking men's dresses now that we'll be taking up permanent residence here?"

Lady Maccon coughed. "Come away, dear. Let us allow the gentlemen to continue their work. Do pardon my husband, good sirs. He has been enduring a protracted illness and has only just left his" – she paused, grappling – "bath."

The officials nodded gravely. Presumably, they understood the importance of baths.

Lady Maccon steered her enormous spouse, the only man who made her look delicate, down the hallway towards the guest quarters. No doubt an officer would check their papers later.

"Well, may I?" Rue heard Paw press the issue with Mother.

"You'll look utterly ridiculous."

"But I'll be *comfortable*. It's almost kilt-like."

Rue wanted to run after her resurrected father and leap into his arms. He looked better than he had in ages, even with the slime. It was a joy to see him safely out of that horrid tank. But she was captain of an airship and had a role to play, particularly with foreign officials. She and Prim were required for feather-brained chatter. Familial reunions could wait.

Primrose had all the *Custard*'s paperwork in order. Although, she had passed it on to the head steward because they'd agreed record-keeping might be better coming from a soberly dressed man.

The officials checked the numbers against the roster and counted up decklings, sooties, deckhands, greasers, and house-hold staff. They clearly weren't interested in laymen, for they quickly moved on to the officer's papers. They insisted on interviewing every one of *The Spotted Custard*'s passengers as well. Lord and Lady Maccon and Tasherit Sekhmet came under considerable scrutiny.

However, of the entire company, only that last proved to be of concern.

The chief officer closeted himself with the werelioness for a good half hour. The fluted notes of an animated discussion emanated from Tasherit's cabin. It being in a foreign tongue, Rue and Prim couldn't even eavesdrop.

Once he emerged, the officer insisted on speaking to Rue privately, as the captain, in order to finalise the ship's approval. Rue insisted that Primrose accompany her, as chaperone. He agreed and they took to the stateroom.

He stamped her application for an air tourist licence, then had her sign several documents of writ and disclaim. He then shuffled through the resulting stacks of papyrus sheaves awkwardly.

Finally he said, his English heavily accented, "Very well, missis. You hitch to a red obelisk for twenty-four hours." He whipped out a map of Cairo, pointing to several red x marks along the southern part of the Nile. "Until you clear Quinton."

"Quinton?" Rue hissed to Primrose, confused.

"Do you mean *quarantine*, sir?" Primrose asked gently.

"As I said, missis, Quinton. After that, you free to travel

around our land. We give you flag. Guard it well. There are many who want flag, missis. Value is high."

Rue smiled at him vacuously.

He passed over a little triangle-shaped flag, like those of the standard bearers in medieval tapestries. It was bright blue with an eye embroidered in yellow and gold thread.

"After Quinton, you free to partake of Cairo. Here are your teskireh."

He went to pass over a stack of papers, then paused to examine one particular note.

"Teskireh?" Rue whispered to Prim.

Prim consulted her *Baedeker's*. "Viceregal recommendations for the allowance of scientific study."

Rue squinted her tawny eyes. "Percy or Quesnel?"

Prim considered. "Likely both. On the bright side, Teskireh carries with it a weapon's licence for the acquisition of big game."

The official jumped on that. "Speaking of big game, your dreaded one is not free."

Rue blinked. "My *dreaded* one?"

The man waved the papyrus at her, as if Rue could read the funny curly dotted writing as anything more than something that most closely resembled, in her experience, musical notes.

At her continued confusion, he explained. "She who mauls, before whom evil trembles. She who speaks with hot breath of desert wind."

Rue screwed up her nose. "Miss Sekhmet?"

The man's smile from behind his tidy beard was startlingly white. "A good name. Yes. She not leave ship. Egypt does not welcome damned."

"Naturally." Rue did not feel it necessary to point out that even with the God-Breaker Plague, Tasherit was cat enough to take any attempt at confinement as a challenge.

After the officials left, Rue bearded the lioness in her den.

Normally, Rue respected the werecat's privacy, but this was a matter of ship safety, which gave her licence to pry. She left the door open so as not to cause gossip.

"You're not technically allowed out of quarantine while we're in Egypt."

The werecat rolled her brown eyes. They were big and almond-shaped with thick lashes so monumentally unfair that combining them with flawless coffee-coloured skin, a straight nose, and full lips was basically an insult to every other female. Some supernatural creatures looked tired or old when they lost the shine of immortality. On Tasherit, the mantel of death turned her approachable, and by extension, Rue thought, more deadly.

"I'm not surprised." The werecat wasn't offended. "They do not hold with females who have lost their faith. Even if I am older than its arrival in this country."

"You were born here?" Rue pounced on the clue, catlike herself.

"I am a daughter of the desert sands, at least in part. I took my name from an Egyptian queen, as is our custom," was all Tasherit would say.

The phrase reminded Rue of the officer's comment. "He called you 'she who speaks with the hot breath of the desert wind'."

"A fair accusation."

"How did he know?"

"I do not exactly match the rest of your crew, Lady Captain."

Rue narrowed her eyes. "You understand very well what I'm asking."

Tasherit fiddled with the thin chain around her neck. "He noticed this."

From the chain dangled two small gold charms. Rue had never seen them up close but judging on general shape they appeared to be a shield and a sword. They were not only tiny but also worn with age, so it was difficult to discern details.

The werelioness explained. "Even the followers of Mohammad have not forgotten all the old symbols. It does not pay to count entirely on the God-Breaker to protect one from the outside world. The smart ones remember that borders shift, even anti-supernatural ones. It is best to know the signs of the damned, even if you believe them long gone."

"You don't mind being trapped aboard?" Rue had made the promise on Tasherit's behalf.

"I don't mind that they wish to pretend." At Rue's worried look, she added, "I will not go exploring this city. And Cairo doesn't mind what happens to the south."

"Good." Rue figured it was only the appearance of compliance that mattered. "Will we see you at supper?"

"Indeed. I find my fragile mortal self is quite hungry. How do you people manage?"

Rue laughed and stood.

A veritable roar emanated from the guest quarters across the hall.

Tasherit's voice went bland in an effort to hide amusement. "I believe your father may be objecting to something."

"Probably my mother."

Rue went and knocked on the door opposite.

The roaring continued.

Rue knocked louder. With no response forthcoming, Rue let herself in.

Paw was striding about the chamber yelling, mostly dressed and no longer covered in slime.

His wife sat in calm tolerance at her dressing table, brushing her hair and replying in a maddeningly reasonable tone. "Conall, do put a cork in it. People will hear you."

"Too late." Rue shut the door behind her without bothering to ask if she could stay. It was, after all, her ship. And these were, after all, her parents. "Must you make a scene, Paw?" She walked over to him for a hug. "It is good to see you looking so well."

"Ah, little one!" He snaked her into a smothering embrace.

Rue relaxed against his familiar rough affection. He did not smell quite as he used to – a product of mortality or time in a Lefoux tank; it was difficult to know which.

"Are you feeling better?" The question was partly muffled against his broad shoulder.

Paw released her. "I'm as hale as a man one third my age."

Lady Maccon began coiling and pinning up her hair. "One sixth, my dear, I think it is."

Paw shrugged. "Mathematics never was my strong suit."

Rue didn't know quite how to ask if he was still suffering Alpha's curse. How did one enquire as to the mental capacities of one's own father?

"Do you have any *odd* inclinations?"

Paw looked confused. "Pardon?"

Rue scrambled for some other delicate way of putting it. "Oh, I don't know. A preference to don one of Aunt Ivy's hats? The sudden feeling of euphoria and an inclination to polka with a palm tree?"

Mother put down her pins. "Your daughter would like to know if you are still going insane, dear."

Paw considered this. "I've been married to your mother for over two decades. You might allow me certain dispensation for eccentricity."

"Paw, please be serious. I must consider the welfare of my ship."

"I love you too, sweetheart."

Rue crossed her arms and glared, looking, many might have pointed out, rather more like her Paw than she ought being half his size and female.

He grinned. His Scottish burr became more prevalent. "Och, you fretful bairn. Whatever it is that pulls the senses out my head, 'tis linked to pack. I'm mortal, so that's all gone, along with my pack." A flash of pain cut across his face, quickly smoothed away with long practice.

Rue had felt that same pang when Uncle Rabiffano turned his back on her. And she'd had only a short time within a pack.

Paw had been with a pack for hundreds of years, in some form or another. He must be awfully lonely.

Mother clearly thought the same, for she stood and walked to her husband, slipping her hand into his.

Dama had once said, "Although they're careful not to use the word *tether*, never you forget, Puggle, that werewolves are tethered to pack, just as vampires are tethered to place. That's why they get stuck. It's a tragic weakness." Dama had looked thoughtful rather than sad. "You may need to exploit it someday. Of course, it's also a strength, like Hollandaise sauce."

Rue hadn't followed. "What's like Hollandaise sauce, Dama?"

Her vampire father had given one of his tight secret smiles. "The thing that links us up. Wolves to the packs. Queens to the hives. Even me, in my way, to my *darling* drones and beloved home. Hollandaise sauce – delicious and a vital part of many superior dishes."

Rue understood that reasoning, being a frequent partaker of sauces. "But?" she'd prodded, knowing a classic Dama analogy was imminent.

"Well, my *buttercup*, it splits easily, does Hollandaise, if you aren't careful. Just divides up into its component parts and becomes inedible."

Rue hadn't asked how he knew so much about cooking a sauce, being one who didn't eat anything. But she did take his point.

Paw had gone and split. The question now being, was he edible any more? She tried to catch her mother's eye, get her assessment, but Lady Maccon was focused on her husband.

Rue prodded. "Well, if you aren't deranged, what are you in a temper about?"

Lord Maccon looked confused.

"I heard you from across the way, howling like a buffoon."

Lady Maccon looked suspicious. "What were you doing in Miss Sekhmet's room?"

"Talking to Miss Sekhmet."

"Just *talking?*"

Now what is Mother on about? "Yes. Now stop avoiding the question. Paw?"

"Oh, I was just yelling a bit. Alexia and I were discussing the pack transition. Ill handled, I think. I could have stayed longer, seen young Biffy settled into his new position."

Lady Maccon snorted. "Don't be preposterous."

Rue said simultaneously, "Oh, Paw! Even I know the old Alpha can't be overseeing the new one."

Lord Maccon harrumphed. "Well, still, I might have done some good."

"You see what I put up with?" Lady Maccon appealed to her daughter.

Rue knew an exit cue when she heard one. "Supper will be served at nine tonight. *Spotted Custard* is assuming daylight hours while everyone is mortal. There's a great deal to see in Egypt; might as well take it in. Although, we're under quarantine for the next twenty-four hours."

"Are we dressing for dinner?" Lady Maccon resumed fussing with her hair.

Rue gave her father an evil look. "Might as well."

She heard him groan as she closed the door behind her.

Dinner went off without incident. Paw behaved himself. More to the point, so did Mother. Primrose and Tasherit ignored one another. Quesnel was as engaging as ever, and Percy as lacklustre. After pudding, everyone trooped to the forecastle for cigars and drinks – brandy for the gentlemen, sherry for the ladies. The moon was a bulbous yellow orb over a fairy-tale city below.

Tasherit and Paw were obviously unnerved at basking in full moonlight, no curse shining down alongside.

"I forgot how very beautiful she is." Tasherit was moved to something approaching sentiment.

Gail Carriger

"We could buy a silver cutlery set now, couldn't we, wife?" Paw sounded as though Lady Maccon had done nothing their whole marriage but lament the fact that they must use brass at the dinner table.

Rue's mother made a funny face. Rue was in no doubt that Alexia Maccon had never given cutlery a second thought.

Rue went over and touched first her father and then her were-cat friend with a naked hand to the cheek. Nothing happened. The numbness was still on her. There came no indication of gaining supernatural abilities with her touch. No strength. No shift. No nothing.

"Odd," she pronounced. "Paw, are you normal strength now?"

Lady Maccon laughed. "Infant, look at him. He's still built like a Clydesdale."

"Thank you, wife."

Rue smiled. "You know what I mean. Tasherit, what about you?"

"Normal. Slow healing and all else that goes with mortality." Tasherit examined her snifter with pursed lips. "Susceptible to alcohol, too, I suppose. What bliss is that." She drained the last of her brandy. She didn't hold with sherry. She'd been offered a cigar as well, since brandy was already quite manly, but declined, muttering something about hookahs being preferable.

Tasherit twirled the empty glass. "To tell the truth, young-lings" – Rue supposed there was a good chance even Paw was younger than Tasherit – "it makes me feel odd and exposed." She shivered, although the evening was warm. "I'm for bed. I shall enjoy the novel experience of sleeping at night."

Rue finished her sherry. "Me too." She gave Quesnel a slight smile.

He lowered his eyelids in a blatant lure. Pansy eyes glittering from behind fair lashes.

She wanted to nibble the back of his neck as she passed.

Lady Maccon gave Rue a dour look as she made her way to the stairs.

"Leave it, wife," she heard Paw say.

Despite whatever it was her mother thought was happening, Rue entered the captain's quarters alone. She changed into a tight red velvet top, beaded about the neck, and a narrow satin skirt. Remembering Quesnel's reaction back in India, she put a bit of kohl about her eyes and rouged her cheeks and lips. With her abundant curves, Rue looked like a ladybug and felt silly. But Quesnel had liked it so much last time. She had this notion that if she dressed for him *now*, he might wear his leather workman's apron and nothing else for her *later*. Privately, of course. She was rather too intrigued by the idea of a smudged and sweaty Quesnel wearing leather on the front and nothing at all over his back.

She sat on her bed and waited.

Rue was not a bad captain, not by any accounts. Spoo would not hear a word against her. She always posted a watch. Tonight it was a light watch, as they were moored at the top of an obelisk on the outskirts of town, only a long rope tying them to the world below. The spire could not be ascended; unlike other mooring posts, the red quarantine obelisks had no lifting platform, no tracks, no stairway winding about, not even a rope ladder. The *Custard* shared the obelisk with two fat luxury merchant vessels with skeletal crews and disinterested staff. No one would have thought any risk inherent in such an isolated position.

No, Rue could be excused for not being wary while they were in quarantine.

They were attacked anyway.

ELEVEN

In Which Percy's Unbearable Smugness Is Revealed

It was a much fairer fight this time. Rue and her crew no longer had a werelioness or a werewolf on their side. Although, no one tried to stop either former werecreature from rallying round.

Tasherit was spoiling for some kind of battle, tetchy from arguing with Primrose. Lord Maccon was never one to sit idle and waded in, meaty fists flying. Rue might have said something, not sure if Paw was up for it. Lady Maccon might have said something, because she was accustomed to an immortal husband and not particularly fond of the idea of losing him. But both had been with him long enough to know that any attempt at mollycoddling would be met with outraged disgust.

These men were different from those at Wimbledon. These were comprised of some species of bandit in native Egyptian dress, all swirling robes, fierce dark skin, and bearded faces.

Rue supposed that could all be faked – beards, swirls, and skin colour. But they spoke to one another in some form of Arabic, so she had to assume they were of local extraction.

Percy and Primrose, showing admirable restraint, poked their heads out of the main hatch, ascertained the violence of the activities, and disappeared back below. In this the twins agreed: fisticuffs were not worth their time.

The decklings took potshots at the fray from various vantage points. The crew was mainly represented in combat by deck-hands, two footmen, and the cook. Rue worried about the cook. Good cooks were hard to come by, and this one was a whizz with puff pastry; she didn't want him damaged. Still, he seemed to be enjoying himself, brandishing a nasty-looking cleaver in one hand and an iron skillet in the other. Lord Maccon had acquired a cutlass from some unfortunate. Tasherit held forth employing a weaponless kicking technique that turned her into a blur of vicious intent. Lady Maccon wielded her ugly parasol with remarkable precision both as a blunt instrument and via emission of various darts. It also sprayed acid, which Rue's mother used to admirable effect, backing a couple of bandits up against the railing and then over it, in their desperation to avoid the burning liquid.

Rue did her level best. Dama had given her some instruction in the defensive arts, but his was an old-fashioned soldier's technique. "It's been a very long time since I fought in any *actual physical* battles, Puggle dear. As a rule, try to avoid altercations. One doesn't want to sully one's gown with blood. This is why gathering information is so important. If you know what's going on, you can avoid it."

Classic mistake. Rue ducked a punch, knocking her assailant in the throat with her elbow. *I didn't know enough about Cairo when I came in to port. I had no idea an enemy might be waiting in ambush. I ought have taken precautions given our previous incidents.* No dirigible, not even *The Spotted Custard*, could move faster than an aethographic transmission. Someone must have arranged from London for Cairo's premier bruisers to take on the *Custard*. Rue had to assume, with no other evidence presenting, that they were still after the Lefoux tank.

Speaking of which, a holler rent the air and Quesnel Lefoux bounded into the mêlée followed by Aggie Phinkerlington and two of their biggest greasers. Quesnel had his dart emitter out, deploying one after another with impressive accuracy. Aggie and the greasers were wielding iron firebox prods with deadly skill.

Once out of darts, Quesnel was about Rue's ability with intimate combat. Someone had taught him the basics, but he was no proficient. All his muscles, which Rue could personally attest to, were from labour in the laboratory, not sporting at White's.

Rue grinned at him during a lull in the proceedings.

"More of a lover than a fighter, pretty boy?"

He winked. "You should know, *chérie*, I was on my way to your room. Your week's wait is up."

"So it is. Bother this interruption. So rude!"

The odds having been evened by Quesnel's arrival, it was merely a matter of sorting through who was more tenacious in pursuit of their ends: the bandits in securing whatever they had been sent to secure or Rue's crew in defending the ship.

Rue had complete faith in her crew. The invaders may be many things – more prepared, more powerful, and more ferocious – but Rue's people were most assuredly more stubborn.

"I know. I was so looking forward to it. Speaking of, I *adore* your dress." He winked at her.

Rue whacked a particularly harassed-looking beard with a mop handle. For some reason mops were the first things she grabbed in a scuffle. She twisted it about and shoved the dirty rag end into the offender's face, twirling it savagely.

"Take that!" she said, knowing the man likely couldn't understand her. "You have interrupted my deflowering. There's no excuse for that kind of thing!"

Quesnel laughed. "Especially when we've been practising for days." He danced around Rue's opponent in a fair imitation of a Highland Fling and, applying the principles of leverage and fluid dynamics – because he was an *excellent* engineer – utilised a bit of a ramp and some machine oil to slide the confused bandit over the side.

"Exactly!" Rue turned a manic grin on her next opponent.

Lord Maccon had led the front lines in several wars, not to mention the fact that Scotsmen had a well-earned *reputation*. It wasn't for flower arranging. For Conall Maccon, a nice brawl under the moonlight was, to put it mildly, old hat. Trusting in his wife to know the way of things – Lady Maccon wasn't a great fighter, but she was an unrelenting one – Rue's father, nibbling a date, came to secure his daughter.

Only to find her dressed like a dollymop and flirting outrageously with a Frenchman. In terms most indelicate and, frankly, alarming for any father to hear.

"Your what?" he roared, banging together the heads of two attackers and looking as if he would like to bang Rue's and Quesnel's heads together next.

Rue did not desire her father's input in this matter. Nor did she feel he could add anything of value to the situation. "Flouring, Father. Quesnel and I were to learn baking techniques from Cook this evening. We were interrupted before we could get started. That's why I'm wearing this old dress."

Lord Maccon was not mollified. "And face paint?"

Rue turned big innocent eyes on him. "Didn't you know? All the best cooks wear face paint."

Lord Maccon had nothing to say to that, only glared at Quesnel and turned to bash his fist into the face of some luckless scrapper.

Quesnel gave Rue a look of profound cock-up.

Rue nodded her agreement before returning to the rumpus.

It didn't last much longer. Fully half of the invaders had been repelled, and upon realisation that they were losing the battle, the others ran and jumped over the railing. Rue thought it a tad extreme to die simply because one didn't get one's way, until it became clear that just below them were two dirigibles. What the men were doing was leaping off *The Spotted Custard* to land comfortably in a net held taut between the two gondolas and then scrabbling over to one ship or the other.

"Ingenious," said Rue.

"Drifters have them." Lady Maccon sprayed down the last of her acid, perhaps hoping to eat away at the net. She either hadn't enough or the net was resistant to such things. A few hapless malingerers squeaked at the burn, but nothing else resulted.

"Bother," said Lady Maccon. "Now I require a refill. I don't suppose you happen to stock lapis solaris in acid as a general rule?"

Rue pursed her lips. "You'll have to ask Primrose; she handles provisions. I wouldn't be surprised. Acid is one step removed from citrus, and she's convinced we must always have a full complement of limes. Very paranoid about scurvy, is Prim."

Rue considered manning the Gatling gun. However, it was on the port side, which would make for some wonky manoeuvring to get a clear shot. Plus she wasn't certain they were allowed to fire on native craft while under quarantine.

Instead, she looked at Quesnel with overly bright eyes. "This is rather fun, isn't it?"

"Feral little beastie, aren't you?" Quesnel's tone was affectionate.

Primrose appeared on deck at that juncture. She evaluated Tasherit from under her lashes before becoming quite business-like. "Right, who's injured?"

The crew numbered an assortment of scrapes and bruises. On the more serious end of things, one of the greasers had a long cut up his left shoulder and one of the sooties had fallen and broken an arm. Prim did what she could. She stitched the wound neatly. She had a fine hand with the needle, and the man, fortunately for everyone, fainted. She set the arm, such as she could.

"I'm no leech," she said crossly to Rue. "If you insist on taking us into dangerous territory, you ought to hire someone."

"That's fair."

Primrose blinked. She hadn't expected such rapid capitulation.

Rue turned to her crew. "Deckhands, I'd like one of you on duty rotation all night long, plus at least two decklings, armed with crossbows. I do apologise. I believed quarantine was an opportunity to relax but apparently not. Walk the railing every half hour, please, and keep an eye below. I'd rather we weren't boarded again. Man the Gatling gun at any suspicious approach portside; fire a warning shot into their balloon. Hang the restrictions. If the authorities don't like it, they should protect us better."

"Hear hear!" said a few voices at that.

Rue continued, smiling her approval. "Thank you all for your defensive work. I hope it goes without saying that hazard pay will be forthcoming."

As usual with that statement, a rousing cheer went up. The decklings began their Custard Doom war chant.

Primrose said to Rue, under cover of the noise, "You might also consider a small complement of militia. I know we aren't a military ship, but this is getting absurd. And, frankly, expensive in hazard pay."

"I'll think about it." Rue raised her voice. "Bedtime, the rest of you." She gestured roundly to the assembled nondeck crew.

Another more half-hearted cheer met that and the defenders dispersed, feeling victorious.

Rue would not have been surprised if Paw posted a guard at her door. However, Quesnel let himself in after only an hour with no impediment. Paw either hadn't set a watch or Mother had interfered.

"You made it." Rue let the pleasure colour her voice, still euphoric after their battle.

Quesnel tossed his hat to one corner of the room and charged over, scooping her up like some Lothario from a novel.

"Stop it, you ridiculous creature. You'll strain something."

He dropped her onto the bed and she bounced.

"Rue, my deadly darling, I worship that dress."

"I thought you might. Sometime we must talk about what I'd like to see you wearing."

"Oh yes?" He began unwrapping his cravat and removing his

jacket at the same time. It was not particularly dexterous – he got the long tail of the first caught in the sleeve of the second.

"I was ruminating on your leather apron."

Quesnel was momentarily arrested by confusion. "Oh, indeed?"

"You know, the one you wear to work the boilers, all smudged and such."

"Yes?"

"And nothing else."

Quesnel blushed cherry red and, having nothing much to say in response, tried to extract himself from cravat and jacket, only to get more muddled.

Rue tsked. "Allow me?" She began to detangle him with no little delight. "Did you lock the door behind you?"

"Of course. Wait. Why, do you think it necessary?"

"My father is suspicious." She removed his outerwear.

Quesnel paused. "Could we *not* discuss him, perhaps? A most uncomfortable topic."

Rue grinned and leaned back in the bed, pushing to make her chest press against the outrageously revealing bodice. It seemed to be sufficiently distracting because he pounced on her with a murmur of French.

There was a goodly amount of kissing at that juncture, now daily established as popular with both of them, and then some fumbling while Rue got him out of the rest of his clothing, albeit with greater skill than he had yet displayed.

He rubbed up against the satin of her skirts with a purr of approval and did a deal of petting and stroking all over as if trying to memorise the shape of her body beneath its smooth texture.

Eventually, he began to attack the buttons down the front of the velvet bodice.

"I thought you liked this gown."

"Rather too much, which is why it is now time for it to come off."

Come off it did, and Rue's silk combination. They were both bare but for foolish smiles and rosy cheeks.

Quesnel took great care with her, as if he had ever taken anything less. In fact, he was almost inexcusably gentle. To the point where Rue resorted to frustrated wiggling to get him to move faster.

"I won't break, I promise."

"I've never actually done this before," he admitted.

At Rue's expression of extreme doubt, he corrected any assumption as to his lack of prowess. "I mean to say, I've never done this with an unsullied lady. I don't want to hurt you."

Rue pulled away and took his face in both her hands. "Dear boy, I change shape regularly. There is nothing more painful than shift."

He looked miserable. "It's still not exactly fun for me to know I will cause you suffering."

Rue, in the end, rolled her eyes, flipped him over, and took matters into her own hands . . . so to speak.

It did indeed hurt, but as she had said, not nearly so much as changing shape. After a bit, it was decidedly fun, and Quesnel was perfectly sweet. Having established that she was enjoying herself – she had to nibble his neck to convince him – Quesnel gave over sweet for fierce and intent, his violet eyes dilated. He made sure she was coasting those marvellous waves of joy before he let himself go at all. Rue loved the way his face twisted, almost wolflike, and that he was careful all the way to the end. Ensuring her satiation before taking his own and pulling out so as to minimise any chance of a future inconvenience.

"Most excellent." Rue lay staring up at the ceiling for a long time after, exhausted and happy.

Quesnel's voice came sleepy soft. "Battle fever. I've read about it."

"You mean it's not always that fun?"

"*Chérie*, I shall attempt to ensure so." He'd recovered most of his cheeky arrogance now that she was safely deflowered. "It's usually not so intense. They say there is something about facing down death that drives a body to ecstasies after."

"I shouldn't worry. Given the way I run things, we'll face death again soon."

Quesnel rolled to his front and up on one elbow. With his free hand, he traced a pattern on the skin of her stomach. "I'm not sure whether to be consoled or terrified."

There was silence for a bit while he continued stroking.

Rue closed her eyes and let herself drift, dirigible-like, under his ministration. His hand moved up to her neck and face.

It stopped against her cheek, now mostly rubbed free of the face paint. It was a silly thing for ladybugs to wear, Rue felt, as it seemed designed to come off on positively everything with the slightest provocation.

Rue opened her eyes.

There was something unfathomable in his violet gaze. Something serious and frightening. Did it herald rejection or declaration? Rue was fairly convinced she couldn't withstand either, so she wilfully misinterpreted his focus as critique.

"What'd I do? Was it not good? Is there a smudge on my face?"

He smiled but remained intent. "No, *chérie*. It's only that I am sometimes reminded of how beautiful you are."

Rue was having none of that. "Only sometimes?"

He kissed her softly, as if she were skittish. She was a bit.

"You know what I mean."

Rue batted him off. "Pish-tosh. Miss Sekhmet is beautiful. I'm passing fair at best."

"Miss Sekhmet is pretty in her way. You are also beautiful – silly of you not to see it."

"I'd as soon you said I was brilliant."

"Oh yes, that too. But I suspect you're more ready to accept a compliment on your intelligence and I prefer to keep you on your toes."

"Here I was thinking you liked to keep me on my back." Rue

didn't like it when Quesnel got overly sincere. She didn't know what to do with an earnest Frenchman.

An unwarranted air of bitterness coloured his reply. "And here I was thinking it was you taking ruthless advantage of me and my vaunted vast experience."

"Quite vast, considering this was your very first deflowerment." Rue tried to tease, but he rolled away from her, leaving her bereft and confused as to how the conversation, and the evening, had so quickly twisted into awkward unpleasantness. Was he honestly not that experienced? Was his reputation cultivated but not earned? Had she somehow *actually* taken advantage of him?

"It is a wonder that I have lived so long without the privilege." Quesnel stood and began to dress.

That hurt. Not the comment, because that was only his usual flippancy, but the fact that he was pulling on his trousers. Rue had thought, after the long-anticipated *event* finally occurred, that Quesnel might, finally, sleep the night through next to her.

"Going so soon?"

"We have your reputation to consider, *mon petite chou*."

"Of course, my reputation." Rue felt the inexplicable need to repress tears. She turned her head to the side and pretended exhaustion.

Silence followed until, fully dressed, Quesnel returned to her bed, gentleman to the last. He stroked her once more – a hesitant touch.

"You don't entirely trust me, do you, *chérie?*"

Rue gestured to herself, where she lay, naked. Didn't society dictate she had just given him the ultimate trust?

He took the hand she waved within both his and sat down gingerly on the edge of the mattress. He looked away from her confused tawny eyes, down at their clasped fingers. "Not that kind of trust."

Rue dug about for reassurance. Was he feeling inadequate? "You're a wonderful lover, a good friend, an excellent inventor, and very easy on the eyes."

"But?"

"You're a hardened flirt. You've always been a flirt. I never expected anything more from you than we have. That would be foolish of me, would it not? And I'm tired."

He kissed her on the forehead. "Ah. So, treasure what we have and never mind the rest? Sleep, then, *chérie.*"

He let himself out.

Rue was left with the distinct feeling of having handled something badly, yet she was utterly befuddled by what exactly it was.

Quarantine ended with no further surprises. *The Spotted Custard* found herself a mooring obelisk over the city proper in a prime location near Shepheard's Hotel. She shared the post with three other dirigibles of standing. The sober sleek pleasure barges drifted slightly away when the *Custard* joined them, much in the manner of matrons at a party when a brightly dressed dandy tries to infiltrate their gossip. Rue wasn't sure dirigibles had noses, but if they did, these were all looking down them at *The Spotted Custard.*

Paw had procured both a warehouse and residence in Cairo some twenty years ago, but he needed to consult his broker as to the location and condition. In classic Lord Maccon fashion, he had purchased it at some expense sight unseen on a whim, thinking of his wife and tea. Many a man have committed worse sins with far less justified instigation. The property turned out to be relatively close to Shepheard's, near the bank of the canal, and exactly far enough from the newly built Principal Station to make the warehouse a practical business concern and the residence not dirtied by overexposure to modernity. With Abbasiyeh Station and the skyrail nearby, it was a tradesman's heaven, and an unexpectedly fortuitous investment. Paw took full credit. It was, however, still occupied by tenants whose lease had yet to expire.

In the interim, Lord and Lady Maccon would stay at Shepheard's in fine style with no one the wiser to the fact that they intended their retirement to be one of dabbling in the tea trade – a most ignominiously mercantile end for a pair of vaunted aristocrats.

Rue was proud of them. It would suit her mother to have something to do under the desert skies. Otherwise she might end up Queen of Sheba or on a mission to save the local crocodiles from embankments, or whatnot.

Rue, Percy, Primrose, and various decklings laden with baggage accompanied the Maccons to their hotel. The decklings and the luggage were lowered from *The Spotted Custard* to the ground in porter's nets with balletic aplomb. The officers utilised the Egyptian passenger swing with a great deal less aplomb. Rue tried to be graceful, but grace wasn't her strong point, and upon dismounting from the wooden bar got the single long rope tangled in her skirts. Prim attempted sidesaddle and nearly fell off. Percy, white-faced, lost his top hat and then his dignity in a flailing of limbs and curses. However, once groundside they were rejuvenated by coffee from an enterprising nearby vendor.

Rue's mother complained that this was a sign of how great the need was for proper tea in this country. "Here we are, after a harrowing yet commonplace occurrence, and all that is on offer is *coffee*."

It was a quick march from the mooring obelisk to the hotel. Quesnel did not accompany them. He could not meet Rue's gaze and insisted he must stay to supervise the maintenance and restock.

Tasherit stayed aboard, as ordered. Rue also officially requested that she ensure the safety of the crew. Catlike in protection of her territory and her people, Miss Sekhmet adored official sanction to cause maximum bloodshed. She wore her favourite tan skirt and red hunting jacket, which looked very like a military uniform, and tucked a pistol of indeterminate make into the sash at her waist. Rue didn't ask if she could use the gun, let alone

where she had purchased it. Tasherit would never arm herself
with a weapon she couldn't wield, and her means of acquisition
were mysterious and likely to remain so.

With her ship in good hands, Rue marched along, taking in
the wonders of the city around her. In the comparative cool of
early morning, the streets were alive with activity – performers
plying their arts, vendors selling wares out of stalls or off the
backs of donkeys, and all manner of street urchin. On the short
walk to the hotel, they stepped to the side to allow not one but
two processions. One was religious and the other military. They
were passed by several open-topped steam carriages and a cara-
van of impressive camels – no doubt off to view the pyramids.
A massive omnibus scuttled by, steam-powered and covered in
passengers, so many they appeared piled and draped over a box
on wheels, dangling in such a way as to be both precarious and
decorative.

Cairo was a desert child dressed in soot and sand. The
men wore flowing robes of rust, soft blue, and cream with the
women confined to darker shades. There seemed a great deal
of importance placed upon the type and style of a gentleman's
headwear, more so than even the top hats of Rue's home country.
She could only respect that, given her familial relationship to
Uncle Rabiffano and Aunt Ivy. The street was loud, full of
chatter and music. The laymen sang as they marched towards
the Nile and the railway stations beyond. Even as Rue delighted
in her new surroundings, she dreaded the impending horror of
abandoning her parents in this dusty place.

Shepheard's was very impressed with itself and with the
honour of housing Lord and Lady Maccon. Certainly, the hotel
was accustomed to entertaining persons of great wealth and
privilege, even occasionally great title and power, but rarely all
four at once.

The Maccons were let the best rooms. The owner himself saw
them settled before bowing out in an obsequious manner. Rue
gave the decklings some coin and the afternoon off, to be home

before sundown. Thus the aristocrats found themselves alone in the sitting room as the heat of the day pressed down.

"Young Percy," said Paw, "a private word if you would?"

Percy, surprised, followed Lord Maccon into a separate chamber, leaving the ladies to enjoy a light repast of tea and sandwiches.

"Not bad tea, actually." Lady Maccon was begrudging. "I suppose they must cater to British preferences. I wonder how much it costs them to import?"

"Mother, are you sure of this decision? I worry about leaving you two in this foreign place alone."

"Don't be silly, infant. We're well equipped to handle ourselves. He's looking better already, wouldn't you say?"

"He's certainly looking older, if that's what you mean." Rue nibbled at a funny honey nut biscuit thing.

"Good. He may catch up with me and we shall look the same age."

Primrose came over perturbed by illogic. "I don't think mathematics quite work that way, Lady Maccon."

Mother laughed. "I was trying to lighten the mood. Infant here looks so concerned about life. Or death, as it were."

Awkward silence permeated the room. Prim poured more tea rather desperately.

Finally, Lady Maccon pulled out her parasol, the ugly one that sprayed things when it wasn't shooting other things or being used as a blunt instrument. "Prudence dear, I should like you to have this now." She passed the accessory over. "You know its worth."

Rue took it gingerly. "Certainly I do, but, Mother, are you certain? It's very important to you, and you should find a weapon far more useful than I. Particularly as you are residing in a *public* hotel."

"Ah, but you, my child, can't steal immortality inside the God-Breaker Plague. It should make me feel better knowing you had a good weapon. When you leave Egypt and can be metanatural again, I thought Miss Primrose here might be interested in the accessory."

Primrose was shocked at being included in a family concern. "Oh, I shouldn't want to take on a family heirloom."

Lady Maccon snorted. "Don't be ridiculous, girl, I'm not sentimental. I've had half a dozen or so of the bally things."

Primrose whispered into Rue's ear in an excess of shock, "Your mother is gifting us with a *second-hand* parasol?"

Rue hid a smile. Her mother was, at her best, overbearing. She was also not one to be challenged on points of generosity. Best to accept her dubious gift and have done with it.

"You've ordered a replacement from Madame Lefoux already, then?"

Lady Maccon grinned at her daughter. "Naturally. With new features designed specifically for a desert climate. I'm looking forward to the modifications about as much as Genevieve is looking forward to designing them. She does love a challenge." Her mother's words were coloured with that peculiar affection reserved exclusively for Quesnel's mother. "And there will be a nice *new* one for you, Miss Tunstell, eventually – full of useful and ladylike necessities, like perfume, and handkerchiefs, and piccolos, and very small truncheons, and what have you. You'll want to consider the practical applications to your own daily activities. I find it is always best to go custom in these matters."

Primrose looked startled. "Thank you kindly but I've plenty of perfectly lovely parasols."

"It's the principle of the thing." Lady Maccon was not making a lick of sense.

"Well, then, I cannot wait to return to London to oversee its creation." Prim's expression spoke volumes. She was hoping to intercede with Madame Lefoux in order to ensure it was fashion forward, perhaps with a removable shade so she could change the colour.

"I don't think Genevieve would like that. She doesn't like to be watched while she works."

And Primrose didn't like to be surprised with ugly accessories. There was a battle in the future. But for now, Prim was lady
enough to accept her fate, ugly as it was likely to be.

"Well, thank you for my part, Mother. It will be nice to hit
people with something more elegant than a mop."

"A mop!"

"Too long to explain. Now, would you show us how this one
works please?"

Lady Maccon did so. "Twist the handle just so and blades
come out the tip. See? Very sharp, one silver, one mahogany.
Press this button here and the dart emitter is open and activated.
You've only four darts left, so use them wisely. Normally you
get six. They're a species of numbing poison – works well on
humans, not quite so well on immortals." She reached down to
point to a dial at the base of the ferrule, before the fabric started
and hidden by a top ruffle. "You have three mists – lapis lunearis
in water, lapis solaris in acid, and a lemon basil tincture. The
first is for werewolves and it will also discolour human skin.
The second is for vampires, and it's acid, so it will burn almost
anything else. The last causes a nasty reaction in supernatural
creatures but does no permanent damage. You're out of the acid,
I'm afraid. There are pockets here and here in the ruffle to stash
things."

"Mother, that's amazing. I had no idea it was so comprehen-
sive." Rue took the parasol, handling it with more respect than
she had ever thought to show an accessory.

Lady Maccon grinned. "It's most useful."

Another awkward silence fell.

Rue felt the finality of it engulf her. She cleared a throat
choked with sentiment.

"Perhaps we should make our goodbyes?" Rue thought a clean
break might be best. She and her mother had never been very
good at this kind of thing.

Lady Maccon raised one hand. "There is something I should
like to do first. It is a bit silly. Which, to be fair, is all your

mother's fault, Primrose dear. I had to invent something, you see, rather on the spot. And now it is tradition. Ridiculous, but tradition."

Primrose was serious. "Most traditions are ridiculous, Lady Maccon. Look at Eton."

"Point taken. If you ladies would please stand?"

Mystified, Rue and Prim stood, skirts rustling.

"And open your parasols?"

When Mother got this way, it was best to play along. Rue opened her second-hand parasol, surprised at how heavy it was – full of deadly fluids and armaments.

Primrose objected. "Lady Maccon, we are indoors!"

"This will only take a moment."

Prim popped open her own lavender confection, edged in black chiffon ruffles and black velvet bows to match her dress.

Lady Maccon looked like she would blush if her complexion allowed it. "Please spin your parasols three times and repeat after me: _I shield in the name of fashion, I accessorize for one and all, pursuit of truth is my passion, this I vow by the great parasol._"

Wide-eyed with suppressed amusement, Rue and Prim did as requested, reciting the strange pledge in unison.

"Here I was worried about Paw going balmy. Now I think it might be you, Mother."

"Hush, infant. Now, raise your parasols to the ceiling."

Rue and Prim raised happily. But when Lady Maccon produced a small knife from her décolletage and unsheathed it to show a sharp silver blade, they exchanged worried looks.

The strain of Paw's illness was too much for her – Mother really has gone barmy.

"Come here, girls." Lady Maccon gestured.

They pottered reluctantly over, baffled.

"May the blood of the soulless keep your own soul safe." Lady Maccon sliced into the pad of her palm. She grabbed Rue's hand and did the same, pressing the two cuts together.

"What!" said Rue. But then it was over.

Lady Maccon gestured at Prim in her most commanding way.

After a long stare, Primrose reluctantly took off her glove and allowed the same.

"Mother, you're a loon." Rue sucked the cut to stop the bleeding.

Lady Maccon sighed. "Let me explain. Sit down, both of you." They sat.

"For years now I've been running a sort of secret club. It's for emergency use, communication, and generally keeping an eye on things around the empire. Your mother is a member, Lady Primrose. She goes by the moniker Puff Bonnet."

Primrose tied a silk handkerchief in a neat bow about her own cut. "Not a very covert name. Anyone could guess."

"Yes, well, she hasn't made many contributions since turning vampire. I go by Ruffled Parasol. And Biffy by Wingtip Spectator."

Rue was startled into commenting. "Uncle Rabiffano is part of your club?"

"Indeed, as are you two now. You're all grown up, infant dear. Gained your majority and all that entails. I thought it time to pass along my connections. I have a feeling you will need them more than I." She handed over a stack of documentation. "Other informants of note: the top sheet lists those in Egypt, plus any additional code names I know of. These aren't members, mind you, just contacts. Not all are trustworthy. Watch out for the Wicker Chicken in particular, very tricky, that one. Weapons and weaknesses are noted in cipher. It uses the Isinglass cypher. I fancy you are already familiar with that."

Primrose took the package delicately. "I'm better with paperwork."

Rue only stared at her mother.

"You'll need code names." Lady Maccon cocked her head in enquiry.

Rue and Prim exchanged glances.

Eventually, Rue gestured at her friend with a thumb. "The Ledger for that one."

Prim grinned. "Makes me sound all dark and ominous. And organised. I like it. And you, Rue, you should be . . . ?" She trailed off, frowning.

"Hot Cross Bun." Rue was firm on this.

Lady Maccon sputtered. "Infant, that sounds quite rude."

Rue was unwavering. "I always said I'd rather be called a hot cross bun than a bit of crumpet and I'm sticking to it."

"Tradition demands you both be accessories of some kind."

Prim produced a dainty little ledger from her reticule, the one with the lavender leather cover in which she tallied the daily accounts. "Ledgers *are* accessories."

"So," added Rue, "given the right set of circumstances, are hot cross buns."

Lady Maccon could not argue with that.

Rue pressed for further information on this club of her mother's. "Dama is a member? I learned Isinglass from him."

"Somewhat. We do share the cypher, just in case. He has a code name, Goldenrod, but I didn't give it to him. It doesn't pay, my dear, to involve Lord Akeldama in *all* one's secrets, much as I adore him."

"You adore someone who isn't me, wife?" Lord Maccon returned, Percy in his wake.

Rue looked to her mother.

Lady Maccon shook her head. Nothing else needed to be covered that afternoon on the subject of secret societies and code names.

Primrose squinted at her brother suspiciously. "Percy, you look priggish. Well, more priggish than usual. It's unsettling. Stop it at once."

"I've had some good news, sister darling."

"That's no excuse."

Rue made the motions of departure. It was past time to make their farewells. Prim and Percy could argue for hours if given the right incentive, like priggishness.

"Mother, Paw, it's been a pleasure transporting you here. I shall be certain to visit as often as I can. I do hope your tea endeavours prove both profitable and distracting."

Lady Maccon stood as well. "Thank you, infant." She held Rue in an oddly fierce embrace for a long moment. Rue relaxed into the unexpected joy in her mother's touch. There was no reason for it. Lady Maccon had nothing to steal from her that plague and sunlight hadn't already rendered moot. It was nice, once in a while, not to be frightened of her mother.

"You'll look after Paw, won't you?" Without his supernatural abilities, Lord Maccon could not hear his daughter's whisper.

"Since the day we married, I've watched over that lummox. I'm not stopping now," Mother answered equally softly, with a wealth of love in her voice.

"Good. Someone has to."

"And you?"

"I'm fine on my lonesome." Rue drew back, smiling into Lady Maccon's worried brown eyes.

"Fortunately for me, you aren't alone." Mother tilted her head slightly towards the twins who were still bickering amicably.

"Too true."

"You'll be careful, infant? Now you're officially grown up and legally autonomous?" It was both a question and a statement rolled into one, as if Lady Maccon were trying to reassure herself.

"'Course I shall." Rue was unused to hesitancy from Alexia Maccon. "I'm your daughter after all."

Mother seemed to lose her voice and with a funny little wince, let her go and twirled away. Fishing about for a handkerchief, she dabbed at her eyes. "Blasted desert dust."

Primrose moved to distract her with more formal farewells.

Rue turned to her Paw.

He engulfed her in a fierce hug, fairly cracking her spine with affection. He snuffled into his beard unashamedly. He hadn't his wife's sense of propriety or gravitas. "Take care of yourself, little one. Try not to get into too much trouble."

"We'll keep an eye on her, Lord Maccon," said Percy in a most un-Percy-like cheerful manner.

Lord Maccon grunted at him and let his daughter go.

Rue and Prim gathered up their parasols. Percy went to find his hat, which he'd naturally forgotten in the other room.

"Oh." Lady Maccon gave a little sigh of annoyance. "One more thing. I really shouldn't but I think you ought to know."

"What is it, Mother?" Rue felt a tinge of fear.

"It's that ragamuffin's tank. The one we used for Conall."

"Yes?"

"It's not meant for werewolves or vampires or anything similarly animate. It's a ghost holder, for the preservation of dead bodies and the maintenance of a tether. Keeps a ghost from going poltergeist for much longer than normal, as long as you stick the dead body in quickly."

Rue frowned. "How much longer?"

"I don't know. Genevieve used one similar on her aunt, but that was decades ago. I'm sure both she and her son have made extensive improvements since then. It's possible it could hold a ghost interminably."

Rue let out a sharp breath. "Useful little jobbie."

"Very useful. The question is, why do the Lefouxs think such a thing needed in Egypt?"

Rue nodded. "Yes, that is the question, isn't it? Thank you for telling me, Mother."

Lady Maccon looked almost sympathetic. "I take it that he didn't tell you?"

Rue wasn't going to give her mother that kind of insight into her relationship. So she smiled at her without commenting further.

Percy returned and they made their final goodbyes.

Once free of the hotel, Primrose took Rue's arm, pulling her close for private consultation.

"What was that about a ghost holder?"

Rue felt her skin prick, even though it was a hot afternoon. "Someone is going to die and Quesnel knows who it is."

"And he never told you?"

"He never told me."

Prim looked even more upset than Rue. "You don't think he intends to kill someone and stick them in there, do you?"

Rue winced. "The fact that he has been so secretive certainly doesn't bode well. Although we do have one advantage."

"What's that?"

"There a good chance he's forgotten that one of a metanatural's *other* skill sets is exorcism."

Percy bounced up and insinuated himself between the swishing skirts of the two ladies, taking their arms in his, in a crude imitation of a gallant escort.

"Percy, really, what has got into you? You're bubbly. It's horrid." Primrose was sharp in her exasperation.

Percy didn't notice. "Lord Maccon had a letter for me, and a few bits of other post. I had my club send it on to Shepheard's just in case. It beat us here."

Rue took offence on the *Custard*'s behalf. "We've the fastest ship in the skies!"

Percy shrugged. "Post doesn't have to clear quarantine. Anyway, look at this!" He flapped a pamphlet against his sister's skirt. Rue realised he had been holding it the whole time.

"So tell us about it. We aren't going to stop in the middle of a public thoroughfare to *read*." Prim tried to limit her encouragement, but she did love her brother.

It was nice to see Percy animated about something, Rue thought. But she wasn't really listening to him. She was thinking about the ghost holder. She and Quesnel were already estranged; now she was questioning ever trusting him at all. Thank goodness she hadn't allowed herself the luxury of falling in love. She was upset because, as his captain, he should have told her the tank's true function. Not for any other reason. Of course, not for any other reason at all.

Percy crowed. "*This* is a copy of a recent Royal Society Bulletin in which it is announced that my paper has been accepted and will soon be published. I shall be famous."

"Your paper?" Rue was suddenly suspicious.

"Your paper about what?" So was Prim.

"Werelionesses!" Percy crowed.

Rue and Prim stopped dead in their tracks. A garble of outraged dialects met the three tourists impeding the walkway.

"Percy," hissed Rue, "you didn't."

"I most certainly did! Far more romantic and exciting than weremonkeys, don't you think? And I'm the *only* author."

"Primrose, and I mean this kindly, would you be awfully upset if I strangled your brother?"

"Go right ahead." Primrose's fine eyes were flashing. "Percy, how could you! Tasherit explicitly asked that her status as a supernatural be kept private."

"I perjured myself in an official report to the *queen* by not mentioning her!" Rue added.

"We all agreed!" insisted Prim.

Percy came over truculent. "I didn't agree. And I couldn't very well let that insufferable inventor and his female confidante get the credit for the second most important discovery of the century."

"Oh, Percy, Miss Sekhmet is going to be so upset." Prim nibbled her lip.

"And that's what really concerns you, isn't it, sister?"

"I've no idea what you're talking about." Prim began walking again and the other two were forced to keep up.

"As if I don't see those whiskers sniffing around—"

Rue could see where this was heading. "Stop it, both of you. Percy, you're insufferable. You did this to get back at Quesnel and there is good chance we might lose Tasherit because of it. We need her desperately right now. She's the best defence our ship has. Not to mention a fine friend and stalwart companion. How thoughtless of you."

Percy narrowed his eyes. "Footnote doesn't like her."

"You can't possibly tell me you feel the same? I thought you enjoyed Miss Sekhmet's company. Or at least tolerated her more than most." Rue was not going to let him sidle out of a bad decision.

"Well, yes," Percy muttered, "but this is a matter of academic pride and standing! Surely she'll understand the seriousness of my intellectual position."

CHAPTER
TWELVE

Up the Nile Without a Puff

M iss Sekhmet, as it turned out, did not understand the seriousness of Percy's intellectual position. This was made evident shortly after Rue and Prim marched him belowdecks to face Tasherit and confess all. If she had been a lioness at that moment, she would have gone straight for his neck and no gentle nibbles about it.

Lacking cat form, Miss Sekhmet used language to eviscerate instead. "Idiot child! Have you any idea what you've done? The danger you've brought down on us?" Even lounging in a chair, she seemed to loom, vibrating like an ill-struck chord.

Percy was defensive. "*The Spotted Custard* has weathered worse. You'll be safe here."

Tasherit bared her teeth, square and human but still menacing. "That is not the *us* I'm worried about. You can't possibly have thought me the last of my kind?"

Percy looked guilty. "Well . . ."

"You have endangered my pride. What little is left of it."

"I don't understand." Percy, being a frightful booby, was never one to take his cherished book learning and actually apply it to reality. Presumably, he would find such a logical step quite silly.

"Werecats have been safe, forgotten, lost to antiquity, free of the concerns of you paltry mortals with all your petty wars and sad little dynasties. Our safety is in anonymity, not numbers. And what now? Now your ships with their nets and sundowner guns will be after us."

"Why would they do that?"

"Supernatural status is a legal right, one that needs to be granted, not assumed. Without the Crown's protection, we are the world's most exciting big game. Did you forget your own past? Your Dark Ages, before werewolves were part of society? Perhaps you should go and discuss history with Lord Maccon. I am certain *he* has not forgotten. You wanted academic credit, Percival Tunstell? Now your name will be recorded for all posterity as the architect of werelion genocide. It wouldn't take much. We haven't many breeding males left."

Percy was white, his freckles popping out like currents in a fruitcake. "How do you know?"

Tasherit slapped both hands to the table and leaned forward. "Muttonhead! It's what the British Empire does. You couldn't possibly think your expansion a glorious, enlightening, civilising force? All those books and you never once realised that is the song all conquerors sing?"

Primrose was moved to speak. "Now, now, I wouldn't take it so far."

Tasherit, colour high, eyes fairly shooting sparks of disgust, turned on her. "Wouldn't you? And how might the Tasmanians feel about that? Wait, we will never know, will we? There aren't any of them *left*. Or the rubber-workers of the Putumayo? And both are peoples classified by your government as *human*. Without any protection at all, my people are mere animals."

She turned back to Percy. "Collectors. Explorers. Hunters. It doesn't matter what you name them. You – you insect! – have let them loose on my people. Mine. I was a fool to trust you. Any of you." She glared, including both Prim and Rue in this statement.

Rue could not argue; the werecat's anger was justified.

Primrose looked miserable.

Even Percy was cowed.

But Tasherit's statement made Rue think. "Percy, did you send your paper to an academic review committee?"

"Naturally. Why do you think it took them so long to announce the finding? Shockingly bad form to delay, if you ask me. But they wanted verification."

"So people outside the Royal Society know, likely *have known*, since before we left London?"

Percy was not interested. "I suppose so."

Miss Sekhmet sagged, her face drawn, cheekbones even more prominent.

"You can be quite the insufferable nib, Percy. You know that?" Rue scrubbed her face with her hand and began to pace.

Primrose followed Rue's reasoning. "You think the attacks back in London and during quarantine are related to Percy's paper, not Quesnel's tank?"

Rue nodded. "Our attackers are likely after Tasherit. If Percy used her as the only known example and if he reported her presence in our crew as proof."

"Only to the review committee," interjected Percy. "As evidence. I didn't need it in the paper proper for publication."

"Committees talk." Rue squeezed one hand with the other as she moved.

"You think they attacked in order to get me to change shape?" Miss Sekhmet put effort into calming herself. Long practice, Rue suspected, from an old supernatural creature.

"I think the presence of a pet lioness fighting smart to defend *The Spotted Custard* is awfully substantiating."

"They're after me?"

"You'd make a pretty nice addition to any unscrupulous natural historian who wanted to collect the world's only known sample of werecat. Caged on display or pinned like a butterfly to velvet backing, I imagine they care not which."

Prim scooted closer to Tasherit and put a cautious arm around the werelioness's shoulders. "Oh, Percy, how could you?"

Tasherit didn't shrug her off.

Rue paused at the head of the table. "I thought they were after Quesnel's tank, but Mother tells me that it's an established invention with patents. It makes more sense that they are after you. The weremonkeys have a treaty and the werecats do not. Which makes them fair game by empire law."

Percy looked as if he would protest, so Rue held up a fore-stalling hand.

"British policy doesn't recognise supernaturals as people, not in the broader sense. We've only legislation to cover vampires and werewolves specifically. I made a cock-up, as far as the queen was concerned, with weremonkeys when I granted them legal standing."

Primrose nibbled her bottom lip. "So Miss Sekhmet is right?"

"Yes. Percy has let the cat out of the bag in a big way."

Tasherit looked up, her almond eyes wide with fear.

"Oh, mercy." Prim finally understood the full scope of the implications. There were fates worse than death, especially to immortals.

Percy squinted, confused. "Rue, are you worried people will want werelions for pets?"

Miss Sekhmet curled a lip at him.

"No, you idiot!" Primrose lashed out at her brother, almost physically, shaking in repressed fury. "She is saying they will want them for slaves."

Rue sat heavily, slumping forward in a manner most indec-orous for a young lady. But such a situation as this warranted bad posture. "Recriminations are all very well but what's done is done and Percy will have to answer for it. I leave the manner of his punishment up to you, Miss Sekhmet. Meanwhile, we have a responsibility to your people. How can we help protect them? *The Spotted Custard* is at your disposal. We will do whatever we can to fix this."

Tasherit took a long, shaky breath. "We must get to them *first.*"

Rue nodded. "We run the risk of being followed and leading the enemy straight to them."

"Do you, or do you not, have the fastest ship in the British Empire?"

"So they tell me."

"Then prove it. It's most important to warn them. At this juncture, the British are coming. We simply must to beat them there."

"Very well." Rue assumed her captain voice. "Primrose, please check we've restocked sufficiently for a long journey and ascertain the whereabouts of the crew. I know some are on shore leave. We must get them back as quickly as possible. Percy, you'll have to consult Miss Sekhmet as to our course. I'm sorry, Tasherit, but he's the best we've got. I advise planning it in such a way as to make it look as if we are tourists. The longer we remain innocuous the better. Is that practicable?"

Tasherit nodded.

Everyone was somewhat emboldened with the possibility of action.

Rue turned to mobilise the remaining crew for departure. It would be best if they were ready to move as soon as the last straggler boarded. Then she thought of something else.

"Percy, after you've done all you can to get us ready, I want you researching that treaty of ours with the weremonkeys, plus any supporting texts. See if we can't graduate other species in or use it as legal precedent to get the werecats a similar treaty. You're the closest we've got to a solicitor, and you've amends to make."

Percy sputtered a protestation.

Rue cut him off. "I don't care if your brain rots reading while airborne. You'll take that risk or I'll jettison you in the middle of the nearest desert. Don't test me."

She left the buzzing atmosphere of confrontation for the slightly less oppressive heat of the upper deck. Most of the decklings were slumbering in their hammocks. Rue hated to rouse them, but rouse them she did.

"How many are off on leave?" she asked once they'd rallied round.

"One of the deckhands and four of us, including Spoo," piped up a sleepy voice.

"And the staff?"

Another deckling wrinkled his nose. "We don't much steam with those belowdecks but Cook certainly sent a few off to the market."

Virgil chivvied up at that juncture. "What ho, Lady Captain? Himself is in a tizzy and has me running all sorts of places. What's flipped his pikelet?"

Rue sniffed. "*Himself* has put us all in a bit of a bind. We float out as soon as full complement is aboard." She returned to the patient decklings. "I'm sorry, you lot, but all leave is cancelled. Plus you'll have to spread the word to the other unluckies all over the ship. I want us ready to go as soon as may be. Double shifts and double pay if you can get us ready by sundown."

A chorus of groans met that.

"Now, please."

The decklings scampered off, with a little less enthusiasm than usual given the oppressive heat and curtailed fun.

Virgil turned to go about whatever business Percy had set him.

"You keep an ear to most things aboard ship, don't you, Virgil?"

Virgil grinned.

"Who else of ours is loose in Cairo?"

Virgil considered. "Steward took a log, so Miss Tunstell should be able to get the details for you. I'd guess about half the sooties and two greasers went off to explore. Old Aggie is still flapping below, though, so we won't fall out of the sky."

"I certainly hope not."

Virgil turned to go, giving her a final tidbit over his shoulder as he moved off. "And your Mr Lefoux left about an hour ago."

"Did he, indeed? And where, exactly, did he go?"

"Search me."

About an hour or so later, Rue went to visit Percy in his lair.

"Come to yell at me again, have you?"

"No. I think you know well enough what you've done."

Percy sighed. "I do now. Rummy business. I didn't consider it from Miss Sekhmet's perspective. I thought her wanting to stay undisclosed was a whim."

"Percy, she's hundreds of years old. Does anyone with that much experience have *whims* any more?"

"Lord Akeldama is comprised of nothing but whims."

"Fair point. I think it's how he keeps going. But I never once made the mistake of thinking them trivial. He isn't all brocades and pomade, you know. He's still a *vampire*. Vampires run deep."

Percy looked at his charts. "Consequence of being the son of a very young and very silly immortal, I forgot how the old ones operate."

"Or you lack the necessary interpersonal empathy."

"That's not a very nice thing to say, Rue."

"I'm not feeling very charitable at the moment."

Percy looked so crestfallen at that, Rue decided to gentle her abuse. She needed him functional to fly the ship.

Footnote appeared at that juncture, intent on sniffing her shoes. Rue could sympathise. She was fond of footwear, too. She nudged him in Percy's direction, hoping the cat might alleviate his depression.

Footnote chirruped at the academic autocratically.

Percy chucked him under the chin as ordered.

Rue explained. "I came down to find out where we are going. She never said."

Percy pointed to a map of Africa sprawled out over a pile of books. The Nile snaked down the right-hand side. He traced the long blue line with one finger out of Egypt, through Nubia and the Sudan, and into the contested wilds around Lake Victoria.

"We're going here, to the Source of the Nile."

There was a march of letters across the map: *unexplored*. Rue felt a tinge of fear but refused to show Percy. They had travelled quite a bit in her wonderful little ship, but they had yet to leave the comparative safety of the empire's fortified territories.

"Well," she said, "I made a promise on the back of your mistake. Let's hope we can survive them both."

Percy returned to his charts. "There is a difficulty. No aetheric currents flow in that direction. Plenty of lower atmosphere wind, though. The locals have a saying: 'sail the Nile south with the wind and north with the current'."

"Is that what normal tourists would do?"

"Normal tourists wouldn't go uncharted."

"Then we drift astray."

"You should know."

"Percy."

"Sorry, Lady Captain."

"It's not the fastest, and it'll take more propeller – we'll go through coal. You're sure atmosphere is our best option?"

Percy grimaced. "It's our *only* option."

"South with the wind we go, then."

Rue left him to it and went down to beard her ship's second fiercest lioness in her den.

Aggie Phinkerlington was more than normally impossible.

"I've no idea where he scuttled off to," was all she would say to Rue's enquiry.

"Well, then, you had better prepare the ship for float yourself. We leave at sundown whether Quesnel Lefoux is back aboard or not."

"Like that, is it?"

"We have an urgent mission and his private business cannot be allowed to interfere."

"Taking it out on him, are you?"

"Oh for goodness' sake. Taking *what* out?"

"Your lovers' spat."

"We aren't having a lovers' spat. This has nothing to do with me or him or us."

"Oh no? And the fact that he was in here this morning looking like a depressed baked potato has nothing to do with an evening spent in your bed and not his own?"

Rue blushed, hot and humiliated. "You keep a careful watch on his comings and goings, don't you? Or is it me who interests you so strangely?"

Aggie sputtered in a rage so overpowering it rendered her speechless.

Rue followed up her advantage by calming her voice into condescension. "Your obsessive interest in my private affairs notwithstanding, you cannot go around besmirching my reputation."

Aggie snorted. "You have no reputation. All your vaunted aristocratic connections and you're little more than an unmarried strumpet with parents in *trade*."

As that was a concise if not particularly flattering assessment of her current situation, Rue could hardly protest. "You know a great deal more than you ought, don't you?"

"The old boffin is my friend. And he's my kind. You think you're too good for him with your snobbish ways and your fast connections."

Rue frowned. "I'm confused. You're angry because I won't make an honest man of Mr Lefoux? You're protecting his interests against predatory little me?" Rue gestured to herself dismissively. "Because I'm known to swallow men whole like oysters in season? Look, if you must know, neither of us took advantage. It was a mutually agreed upon arrangement that is likely now over and *was never any of your concern*! Now, as a matter of official business, if you won't tell me where *my chief engineer* has gone, you had better get a message to him instructing him to return immediately. Is that clear?"

Aggie grunted.

Rue, in a temper, took that as a yes. She marched away muttering, "Is *nothing* secret aboard an airship?"

To which one of the sooties answered with feeling, "Not much, Lady Captain. Worse than a small town. If there ain't something interesting to talk about, we make it up, including each other's doings."

Rue looked at the soot-covered scrap of humanity, feeling a sudden kinship. "Got you, too, did she?"

The boy rolled his eyes expressively. "You've no idea."

Rue nodded and continued on her way. *Everyone's got problems, I suppose. Silly me to think mine so much more profound.* She wondered what Aggie's problems were, for certainly they were made manifest whenever Rue was in the room.

Fortunately they did not have to leave Quesnel behind. Although his manner of return was unusual: he bobbed abreast in a hot air balloon – a balloon that wasn't his. And he wasn't alone.

At first, when the balloon approached, Rue thought it was coming to share their obelisk. However, it was not a style of craft welcome in Shepheard's part of town. It was one of the roughed-up patchwork jobbies piloted by local tribesmen. It was small and nimble, retrofitted with a manual propeller to give it some manoeuvrability. It was more primitive than even Dama's old dirigible, *Dandelion Fluff Upon a Spoon.* However, it had been lovingly maintained, for all it showed its age in the smoothness of its gondola's wicker edge, rubbed by hundreds of hands pressed to lean over.

Quesnel hailed *The Spotted Custard* as soon as they were in range, although the deckling in the crow's nest had already shouted down details of who was on intercept.

Quesnel cast a line over and the deckhands winched him

in until the two airships bobbed as close as they may without balloons clashing. At this juncture, Quesnel and his friends cast out a thick net between the two ships. Rue's crew scuttled to anchor their side taut, so that it became a hammock meets walkway.

Quesnel trotted across. He was uncommonly graceful, bouncing only slightly. Two other figures climbed up to the net behind him and followed.

Rue met him at the rail. "You're late."

"Now, *chérie*, you said we might have the afternoon. It's not yet teatime. Not that I wasn't perishing for lack of your scintillating company."

"Yes, yes, you're horribly charming. Sadly, circumstances have changed."

"I'm no longer charming?"

"Cairo is no longer charming."

Quesnel sobered. "What *circumstances*?"

"Percy is an outstanding rotter, not to mention a terrific chump."

"Well, I know that! You know that. That's nothing new."

"The problem is that now *everyone* knows." Rue glanced away from his twinkling violet eyes. The two strangers moved more slowly over the mesh than Quesnel, although they were clearly accustomed to the technique of net strolling. Both wore the flowing robes favoured by natives. The man was swathed in white, bent and frail, assisted by a younger female in black.

Rue explained. "Percy has exposed Miss Sekhmet's existence in an effort to get back at you. Now we are all on the hook to make it right with her and the werecats."

Quesnel took this in stride. "I take it you'll relay details later?"

Rue nodded. "Over dinner."

He flinched.

At which she realised he might be implying later *later*, over pillows instead of port. Not knowing how to react, she kept the conversation on business. "Do we have passengers or visitors?"

"That will depend on you, Lady Captain." Quesnel's tone became formal.

"There could be a more convenient time."

"On *The Spotted Custard* it's rarely convenient. I will go down and resume my duties, if you would only talk with them? They've come a long way to meet you."

"Me? Oh dear. Is this a metanatural thing?"

Quesnel tilted his head, giving nothing away.

"If you insist. Come and see me later, once we're in float? Official business. There's something we need to discuss. I'm afraid my mother has spilled the beans." Rue could hardly believe this man had concealed so much from her. *Who is going to die?* she wanted to ask. *Why didn't you just tell me about the true purpose of the tank? Why don't you trust me?*

"Ominous."

"You've no idea."

"I'll just make introductions and be off."

Quesnel helped the old man and the younger woman down from the net.

"Lady Akeldama, please allow me to introduce Grandfather Panettone and Miss Panettone. Grandfather, Miss Panettone, this is my captain and friend, Lady Prudence Alessandra Maccon Akeldama."

Quesnel bowed and then left.

Rue, conscious of her duties as hostess, led her strange visitors over to Prim's shaded sitting area.

"Mr Panettone, Miss Panettone? Do sit. Tea? I'm afraid we stock the English variety."

The old man nodded, looking as if he would like to smile in pleasure at the idea. But he did not have the kind of face that smiled well.

Rue hailed a footman and sent him for tea, hoping Cook wouldn't be too mad at the disruption to float off preparations. Apparently not, for the footman reappeared promptly with a fresh pot and a few biscuits.

Miss Panettone was a lively little thing, thin but with a round cheerful face darkened by the sun. She did not wear the full veil as Rue had seen on most women in Cairo and her hair was pulled out to frame her face. Her features were pleasingly symmetrical, with serious liquid black eyes and thick lashes. She wore black robes, fitted at the top, with a velvet belt around her hips from which hung colourful tassels. Her robe's skirt and sleeves were richly embellished with gold embroidery. Over the top she wore a dark blue velvet vest with yellow embroidery which reminded Rue of a Spanish bull dancer. The embroidery was a repeated motif of a stylised balloon.

"A pleasure to meet you, Lady Prudence." Miss Panettone had a strong accent. Her voice was oddly familiar. As were her eyes.

"We have met before." Rue poured tea, frowning. It was not a question.

"I did not think you would remember."

"You wore a fuller veil and you called me *Puggle*. Anitra, I think it was."

She dimpled. "He trained you well."

Rue thought of Dama drilling her on names and faces and how to remember them. She'd thought at the time it was merely for society gatherings. "Do you have another message for me?"

Anitra's smile widened. "Not this time."

"And this is your grandfather?" Rue wondered if the young lady's elderly relation knew she was a spy for a British vampire rove.

Anitra inclined her head. Unlike other Egyptian women, she wore no jewellery except tiny glass jars dangling from her ears.

Rue turned to the gentleman. He was very old, perhaps in his nineties. It was hard to tell with a face so wrinkled and leathery from sun and wind. His features were undistinguished, as if they were trying hard to be forgotten. His eyes may have been blue. His expression was mild, almost self-effacing, as if he were accustomed to being overlooked.

Rue inclined her head. "Panettone is not a Drifter name."

"Indeed it is not. It's Italian." His voice was clipped and perfect. He spoke English as if born to it. "And Anitra is not my real granddaughter. In the desert skies, *grandfather* is a term of respect." Was he British or Italian or something else? It was difficult to tell under all those wrinkles – robes and skin.

Rue sat back, sipping her tea. "I'm afraid my ship must depart soon. What can I do for two friends of Mr Lefoux's? And, perhaps, my father's?"

Anitra dimpled again. "Goldenrod has not called upon my services recently. Although my family will always respect him."

Her grandfather added, "And Mr Lefoux was merely a means of introduction. I once travelled with his mother."

"So, why *do* you visit *The Spotted Custard?*"

The old man tilted his head, as if lost in thought or in imminent danger of falling asleep.

The young ladies waited.

Finally, Anitra put a hand to his arm. "Grandfather?"

"You are not as much like your mother as I thought you might be."

"I shall take that as a compliment. You knew my mother?"

"Quite well."

"Then you'll be pleased to know she has taken up permanent residence here in Cairo. Perhaps it is her you wish to call upon, not me?" Rue did not want to be rude, but she had a ship to see to.

"I think not." Mr Panettone's voice held no emotion.

Rue struggled to fill the awkward silence. "I will miss her, despite our differences. More than I realise, I suspect." She was babbling. Something about these two made her nervous.

"She is easy to miss." The old man's voice still held nothing but calm, almost servile, support. Was this some old family retainer? Living among the Drifters of Egypt? Preposterous.

Rue put down her teacup. "Easier to miss than to live with, I find. So, what is it you require of me?"

"Now you sound like your mother." The old man settled back,

stiff in posture but tired, gesturing for his granddaughter to take over the conversation.

She did so. "It is not so much that we wish something from you, Lady Prudence. Instead it is that we believe we may offer our services as interpreters. Plus, we understand you are being followed."

Rue sat up. "How do you know that?"

Anitra inclined her head. "Goldenrod may not require me these days, but that does not mean I have lost my training. Grandfather likes to know what is going on, particularly where the supernatural is concerned."

"So they *are* after Tasherit?"

"Who?" The old man's tone could almost be qualified as interested.

So these two, who seemed to know much, did not know about Miss Sekhmet.

Anitra continued. "Or they are after you, skin-stalker. Or they are after something or someone else. They have been asking questions. They have been watching, preparing. Yet when they made their move, you were able to repel them. It is . . . impressive."

"They were clumsy. So you do not know what they are after, but you do know who they are?"

Anitra cocked her head. "We have theories."

Rue did not like obfuscation. "How do I know I can trust you?"

The old man reached into a fold of his sash belt and produced a folded bit of paper, yellowed with age. He handed it to her.

It looked like one of those privateer letters of marque and reprisal from centuries ago. Only this one was dated 1855. It turned out to be a writ of legal safeguard granted by the British government, to the bearer, over one Alexia Tarabotti.

"You really *did* know my mother well."

He inclined his head.

"She never mentioned you."

Something died in his eyes.

Yet, even as she said it, Rue remembered something from years ago. It was vague. They'd been talking about death for some reason. What had Mother said? *"I've an old friend, in Egypt now so you'll never meet him. Well, more like an estranged family member. He killed the wrong person. Oh, don't look so shocked. I've killed a few people in my day. Your father's killed hundreds, I shouldn't wonder. Both your fathers. And then there was that time London caught fire. Occasionally, my dearest girl, one has to kill. Take my advice: choose wisely and be tidy about it."* At the time, Rue had been too shocked by all Lady Maccon's talk of killing to think much on the random mention of an estranged friend in Egypt.

"You killed the wrong person."

"So she *did* mention me." His eyes flickered back to life.

Rue handed the man back his marque of guardianship. "Gave it up, did you? I imagine she'd be a hassle to keep safe."

He gave a funny little smile. "She's still alive, is she not?"

"Ah. Very well, welcome aboard." Trust might be too much to require so soon, but with both the man and his granddaughter being friends of Quesnel's – the one having tolerated her mother and the other her Dama – she would allow them to stay. It'd also give her the opportunity to satisfy her now wild curiosity.

Anitra brought them back to the present. "We do come bearing gifts. Or should I say reinforcements?" She gestured expansively with both hands.

Rue looked.

The sun was setting and up on the breezes of the cooling skies, balloons were rising all over the city. Patchwork balloons, small and nimble, old and well loved, brightly coloured and drifting together. Rue had never seen anything like it. They rose like champagne bubbles in a crystal glass, bobbing together.

"What?"

Anitra smiled broadly, easy and open. "We Drifters were thinking if you need to leave Cairo, it is better done under cover of airship than any other way. You, after all, have one of the brightest painted crafts I have ever seen. She will fit right in."

Rue grinned back at her. "That she will."

Anitra and her grandfather stayed aboard. Their balloon, which Anitra explained was more properly her family's balloon, piloted by her older brother, Baddu, would join the others in escort service. The young man with Anitra's eyes waved cheerfully after retrieving the net.

Spoo was the last to return from leave. "Apologies, Lady Captain. I'd no idea we were biffing off. No pyramids?"

"Sorry, Spoo, next time we're in town."

"That's what they all say."

"Spoo, my parents live here now. We will be back."

Spoo brightened and ran to stash her market goodies and assume her post.

The Spotted Custard cast off her mooring rope and rose to join the Drifter balloons dotting the sky. It was difficult to count but Rue would have said near to a hundred or so were participating in the protective cover. Among the classic onion shapes she noticed a few almonds as well. One or two proper dirigibles had joined their party. None were as sleek as her pride and joy, but certainly they were more up to snuff than the standard Drifter fare.

"You've some corkers in the mix."

Anitra nodded. "Grandfather's. He likes to dabble in modern technology."

The old man appeared to be slumbering in a deck chair, but Rue got the impression he was still paying attention to everything going on around him.

"Sound investments." The airships were backlit by the setting sun, so Rue could make out little else but their silhouettes.

Together the flock of airships drifted up the Nile, southwards, high enough to spot the great pyramids far to the right – Spoo waved as if they were old friends – and then moved on into the nomad's land of river, sand, and stone.

Rue left her new passengers – one napping, the other making fast friends with the loquacious Spoo. Spoo was delighted to explain the workings of the *Custard* to an interested Anitra. Rue was suspicious of such interest, but Anitra did carry Dama's seal of approval. And it wasn't as though they weren't surrounded by hundreds of her people. *In for the boil, might as well steam.* Plus they did need an interpreter.

With Mother gone, Rue declined to change for supper. Primrose might be upset since they had guests – *Oh dear, I had better tell her we have guests* – but Rue couldn't be bothered. She sent a message to Prim warning her of their new passengers and wandered off to the dining room in hopes of finding the beginnings of food.

Instead, she found the beginnings of an academic. Or the endings of one.

Percy was still in a bit of a state, whether it was guilt or arrogance it was hard to tell, as he'd hidden all but a nervous eye twitch under his customary persona of first water prig.

"Percy, how's the research going?"

"Not great."

"Tasherit will not be pleased to hear that." Primrose joined the conversation, entering the room carrying a tray of barley water.

Percy blanched. "Don't tell her, please? I've recently escaped. She's pacing my library. Traumatising poor old Footnote."

Since Footnote was currently sprawled in one of the dining chairs licking his white chest fur in a most untraumatised manner, Rue raised both eyebrows.

Percy continued defensively. "I've only just started. That

treaty, the one you made with the weremonkeys, it assigned them legal status, as people."

"There was precedent; the local Rakshasa had already been granted rights." Rue took a seat.

Primrose distributed the barley water. "Drink up; it's good for you in this heat. I'm beginning to understand why Queen Victoria was so angry with you, Rue. You made it so they couldn't be exploited. Bold move."

Rue sipped the cloudy drink and made a face. "I wish I were that noble and full of foresight. I didn't do it intentionally, although I would do it all over again. The empire is a yearning maw of exploitation, Prim. You didn't know?"

"Miss Sekhmet is clearly a person!"

Rue drained her cup, to get it over with. "By whose definition? She lives for ever. She changes shape. She looks like a goddess, not a human."

"That's horrible! How can you even think such a thing?"

Percy sipped his barley water with evident enjoyment. Either the boy had no taste or he was delighted to see his sister's ire turned on Rue for a change.

Rue covered the top of her empty glass to forestall refills. "It's not what I *think*, Prim. It's the way the law *acts*."

"But that's awful."

"My dearest friend, how do you think I'm classified?"

Primrose put a hand to her mouth, eyes wide. "I never thought. Are you . . . ? I don't even know how to ask the question."

Percy was intrigued despite himself.

Rue gave a little laugh. "Last I checked I was a national asset with permitted autonomy, not necessarily a *British citizen* with all the privileges thereof. There's some question, Dama said, of me even being considered human. And now my mother is no longer muhjah, and I just upset Her Royal Majesty with weremonkeys. Even with Dama on my side, who knows how the Crown might try to control me. Powerful creatures are dangerous. The government doesn't like dangerous."

A tap came on the stateroom door. Quesnel stuck his blond head in, hat off, face freshly washed. "You asked to see me?"

Primrose rose to leave. "Come along, Percy."

"Stay, please." Rue's voice was harsher than she intended.

Prim reluctantly sank back down, looking like she would rather be anywhere else.

Percy looked smug. Well, smugger than usual.

"Come in, Quesnel, sit."

Quesnel came in, but he did not sit; he leaned back against one wall, attempting to look unperturbed.

"I understand you have a ghost holder in my . . . hold."

"She told you, did she?"

"I would have rather it came from you."

"Family matters."

"I hope your family will understand that, as captain of this ship, I wish to know if that device is patented and registered."

Quesnel blinked at her. This was taking a turn he hadn't expected. "Of course."

Rue sighed. "I wish you had, at the very least, said *that* much. These attacks, I thought they were after that bally tank of yours."

Quesnel shook his head. "Goodness no. I imagine they'll be up for sale on Bond Street soon, with Woolsey Hive's backing. Last I heard, Mother was entertaining the possibility of mass production. I see no reason for technological espionage. I shall be a rich man, in the end. Will you still love me then, my cold beauty?"

Rue glared at him. "That settles the matter. They *must* be after Miss Sekhmet."

"Who?" Quesnel looked confused.

"Yes, that is still the *real* question. *Who?*" Rue sighed. "Are we ready for speed?"

"Of course." Quesnel straightened in offence at any question of his people's efficiency. "You going to tell me where we're going?"

"Miss Sekhmet is taking us to the Source of the Nile. We are at her disposal in order to fix his mistake." Rue gestured at Percy.

Quesnel blanched. "The source is in contested lands. Is that wise?"

"Probably not," Percy muttered.

Rue glared at him.

Quesnel remained focused on Rue. "Why there? What's happened? What has he done?"

"Why don't you try living for a while without all the necessary information? See how pleasant it feels, *chérie*." Rue was not above revenge.

Quesnel gave her a little bow. "Yes, Lady Captain." With which he twirled and marched from the room.

"Oh, Rue! His face. Did you have to be so mean?"

Rue glared at Primrose. "He should have given Percy that darn byline! We'd never be in this mess."

"Thank you, Rue," said Percy.

"Don't start," Rue shot back. "And he should have told me about the ghost holder from the beginning. Who, exactly, does he think is going to die?"

"But he's awfully fond of you," defended Prim.

"He's awfully fond of withholding information. And he's awfully fond of my enthusiasm under the duvet."

"Rue!" Primrose was appalled.

Percy stood abruptly and marched from the room.

Primrose took control of her shock. "I think you malign Quesnel's character."

"Which of us has been kissing him lately?"

"Exactly why you're in no condition to properly assess his intentions."

Rue was past caring. "I'm small, round, outrageous, and – as I just explained – possibly not legally a human being. What makes you think that man takes anything seriously, least of all me?"

Prim took a breath. "Wouldn't you like to be taken seriously?"

"Oh, Prim. You're such a romantic."

Prim frowned. "I believe you're rendering a disservice both to your worth and his attentions."

Poor old Prim – she always wants to see the world in the best possible way.

"Primrose, I just drank barley water for you. For the moment could you leave off my entanglement, such as it is?"

Primrose nodded. "I'll say no more on the subject."

"But?"

"I'm worried about you, Rue. You're isolated."

"I'm on a ship full of people, you chump."

Prim shook her head, annoyed with her own inability to articulate. "You've lost your family. Well, left them all behind."

"To be fair, some of them left me."

"Exactly my point. I don't like you feeling so . . . abandoned."

Rue couldn't deny that. Even Dama had left her to her own devices. *And I was so glib with him about gaining my majority, so glad to be free. I did not realise what else the world would take away as well as his guardianship – my pack, my parents.* "It's not so bad, Prim. They're all still alive, further away but alive, and less mine than they once were. Isn't that growing up?"

"Well, if it is, it's pretty darn awful for you. Excuse my language." Her dearest friend pushed on, embarrassed but determined. "I only mean to say, we're still here for you, Percy and I."

Rue tilted her head, suspicious.

"Fine, me more than Percy. But we're twins enough for me to speak for both of us. It's just . . . We are also your family. You do realise that?"

Rue came over a little teary and said what Primrose couldn't quite muster. "I love you, too."

The presence of Anitra and her grandfather at supper mitigated any possible emotional outbursts into tense small talk. Rue never thought she'd have reason to be grateful for polite niceties, but at that meal she certainly was.

Quesnel was at his flirtatious best; perhaps his eyes twinkled

less than normal but his words were even more than commonly
facetious. Anitra enjoyed his attentions. And why shouldn't she?

Both visitors were curious to meet Miss Sekhmet, who sat
in glorious dignity nibbling a kipper. Anitra was almost reverential when speaking to the werecat. Tasherit took this as her
due. Primrose took this as offensive. Mr Panettone was more an
observer than participant. Something about sitting at the supper
table unnerved him. Rue treated him as gently as she could but
was happy for his sake when he excused himself early for bed.

"Please forgive Grandfather. He isn't well."

"Oh, I am sorry!" Rue had noticed real affection between the
two, even if they were not actually blood related. Being adopted
herself, she understood entirely.

"It's mostly age, I think."

Everyone was grateful when the pudding course was served
and the party could disperse. In the old days, Rue and her friends
would have taken to the upper deck for drinks and cigars, but
in this instance they all took to their rooms.

Rue was entirely unsurprised when Quesnel did not come
to her chamber that evening. She forced herself to drink more
barley water and cried into the glass. Tears, as it turned out,
didn't improve the taste in the slightest.

CHAPTER

THIRTEEN

In Which Rue Learns About Antiquity

Next morning found *The Spotted Custard* floating some distance south of Cairo following the course of the Nile towards Luxor. Ill-rested and sandy-eyed, Rue donned a set of advanced ocular magnification lenses and took a closer look at the flock of balloons surrounding them in the morning light. Most of the airships were similar to Anitra's, small and family-run with a tendency towards comfortable well-tended shabbiness. The four dirigibles were more modern, of fine workmanship and able floating, although certainly nothing on her *Custard*. Whatever Mr Panettone did, he made good money doing it. *Unless, of course, his wealth was inherited.* Rue put the lenses down. He didn't *act* like a nobleman.

As if her thoughts had summoned him, the antiquity in question joined her on the forecastle.

"Lady Prudence." He greeted her with a painfully formal bow. Rue was afraid he might fall over with the effort. He looked so frail, the slightest breeze could tip him spout over handle in the manner of a porcelain teapot.

"Mr Panettone. How are you this morning?"

"Tolerable."

A man of brevity, this one.

Rue gestured for him to sit in a nearby deck chair. He did so

with relief. Rue was sympathetic; the stairs and ladders of her
ship were not designed with the aged or infirm in mind. Quite
the opposite, having been conceived of by an ageless vampire and
executed by a series of disgustingly healthy drones.

Rue turned back to their surrounding flock. "I find it interesting that these dirigibles of yours are all painted red with black
spots. Newly painted, unless I miss my guess. Surely this is no
coincidence? Not that I think my taste unique, simply eccentric."

The man barely cracked a smile. "I had word of your coming."

"And somehow knew I would need ladybug decoys?"

"You may be different from your mother, but not that
different."

If that wasn't the perfect opening for more questions, Rue
would eat her hat. "Eighteen fifty-five was the date. Mother
would have been around eight. How did you—?"

"I was in service to your family."

That explained his general demeanour. "Oh yes?"

"It is a family in ever great need of decoys."

Rue wrinkled her nose. Truer words were likely never before
uttered.

She prodded. "Grandmother's household?"

He inclined his head. "Butler."

"I do apologise." Rue had little to do with Grandmother
Loontwill over the years, first at her mother's insistence and later
at her own. Grandmother Loontwill was unpleasantly silly and
had produced two equally silly follow-up daughters to Alexia.
Aunt Evelyn came to the pack's Sunday roast once or twice a
year but Grandmother Loontwill wasn't welcome in the Maccon
household. There was another aunt, Felicity, but she and Mother
did not speak. She'd left London and was reputed to be worse
than the whole rest of the family put together. "That could not
have been a very pleasant house to work in."

Mr Panettone did not acknowledge this statement. "Before
that, I worked for your grandfather as valet."

Rue was totally floored by this. "The Italian one?"

"Alessandro Tarabotti."

"Is that why you have an Italian name?"

"That's why I use one."

Ah, then it's not his real name. "Mother said her father was an unsavoury sort but that he'd died heroically and was burned without headstone."

"True enough."

"Dama said he was one for both women and men."

This seemed to rather shock Mr Panettone. "One does not discuss such things, Lady Prudence."

Rue grinned. Of course, he was from a different generation. "I assure you, one certainly does. We're very frank aboard this ship, quite modern. Well, not Primrose. I'd wear bicycle bloomers all the time if shape-shifting weren't easier in tea-gowns. And you've seen Miss Sekhmet marching around in split skirts and a military jacket."

The gentleman went silent.

"Mr Panettone, have I offended? I beg your pardon."

He sniffed. "You might as well call me Floote. It seems odd to use any other name with Alexia's daughter. You may not look like her, but your voice is reminiscent."

"Mr Floote, then."

"Just Floote." That rang another bell in Rue's memory. Hadn't she heard him mentioned by the Maccon staff in a reverential manner? *The Great Butler who came Before.*

"I remember that name. They missed you."

A tiny smile crept through the wrinkles. "Nice to know I made an impression. *They* wouldn't include Lady Maccon, would it?"

"No."

"I thought not. We parted badly." He appeared impassive, but there was something stilted in the way he spoke.

"Not uncommon with my mother." Rue's voice held a trace of bitterness. On more than one occasion, she had been on the receiving end of her mother's militant obstreperousness.

"Not her fault."

"I suppose not." Rue was dying to know more about this *wrong person* that Floote had killed. "She apparently objects to untidy death." She prodded.

"To be fair, so do I." He did not take the bait.

"Then you disagreed over the individual in question?"

An inclination of the head.

"Not going to tell me more, are you?"

A slight shake.

"And my grandfather?" Rue shifted forward. "What about him?" It was rare Rue got to ask anyone about her grandfather. Lady Maccon had told Rue some things – things relevant to being preternatural. After all, Alexia had inherited her soullessness from Alessandro Tarabotti. Which meant Rue owed half her metanatural powers to this long-dead ancestor. But Mother was more circumspect about her paternal line than she was about anything else. Which must have been difficult for her.

"Very tidy about death was Mr Tarabotti. Not to mention, good at doling it out. A curious man. He had his own morals, although they were not always commensurate with that of society."

"Which society?"

"British. Italian. Egyptian." The old man looked thoughtful. "I suppose he never did fit in."

Rue nodded. "Like Mother. Preternaturals find it hard to fit in. I sympathise."

He raised an eyebrow.

Rue was surprised to find herself saying, "Imagine being the world's only metanatural."

"You have Lord Akeldama as guardian."

"Not any more. I reached my majority."

His eyes narrowed. "Have you indeed. I *am* getting old."

"And Paw lost the pack."

"Inevitable, of course."

"So I don't belong anywhere." *I'm supposed to be getting him talking, yet here I am babbling about my problems.*

Floote looked around, taking in the ship, decklings chattering away as they shifted from night to day watch. The deck vibrated slightly as the boilers picked up steam. Soon Primrose would appear and herd them to breakfast.

"I think you've found your place."

Rue smiled. "She's called *The Spotted Custard*."

"You always did like ladybugs."

"I did?"

"Indeed. Your grandfather was fond of crimson, too. His favourite jacket would have matched your balloon to perfection." The old valet stopped himself before relaying anything further.

It must be hard, thought Rue, *to always curtail one's speech*. The elderly folk she knew liked nothing more than to mutter about the past. With Floote it was like pulling essential gears from an ornithopter, painful and possibly resulting in a crash.

"I wager you know all the stories," she tried to encourage.

He inclined his head. "Which is why I had my dirigibles painted red with black spots." He closed his eyes then.

"You don't really want to talk about Grandfather, do you?" Rue put some of Dama's training to work reading the man's tone, even as his face remained impassive.

Floote did not respond or move.

"Would you tell me about my mother when she was little? I am beginning to think there is much I do not know. Or did not think to ask. Or heard and forgot."

The old man smiled like a proud parent. "What do you want to know?"

"What do I need to know?"

"Once upon a time," he started, clearly humouring her, "the Templars kidnapped Alexia."

It turned out to be a most entertaining afternoon.

The day passed in sleepy progress. It was gruellingly hot, although the proximity of their companion Drifters cast shadows over the *Custard*'s deck, alleviating some of the direct sunlight.

"The heads of the families will want to meet with you," said Anitra. "Discuss plans."

Rue nodded. "I'm afraid I don't speak your language."

Anitra shrugged. "Grandfather and I will interpret for you."

Rue didn't like that this put her in a dependent position but she supposed she was already dependent upon these two for this whole arrangement, so she might as well cast herself adrift on the Drifters' whims.

"About your grandfather . . ."

"He told you more?"

Rue nodded.

"He's a good man, loyal. It has cost him much, I think, that loyalty."

Rue wondered if that loyalty was to her mother or her grandfather or someone else further back in time. He was, after all, ancient. Instead she asked, "The name, Panettone?"

"Is an old one around here. He is not the first to use it. We remember only because we Drifters have dancers of record whose steps stretch back for a thousand years. Panettone is not as old as Goldenrod, but whose name is?"

Rue gave a small smile. "Tasherit perhaps?"

"Ah, that one. Best if she not come to our meeting this evening."

"Are Drifters not fond of the shape-shifters?"

"It depends entirely on the shape. They ruled the Two Lands as gods for a very long time, before they didn't. While the fettered of the earth remember only their harshness, we Drifters remember more. The Daughters of Sekhmet left of their own volition. They were not thrown over. They have ever been the hot breath of the desert winds. We make our living by those winds.

Your deadly lady, without her shape, unable to prove her true nature, with all that beauty, she would be unsettling, confusing. Confusion is dangerous to negotiations."

Rue thought about the God-Breaker Plague. Even floating as they did, high above the river, she could feel its oppressiveness — so much like her mother's touch. It was getting worse the closer they got to Luxor. Taking away the sparkle of opportunity, the possibility of other's shapes. Rue didn't like the sensation. *Perhaps I truly am the inhuman parasite some have thought me to be.* Rue shook off that depressing thought.

"Are you Drifters against the God-Breaker Plague?"

Anitra tilted her head. "How is one to be against reality? It is what it is, a plague of unmaking. It is no political party to protest. We have accepted it but we are Drifters, so we need not live within it. It no longer expands, of course, not now, but it will remain as long as the Creature in the Sands still reaches out into the desert."

Rue didn't follow. "If you say so. I suppose it has its uses. If you're a supernatural who wants to die, for example." She tried to keep the hurt out of her voice. To lose her father in such a way . . . it was still difficult to face.

The closer they got to Luxor, the more profound the nullifying feeling of the plague. Rue learned to tolerate it. She spent most of her time standing on the main deck, eyes glued to magnification lenses, watching the Nile below. Paddle ferries chugged along while old-style dahabiyas, with their two triangular sails, nipped in and around them. Closer to the embankments, small reed rafts floated, from which scantily clad young men slapped the water with big sticks in a pretty, if confusing, method of fishing. Or was it crocodile control?

They arrived in Luxor as the sun set on the third day. It seemed to grow larger as it sank, a massive orange globe tinted red at the bottom by the dust of the desert. Primrose owned a dress that did that.

Luxor was greener than Cairo, the Nile near the city dotted with half-formed islands. The banks were thick with palm trees, which crowded into the sandstone of the town, while rocky grey monoliths spiked out of the desert beyond. *The Spotted Custard* floated in over the massive statues of Memnon, sitting in faceless judgement over those little islands, like two stern governesses. Primrose – *Baedeker's* in hand – pointed out Karnak at one end of the town and the Temple of Luxor at the other.

At Rue's orders, *The Spotted Custard* and company remained high above the city. The feeling of the plague was simply too unpleasant if they de-puffed even slightly. The decklings were disappointed. They wanted to see the Valley of the Kings up close.

That evening, Rue was to host a Drifter gathering. Quesnel declined to attend. Primrose didn't feel it was her place and Miss Sekhmet made herself obligingly scarce. Which left Rue and Percy, of all people, to welcome their guests.

It was a still night, with little wind, so the balloons performed their dance in stately majesty. Slipping about each other like the most dignified of matrons at a church ball, they collected into pods of ten or so family groups and cast out more of those massive nets. Each pod netted to another, until all hundred-plus airships were linked together.

Quesnel, on deck for this occurrence, was impressed despite himself. "I had a friend at university, used to draw schematics of molecules in just such a manner. He theorised that chemical bonds were more net-like than stick-like in the Kekulé model." He spoke mostly to himself.

"Preposterous." Percy overheard the mutter.

"Yes, so our professor always said. But if one were to conceive of molecules on a two-dimensional plane and then extrapolate into three dimensions? Perhaps netting bonds is not quite so outlandish."

At that juncture, a holler and a thrown net saw the *Custard* bonded to the greater molecule as well.

"Note how the nets allow for each individual ship to sway and bob about where a stiffer material would not? Is it so far-fetched to imagine a molecule might enjoy equal flexibility?"

"Oh, go below, Mr Lefoux, do." Percy's tone was only mildly annoyed. "No one is interested in your ridiculous theories on the chemistry of airships."

With a bow, Quesnel unexpectedly did as instructed.

Percy was disappointed at being denied a theoretical debate.

Rue felt a twinge of pain. It wasn't like Quesnel to cede an intellectual point, much less take an order from Percy. He must be feeling quite low. She stopped herself from following him.

Around them, the nets became walkways by which matters of business were conducted. Women began paying social calls on other balloons. Children commenced games with one another. After a complex series of greetings and gift exchanges, each group decided upon a representative. These converged upon Rue's dirigible.

Rue felt a distinct pressure to make her guests welcome and not to commit any outrageous social gaffes, if she could possibly help it. Considering social gaffes were her forte, she was nervous.

Twelve leaders from the various family groups – plus Anitra, Floote, Percy, and Rue – were too many for the *Custard*'s stateroom, so they held the assembly on the main deck. The Drifters seemed not at all insulted by an al fresco setting. Nor were they disturbed by the delighted shrieks of the decklings, who had discovered that the net walkways were particularly amenable to a modified game of cricket.

"Spoo," ordered Rue from over the railing, "don't let anyone fall off!"

Spoo waved at her from the middle of the net where she was bouncing higher and better than anyone else. "Course . . . not . . . Lady . . . Captain," she yelled at the apex of each bounce.

They hadn't enough chairs for all their visitors, which turned out to be no bad thing, for the men – and by clothing and prevalence of beards they were men – chose to sit cross-legged directly on the deck.

Primrose, blushing and desperate, fetched cushions from everyone's beds so the visitors need not sit on the hard wood. This seemed to be both a kindness and a luxury. The cushions were met with murmurs of approval. Prim saw to the distribution of cups of tea, which seemed to be a kindness and a confusion, and then scones with strawberry preserve, which were universally regarded with suspicion and then delight. The niceties having been observed, she made herself scarce with almost improper haste. Rue couldn't blame her – there were men, in robes, sitting on the floor.

Rue, with a shrug, joined them. Percy, askance, followed suit. He looked uncomfortable and unsure as to why he had to be there. Floote took a seat next to Rue, and Anitra next to Percy.

Floote asked in her ear, "Is that *the* parasol?"

Rue patted her mother's hideous accessory where it rested tucked against her side. "It's one of them. She's had quite a few over the years."

Floote raised his eyebrows. "Two while I was with her."

Rue smiled. "Tough on parasols, my mother. She already has a desert-edition replacement on order."

"I never doubted." Floote gave a little seated bow, either to Rue or the parasol it wasn't clear which.

One of the few men without a beard spoke first. Despite the fact that he wore light-coloured robes and no veil, he had a voice that was – without question – female. This confused Rue. Particularly when Anitra translated, "He is welcoming us all to the circle and thanking you for the generosity of food and drink."

Rue wasn't one to question; if the handsome older woman across from her wished to be a *he*, why gainsay?

Anitra continued her role as interpreter. "Ay asks if the young lord will be speaking for himself or if the fire hair is his voice in matters of barter."

"I'm sorry, what?"

Anitra dimpled a little. "You are the *young lord.* Mr Tunstell is the *fire hair.*"

"I'm *what?*" Rue looked down at her considerable bust. The light blue tea-gown she wore was not as daring as a ball gown, but the square neckline for all its lace trim did nothing to conceal the fact that she was, most determinately, a woman. If anything, it advertised this fact. There were *bows* all the way down the front.

Anitra tried to explain, "You captain this ship, and you are wearing something similar to a blue robe."

Rue continued to blink.

Floote said, his voice cracked with age or exhaustion or humour or all three, "They think of you as male."

Rue regarded the leader who had started the talks with new interest. "Women in charge are thought of as men?"

Floote nodded.

"Right, then, do continue. Please inform them that I shall speak for myself."

The woman who was no-woman, Ay, waited politely until Rue nodded at her and then continued.

Anitra said, "He is congratulating you on the beauty of your airship and your crew." After another lengthy statement from Ay, Anitra blushed and covered her mouth to hide a smile. "And wishes to know if your woman is entertaining suitors? Ay represents a very powerful family and he thinks she would make an excellent wife. He enjoyed the little fluffy breads very much."

This was getting most bizarre. "Primrose? She – wait, *he* – is interested in *marrying* Primrose? Because he liked the scones?"

"Oh I say!" said Percy. "That's not on. That's my sister you're haggling over."

Rue kept a straight face. "Please thank her – er, him – for the compliment and inform him that Miss Tunstell has a prior commitment." Primrose, Rue realised, had been wearing a navy dress. That colour seemed the provenance of women. Rue supposed it wasn't so odd to have attire intimately linked to social conventions. After all, back in England, an inordinate amount of time and attention was spent on the niceties of mourning garb. The presence or absence of black crêpe in British society was certainly as esoteric to an outside observer as gender-determining robes were to Rue.

Ay inclined her head and then waved in a dismissive manner.

Anitra said, "It is of no great import."

Floote whispered to Rue, "Good response."

Anitra explained, "Ay's offer may have been sincere or it may have been a compliment. In either case, it is now acquitted without shame to either party."

Rue whispered back, "You mean, she might actually wish to marry Prim, in that also acting as a man?"

Floote inclined his head.

Anitra laughed. "Ay has two wives already. And three children."

Rue reeled. "How is that possible?"

Floote went deadpan. "To know, I believe you must ask the wives. Now focus."

Rue focused. She was aware that she must play by Drifters' rules. *The Spotted Custard* could not afford to be abandoned on its own so far from Cairo. Now that they had the escort, it would be better if they could keep it.

The other leaders around the circle introduced themselves. They all seemed, by voice and facial hair, to be biologically male, although Rue decided not to take anything as truth until told so.

Rue tendered her gratitude for their assistance thus far and the meeting proceeded apace. With Anitra's and Floote's help, Rue believed she avoided cultural pitfalls. But she wasn't entirely certain, given the fact that she comprehended neither language nor expressions. Percy, too, although adept at foreign tongues, could no more follow this conversation than he could a school of gossiping goldfish. He stuck his nose in the air and whispered to Rue that it was, "Quite a primitive tongue," in a tone that suggested he was annoyed that the language was outside his comprehension and that the opposite was actually the case. It was too sophisticated for even his vaunted brain to follow.

Anitra explained that the family leaders had gone as far as they felt necessary in helping Goldenrod and were reluctant to continue floating south. "They understand you are hunted but not why they should involve themselves further."

Rue wondered if they had any idea why the *Custard* was being chased. Given Anitra's reverential attitude to werecats, should Rue present Tasherit's case? Would that work for or against them? But Anitra had insisted Tasherit not attend this meeting, so perhaps it was best not to petition for werelioness protection.

Rue decided not to mention cats. "I understand your position. I'm most grateful for such assistance as you have rendered thus far. I would beg your indulgence a little further on my journey."

Anitra shook her head. "They are not ones for charity, Lady Prudence."

Rue frowned. "Trade?"

Anitra said something, making a gesture with her arms. The men all sat up straighter, suddenly very interested.

Anitra said, "Do you have coffee? It is the custom upon opening a barter."

Rue grimaced in disgust.

"Wine?" suggested Floote.

Rue narrowed her eyes. "Will port do?" She hated port, yet for some reason Cook had seen fit to stock a very great deal for the journey.

"Splendid."

Rue leaned back out of the circle and gestured with one arm at Spoo. In classic Spoo fashion, she'd left her game to sit nearby in the guise of some vital task – whittling a wedge of cheese or what have you. "Run to Primrose, please, Spoo. Have her release two—"

"Four," interrupted Floote.

"Four bottles of port from stores. Have the footman bring

them up with some of those little serving glasses Cook likes so much. The footman, mind you, *not* Primrose herself."

"Consider it done, Lady Captain."

"Thank you, Spoo."

"Lady Captain?"

"Yes, Spoo?"

"Please don't say or do anything exciting until I get back?"

"I have a feeling nothing untoward will occur until the port arrives. Now hurry along."

Spoo dashed below.

Ay leaned forward. Anitra translated for her. "You wish to open negotiations?"

"I do."

"You need to know exactly what you're asking for. Request more initially. Then back down. Saves face for everyone." Floote seemed invested in helping Rue through this murky situation. It was the most sentences she'd yet heard him string together.

Rue could only be grateful.

They waited for the port.

It arrived, along with Spoo, the footman, and many small glasses. Ay seemed disappointed it wasn't Primrose but cheered considerably when the port was passed around. More bottles were placed in the centre of the circle where anyone could reach them.

Everyone sipped gravely. Delighted smiles crossed the faces of the men.

To each their own, thought Rue. "I should like to continue our escort for the next week, into the deep desert, plus escort for the four decoy dirigibles going in opposite directions."

"A large request. You take us away from our normal trade routes and hunting grounds, simply because you are being hunted yourself."

"Those with the decoys may follow any path they wish, hunting or trade. It is only those who accompany me who are required to stick to a specific path."

"That does lessen the inconvenience. What will you give to the decoys, and what to your own personal escort, all of whom undertake a certain amount of risk in your protection?"

Good question, thought Rue. *What will I give? What do I have to trade that these men might want?*

"I offer contacts with a new trade concern in Cairo. A lucrative tea import business that will need middlemen."

"And why would a tradesman use Drifters with small balloon capacity over faster and more effective trains?"

"Fair point," said Rue. She regarded Ay. *How much is Primrose really worth?*

Percy seemed to follow this line of thinking and elbowed Rue. "Don't you dare trade my sister."

"Well, what else do we have, Percy? Your books?"

"No! Fine, by all means, offer them Primrose, for you are not trading my library!" He paused, frowning. "How about aetheric current charts? I could copy those over."

Rue thought that a pretty good idea; although the Drifters' balloons were not designed for aetherosphere puffing, they could float short ways if they wished to. She made the offer.

The Drifters looked intrigued but doubtful.

Rue consulted Anitra and Floote. "I could have Cook make up all the scones our stores allow. And they can have the rest of the bally port. But really I can't offer much more from our supplies. We've no idea when we might get supplies again. We will need to eat."

"How much sugar do you have?" Floote asked.

Rue raised her eyebrows. "I'd have to ask Primrose, but quite a lot. I've a terrible sweet tooth."

"Like your mother."

"Be fair, she has a general tooth."

"Offer them all you can spare."

Anitra explained, "It's a coveted delicacy in these parts."

Rue took a breath and sacrificed her beloved lemon tarts on the altar of human safety. "A sugar loaf of this size" – she made the shape with her hands – "to each family group that remains to help."

That resulted in murmurs of delight. Several of the men nodded; they were temped, but it still wasn't enough.

Rue looked to Floote. "What else might they like? I have a great number of shoes and Primrose has hats and parasols and such. I don't suppose . . ."

"They might like the parasols."

"I'm going to need Primrose at this juncture. I can't trade away a lady's accessories without her knowledge any more than I can trade away her person. In Prim's case, the accessories likely carry more weight. Percy, go and fetch your sister, please. And ask her to bring as many of her least favourite parasols as she can spare."

Percy stood, grumbling. "Don't you dare give them my books while I'm away."

He left.

Floote said, "I suppose he knows they can't read?"

"It would never occur to Percy that *anyone* couldn't read. Don't burst his bubble. I prefer him worried. And nothing makes Percy more worried than the possibility of diminishing his library."

The twins returned momentarily and there was a murmur of dissent as Primrose drew up a deck chair, joining the circle behind where Percy and Rue sat. Primrose would never sit on the floor of anything for any reason. Ever. International incident or not.

While Anitra said something that seemed to soothe matters over the presence of a foreign female in a deck chair, Rue turned to her friend.

"We're in sticky negotiations, asking them to continue escorting us. I've had some luck offering up most of the ship's sugar stores. Sorry. Now we were thinking maybe your parasols would appeal."

"Oh, were we?"

"I'll buy you replacements when we return to London."

Prim grinned. "Only funning. Of course you may have them. Well, not all of them, but most will be out of fashion by the time we get home anyway. I'll be receiving one of your mother's specials as well. I have decoration plans for that, which should result in not needing most of these." She gestured and Spoo staggered forward to dump a full dozen parasols of different shapes, sizes, colours, and decorations in the centre of the circle.

While the visitors crowded forward, grabbing for their favourites, Rue said, "That's very generous, Prim. Thank you."

"And you mock me for my excessive accessory collection."

"Never! I'd give them my shoes if I could."

"Just goes to show you that parasols trump shoes every time."

Rue didn't argue because, really, Primrose was being very philanthropic.

"Any other ideas?"

Between them they managed to come up with more offerings. All their available perfume oils, several bars of soap, glassware from the table setting, two silver candlesticks, three thick fuzzy carpets showing Uncle Rabiffano's impeccable taste, two dozen scones, some muffins, several tins of spices, and four of Prim's least favourite hats were offered up.

And they had an agreement.

Still the Drifters seemed reluctant to make any concrete promises.

"It's not that they don't find the goods sufficient," explained Anitra, when Rue and Primrose began scrabbling for more disposable offerings. "It's that they believe the quest ill-omened."

"Why?"

Anitra shrugged. "There has been no sign or portent."

"How do we arrange a portent?" Rue was not above fabricating fate, if it would not be tempted.

At which moment Footnote came striding up, because cats have perfect timing when they care to use it. Tail high, the little tuxedo was enjoying full run of the ship with Tasherit confined to her room. Upon seeing the assembly, Footnote, being a social beastie, strutted into the exact centre of the circle. Naturally, with everyone focused there, he assumed the pile of objects was his by rights.

The crowd fell into a shocked silence as the cat trotted around, twitching his whiskers at hats, parasols, perfume bottles, and sugar loafs, batting at this or that. The silence stretched as he made a second wider circle, sniffing everyone's feet. The Drifters held perfectly still. Satisfied that he had claimed everything for cat-kind, Footnote flopped in front of Percy, showing his belly – cat language for "scratch my neck but don't you dare actually touch the belly". Footnote had handsome white tummy markings which went up to his throat. He also had white spats, impressively long white whiskers, and a white tail tip. He was quite the natty dresser. After receiving the requisite neck scratches, he sat back up, stuck his rear foot high into the air, and proceeded to give himself a good wash in a most indelicate area.

Primrose was enormously embarrassed. She bent forward from her chair to shoo him away.

Floote stopped her. "No, Miss Tunstell, watch."

A murmur of excitement buzzed through the circle. The visiting leaders began talking to one another in hushed tones.

The suppressed tension made Rue nervous. She reached for her second-hand parasol, gripping the knobby handle that activated various secret weapons. She began categorising the armaments in her head, wondering what might be most effective on such a large number of people.

Floote said, "I don't think that will be necessary, Lady Akeldama. See?"

Ay spoke and Anitra translated. "We have a deal."

Rue was shocked. "What?"

"The decoy ladybugs will have their escorts away from here. My family, along with Ay's, have agreed to continue southward with you."

"But how?"

"They like your cat."

Only Percy was unsurprised by this. "He is a very nice cat, as cats go. Spoiled rotten, of course. But what cat isn't?"

"Just like that?" After a long session of tense negotiations, Rue couldn't believe her luck.

Anitra laughed. "Cats are considered the visible soul of a ship, to have a black and white one is very rare and very lucky in these skies."

Ay tilted her head back and swallowed the last of her port. Around the circle, the others did the same. Rue and Percy followed suit.

Without further ceremony, the party dispersed. No farewells were made to Rue or her companions. Although a few of the visitors made an effort to approach Footnote and give him a head scratch. Footnote took this as his due.

They watched from the deck as the departing leaders bounced across the nets.

"Why do you think they wanted the hats?" Primrose asked. "Not that I'll miss them: Mother's gifts, every one. Frankly, they couldn't have gone to a·better home than the middle of an Egyptian desert where no one is likely to see them ever again."

"From what I could gather, they mean to use them as balloon toppers. Sort of like figureheads on a boat," Anitra explained.

Rue grinned hugely. "You mean, like an actual tiny hat atop a big balloon head?"

Primrose started to laugh at the picture this presented.

Anitra nodded.

Percy said, "I don't see what's so funny. It's a perfectly acceptable way to display a highly decorated object of high rank. Mother would be proud."

Prim snorted. "No, she would not, and don't you dare tell her. Better the hats sacrificed themselves for our continued survival than ended up cultural curiosities collected by floating nomads."

The sound of a horn broke through their merriment.

"What's that mean?" Rue asked.

Anitra winced. "That's lookout scouts on the far edge balloons. Incoming hostiles. Grandfather, why don't you go below? You're looking tired."

Floote gave his adopted granddaughter a funny sigh but did as she suggested. He did look tired, bent over and shaky as he approached the stairs.

Rue frowned. Floote's eyes were always so alert that sometimes she forgot how old he was. And he'd just spent the better part of an hour sitting on the floor. "Poor thing, someone should help him. Those stairs aren't easy for anyone save decklings. Primrose, would you?"

"By all means."

"And if there's going to be trouble, you might stay below yourself."

Primrose nodded and trotted after Floote, offering him a supporting arm.

"Not you this time, Percy." Rue forestalled the redhead when he would have followed. "Don't look so worried. We aren't going to stay and fight. I need you at the helm. It's time to test the *Custard*'s mettle and make a break for it. Come on."

"Oh good. I prefer running away." Difficult to tell if Percy was being sarcastic.

Rue accompanied him to the navigation pit and picked up the speaking tube.

"What?" Aggie barked at the other end.

Rue hadn't time for animosity. "Grab that nasty-looking crossbow of yours, Miss Phinkerlington, and get up here on the double. No arguing. And put Mr Lefoux on the line."

Surprisingly, Aggie did as ordered.

"*Chérie?*"

"We've got unwelcome visitors. Heat up the engines. We're testing her mettle."

"Do we have an escort?"

"That we do."

"Nicely done."

"It's all Footnote's fault."

"I won't ask."

"Probably better that way. You ready?"

"Always."

"Bring them to the boil, then, immediately, please."

"Consider it done." Quesnel set down his end of the tube with a soft click.

With remarkable efficiency, all around them, the nets were reeled in. The decoy dirigibles began puffing, while the Drifters divided into clusters around each one.

The warning horns sounded again. Taking that as the signal to depart, they began heading in different directions. One group of Drifters even floated due north, down the Nile, towards the attackers.

Rue put the spyglass to her eye and gasped, for charging them at speed were a dozen airships. Not just dirigibles either, but ornithopters and other flying machines. There were nimble and manoeuvrable and not dependent on wind. Not able to float the aetherosphere but good for close-range combat.

Rue never thought there might be so many working together. It conflicted with her imagined solo collector out for reputation and glory.

FOURTEEN

Drifters Like Cats

Aggie Phinkerlington appeared at Rue's elbow. "You summoned?"

Rue handed her a set of glassicals and pointed north. "We've got company."

Aggie looked through, her eyes wonky with magnification. "You always did attract the nicest types."

"And here I thought you *liked* Mr Lefoux."

Aggie handed her back the lenses. Was she trying not to smile?

"I take it you know how to shoot that thing?" Rue gave a chin nod to the crossbow.

Aggie didn't bother to answer, simply made her way to the best vantage point on the forecastle, propped her massive crossbow up on the railing, and winched the string back to load a bolt. *Old-fashioned*, thought Rue, *but serviceable*.

"Spoo," she called, "leave off prep work, grab a friend, and man the Gatling gun. I take it you've figured out how to use it?" Rue had confidence in Spoo's general interest in violence. She was eleven, after all. All eleven-year-olds were, by nature, bloodthirsty.

"Aye, Lady Captain."

Spoo grabbed, of all people, Virgil, who had been herding Footnote belowdecks. They ran to ready the massive gun.

"Don't go shooting any friendlies. I spent far too long, and too much sugar, acquiring that escort for you to go potting a Drifter. Spoo, take your instructions from Aggie."

Aggie didn't respond except to nod at Spoo.

Spoo gave a reluctant, "Aye-aye." A former sootie, Spoo had transferred up to deckling because she didn't like Aggie.

Nevertheless, Rue was pretty darn certain that if anyone could forge a working relationship under pressure to kill people, it was those two.

Rue picked up her mother's parasol, trying to decide which of its armaments would be most useful long range. "Percy," she said, "set course due south and take us up. Not into the aetherosphere. Find us a good breeze so the balloons can keep pace but be prepared to boil up to full propeller if needed. Hold us towards the back of the pack so the gunners have shooting lines."

The Spotted Custard let out her usual noise of petulant flatulence but responded with eager nimbleness to Rue's commands and Percy's touch. They puffed smoothly upwards, shadowed by an escort of seven balloons. Fortunately they found a favourable southern wind and hooked in, moving quickly.

Rue watched their hunters with her glass. They were obviously confused by the multiple ladybug dirigibles and their multiple Drifter companions.

Anitra appeared at her elbow.

"Floote's plan seems to be working." Rue gave her a cheerful smile. "They are dividing to follow, not sure which of us is the *real Spotted Custard.*"

The young woman smiled back. "Best keep your distance, then. As soon as they have deck view, they'll spot you as a female captain and know for certain which is which."

"I take it he didn't go as far as to have all the decoy captains dress in decoy Worth tea-gowns?"

"Bit pricy."

"Good point." Rue kept grinning. "Could disguise myself with one of those Drifter robes. Got any spares?"

Anitra shook her head. "Not with me."

Rue gestured to a deckling. "Run down and raise Miss Sekhmet. We could use her military prowess. Ask her to bring me one of those silk robes of hers and a scarf or two."

The deckling scampered off.

Moments later Tasherit arrived. They were floating high but the plague remained strong; while Rue still felt the oppressive numbness, Tasherit seemed nothing more than blithely mortal under its sway.

"Rue?" The werecat wasn't one for formalities. She handed over a silver robe and some colourful scarves. Rue handed her the parasol and glassicals. Rue pulled the garment on, wrapping one of the scarves about her head, including her hat. She must look rather ridiculous, like a silvery beekeeping nun, but she hoped it would confuse their followers.

"We've got ourselves a spot of bother." Rue filled Tasherit in on the particulars of their new escort, the decoys, and the attackers.

Miss Sekhmet handed her back the parasol with a lip curl. "What *is* that colour?"

Rue looked at the ghastly thing in surprise. It was some species of brown, although in certain lights it had a red tinge, in others a green, and in still others a yellow. It was trimmed with a great quantity of lace and chiffon of the same not-quite-anything-reliable colour. She supposed it was meant to match any outfit, which of course meant it clashed with everything.

"It is a Parasol-of-Another-Colour," Rue announced in a formal manner.

Tasherit sniffed and looked through Rue's glassicals at the enemy, as if in an effort to avoid the parasol. "There are more of them this time."

"More even than that. See there? The decoys are drawing some away." Only four airships remained tailing the *Custard*.

"Strange that collectors would pull together. Isn't the point to make the catch for yourself, alone?"

"I thought that, too." Rue nodded.

"So, maybe not collectors?"

"Whoever they are, they're hostile. You got a gun with any range on it?"

"No." The werelioness looked over to where Spoo and Aggie were tensely pointing their weapons at the slowly encroaching enemy and bickering mildly with one another. "But I'm better at a Gatling than Spoo there."

"I wager you are. By all means, go and tell her to do something more useful, then."

"Oh, great, thanks for that. I was hoping you'd tell her. You know, for truly rapid fire we really need four operators."

Rue wrinkled her forehead. "I'm hoping it won't come to that. Just a warning shot."

The werecat nodded. "Two of us will do, then."

She went and ejected a dejected Spoo from behind the gun but showed her how to feed in the Bruce instead. Virgil, looking relieved, was free to take on more valet-like duties. He went immediately to see to Percy's cravat, which had, in the chaos, come undone and was wafting. Cravats should never be allowed to waft.

One of the ornithopters pulled away from the pack and began closing in on them.

"Bring him out of the sky, please, ladies." Rue didn't want him seeing their personnel and reporting back that this was the *real Spotted Custard*.

The Gatling gun *rat-tat-tatted*.

Aggie's crossbow twanged.

The bullets took the ornithopter in the engine block. Aggie's bolt tore out one of the wings at its midway joint. The craft spiraled down to the desert. After that, their followers, now numbering only three, kept a respectful distance.

They remained some leagues off for several hours until the

other Drifter groups were mere dots on the far horizon. By which time Rue had formulated a plan.

"Quesnel, could we simulate a mechanical malfunction? Gouts of black smoke out of the stacks or something? I'm thinking to try a lame-duck gambit."

At the other end of the speaking tube, the Frenchman didn't sound surprised by this request. "Most assuredly. When would you like it?"

"Five minutes enough time?"

"Certainly."

Rue hung up the tube and turned to her navigator. "Percy, prepare to de-puff and cycle down the propeller."

"Aren't we in the middle of a chase?"

"We are, but we can't keep this up into nightfall. I'm thinking, I have some good gunners – we might was well turn this into an attack."

Percy grumbled, "I don't know why I expected anything different from the daughter of a werewolf. Didn't that vampire father of yours teach you any subtlety?"

"That's rich coming from the son of Aunt Ivy."

"Touché."

"You've a better idea, Mr Tunstell?"

"Well, no . . ."

Rue went to talk to her gunners.

"I'm luring them in. I want you to take them out as soon as they are in range."

"You got a lot of faith in our abilities." Aggie registered displeasure out of orneriness, not lack of confidence.

Rue arched her brows. "I never doubted you for one second, Miss Phinkerlington. Remember, it was always the other way around."

Tasherit nodded at Spoo to prepare the Bruce. Spoo checked the cartridges with an intent face.

"Anitra?" Rue called to the young Drifter woman, who was busy pacing the decks with no concrete roll to play aboard ship.

She clearly wished to pitch in, being born to the skies, but knew that on a well-run airship she was likely to be a hindrance until she got their rhythm.

Rue paused, seeing her crew through another's eyes. Competent and sure, with a ballet-like grace to their movements. *Not too shabby, if I do say so myself. Is that because of, or despite, my leadership?*

"Looking bang-up, everyone!" Rue wanted to ensure they knew she appreciated them. A few of her decklings waved at her without pausing in their duties.

Anitra came over. "Yes, Lady Akeldama?"

"Can we get a message to your family and Ay? I'm assuming you have way of communicating while afloat?"

"But of course." Anitra pulled out two small bright red scarves from her sleeves, as if she were about to do some exotic dance. She waved them high above her head, signalling for attention from their escort.

"What should I say?"

"Ask them to please prepare their nets."

"We're going to stop?"

"No, we're going to set a trap."

The Spotted Custard pretended weakness, puffing out gouts of smelly black smoke and sinking down and away from any protection afforded by the balloons.

The hunters closed in, ignoring the Drifters.

Tasherit and Aggie engaged in a solid exchange of fire. Aggie managed to take down a second ornithopter while Tasherit and Spoo annihilated the balloon of the smaller dirigible. Neither one was permanently damaged, but they were limp and grounded for the time being. The largest and best manned of the ships got in a few good shots of its own. One bullet splintered the aft section of the *Custard*'s gondola, while a second

put a sizable hole through her balloon. It was enough to make
their fake fall not quite so fake. Decklings scuttled to climb
the lines and patch the tear. Rue let them, despite the danger
both from falling and further gunshot. They couldn't afford to
actually be weak.

Meanwhile, the Drifters dropped back and were coming
around the enemy from above. They only boasted a couple of
pistols among them, nothing like a Gatling, but they weren't
intending to join the fight. Instead, they hovered over the
remaining hostile like a small swarm of chubby honeybees.
When the time felt about right, they dropped one of their
massive heavy nets. It slid over the aft point of the dirigible's
almond-shaped balloon and fell with a thud to drape over the
gondola below. Nothing happened for a moment, and then the
net, swaying, got tangled up in the propeller beneath.

The propeller cracked and splintered, one paddle falling
completely off.

The crew of *The Spotted Custard* cheered.

"Rev her back up," said Rue to both Quesnel via the speaking
tube and Percy at the helm. "No puffs yet – let the sooties fix
our balloon first."

Percy nodded.

"Fix? What happened to the balloon?" Quesnel's tone was
accusatory.

"She got a bit of a hole. Should be patched shortly."

"Squeaker?"

"Yes. Helium, not ballast. We're sinking."

"Well, don't let her squeak too much or we'll need a refill at
Wady Halfeh. We already have to stop for coal and water; add
helium to that list and we'll lose all the time you just bought
us. I thought we were in a hurry."

"Thank you, Mr Lefoux, for telling me something I already
know."

"You can count on me, *chérie*. Too bad other blindingly obvi-
ous truths elude you."

Rue wasn't going to let him bait her. "You're too kind."
He'd already hung up the tube.

Their little skirmish garnered them a good day's lead, possibly
two. Some more red handkerchief communication saw them set
as brisk a pace as the Drifters could manage.

Rue consulted her friends and fellow officers over a light tea
in the stateroom. It was stuffy and hot but she wanted the privacy afforded by closed doors against prying ears – otherwise
known as Spoo.

"If we manage a coal and water suck and get out of Wady
Halfeh before our friends repair and catch up, could we take to
the deep desert here?" Rue pointed to a place on the map.

Percy stood next to her. The others were seated casually, in
such a manner as to stand and come around if they felt they
had something to add. Out of necessity, Floote and Anitra were
included in the discussion. They were, after all, the closest Rue
had to local guides.

Percy nibbled a date. "Depends on the wind direction. If
we want to keep with our Drifter friends, we are reliant on the
winds."

Rue frowned. "They have propellers on their balloons, do
they not?"

Quesnel shook his head. "Those are for catching and slowing
a spin, not momentum assist. More like the rudder of a boat.
Unless my understanding of aeronautics is entirely off." He gave
a depreciatory little bow in Anitra's direction.

He was being falsely humble, for he knew perfectly well how
Drifter balloons worked and had an impeccable understanding
of all things aeronautical.

Rue tried not to sneer at him.

He passed Anitra the plate of toast tips in a solicitous
manner.

Anitra took one. "He's right. We need wind, and reliable winds stick to the Nile."

Rue moved her finger further down the map. "What about here, at the second cataract? We go due south while the Nile veers west. We'd save considerable time cutting across the desert both there and later, at the third. We start following the river again at the sixth, here at" – Rue craned her neck about to read the city name – "Khartoom."

Floote, who apparently didn't need the benefit of a map to follow, sipped his tea. Tea in this weather! Rue supposed that as a frail old man who ate little, English tea was both his main sustenance and a comforting reminder of his former life. She was happy with water. Quesnel, Percy, and Anitra partook only of barley water tempered with a little lemon. Primrose, stubborn to the end, drank her tea with a will, something to be endured for the sake of tradition. Tasherit sipped iced milk from a teacup.

Floote said, "Nubia is dangerous."

Anitra added, "Not exactly friendly. Not to Drifters, and certainly not to the English."

Rue shrugged. "War is in the air, I know. But tracking the Nile is no way to ensure safety either. We're over hostile territory, desert or river, and at least this way we save time. What do you think, Tash?"

Tasherit twitched, as though hoping for a tail to suddenly appear that she might lash. "Directness is not in my nature, but with an unknown enemy on our tail, I say risk the desert at speed."

"Unknown enemy?" Quesnel's eyes narrowed at Rue, as if it were her fault. "I thought we'd settled on them being some big game hunter."

Rue sighed. "Too many attacked us back before we split the escort. Not even the Royal Society could float that many ships at once, nor would they spend all their might on collecting one werecat, rare though she may be."

Miss Sekhmet's brown eyes were grave. "That takes me down a whisker or two."

"No insult intended." Rue hurriedly backtracked, until she realised the werelioness was joking. *Cats, terrible sense of humour, the lot of them.*

Prim looked up from pouring herself another cup of endurance tea. "You mean to say, we're back to not knowing who's after us?"

Rue turned an enquiring look on her mother's former butler. "Mr Floote, would you care to enlighten us as to who might be attacking *The Spotted Custard*?"

The old man put down his cup. His hands shook a little, with palsy, not fear.

"Hunters you call them?" He turned the question back on her, very Socratic.

"Back in London, Percy let it out that we had a werelioness aboard. They likely think she's the last of her kind. We think that made her a pretty tempting prospect."

"And if they knew there were more of her kind?" Floote cocked his head.

Tasherit hissed at this.

The elderly man held up a hand. "Would that diminish her value?"

Rue considered this. "Difficult to determine. But there's no legal rights for Miss Sekhmet's people either way, so we thought it had better be us doing the protecting."

"Unless you are guiding the enemy straight to her pride."

"That was my point," put in Quesnel.

Rue glared. "It was Tasherit's call and she said we go. So we're going."

Floote nodded his grey head. "I see. But you now think that many ships refute the hunter-collector theory? They could have help."

"And who might be helping?" Rue was pleased they were back on her initial question.

Floote raised a liver-spotted hand and ticked off one gnarled finger after the other. "Templars. Order of the Brass Octopus.

Some other secret society. Members of the British Royal Society. Museum, contract, or independent collectors. Sportsmen after exotic game. Or a coalition thereof."

Primrose put down her teacup with a clatter. Her eyes were fixed on Tasherit. The werelioness looked like she was trying not to be ruffled by such a long list of enemies.

Rue let out a breath. "That's a surfeit of interested parties. Could you elucidate further?"

Floote tilted his head. "The Templars are more concerned with your mother's kind, and likely you, than with shape-shifters, but that doesn't mean they don't want to kill them. A new kind of immortal is a new kind of threat, so the Templars might send agents out of curiosity. Or they might prefer to finance others. Depends on how taxed their resources are right now. I'm afraid I've been out of the European loop. Regardless, it never pays to discount the Italians."

Rue nodded. Her mother had mentioned Templars. She'd called them *disagreeable fellows with a predilection for delicious food and lopping the hands off of preternaturals, religious zealots with funny ideas about immortality, nightclothes, and daemons. "You take my advice, infant, avoid Italy. It's not worth it, even for the pesto."* Since Rue did not want her hand lopped off – preternatural policy likely extended to metanaturals – she had stayed out of Italy. Regretfully, as they were renowned for their pastries.

"And how would we know them?" Rue asked.

"Templars wear white tabards with red crosses. They aren't above hiring outside aid, but there would be at least one present to watch the operation."

Rue had to be grateful for Floote's knowledge and his willingness to share. There was a lot, she was beginning to realise, that her mother and father had tried to teach her about evil and enemies and secret societies. She had either blithely ignored it, or thought it unlikely to apply to her, or not realised its import at the time. If she had, she might have asked more questions.

"And the Order of the Brass Octopus?" she asked, hopeful.

"They're different, vested in keeping themselves secret."

Rue pushed. "And they are?"

"A society of concerned scientists that occasionally interferes in politics when they feel the world needs a nudge. I haven't seen hide nor hair of them for" – he frowned – "well over a decade, possibly two. You might ask our young friend there." He tilted his head in Quesnel's direction.

Quesnel flushed as the entire table turned various levels of anger, interest, and concern in his direction. He raised both hands. "Whoa there. You can check me for the tattoo. I'm not a member."

Rue was tolerably certain, and she could feel herself heating up at the possibility of having to acknowledge this to everyone in the stateroom, that Quesnel hadn't a single tattoo anywhere on his body. She'd conducted a complete inventory on more than one occasion. She would defend him if it came to that – no one deserved to be wrongly accused. However, it was one thing to hint to her friends about fraternisation and quite another to confirm it publicly.

Fortunately Quesnel said, "My mother was OBO. Is she up to her old tricks? I don't think so."

"It's not her we're worried about," said Rue. *At least I don't think it's Mother's old chum.* Rue had never entirely trusted Madame Lefoux. Partly because on those occasions when she'd observed them together, they did seem so *very* chummy.

Quesnel watched her for signs of suspicion. "You want to know if the OBO is still active?"

"Is it?"

"Likely, yes. I declined to join. Secret societies are too old-fashioned for words. Haven't heard from them since. Regardless, I doubt they'd ally with the Templars – opposing views."

Floote agreed. "The OBO is likely a better ally for sportsmen and collectors. Of the two, let's hope it's them."

"Why?" Rue asked.

"Templars like to kill first and ask questions later. The OBO would rather experiment first and kill later. Either way you end up dead, but at least with the OBO there's a chance of escape."

"Very optimistic." Miss Sekhmet looked, if possible, even more worried.

Primrose poured her another cup of iced milk.

They were two days out from Wady Halfeh. All that first after-noon, they floated high and fast over the gates of the cataracts. Anyone free of shipboard duty hung over the railings staring down at the widening of the Nile below. The great river became a near lake, dotted with white rapids and the peaks of a thousand varied islands – rocky, sandy, or covered in palm trees. During the night, they floated over Assûan, a town so small they barely marked it passing. Dawn had them at the second cataract. Rue had never before wished to explore groundside so badly. The fierce beauty of the place drew her, the rapids forming a barrier so inhospitable that no villages edged this Nile, yet the scattered lush islands were the stuff of fairy tales.

They continued on, over the unmarked Nubian border, finally arriving at Wady Halfeh. At first glance it was similar to all the previous villages in Egypt. The buildings built of mud-brick with tile roofs, all tan, yellow, and orange. Paths cut from it out into the desert in sand wheel-whorls. But as they de-puffed, it became apparent that Wady Halfeh was different.

The town jutted up on pillars fully three storeys high, out over the Nile. It was constructed to allow for the annual flood, but its focus seemed turned to the desert, looking to the camel trails for trade because the river was too fraught to provide. Tall industrial pipes spiralled into the skies like obelisks, smoke gusting out. This shrouded the town in sooty gloom, not as much as London, but only because the Nile's persistent breeze carried some partic-ulate away. Still, it covered much of Halfeh in a layer of grime, making the town grungier than the desert around it.

From above, it looked like a great big smudge.

This place was more a creature of the modern age, as Rue had come to understand it, than any she had seen in Egypt. She half expected to find a railroad, spearing out into the desert towards Abu Hammed.

"The desert eats it up," Anitra explained when Rue asked. "The tracks, I mean. It's been tried but it never lasts. One could parallel tracks along the Nile, as they do in the Delta, but the flooding is less predictable here. It'd have to stop half the year and then be dug out after. So, with no train, Wady Halfeh does the heavy lifting for aircraft in these parts."

Rue nodded her understanding. "There's always lot of airships where trains can't go."

"Exactly."

Rue nodded. "Can't complain. After all, we intend to refuel here."

"Nubia has a few way stations further south. But respectable dirigibles don't moor there unless it's an emergency. Even then I wouldn't recommend it. At least Wady Halfeh has *some* laws."

Rue nodded. "Understood. Percy, take us down."

The Spotted Custard sank down, de-puffing in stages towards what looked like the main dockyard. It wasn't designed up, like most dirigible service ports; instead it soared out over the Nile, bringing airships in low to tether to one island or another.

"We are responsible for our own water intake while moored?"

Anitra nodded. "Coal transfer takes place via a centralised venting system in the centre of town. See there?"

"Percy, take us there first, please."

The coal-dispensing station looked like a massive cauldron, with holes plus anchor points at various junctures, like a strawberry pot. They were hailed the moment it became clear they were in need of fuel and directed into one vent by the gesticulations of a precariously stationed native boy.

Spoo supervised as they let out the lines to a group of eager local sooties whose hands reached out from the cauldron interior in an eerie disembodied manner. Like a poltergeist.

Anitra undertook a rapid haggle over cost.

Primrose, as ship's purser, stood by wearing a deeply contemplative expression more common when deciding how to dress for a ball.

For a price that Prim deemed just shy of extortionist, a tube was ejected outward and connected to the open porthole of *The Spotted Custard*'s boiler room. Coal was transferred aboard and gold transferred off. Transaction complete, they were gestured rudely away by the disembodied hands.

Rue directed Percy to moor far out over the rapids, at the most isolated island.

She still felt their position exposed. True, there were white-water rapids between them and shore, but there were also rope bridges aplenty and small light aircraft developed exactly to deal with the difficulty inherent in living near cataracts.

"I don't like this, Lady Captain. We're awfully easy to board."

"Agreed, Spoo. But what can we do? We need water and this is the only way to take it on."

Tasherit joined them, leaning over the forecastle rail.

"Not a particularly defensible military position." Her attitude was deceptively casual.

"Nevertheless," said Rue, "I'm afraid you must guard us against attack." She looked down at her small shadow. "No shore leave, Spoo. Apologies."

"Understood, Lady Captain."

Quesnel appeared.

"Must everyone come up top right now when we are at our most vulnerable?" Rue asked the world at large.

"Got to supervise the water coming in, Lady Captain. It's not easy to draw off rapids."

"Fine. Just please be careful."

"Didn't think you cared."

Rue glared.

Quesnel glared back.

"Softly, you two." Miss Sekhmet was the only one brave enough to modulate the crackling friction between captain and chief engineer.

Rue considered Spoo's finer feelings and relented by walking away.

Miss Sekhmet strode the deck, stationing armed deckhands and decklings at various points, including up the sides of the balloon in lookout positions. She kept her own pistol at the ready. Spoo and Virgil manned the Gatling gun, although they were under orders not to use it in port unless given a direct command. Meanwhile, Quesnel, with Anitra on his arm, oversaw the sooties as they telescoped the hydrology tube down to sink into the rapids. It took seven tries to find a point deep enough not to break the pumps with too much air intake.

Rue carried her Parasol-of-Another-Colour open against the sun – it was greenish today – reassured in the knowledge of its armament. Acid was effective on everyone, and she wore goggles on her hat to pull down upon emission. She'd refilled its complement of lapis lunearis, lapis solaris, and lemon and basil tincture from the ship's medical cabinet. Thank goodness Primrose kept that fully stocked. She'd ensured the parasol's remaining four numbing darts were loaded. It occurred to her that, if necessary, the lemon and basil tincture might be added to barley water, improving taste and mood in one dose. The idea put a spring in her step.

Primrose wanted to leave *The Spotted Custard* in search of a marketplace.

"Absolutely not." Rue twirled her hideous parasol in frustration.

"But, Rue, we'll run out of food eventually."

"How soon is eventually?"

"Well, three weeks. But we've no milk at all."

"Too hot for tea anyway."

"You aren't being reasonable. I'll be safe."

"No, Prim, I can't spare the manpower to guard you if we don't need stores that badly."

"Tell that to Cook."

"You tell it to Cook. Needs must."

"I hate it when you say that. You sound like your mother."

"Don't be cruel. Now go below, please. And take your brother with you."

Primrose sulked but did as Rue asked. "Come along, Percy. I'm sure there is something you need to research and we should keep an eye on Footnote."

Percy was remarkably docile. "Indubitably. I was wondering about desert fauna and the relative frequency of sand fleas only yesterday."

Rue was suspicious. She had long since realised Percy only got publicly pedantic about his studies when he was trying to cover something up. His emotions. Or his real interest. Or his activities. Or some less savoury research.

Perhaps it was because they were so very prepared.

Or perhaps their mysterious enemies hadn't any contacts in Wady Halfeh.

Or perhaps the town was simply too wrapped up in its own business.

But no attack came.

The *Custard* was able to set back out only a few hours later in relative harmony.

Everyone stayed tense, though. A gaggle of off-duty decklings remained glued to the aft railing, scanning the northern skies beyond their Drifter escort for hunters to reappear.

Perhaps the enemy's repairs took longer than estimated. Or perhaps the *Custard*'s refuelling in record time gave them a consistent lead, but no one else broke the skies. They had the whole world to themselves as they left Wady Halfeh far behind and headed into the desert. The Nile disappeared. The moon rose into the sky, and below them was nothing but rolling sands and the jagged shadows of craggy rocks.

For the first time, Rue moved beyond the long arm of the British Empire. It felt terrifying and freeing all at once. A little like attaining her majority. They glided into skies even the East India Company feared to float. It was dangerously peaceful.

That evening they dined under the stars. Their Drifter escort made silent shadows about them touched by the occasional glimmer of lantern light.

After dinner, Rue, feeling antisocial, leaned over the rail near the quarterdeck, watching Primrose, Percy, Tasherit, Anitra, and Quesnel talk on the forecastle. The gentlemen and Anitra puffed small cigars. A marker of how casual shipboard life became was that they did so without smoking jackets. Quesnel's blond head bent solicitously as he listened to something Anitra said. The group laughed. Their humour tinkled out over the silent night and died in the sands below.

Floote caught her staring. "He turned out a better man than I expected."

"Quesnel or Percy?" Rue paused and then added, "Or Tasherit?"

The former valet gave a chuckle. "Quesnel. He was quite the rascal."

"And now he is quite the rake. You might warn your granddaughter."

"Might I?"

"I would."

"For your good or for hers?"

"Ouch. Were you this blunt with my mother?"

"I said very little."

"Because she didn't need help?"

"I'm too old to sit idly by and watch young people be foolish with their hearts."

That made Rue smile. "I thought that was what old people did – allowed us to repeat their mistakes."

"Perhaps."

"You think he is really interested in Anitra?"

"I think we seldom regret the risks we take as much as the times we did not try at all."

Wonderful, now he talks in riddles. Rue looked at their balloon shadows, grateful that they weren't alone above an unkind world.

Floote followed her gaze, leaning his old bones against the railing. His breath was shallow and quick, although he had not exerted himself.

"I am still amazed they agreed to come." Rue thought it might be intrusive to ask about his health.

"They are curious about you. And about Lady Sekhmet." He gave the werecat a title, as if she were nobility. "One of the reasons to keep her from meeting them initially."

"Ah, I see now."

"Ironic, really. That they rush to keep her kind from becoming slaves, when shape-shifters once enslaved all Egypt."

"I know Ancient Egypt was once werewolf ruled. The God-Breaker Plague was born to cast the wolves out. Are you saying it wasn't wolves or that it wasn't wolves *alone?*"

Floote's lined face was thoughtful. "Your grandfather once uncovered a tomb containing the mummy of a jackal-headed creature. There is good reason to call it Anubis form. Mr Tarabotti kept it secret. He was a man who preferred secrets. Ironic that it is you, half a century later, who broke that seal and exposed the world to the fact that there are more than just werewolves changing shape around us."

"To be fair, it was Quesnel and Percy who did that."

Floote raised one eyebrow at her.

Rue considered the past, frowning. "How many animal-headed gods were there in the Egyptian pantheon?"

"Enough to keep you busy hunting a long time, Alessandro's granddaughter."

"Back then, were werelionesses really so bad?" Floote was clearly a resource. Rue was surprised to find she admired him for it. She was beginning to realise she'd wasted opportunities to learn from her parents. Her mother's history was fascinating. Rue had always thought her so staid and old-fashioned! She refused to be so foolish now.

"The pharaohs of Egypt controlled vast numbers of slaves with crook and flail. And the living gods controlled the pharaohs. I would say the werecats were as bad as any other. Until they realised their mistake might be deadly."

Unheard, for she had silent feet even without a cat form to call upon, Tasherit joined them. Rue jumped when her perfect profile suddenly appeared on the other side of Floote, silhouetted against the waning moon.

She said, "We were the first to abdicate."

Floote nodded at her. "There are no great cats on the walls of tombs built after the Middle Kingdom."

"There were so few of us left at that point. And we were tired of ruling. Cats have never played nice with others."

Rue gave her a suspicious look. "Are you trying to tell me *cats* gave up being *gods*? Preposterous."

Floote gave a dry chuckle. Tasherit did not respond.

Rue tried another question, gesturing at the nearby balloons with a sweep of her hand. "You think the people of Egypt forgive you their long imprisonment?"

"Humans have short memories."

Rue cocked her head. "Even Drifters?"

"Ah, but they were never ours to begin with. They had no flight back then, but they were always nomads. We could no more hold them than we could the shifting sands. This is no betrayal of history, them helping us now."

"Interesting," said Floote. As if Tasherit's one statement had changed his whole perspective on the situation.

The werecat flashed them both a wide smile. "Drifters like cats."

Then suddenly, just like that, she shifted form. A large lioness stood on hind legs next to them, with paws against the railing and tail swishing behind her.

Instinctively, Rue raised her hand to provide the necessary control with touch. She looked to the moon. It was not full.

Miss Sekhmet shook herself, like a dog after a swim, her thick golden fur silvered in the moonlight.

With instinct dampened and safety assured, Rue realised that she, too, had felt it lift. The numbing oppression that surrounded her since they entered Egypt was gone.

They were outside of the God-Breaker Plague.

FIFTEEN

Coal and Consequences

It took them another full day of floating to meet the Nile again where she bent, eastwards this time, below the tiny Nubian village of Abu Hammad. There the dervish met them with a porcupine of bristling guns. Rue had no interest in encountering those whirling automated cannons. They gave the town a respectably high float-over.

Several miles upstream, the Nile narrowed, digging out a deep undulating blackness with sheer cliffs to either side. Miss Sekhmet scented the air, pronounced it safe, and they dipped down to the river to take on boiler water.

At Quesnel's request and Spoo's big eyes, Rue allowed the crew a short swim. They deserved some little luxury. Rue envied them their delighted splashing, but it was beneath the dignity of a captain, let alone a lady, to submerge herself in water. That was assuming Rue could swim, which she could not. In fact, Rue had never been a great bather of any kind. There was something about being surrounded by water that made her feel dulled, half her senses cut off from the world, rather like the God-Breaker Plague. She preferred a shower, although rarely available, or a sponge bath.

Quesnel, who had no dignity, joined the crew. He kept his smalls on, although the way the cloth fairly stuck to everything, he might as well not have. It seemed more scandalous than nudity. You'd think, since she'd seen it all already, Rue could pull her eyes away. But she was hypnotised watching him cavort about, tossing Spoo and Virgil up into the air. The youngsters shrieked in delight.

"Lovely." Tasherit came to watch. She shared Rue's abhorrence of bathing.

She was shrouded in robes to protect her from sunlight, wearing a hat and carrying one of Prim's surviving parasols. She looked tired. Were she the type to obey, Rue would have ordered her back to her quarters to sleep the day away like a respectable immortal.

Orders being wasted on cats, Rue said instead, "I didn't think you favoured men."

"I make exceptions. However, in this instance, I wasn't looking at your pet. See, there?" The werecat pointed to where Primrose joined the bathers.

Prim was in a full swimming costume, navy blue with white piping. She was a darn good swimmer for an aristocrat, as was Percy, who paddled next to his sister in a striped costume of white and red contrasting with his hair. Incongruously, he wore a top hat as he bobbed about.

"Oh, sir." Virgil was distracted from his play into noticing his master. "This is the one time you are supposed to leave *off* your hat!"

Percy only floated by, looking dignified and pleased with life. Rue would never have thought Percival Tunstell fond of a nice swim. Funny, she had known the twins her whole life. When had they become sporty?

Primrose completed her exercise and went to paddle in the shallows, retrieving a wide-brimmed straw hat. Even damp she was pretty as a picture, her waist enviably small without a corset. Rue sighed. She'd never have Prim's figure, not without giving up her beloved puff pastry for ever.

Tasherit couldn't take her eyes off the girl.

"She's not ready for you." Rue wanted to urge caution without discouraging too much.

"Can't help chasing. It's my nature."

Rue grinned. "I think perhaps you are old enough to control your nature, should you really wish it. Admit it, you like chasing."

"It's been decades since I've been this intrigued."

"Well, tread lightly." Rue wondered if she ought to stop this conversation. Primrose was her dearest friend; she didn't want to say anything that would betray that friendship.

"That, too, is in my nature." The werelioness smiled. Her liquid brown eyes gleamed when Prim laughed at Quesnel and Spoo's antics. "I'm patient."

"You'll have to be."

"She's special."

"I know."

"He's special, too." They both knew the werecat was talking about Quesnel.

"Don't matchmake me, old godling."

The werelioness wheezed out a laugh. "Mortals! Everything is fuss and bother with you."

At that, Rue decided it was time to hurry everyone back aboard.

Rue watched Quesnel that evening at dinner, more than usual. He was solicitous of Anitra, even attentive. He also took great care of Floote. Really, Quesnel flirted with everyone, except maybe Percy. He'd probably flirt with Percy if they hadn't been perennially at odds over the finer points of academic publication theory.

After dinner, when the gentlemen would have gone to partake of brandy on one side of the deck while the ladies drank sherry on the other, Rue put a hand on Quesnel's arm.

"A private word, Mr Lefoux, if you would be so kind?"

The others looked curious but no one was brave enough to insist on a chaperone.

Quesnel followed Rue belowdecks to the stateroom.

Rue didn't know what he was expecting, but from his expression it wasn't what she asked. "Quesnel, have you figured out a way to determine excess soul?"

His answer was flat, with no artifice to it, almost shocked. "No. Of course not."

Rue let out a breath of profound relief. "Oh good. Because a whole lot of people would want to kill us if we had that technology on board."

Quesnel frowned. "It would save lives. To know beforehand if someone could survive the bite. It would be a miracle."

"It would also limit the number of people who would petition to be drone or claviger. Society as we know it would collapse. Vampires would have much less blood to draw on and werewolves fewer guards at full moon. Both would have to hire out. The balance of power would shift."

Quesnel nodded. "It's not possible to measure the soul, last I heard. Although there is always someone researching it. It's only a matter of time."

"Well, I hope I'm not in London when it happens."

"Why did you think I might, *chérie?*"

"That preservation tank of yours. You brought it with us on purpose. You brought it because Mr Floote is dying."

Quesnel didn't try to deny it. His face shuttered.

"Is he particularly creative? Do you think he has excess soul?"

"Mother says the man always did come up with the most original cravat knots."

"Is that enough?"

"He expressed a fondness for flower arranging."

Rue quirked an eyebrow, hoping she looked sardonic.

"He fights as if he were dancing."

"My grandfather's valet, my mother's butler, *fights?*"

"According to *maman*, quite beautifully."

"So the preservation tank *is* for him. Why?"

"He knows too much."

Rue narrowed her eyes. "According to whom? Your mother? The OBO? *My* mother? Someone else? Who are you really working for, Quesnel?"

"I'm working for you. For this ship."

Rue snorted.

"You don't trust me at all, do you?"

"Give me one good reason why I should?"

"I can give you ten; my chamber is right down the hall." He moved towards her.

Rue wanted, very badly, to lean in to those clever hands and that sweet mouth. But he was using both to avoid conversation and she knew it. "Quesnel, I trust you to be very good at what you do, under an engine or a coverlet. And I trust you to take that expertise to the highest bidder, in money or beauty."

Quesnel put a hand to his chest as though mortally wounded.

Rue gritted her teeth at his flippancy. "Oh for goodness' sake."

"You already have your answer, *chérie*. I've given it to you. Think. Who would want a man preserved because he *knows too much*?"

Rue's mind clicked over, like a slow but inexorable cog. Who had insisted that Rue put Quesnel to work in engineering? Who knew Quesnel's patroness of old, when Countess Nadasdy and not Baroness Tunstell had ruled the London hive? Who could afford to invest in a preservation tank – new technology at great expense – on the mere whiff of an old man's memory?

"Dama," said Rue. "Blast him. Why didn't he tell me? Why didn't you?" *He's trying to meddle from afar!*

Quesnel gave one of his French shrugs. "It's morbid, *non*? Perhaps he was trying to protect your finer sensibilities."

Rue narrowed her eyes. "Or perhaps Floote knows something Dama wishes me to know. Perhaps this is Dama's roundabout way of helping, of trying to keep me safe." She was thinking about her conversations with Floote concerning her mother's past and all the things he hadn't told Rue about her grandfather.

Quesnel shrugged again. "Information is vampire currency. I shouldn't take it as an intentional slight."

"No, you wouldn't."

"What's that supposed to imply?"

Rue examined the world through her eyelids for a moment. Her nerves hummed, from anger, or discovery, or Quesnel's proximity it was hard to determine which. Unable to cope with any of it, she left the room.

They abandoned the Nile for the desert once more. At one point they saw, far away in the rocky sands to the west, the black smoke of a nomadic centacopper. Powerful, town-carrying, mechanical turtles of the great empty, those major feats of engineering could crawl over the desert for weeks on little fuel and less water. Quesnel came up from engineering at the first word of a sighting and kept his amplified glassicals trained for as long as he could.

"I've always wanted to see one up close." He seemed wistful. Almost subdued.

Rue was briefly tempted to hare off in pursuit of the centacopper; perhaps then Quesnel would smile again. But she was not so foolish. *If only*, she thought, *we really were a ship of exploration and not a ship near constantly under siege.*

"See?" Primrose also noticed Quesnel's odd behaviour, later at supper. He had said only the nicest and most politic things and then left early. "Happy now?"

Rue narrowed yellow eyes at her friend and mouthed, "Not now." Anything Prim had to say to her in that particular tone of voice was best kept for private chambers.

They retreated there as soon as politeness allowed.

"Out with it." Rue faced her demons as soon as they were alone in Prim's room.

"You've broken that boy's heart." Primrose was getting rather dramatic, even for Aunt Ivy's daughter.

Rue let out a burst of surprised laughter.

Primrose was not amused. "Oh, stop it. What is really going on?"

Rue paused to examine her feelings. What *was* really going on? Finally she said, before she could stop herself, "I don't trust him not to break *my* heart."

Primrose sat back with a whoosh noise, pensive and startled at the same time. She took a small breath and spoke slowly, choosing her words with care. "So you break his first? That's hardly sporting."

"I didn't think his heart was something I had power over."

"So are you doing this simply to prove that you can? I did think, from an outsider's perspective" – she blushed – "that you were good together. Was I wrong? Did something not work in, you know, *that* way?"

Rue considered Quesnel's mouth and hands, the smooth feel of one and the rough feel of the other. She considered his eyes, up close, violet twinkling. It had been a great deal of fun, his lessons. Was there something wrong with fun? She was usually in hot pursuit of adventurous pleasure in all other parts of her life.

"Quite the opposite."

Primrose pressed.

"So you are in love with him?"

Rue shied away from that idea. It was utterly terrifying.

Later that evening, Rue unexpectedly encountered Anitra alone on the poop deck. She would have turned to leave the girl in peace but, at a welcoming gesture, joined her. They stood companionably chatting, looking out over the dark desert.

Pleasantries exchanged, Anitra said, quickly, as though getting something pent up out, "Captain, I wish to say something. I do hope you will not take it amiss."

"Yes?"

"I wear no dowry coins." She gestured across her forehead where the edge of her veil rested. "Nor do I wear anklets or bracelets."

"I had not known to remark upon this absence but I do now." Rue was a little confused but it was her business to be polite to a guest.

Anitra bit her lip. "Very well, then, I should . . . um . . . good evening." With which she left.

"Well, that was odd," said Rue to the night silence.

"What was?" Miss Sekhmet emerged abovedecks, looking fresh and chipper. They'd settled happily into their old immortal cycle where she joined them for supper after sunset and then took the night shift. They missed her company during the day, but it was healthier for her not to fight the nocturnal habits of several lifetimes.

"Miss Anitra just insisted on telling me that she wore no jewellery."

Tasherit grinned. "She was informing you that she is not available for courting. Did you make a move in that direction?"

"Certainly not." Rue thought of Ay and that fact that Anitra might perceive her as masculine. "At least, I don't *think* I did."

The immoral nodded. "Ah, so. Then it is your jealousy when Quesnel pays her too close attention. She is trying to make clear her lack of intent."

Rue drew herself up. "Pardon me!"

"No need to fluff up, child. If you do not wish your feelings known, hide them better. On this ship, the only one unaware of your interest in that mechanic is that mechanic. And possibly Mr Tunstell. But Mr Tunstell would remain unaware of a sand tick up his nose." The werecat grinned at her own wit and returned to the point. "Anitra is merely informing you that she is not after your man. A female Drifter without dowry on display is not available."

Rue was forced to accept that she had not been subtle. She would have to sort this mess out before others were drawn into it as well. It was most complicated, being the captain of a ship.

Of course Rue avoided both Quesnel and the mess for the next two days. Instead she dogged Floote, asking him about the past, when he let her. She soon realised that she was telling him more than he was telling her. She found herself reliving her peculiar upbringing with three parents and two house-holds. She reminisced about the things those parents had taught her, which until he asked she'd forgotten. She told the more recent stories of the pack's rejection and about Queen Victoria's anger and Dama's concern over her majority. Rue began to suspect that Floote said so little because others found him easy to talk to.

At which point, they reached Khartoom. The city sat at the junction of the White Nile and the Blue Nile. This was rummy-looking from above; for leagues they could see the two rivers meet but stay parallel, not intermingling, the brown of the Blue Nile alongside the green of the White Nile. The city took her mechanical power from these waters. All along the banks, dozens of great watermills, or what looked like water-mills, spun and whirled, casting droplets to the sky. Khartoom was a beautiful city, all lush green with spires of white. It was also decidedly unfriendly to both Drifter balloons and ladybug airships.

"Odd names for rivers neither white nor blue." Rue chewed a bit of candied orange peel and stared down at the water.

Anitra smiled. "We don't question the ancients."

"No? Why not?"

Several red handkerchiefs were waved at them from Ay's

balloon. Anitra waved back, and as a group, the Drifters caught a breeze eastwards away from the city.

"They're abandoning us?" Rue tried not to sound forlorn.

"They'll meet us on the other side. We're less of a threat without their shadow. They'll keep a long-distance eye on us."

"Khartoom looks calm enough." Rue watched their escort drift away.

"It's been under siege at one time or another for as long as I can remember." Anitra seemed to think that was explanation enough.

Rue swallowed her last bit of peel, looking with sudden suspicion at all the lush graceful peacefulness. "Who holds it now?"

"You didn't check with the council in Cairo before you set course?"

"Didn't know we were coming here, exactly." Rue was put off by the accusation in her tone. And her own guilt. She should have thought to make enquiries. Then again, enquiries would have left a record.

"The Mahdists hold it, but they're stretched with forces out at Adwa. They took some of Khartoom's major defences with them to roust the Italians. It leaves Khartoom vulnerable, and nervous about it. I wouldn't go to ground if I were you."

Rue slouched in dejection. "We may not have a choice."

She put in a call to engineering, not sure if she was more reluctant to talk to Quesnel or Aggie. No choice—Aggie answered.

"Miss Phinkerlington, how are coal reserves?"

"Pants, Captain."

"No need for vulgarity."

A snort met that rebuke.

"How many days?"

"No days. Hours."

Rue hung up the speaking tube, cursing herself for not putting a system in place that warned of low reserves. *I suppose if I were on speaking terms with my chief engineer and not bent on avoiding him for days at a time . . .*

She returned to Anitra at the railing, glum. "No choice. We're dry. Will they even sell coal to us?"

"Can you be another nationality? Raise a flag and don a foreign tongue?"

Rue didn't think they had any other flags aboard. She was not devious enough to have thought of that ahead of time. To be British was, well, British. Why be anything else? That was the general British attitude. Although Rue was beginning to learn, the hard way, the ever expansion of their empire was not exactly welcomed by its recipients.

"What would be less threatening?"

Anitra ticked off on one hand. "French and Italian are all out. Canadians are allied with British, so they're no good either."

Rue mentally ran through her and Primrose's collective wardrobes.

"American? We would only have to try an accent."

Anitra considered. "Might work. Americans do like to play tourist and this ship is garish enough."

Rue nodded. "I'll call a meeting."

She sounded the duck horn, a resonating quack that was, quite frankly, ridiculous but shook the boards of *The Spotted Custard* in such a way as to permeate the airship as far down as the boiler room. Three blasts everyone knew meant the officers were to meet. In very short order, Rue had Primrose, Quesnel, and Percy in the navigation pit. Anitra joined them. Rue decided it wasn't necessary to awaken Tasherit. They'd tell her later, if they survived until nightfall.

"We're desperate for fuel. I'm sorry it's got so bad. I should have asked engineering for an update sooner." She figured she might as well own responsibility, although in future she'd put Quesnel and Aggie under orders to alert her the moment they had less than eight hours at maximum use. She was annoyed they hadn't alerted her and wouldn't put negligent sabotage past Aggie, but there was no point in calling Quesnel out in front of the others.

"So we must refuel here in Khartoom."

Everyone's faces went a little white.

"Unfriendly city at the moment, so we are going in to moor under a different nationality."

No one expected that.

"American."

No one objected. There was no love lost between England and her former colony, particularly over the matter of supernaturals, but that made the Stars and Stripes a better cover.

Rue assumed her most captain-like air, attempting to sound cool and calm. "Primrose, you have that dark blue dress with the white dots; that'll do for the stars. Percy, I'm afraid we need your striped bathing costume. Cobbled together, those two will make for a passable flag. Primrose, Virgil's a valet; he likely has rudimentary sewing skills. Put him to work with a quick baste. Doesn't need to be hemmed or anything – only needs to withstand a glance through glassicals. Luckily we don't fly colours regularly, so there is nothing to take down that might already have been spotted."

Primrose looked like she wanted to object to the conscription of her blue gown but nodded and left to do as she was bidden.

Percy looked dour but did not object. He had very little love of anything material that wasn't typed on paper. "Virgil will have to find me something else to swim in. He's not going to be happy. Made enough fuss about the stripy one."

Rue didn't say anything but she was secretly pleased to hear Percy even slightly worried about the opinion of his valet. Every valet should keep his master a touch terrified of his good opinion.

"I want everyone on high alert, but say as little as possible. I don't think they'll speak much English or can differentiate accents if they do, but best to stay silent unless communication is vital. That includes you, Spoo."

Spoo was, naturally, eavesdropping on the conference. Rue

hadn't even bothered to look where. A disembodied voice said, "Yes, Lady Captain."

Rue turned to Anitra. "Additional suggestions?"

"Speak cockney if you can. To those not fluent in your tongue, it sounds enough like American to pass. Grandfather taught me that."

"Oh, I say!" said Percy.

"Percy," said Rue, "*you* are not to speak at all."

Percy's expression said he felt that silence was superior to cockney regardless.

"Will we be boarded? We haven't United States documents." Quesnel spoke quietly. "I've got French but that's almost worse than British right now. Politically, I mean."

Rue winced. "We must assume trade is more important than hostilities to the laymen. I do have gold. It should speak loudly enough to get us coal. As long as we choose the right vendor."

She looked to Anitra, who nodded but still seemed worried.

"So let's hope we can bribe officials to look the other way, if they do try to check. Meanwhile, let's make ourselves look as innocent as possible. Two hours to nightfall. Recommendations?"

"Wait," said Quesnel promptly. "Better to have an immortal awake than asleep."

"Do it soon," countered Percy. "People are less evil in daylight. And we've better view to shoot with the Gatling, should it be necessary to get out fast. Also I've better close-up manoeuvrability if I can actually *see*."

Rue weighed the options. Percy was right, but they could disappear better at night if it came to a chase.

"Night it is. Percy, set us a course desert side, puff up as well, minimal propeller use, drift, save our reserves. Find us a small refuelling station in a bad part of town that might be more interested in money than morals."

Percy nodded. It was a marker of his growing comfort with her command that he did not object further. She'd listened to his concerns but decided otherwise. He'd learned to accept that this was not a personal affront. Even if it did mean the loss of his striped bathing costume.

Primrose had a tolerably decent, if misshapen, American flag flying from the aft balloon by sunset. Virgil was, it turned out, a dab hand. So were several decklings.

The flag clashed horribly with the ladybug spots.

Miss Sekhmet appeared abovedecks, snorted at it in amusement, and was brought up to speed about the situation. She deemed it prudent to shift to lioness form before they landed. Rue saw no reason to object.

Percy found them a refuelling station attached to one of the southernmost water wheels. It puffed black smoke with enthusiasm, but its owners, a group of robe-shrouded and bearded chappies, did not look favourably upon wayward tourists limping in, desperate for a refuel. American or no.

Rue put on her most supercilious rich young lady airs, her fluffiest dress, a scarf about her head in a mockery of a veil, and a particularly bad cockney accent.

The man who came, cautiously, up the gangplank to meet her didn't seem to know what to do with her.

Anitra spoke to him in some lyrical tongue.

He seemed to mostly understand her.

She explained to Rue, "He'll sell us coal but wants proof we aren't a ship of war."

Rue responded. "Ey up. Why're we be?"

Spoo hissed to Virgil. "What does she think she sounds like?"

The man came further up the plank, flanked by three large friends, each had some kind of small sword, or big knife, strapped to his belt.

The leader, now standing where the gangplank met the gate in the *Custard*'s railing, seemed not particularly suspicious of anything he saw. Not even the Gatling. When he gestured at it, asking Anitra for an explanation, she shrugged and said, "American," pointing to their flag.

The man nodded his understanding.

Eventually, without bothering to look belowdecks or ask after their needs, he left the way he'd come.

"What now?" Rue asked Anitra.

"We wait."

"Why so easy about the gun?"

"Americans have a reputation, guns and flags. Plus that gun of yours is a Colt."

"Ah. British manufacture would mean a" – Rue hesitated, trying to remember – "Maxim?"

"Exactly."

"Well, then, I'm delighted Dama has less pride in national manufacture than interest in an attractive appearance." Rue had no doubt her vampire father had researched the best rapid-fire to mount on *The Spotted Custard*, but she also had no doubt that he was attracted to the round golden sheen of the custom lightweight Gatling. The Maxim was a brutal-looking thing and the Nordenfelt positively unseemly. If one *must* give a young lady a ballistic birthday gift, it should, at the very *least*, be pretty.

"So far, I think they are buying our ruse. I may have convinced them you are the daughter of a South Carolina railroad baron."

Rue blinked at Anitra. "Have you, indeed?"

"Oh yes. Miss Prudence Mayberry."

Rue blinked again. "All righty, then." She'd heard a Southern accent out of the United States once. It sounded, to her ear, slightly like a gramophone playback off speed. She could try to combine that with cockney but had a feeling the results would be disastrous.

"Lady Captain?"

"Spoo?"

"Please don't take this the wrong way, but I'd avoid the stage, were I you."

"Noted."

An hour or so later, the man returned. Through Anitra he quoted Rue a quantity and a price, the quantity less than she'd asked for and the price extortionist. Rue accepted both, tight-lipped.

After some haggling, the tradesmen agreed to bring the coal up to the mouth of the fuel tube and Rue agreed to provide sooties to feed at that point. At this juncture she cursed herself for doing it at night: it would be difficult to check coal quality in this light. Nor could they bring a gas lamp out. So far, all activities had indicated both the airship and supplier wished to keep the transaction private. Rue's guess was that the local government imposed a heavy tax and, with a war on, took it out of the tradesmen's product as well as their coffers. Their host was likely desperate for regular trade.

Rue called down to Quesnel, for the boiler room was always well lit. "Check the quality as it comes down the feed, please? I don't wish to be gypped. Call up to Percy if at any time we aren't getting a burnable seam."

"Are you undertaking the trade yourself?"

"Of course."

"Couldn't you have Tasherit do it?"

"No. I have her in lioness form."

"It's not safe."

"Quesnel, now is not the time to question orders. I've taken precautions. I have my parasol."

"A parasol! What good is that?"

"It's my mother's."

"So?"

"Your mother made it for her."

"Oh."

"Exactly. Now, please check the coal?"

"Yes, Captain."

Rue went to her cabin to retrieve the gold. Dama had been generous. She could cover this refuelling and a few more like it.

She took only the agreed-upon amount back up; she was aware of what a vast sum it was in this part of the world.

The coins were Spanish. Old. Dama preferred hard currency over promissory notes. She marched forward with the cash, flanked by her two largest deckhands. She tried to look like a silly American schoolgirl who nevertheless had enough shopping experience to know what she was doing. Even if this was coal and not hair muffs.

She handed the tradesman the velvet bag. He took it, glanced inside, removed a coin at random, bit into it, and then nodded.

Suddenly things happened very quickly.

He faded to the back, down the plank, and in one fluid motion his bullyboys charged. Presumably to take Rue hostage.

Rue brandished her parasol, pressing a button in the handle. A poison dart imbedded itself into one of the men. The other two, however, had her pinned. Willard, who lately seemed to be more a bodyguard than deckhand, engaged a fourth ruffian man to man. That attacker had leapt up off the gangplank to come at her from behind, as if lifted by coiled springs.

Rue twisted and kicked, trying to get loose from the two holding her. Then she felt the cold sharp sting of steel at her neck and went still.

A roar from one side heralded Tasherit's charge. She was beautiful to behold. Even frightened, Rue was impressed by the intense grace of her leap.

At the same time, the small *pifftt* of a tiny but enthusiastic gun sounded.

One of the men holding Rue jerked. His grip relaxed. The knife at her throat clattered to the deck. Rue spun, kicked, and wrestled herself free of the remaining man. Then Tasherit was there, shaking him by his scruff. Rue would rather not think that the snap sound was his neck. The lioness tossed him overboard. He splashed into the Nile below.

Seconds later, Tasherit had the arm of the man holding the velvet money bag in her mouth. With a gentle but insistent pressure, and only a hint of teeth, she dragged him back up the gangplank. He obeyed her without protest, barely breathing, hypnotised by those teeth closed about his flesh.

"Dreaded one," he whispered.

Tasherit made him stop on deck, right at the point where he might be pushed overboard if necessary.

He began to babble.

Anitra had taken cover so no one understood what he said.

Rue realised with a sick stomach churn that the second man who had held her had been shot, in a hugely unattractive way, in the face. It was most unpleasant to look upon, even in the dark. So she tried not to.

Floote came over, looking almost sprightly as if violence were a cure-all. He evaluated the dead man with satisfaction. "Of course, Miss Mayberry, I was aiming for his chest. These older guns really aren't accurate. Sentimental value, you understand? Or perhaps I'm not what I once was. Ugly shot, I do apologise."

"Say nothing of it. Mistakes will happen." Since he'd saved her life, Rue was disposed to be magnanimous.

The elderly gentleman gave a little bow, whipped out a large handkerchief from somewhere within his robes, and draped it over the dead man's ruined face. Then he drifted away and ostentatiously reloaded his tiny parlour pistol. Rue felt, in that one moment, she had more insight into his role as Mother's butler than ever.

Anitra reappeared. Possibly holding a tiny knife in one hand but it was too dark to make out clearly.

"What's he babbling on about?" Rue pointed to the man with the large cat attachment.

"He apologises but hopes you understand a businessman must seize opportunities."

Rue gave a small nod. "As long as he understands the same holds true for me."

"He suggests that perhaps the deal might continue as originally arranged if the lioness could be persuaded . . ."

Rue shook her head. "I think not. Tell him to shout down to his compatriots. Bring the coal up as ordered. We have the feeder ready, off to the side there. We will keep him hostage until our transaction is complete. Will that work for you, Miss Sekhmet?"

The werecat nodded her massive head, keeping the man's arm in her mouth, so he had to give a clumsy salute.

Anitra told him their new arrangement.

Percy called down for engineering to send up sooties.

After that things went smoothly, although Rue put considerably more thought into hiring a militia. She was even more grateful for Miss Sekhmet's presence than she had been in the past.

The coal shunted down the tube apace. When it began to slow, Rue released two of the sooties to return to their duties in engineering.

Shortly after that, Quesnel came up top in a positive flurry. "Rue!"

Since he rarely called her by her preferred name, Rue was instantly alert. She left Anitra and Tasherit in charge of their hostage, and the deckhands guarding against further infiltration, to meet the Frenchman amidships before he could blurt out anything secretive. After all, she did not know if their supplier really *was* ignorant of the English language.

She kept her voice as low as possible but spoke in cockney just in case the tradesmen had a distance listening tube. "Mr Lefoux, please return below. We have us some bad'uns."

Quesnel was clearly very upset, for he didn't even rib her on the atrocious accent. "So I heard."

"So there be somewhat wrong with them coals, then, me laddie?" Rue was perfectly well aware that she sounded like a pirate in a small operatic production in some backwater hamlet. Spoo was staring with a hand over her mouth.

Rue's question, or performance, dampened Quesnel's anger. "No, it seems fine. If they're trying to swindle us, it isn't through the goods. I even had a sootie test for combustion. It's quality stuff."

Rue let out a breath. At least they had fuel. "Then what's the tick? Did they try for belowdecks?"

"No."

Rue was beginning to lose patience. "Then what? I'm in the middle of taking the egg." She gestured back to where Tasherit stood with her mouth around the man's wrist. "Poor cat, I can't think that tastes good."

"You . . ." Quesnel was scrambling for words.

Rue knew English was not his first language but he had seemed fluent until this moment. Now it was as if vowels were choking him.

"Out with it." She let impatience colour her words. She couldn't think of any cockney slang for getting a man to open his saucebox.

"You shouldn't have done that."

Rue crossed her arms, sort of; she was still holding the parasol in one hand.

"It was a stupid risk, Rue, putting yourself forward." Still angry, he nevertheless softened his tone to a hiss.

Rue flinched when his hand came towards her face. But all he did was touch her neck, fingers shaking. They came away smeared with blood.

The man's knife must have cut her worse than she thought. "I've had worse playing with wolves."

"You should have had a deckhand act as purser. We knew they were hostile and crooked."

"It's just a nick."

Quesnel took a shaky breath, but his hand was back on her skin. An inquisitive finger smoothed along the uninjured part of her neck, stroking the pulse point, tracing the veins. It was as if he was reassuring himself her blood still moved.

"You aren't your father. You aren't immortal."

"I know that."

"Do you? You don't act like it."

It was nice but this was not the right time for whatever emotion drove him.

"Quesnel, this will have to wait!" she said, almost desperately.

Quesnel backed off but did not return below. He stayed up top to observe the rest of the transaction.

Which is how he was on deck when it happened. Which was how he got shot.

SIXTEEN

In Which Percy's Cognac Proves Useful

The gun crack was loud and stark and utterly surprising. Quesnel crumpled.

Rue screamed in a way that was quite melodramatic, but she couldn't help it.

Tasherit twisted and heaved, throwing the man she'd been mouthing down the gangplank over the heads of the remaining sooties. His arm tore, misting blood over the heads of Rue's crew. No one seemed to care much, except for the man.

Rue ran to Quesnel, keening and vibrating with fear like some agitated violin. She slid down next to him, heedless of ripped skirts. Her eyes were instantly drawn to the bloom of red near where his right arm connected to his chest.

Anitra was there, too.

Rue scrabbled at Quesnel uselessly, convinced that the best thing would be to get his clothing off. Ironic that.

The Drifter girl pushed her away, gentle but insistent. "Let me see." She put a hand to his throat. "He's alive."

Rue wasn't sure how long that would last. "We should check for continued bleeding, stop it if possible, right?" Her tone was hesitant. She had no experience with bullet wounds. Mild mauling, scratches, and the occasional neck bite were standard fare in her parents' households, but bullet damage? And this was *Quesnel*!

Anitra did not look up from the fallen man. "I know what to do. Please attend to your ship, Captain."

Rue blinked. The reminder brought her out of the shock. She didn't want to leave Quesnel, but responsibility forced her to stand, trance-like.

She took in the activity around her. The decklings were panicking without Tasherit in human form to keep discipline. Deckhands were torn between establishing order and their own defensive duties. Rue felt a wave of cold flow over her; it carried with it a surreal calm.

She holstered her parasol into attack position.

Another gunshot rang out.

"Everyone, down! Stay moving at a low level." It was unnecessary information to impart, as most had already taken cover, but Rue wanted her crew to know she was paying attention to them.

She yelled out more useful orders. "Sooties, close up the feed, last of the coal is not worth our lives. Then get below – we're going to need you stoking! Percy, puff us up. Whatever speed we can get."

"Not much." The redhead's lips were set firm in either fear or determination or both. Fortunately, the helm was seated in such a way that only his head and shoulders were targets and so far, no one seemed to have aimed for navigation.

"Give us what you can. Tell Aggie she has charge of engineering and must put our new fuel to good use."

Percy activated a puffer and they jerked up with a massive flatulent noise. The gangplank, not properly winched in, crashed down against the side of the ship. There was a plunking sound as coal, and possibly people, fell into the river.

"Decklings in the sky, talk to me!"

Voices called down from viewpoints up on the balloon, crow's nest, and around the deck.

"Nothing, Lady Captain."

"Can't see 'em."

"Bloody dark out there."

"State your location as well as your report, please!" Rue barked.

Decklings instantly responded.

"Aft, nothing."

"Fore, nothing."

"Port, nothing."

"Starboard, man down, dangling plank." That was Spoo.

"Crow's nest, nothing! No, wait—" Top of the mast started his call and then stopped. The boy's voice was high from youth, thank goodness, not a helium leak. "Correction. Ornithopters. Two, sir. No, three. Sorry, Lady Captain, not sir."

"Just report!" Rue yelled back. "Don't worry about formalities."

"They're coming in under the starboard side, must have taken off from land. One looks like it might try to land on deck . . . no, only coasting in close. Watch out, Bennie!"

There came a twang and a curse. Bennie, the deckling stationed on the aft railing, shot at the approaching ornithopter with his crossbow.

"Nicely done," called out the boy in the crow's nest. He was now clinging like a monkey to the ropes of the aft tie point, leaning out and swinging around to get as best a view of their attackers as possible.

Rue said, "Willard, to aft. Give Bennie a hand. Spoo, Virgil, man the Gatling. Tasherit, patrol the perimeter. Everyone, I want line of sight on the other two 'thopters." She made a mental note to evaluate the weight allotment and see about installing a second gun starboard.

Spoo dashed by, making for the gun.

"Spoo! What's the name of my eyes up there?" Rue gestured with a thumb to the boy dangling near the crow's nest.

"Nips, Lady Captain!"

Rue winced. Unfortunate name. Plus "Lady Captain" was quite the mouthful under adverse conditions. "*Sir* will do for now, Spoo."

"Yes, sir!" Spoo ran to the gun.

"Nips!" Rue shouted up. "The others? A location if you would."

"Out of sight, Captain. I think they're below us. Can you have a sootie look out the boiler hatch?"

"Good idea. Percy, get Aggie on the tube. Have her people check."

Percy was occupied with navigation and just as unwilling to deal with Aggie as Rue, especially when engineering was without Quesnel. Nevertheless, he did as ordered.

"Aggie says you're a blowhard doxie and they've two in sight, one heading up port, the other fore and starboard slightly."

"Spoo!" Rue took the information without acknowledging the insult. "Ready to shoot a deterrent blast on my mark. One pass, don't waste bullets. Just keep them from boarding your side. Put the fear of death into 'em."

"Yes, sir!"

"And don't kill anyone we like."

"'Course not, sir. I ain't sloppy!" Spoo's tone was offended, but Rue worried the gun was an awful lot to handle. Spoo was small for her age.

"Tasherit, one's coming up fore and right. Get ready to give them hell, but don't get yourself captured, for goodness' sake. Decklings with crossbows, back up the lioness." Repelling an invasion was harder than it looked.

Another few shots rang out. Loud bangs reverberated through the night, attackers firing on them. Then came the answering *rat-tat-tat* of the Gatling. Mixed in was the twang of crossbows and the hiss of an angry werecat.

Rue went to support her decklings aft, dealing with the first attacker. She flipped her parasol, opening it for acid emission. It was silly to waste lapis solaris on a mortal, but it would, hopefully, eat into the canvas of the aircraft's wings. She reached the railing. The ornithopter was close, a graceful two-seater with one man piloting and another shooting. The decklings were busy loading and firing crossbows as fast as they could. It wasn't easy and most of their shots bounced harmlessly off the engine.

Rue took position, gave them a feral smile, which the decklings appreciated. She held her parasol by the tip and tilted it over the railing. She dialled in the emission and pressed the release button hard, spraying acid upon the attackers.

One of them screamed.

Another shot rang out. A hole appeared in Rue's parasol. *Wonderful, now it's even uglier.*

Rue felt an icy pain in her right arm, worse than shape change, which she hadn't thought possible, and red liquid appeared where her sleeve used to be. *I've been shot,* she thought inanely. Fortunately, she was possessed of enough gumption to pull her parasol back to safety before she began blacking out.

"Tasherit," she called weakly.

The next thing she knew, her bones were breaking and reforming and she was shaking golden fur and feeling the might of immortality in her bones. The extrusion of the bullet from her foreleg, fortunately not silver, was an odd, awful sensation. Her rapidly healing body simply ejected the shrapnel out of the muscle as if passing wind.

Rue should have considered her dress. How many times had she shifted form, and yet she always forgot to consider her dress. *Worths are wasted on me.* She tried to extract herself from the tangle of skirts, hat, and petticoats without tearing anything.

As if agreed upon ahead of time, Tasherit reached in, pulled out Rue's petticoat, and slipped it on. She pulled it up and tied it across her chest, leaving her lower legs bare but otherwise establishing some modesty. She immediately began striding around barking orders. Since these were basically the orders Rue would have given, Rue left her to it. Tasherit had been running drills with the deck crew for months. They were accustomed to obeying her in matters of defence. Rue supposed she'd have to formalise the arrangement – if they survived this journey and Miss Sekhmet stayed aboard.

Percy hauled on one of his nobs and the propeller kicked in. *The Spotted Custard* put on a burst of speed. He puffed them up twice in rapid succession. The *Custard* farted with the exertion but it got them away. A two-man ornithopter with a good pilot could match a dirigible for speed and lateral course correction but hadn't much vertical manoeuvrability.

Tasherit noticed this fact and ordered two more puffs. That put them quite high, not yet in the aetherosphere but close. Everyone's ears were popping. Judging themselves mostly out of danger and giving the decklings and deckhands strict instructions to stay on the alert and fire on anything that closed in on them, Tasherit turned to Rue.

"Should we go into aether cover? I'm assuming they can't follow us there. You'll lose me to sleep, and you'll be mortal again."

"No!" yelled Percy. "It's uncharted, could be an immediate twister or worse."

Rue shook her head as well.

"Right, hold course into the desert. Let's find our missing escort," Tasherit acknowledged.

Rue took a breath and padded over to where Quesnel lay. She sniffed at him, whiskers twitching at the smell of blood, thick and coppery. Rue was lucky she wasn't a true werecreature. The scent did make her hungry but it did not make her crazy. She tried a tentative touch with one paw. He was still warm. Her throat rumbled. *He's alive!* She nosed against his good side, trying for the scent of oil and smoke that always permeated his skin.

She stretched out next to him, for he must be in shock and she was warm in cat form.

Tasherit, judging them safe enough for the time being, came over as well.

"Condition?" she asked Anitra.

"Gunshot to the back, upper right near the shoulder blade. I think it's missed the important stuff. Through and through, thank goodness, out the front here." She pointed.

Rue winced. That had been her favourite place to rest her head.

Anitra continued. "Bleeding's slowed. No sucking sounds. He's unconscious. Blood loss or shock or both."

"Suggestions? Healing mortals is not my area of expertise." Tasherit gave a smile that looked more like a grimace.

"We need it clean. Hard alcohol, the stronger the better. Grain if you've got it."

Tasherit took off.

Anitra evaluated Rue the lioness, her long furry form stretched along the length of Quesnel's body. Anitra had loosened his cravat and unbuttoned his waistcoat and shirtwaist. It exposed him to the cool night air, but they needed to see to his wounds. "Um, Miss Prudence?"

Rue lifted her head.

"Amazing. I mean, I'd heard of your particular skills from Grandfather, but I never thought to see . . . Where is Grandfather? He would be useful right now."

Rue realised that Anitra couldn't go anywhere. She was holding pressure to Quesnel's wound, one hand under his back, the other on his front.

"If you could stay in cat form and keep him warm? Soon, however, it would be better to have you able to issue orders."

Rue nodded.

The missing Floote appeared. He looked older and shakier than ever.

Anitra's face relaxed into profound relief. Until that moment, Rue hadn't realised how frightened the girl was.

"Granddaughter. You are doing well. Hold steady. Is that the werecat or our captain?"

"That's the captain. She was shot, too. Fortunately, Lady Prudence has a quick way of healing. I've asked for strong alcohol to clean the wound. What else?"

Tasherit reappeared with a bottle of Percy's best cognac.

"Good enough." Floote took it. "Now, Lady Sekhmet, we

need linen bandages. If none are available, a clean silk shawl. Lighter colour. Ask Miss Primrose. And blankets, we need to keep him warm."

Tasherit dashed off again.

Several of the decklings appeared with their own blankets at that juncture, the ones they stored about the decks and used in their hammocks. Floote piled them over Quesnel's lower body and arms. They were not very clean, but it was a kind gesture.

Tasherit reappeared with Primrose in tow. Prim had her arms full of linen bandages. Rue had no idea Prim stocked the shipboard medicine cabinet that thoroughly, but she shouldn't be surprised. Primrose did tend to think of everything.

Prim fell to her knees next to Quesnel's body with no care for her lovely dress. In times of great stress, Prim was one of the better elements. She instantly began unfolding the bandages. She was weeping copiously, although it did not affect her efficient handling of the necessities.

Floote grabbed a strip, wadded it up, doused it in cognac, and handed it to Anitra. She used this to swab the back of Quesnel's wound, the side they could not see.

"I've iodine as well." Prim produced a small bottle of the stuff.

"Alcohol first," said Floote. "Iodine once it's clean."

"Should we roll him onto his side?" Anitra wondered.

Floote considered. "Yes, to check. Lady Primrose, you'll be the brace. Decklings, man his legs. On my mark, slow but steady and gentle. We need to know if he is bleeding out."

They rolled.

The entrance wound oozed out from Quesnel's jacket.

"Cut away the cloth," advised Floote. "Anyone have a sharp knife?"

A rustle and then Percy, of all people, appeared and passed over a gleaming blade, from the look of it, silver, kept as sharp as one could keep silver. A vampire's son was raised to take werewolf precautions. He remained looking on, strange given his contentious relationship with Quesnel.

Floote doused the knife with the cognac and then shook his head. "My hand's too shaky. Miss Sekhmet, if you would?"

"It's silver!" the werecat hissed.

"You aren't immortal at the moment."

"Oh, of course. I forgot." She still looked uncomfortable.

Primrose tsked and handed Tasherit the bandages. "You hold these. I'll do it."

Face pale but determined, Primrose took hold of the knife and began to smoothly cut away the layers of fabric around Quesnel's wound. The decklings steadied the Frenchman, who remained blessedly, but scarily, insensate.

Primrose pulled the layers of clothing off. Anitra returned her free hand to the wound in between layers, applying pressure with the alcohol-dampened rag.

Willard came to help her, applying corresponding pressure to the exit wound on Quesnel's front so she might have one hand free.

Once Quesnel's back was clear of fabric, Primrose grimly doused it with more of the cognac.

Rue expected to hear Percy at any moment, objecting to the misuse of his perfectly good bottle of alcohol. But he remained quiet, face set into an odd expression that might have been concern for another human being.

Everyone huddled in, silent as they focused on their ministrations.

One small part of Rue's brain took a moment to be worried about how many were crowded around. *Who is manning our defences?*

She was about to panic when she noticed that Spoo and Virgil were not in the crowd. Nor was Willard's second, Bork. That meant Spoo was still at the Gatling, Bork was seeing to the remaining crew, and Virgil was in the navigation pit – Percy had been training him, by default, as backup navigator.

Rue wanted desperately to have her human form back. But instead she stayed with Quesnel, providing as much warmth as

she could. It was all she was good for at the moment. She cursed
herself for not thinking to hire a shipboard surgeon. As soon as
they returned to London, she'd take out an advertisement. And
for a proper bonesetter, one with real wartime experience, not
one of those academically minded physicians.

Rue growled at Tasherit. She need not sit there holding bandages like a wet blanket! She should get back to captaining the
ship. Rue gestured with her head, tail lashing.

Tasherit shook herself. "Yes, of course. We aren't clear yet.
We don't know what kind of backup those ornithopters had.
Stay on the offensive. You too, Rue. You're no more good here.
Blankets have arrived."

Indeed they had. Someone smart had thought to raid Rue's
closet and brought up a ridiculous fur cape Dama insisted she
pack, despite Rue's protestations that she was "travelling to a
desert country, for goodness' sake."

Quesnel would be plenty warm.

Reluctantly, Rue joined Tasherit in trotting about the ship,
making sure decklings were in place. Occasionally, she reared
up on her hind legs to glare out over the railing into the hostile
night.

Everything looked under control and they'd no followers. Rue
nosed Tasherit towards the poop deck and the helm.

"You want me to take over? That's silly. Virgil's better at it
than I."

Rue jumped down into the navigation pit. Virgil didn't even
flinch at the sudden presence of a lioness. Rue lifted the speaking
tube with her teeth and hissed around it at Tasherit.

"Oh, yes, of course, tell engineering what is happening."

Rue would have liked to give her advice on talking to Aggie.
She suspected that even a werecat with hundreds of years of
experience would be just as awful at it as everyone else.

So it proved to be the case. Although, even with supernatural
ears, Rue could only hear one side of the conversation – tubes
were like that.

"Miss Phinkerlington. Yes. Yes, he's up here. No, I can't send him down. He's been shot. Yes, it is serious. No, you must stay there. We're still in danger. I don't know. Let me ask." Tasherit looked up and shouted over to the medics, "Mr Floote, sir, engineering wants to know if you'd like a hot poker to cauterise the wound?" She returned to the tube. "He says no, and don't be barbaric. Yes, well, I thought it was a good idea, too. But I'm no surgeon. Yes, we should. I imagine the captain will rectify that soon. I don't think you should say such things about the captain!" She held the tube away from her ear briefly and closed her eyes. "That's enough, young lady. No, *you* get stuffed!" Miss Sekhmet slammed down the speaking tube. "What an unpleasant creature. Surely she realises that talk of stuffing to a werelioness brings up taxidermic nightmares?"

Rue rumbled an agreeing cat noise – half purr, half meow.

"Now, how do I get my immortality back? You look healed yourself, and you speaking at this juncture would be a good thing.

"Meroooow!" agreed Rue.

Percy came over and took the helm away from Virgil.

Virgil gave him a look that said clearer than words that even an ornithopter battle full of flying bullets and crossbow bolts was no excuse for a lost cravat.

"That boy," Percy grumbled, sitting down in his customary position, "gets bossier and bossier."

"He didn't say anything," Tasherit defended the lad.

"Didn't need to." Percy was more melancholy than usual. "Rue, could I have a private word? You don't mind, do you, Miss Sekhmet?"

"Not at all. She's all ears." The werecat was perfectly civil to Percy but there was an edge to her voice that suggested she still hadn't quite forgiven him for publishing her existence to the world.

"Exactly why I want to talk to her now. How often does one get to bend Rue's ear without threat of interruption?"

"Rourow!" objected Rue.

Tasherit gave them both an evil smile and drifted back to the crowd around Quesnel to see if anything more was needed. Their balloon escort returned, surrounding them in a friendly flock of chubby shadows. They all hooked into the same southerly breeze and floated along at a nice pace, putting comforting distance between themselves and Khartoom.

Anitra left off her medical ministrations to give a long handkerchief-wave report to the Drifters, under the light of a single lamp. It had a beautiful dancelike quality. The waving handkerchiefs were awfully temping; Rue wanted to bat at them.

Percy snapped his fingers near her whiskers. "Rue! Do pay attention. I'm trying to have a revelatory moment. This is a serious epiphany and you're busy staring at handkerchiefs."

Rue turned tawny eyes on him and blinked slowly. The cat version of, *I trust you. Trust me.*

"Look ..." Now that Percy had her attention, he couldn't seem to find the right words. "I'm sorry. I didn't mean for any of this to happen."

Was Percy being *contrite*?

"I overreacted about the weremonkey publication. I shouldn't have written about Miss Sekhmet without her approval. I treated her like a scientific subject, not a person. It was wrong of me."

Rue gave a *rrupp* noise of agreement, hoping to articulate that perhaps he ought to be apologising to Tasherit, not Rue, but Percy soldiered on. Clearly her *rrupp*s were not nuanced enough.

"And now Mr Lefoux is gravely injured and it's all my fault. If I hadn't let it be known we had a werelioness aboard, we wouldn't be in this mess."

Oh, so now he decides to have a guilty conscience? Rue lashed her tail and grumbled at him.

"It's only that he's so friendly and everyone likes him and he's a great inventor and well regarded and I'm just" – Percy gestured to his rumpled self – "this."

Jealousy? Rue hadn't thought to pry into Percy's motives.

She'd believed his actions spawned from an arrogant belief in his own intellectual superiority. She hadn't realised he felt threatened by Quesnel. Percy never had understood his own value in society or as a friend. He saw other people as either worthy academic opponents, fellow awkward intellectuals, or irrelevant. He applied the same judgement to himself. It was why he found the constant attention of interested young ladies at parties so mystifying. He didn't understand that he was an attractive man, not to mention well connected and reasonably solvent. If only he put himself forward and tried to be polite, he might be just as charming as Quesnel, in his own way. But he never bothered to try.

Rue, of course, couldn't tell Percy any of this. So she lashed her tail and hissed at him.

Percy took this as criticism. "I will try to do better. I never wanted him to die. And now he's injured and we're all in danger and it's my fault."

The last thing Rue needed was to lose another crew member, this time to despair.

"I've ruined everything." Percy was displaying the Tunstell family's flair for the dramatic. "You're one of my best friends and you love him. What if he dies and it's all my doing?"

Percy was slumped over the helm, weighted by guilt. Luckily, they were floating fully in the breeze and needed no course correction, but he'd be pretty darn useless if they were attacked again.

Rue leaned forward and put her damp cat nose against his so he was forced to stare into her eyes. Then she licked his face in one massive swipe of her very rough tongue.

"Rue!" he sputtered, flicking one hand to get her away.

However, it did seem to bring him out of his maudlin humour.

Rue really wanted to talk to him but she needed to break her tether to Tasherit first. It took a whole city block back home, further during dry seasons. They could get the nets out between the balloons and she could run out to the furthest one – that might work. But could they cast nets during fast float? She could get the decklings to lower her in an improvised cat basket. But did they have rope long enough? They could dip up into the aetherosphere, but uncharted currents might yank them leagues away from their escort and course. They could head back to the Nile. Rue could dunk – full water immersion would do the trick.

But all these options would delay their journey. Right now they were making good time and had hunters after them. Aside from waiting until sunrise, Rue could see only one shipboard option for returning to human form. She gave a hiss of annoyance and, tail lashing, made her way down to engineering.

The boiler room was quiet as she climbed down the spiral stairs.

Everything but the absolute necessities had been cycled down, casting the big room in red tones and slowly shifting shadows. They must conserve as much fuel as possible if they were to make it to the source. Most of the sooties were off sleeping or on deck with the drama. Only two still tended the main boiler. Responsible for all the ship's internal functions as well as engine and propeller power, the Big Kettle was never totally cool.

Aggie had, as always, made all the correct decisions. Rue didn't have to like the woman to know she was good at her job.

Rue trotted through, annoyed by how the pads of her paws picked up soot. No wonder Tasherit avoided the boiler room.

"You!" accused Aggie.

Rue blinked at her slowly. *Cat trust, cat calm.*

Aggie seemed to find this annoying.

"Shoo! Get out. You're not welcome here."

Rue sneezed as a bit of coal dust got caught in her whiskers and then continued walking towards the back corner of the room where the preservation tank nested under its tea-cosy cover. She went up on her hind legs and kneaded it with her front paws.

"What on earth?" Aggie followed her.

Rue continued to pick at the cosy.

"You want to get inside it? Why? It's not gassed at the moment."

"Rrrrrourrt," said Rue.

"Oh, of course. If you immerse yourself fully, you should get your humanity back. Certain you want that, *ladyship*? You're a whole lot easier to kill when you're nothing more than prissy human."

Rue continued pawing.

"How could you let Quesnel get hurt? He was only up there because he was worried about you. I told him not to bother." Complaining the entire time, Aggie pulled off the protective cover and cracked the tank top.

Rue leapt inside.

The orange-tinged liquid was cold and weirdly slimy. She took a breath and lowered herself until she was totally submerged in the stuff, even the tips of her ears and tail. At which juncture, the liquid cut off her tether.

She turned back into a prissy human.

Rue reemerged, gasping for air. She'd gone from the painful agony of shift to the general discomfort of the numbing feel of liquid. She hoisted herself out, entirely naked except for the slime, and decided to simply be at peace with this. She was a metanatural after all. She was bound to be naked in front of her crew. The two sooties on duty carefully pretended not to look.

Aggie didn't care. "You've treated him shabby, poor lad. Taking advantage of his expertise and affection. Imagine boldly as to ask for an education of *that* kind!"

So Quesnel told Aggie that, did he? Well, to be fair, I told Primrose. "Now who's prissy?" Rue wiped liquid from her eyes, nose, and mouth. She made a *put-put-put* sound, trying to blow the foul-tasting stuff off her lips.

Aggie almost stomped her foot she was that angry. "You owe him an apology!"

Rue said, "I happen to agree with you. Unfortunately, he was unconscious last I checked."

"Try again!" A pause. "Wait. You agree with me?"

Rue rolled her eyes and marched towards the spiral stairs. "I didn't think he really cared for me."

Aggie followed. "But he's been potty about you since the duck pond incident."

Rue wrinkled her nose. "That's disgusting. I was eight!"

"The *second* duck pond incident, you idiot. Why else do you think he stayed aboard?"

"To see the world? To get away from his mothers?" Rue was flushed with annoyance but tried to keep an impassive demeanour. She was learning much from Aggie's diatribe.

Aggie scrunched up her face. "Well, yes, that, too, but *also* he's in love with you."

Rue's thoughts whirled. *Is Aggie right? Is it really more than a lust-filled whim?* She shied away from the word *love*. It was too bold, even in her own head. The very notion that Quesnel properly loved her was slippery with impossibility, like an oiled ferret. Could they really have that honest constant kind of love? The kind that meant he might stay the whole night in her bed and wake up next to her? He hadn't acted like it so far.

"Oh for goodness' sake, don't you understand anything?" Aggie huffed, her tone modified in her own confusion at Rue's persistent unwillingness to rise to the bait.

By this point, Rue was halfway up the spiral staircase.

"Apparently not. Thank you, Miss Phinkerlington, for a most educational conversation. I may come down and have you yell at me again, next time I need my relationships explained to me."

Aggie put her hands on her hips and glared up. "You do that."

"Now, if you will excuse me, I should get back to the man in question."

"You might want some clothing."

"Yes, thank you, Miss Phinkerlington."

Things were quiet on deck.

Rue, wearing a perfectly respectable brown paisley robe, hair loose but thick with orangeish goop, found the group around Quesnel busy planning to relocate him to his quarters.

Primrose was in charge. "I think we can improvise a litter. It's better to move him to an environment where we can keep him safe, out of the way, and clean. Oh, Rue! Thank goodness. Tasherit said she felt her tether snap. We worried you might be dead."

"Thought Aggie killed you," said a weak voice.

Rue was on her knees next to her chief engineer instantly. "You're awake." She grabbed his left hand. "How are you feeling?" It was an utterly inane question to ask, but everything else she thought of was impolitic.

"Like I've been shot, strangely enough."

"It's no joking matter. You just collapsed. It was horrible." Rue felt the prickles around her eyes from that memory. She shook herself and went on. "Smart of you to choose the right kind. Apparently through-and-throughs heal best. We doused you in cognac as well." Rue caressed his palm with her thumb.

"Percy's?"

"Yes."

"Good. Still, it's a bloody waste." Trust a Frenchman to lament lack of cognac.

"It is not! What better use? We're going to move you below now." Rue let go of his hand.

The two footmen hoisted Quesnel up, trying to keep him as steady as possible. The ship was not made for this kind of transport, but they managed to get him down the main stairs and into the guest room previously occupied by Rue's parents. It was closer to engineering and easier to get to than his actual room.

By the time Quesnel was set on the bed, he'd turned an unbecoming yellow colour and was sweating heavily.

Fortunately, Anitra reported no additional blood loss had resulted.

Rue tried to be nice about it. "You're doing a wonderful job, Miss Panettone. Please don't take this amiss, but did you ask the other Drifters if they had a surgeon aboard?"

Anitra nodded. "I did indeed. I don't want this kind of responsibility. All I've got is limited herb lore and some training for the woman's balloon, when those times come."

"Midwifery?" Rue reached for the outdated term.

"Something like. This is beyond my limited skills."

"We will all do our best. Hopefully Percy has a book on bullet wounds."

Quesnel gave a weak snort. "I doubt it. Books on badminton, possibly, but nothing more useful."

Anitra finished checking on everything. "Are you comfortable?"

"Feeling rather spoiled. Two beautiful ladies tending to my every need."

"He's flirting. He must be feeling better." Rue smiled.

Anitra reached for a small bottle of clear liquid. "Laudanum, for the pain. It'll put you to sleep. Don't take it on your own – we want to keep track of how much."

Quesnel wrinkled his nose. "No fretting there. I loathe the stuff. Makes me feel like I'm being smothered slowly by a flock of malevolent robins, red breasts first, all pushing in against the sides of my eyes."

That was oddly specific. "When have you had laudanum?" Rue bustled about, making certain there was water next to his bed, and a book, and some biscuits.

"Believe it or not, in my childhood I was prone to explosions."

"Liked to experiment, did you?" Rue smiled again, imagining a tiny Quesnel running around mixing noxious chemicals and destroying his mother's laboratory.

"Broke my right wrist once. Seems I have it in for the right side of my body."

"Good thing, too," said Anitra. "Left side this time and it'd be awfully close to your heart."

Rue shuddered.

Anitra helped Quesnel take a nip from the laudanum bottle. He made a disgusted face.

"I can't think of anything else." Anitra turned to go.

Rue nodded. "Send Virgil down, would you, please? Ask him to check in with Cook, eat something, and bring us tea. I'll stay with Mr Lefoux for the time being."

Anitra agreed and left, leaving the door to Quesnel's room wide open. As if anyone still cared about Rue's reputation. As if Quesnel were capable of doing anything with the tattered remains of said reputation. Rue wished he could.

The Frenchman was looking strangely young. His blond hair was darkened by sweat, spiky against the pillow. "Rue, *chérie*, I have to tell you something."

"It's not important." Rue made herself sound reassuring. He seemed so worried. "I'll be nearby when you wake. Send Virgil and I'll come right away."

Quesnel forced his eyes open. "No!" They were heavy-lidded with the poppy's fateful effects. "Robins are here."

Rue drew up a chair and leaned close, wanting to touch him very badly but not wanting to cause any further pain.

"I left it too long, didn't I?" he whispered, slow and slurred.

"What?"

"Why didn't you ever ask me how I felt about you, Rue?"

"I'm frightened."

He was trying to focus on her face through the robin feathers. "No one has ever accused you of lacking courage."

So Rue screwed that courage to the sticking point. "Why did you do as Dama asked, about the preservation tank? You don't owe him any favours."

"Perhaps I wanted to please the father of the woman I loved."

Rue blinked. He said it first. The word was out there, hovering above them, like a tiny explosive dirigible. "Are you secretly traditional and" – she paused, unsure of the right word – "romantic?"

"Perhaps I am."

"But you're so devil-may-care." Rue's stomach went all wobbly.

"You thought that meant I hadn't a working heart under-neath? Perhaps I hide the one with the other." His voice was slurring. His eyes were closing again. "Perhaps I thought you were only curious."

"Oh." Rue was taken with this idea.

"Say it back, Rue. I might not wake up again, you realise?"

"Now who's being melodramatic?"

He smiled, eyes closed.

Rue leaned over and whispered, very quietly, into his ear, "Well fine, then. I love you, too."

He was already asleep.

"Lovely," said Rue into the resulting silence. "Now I have to go through this again."

CHAPTER

SEVENTEEN

The Lost Pride of the Desert Wind

"Go through what again?" Primrose marched into the sickroom.

"Oh, nothing. He's sleeping."

"That's good. Sleep heals."

"Most sagacious, my dear."

Primrose was holding a large reticule, stuffed to bursting, as well as a round pie tin, empty, and an embroidery hoop, full.

"Prim, you know Quesnel doesn't embroider?" Rue shifted a little away from the patient so Prim might bustle.

Bustle Prim did. "But I do and someone should sit with him."

"I sent for Virgil."

"Excellent, then we can take it in shifts."

"You're too good sometimes, Primrose."

"I know."

"What's the pie tin for?"

Prim went very red. "His, um, tender essentials."

Rue blinked and then, "Oh."

Primrose puttered about extracting various additional necessities from the reticule – her embroidery kit, the diminished bottles of cognac and iodine, more bandages, and a jar of calf's foot jelly.

"And the jelly?"

"I don't know. But Mother was always sending round calf's foot jelly to invalids and I knew Cook had some, so I thought I might as well bring it along."

"I'm impressed you stocked laudanum and bandages. Admirable foresight, my dear."

Primrose glowed at the compliment. "We have as complete a medical cabinet as I could manage. I used Steel and Gardiner's recommended list for a family emigrating to India and multiplied the contents tenfold." She stood back, contemplating her stack. "Now, have I forgotten anything?"

"If you have, send Virgil out for it when he gets here." Rue stood, stretching. "Don't be surprised if Quensel wakes up talking of robins."

Rue stayed, looking down at Quesnel while Prim settled in, organising things in that competent way of hers.

His face, without the twinkle and animation, was different, lost. And, of course, she'd never seen what he looked like sleeping.

"Primrose?"

"Yes, Rue?" Primrose put a comforting arm about Rue's waist and rested her head on her shoulder.

"Did I do wrong by him?"

"Did he say he loves you?"

"You knew?"

Primrose wore an expression that said, clear as if she spoke the words, that the entire ship knew.

"Oh." Rue tugged on one hot ear, crestfallen.

"I believe there is a great deal of wagering on the subject. The decklings and sooties have a pool going. Did you say it back? I believe I'll be in for two crowns if you did."

"Does it count if he was sleeping?"

Primrose frowned. "Excellent question."

Rue sighed, letting everything go and bowing to the inevitable. "Why didn't you tell me he felt that way? I might have been nicer to him. Why didn't you tell me *I felt that way*, for that matter?"

"I tried. You didn't want to hear it."

Some day, thought Rue, *I'm going to be saying those words to you. I hope you don't bungle it as badly as I did.*

Primrose looked smug. "Apparently it takes a bullet wound to bring you to your senses."

Rue hung her head, ashamed.

"So, it's done now. You'll have to accept your fate, Rue."

"Why must you be so logical all the time?"

"You know my mother and brother." Primrose's voice held a wealth of familial responsibility.

"Ah." Rue nodded her understanding and left the sickroom.

Perhaps there was a little more bounce in her step than there had been before. Why not just let herself be in love with Quesnel? Seemed silly now, to bother to fight it. Of course, he could still go and die on her and cock it all up. Rue chose to believe he would heal nicely. It was only his right side, after all. Rue knew from intimate experience that Quesnel was left-handed.

Quesnel didn't die.

They set up a rotation of personnel to tend him, with each visitor training the next in keeping his injury clean, changing the dressings, checking for infection, and allowing him the cheat at piquet.

Rue came in one evening to find Aggie, a fireman, a greaser, and two sooties all smoking and dicing with the invalid. The room was full of pipe smoke and laughter. Quesnel had a little colour in his cheeks. Rue had never seen Aggie cheerful before. She might even be called pretty. Although the moment she saw Rue, she scowled.

Rue shook her head and tutted at them for the smoke and the dice because she felt it her role to do so, and then left them to it.

The Spotted Custard was six days following the White Nile southwards ever further into uncharted territory. All the while Quesnel steadily improved. It would take him months to completely mend, and he wasn't out of danger until his wounds sealed over. Anitra worried he'd never regain full use of his right arm. Although by the fourth day he could squeeze Rue's fingers softly when she placed them in his right hand. They chose to be optimistic. Tasherit said that there might be a healer of some kind among her lost pride.

"Why would they have need?" Primrose asked.

"Oh, you think we do not have ... what do you call them? Clavigers."

"A pride lives alongside humans?" Primrose was fascinated.

"We call them our Chosen Ones."

"You make it sound so noble. One step from being a drone." Primrose had grown up in a vampire hive. She was odd about the whole food-source arrangement. She could recognise that werewolves were different, but it still made her twitchy.

Miss Sekhmet looked down her nose at them both in a regal manner. "It is an honour to be one with the Daughters of Sekhmet, to have the option of becoming a cat. Who would not want such a thing?"

Primrose answered, without pause, "Me! Why is it immortals always think everyone else wants to be immortal?"

Rue hadn't given the matter much thought, as by her very nature she would never have the option.

"Lady Primrose, you're an odd duck." The werecat's tone was condescending.

"Not that odd!" Rue leapt to her friend's defence. "Countess Nadasdy had Mabel Dair, the famous actress, in her stable for years. She never asked for the bite. And there's Quesnel's mother, indentured to a hive and never considered metamorphosis even though there's a good chance she has extra soul. She's awfully creative."

"And Quesnel, too, I'd say." Primrose looked at the werecat

with sudden intensity. "Would you have bitten him, if the bullet necessitated it?" Her dark eyes were fixed on the werelioness.

Tasherit dipped her head, embarrassed. "Don't be silly. I've no breeding bite. I'm female."

That surprised the two girls.

Rue narrowed her eyes. "What do you mean? Female vampires are always makers. Female werewolves are always Alphas. It's much harder to survive a bite if you're a woman, but you're awfully powerful once you do. We assumed, you being female and immortal, that it was the same." She looked to Prim for corroboration. Her friend nodded vigorously.

Tasherit gave them the kind of head wiggle that implied they were both insane. "*Lioness*, remember? Can go up high. Not as badly affected by aether. My kind is as different from werewolves in this as in other things. Prides are usually made up of one male lion and several lionesses, whether in natural or supernatural form."

Rue and Primrose exchanged startled looks.

"You mean werecats are mostly *female* immortals?" Primrose was gobsmacked.

"And only *one* male maker?" Rue was slowly puzzling it out. "Like the opposite of a hive?"

The werecat inclined her head. "Exactly. Although, we, too, have a queen."

"So male werecats are harder to metamorphose? And they need to be protected by the others because without him the pride would die out?"

"Yes, poor things. Of course, we need werelions to continue to exist, but the lads are useless without us."

Primrose frowned. "How many of you are left? This pride we are going to find?"

Miss Sekhmet shrugged. "In my pride? A dozen or so last I checked. It's been a while. We aren't on good terms. If this weren't a serious matter of exposure, I would leave them be."

"And how many males?"

"Just the one, Mios. Hopeless buffoon, but sweet. The ladies like him. Not really to my taste."

Rue and Prim both struggled to button down their surprise. They'd never heard of such a thing. The Vanaras, surprising though it was to find a whole herd of shape-shifters that were basically large monkeys, had otherwise fit the general mould of werewolves. They were all male with an Alpha male leader. The idea that a pride of werecats might be mostly female was mind-altering.

An awkward silence descended.

"It sounds lovely," said Primrose finally.

Rue, who'd been raised by large numbers of males on both sides of the family, couldn't even conceive of the idea. She supposed, in general, things would smell better.

They continued south, leaving the desert behind at last. The White Nile became the Sudd, a vast marshland bloated with splotches of floating papyrus islands.

The Drifter escort waved red hankies in discomfort. They were nomadic but never left the desert to float over such an alien landscape. Rue reminded them that they had a bargain, so they stayed, bobbing nervously.

"We will have stories to tell our grandchildren." Anitra was riveted by the swamp, eyes wide in awe. "To see so much green in one lifetime."

Eventually, the Sudd narrowed into a proper river again and on the morning of the eighth day, they floated over the small trading post of Gondokoro. Rue consulted Aggie, who was moderately civil, and said they were fine on fuel, having little used the propeller. Rue instructed Percy to press on.

The Blue Mountains appeared to their left, aptly named. The Nile below them pushed through dense jungle. The next day they passed over Lake Albert, after which the Nile turned white

and perilous, full of waterfalls and rapids. Then, a full ten days
on from their unpleasant stop at Khartoom, low on food rations
and almost out of boiler water, they limped over Lake Victoria.

Lake Victoria was quite the sight from high up, the horizon
an arc instead of a line. It sprawled southwards as far as they
could see. It was dotted with islands, the vegetation around the
edge varied and lush; here and there floated large bright green
blobs of more papyrus.

Even Percy left the helm to stare out over the dark water with
its verdant banks.

"As big as Ireland, they say." He looked pensive. Since his guilt-
ridden confession to Rue, he'd sunk ever more into himself. It
must have taken quite an effort to become even more glum. He
had found a pamphlet on the proper treatment of bullet wounds,
which helped insofar as it supported their initial medical decisions,
but otherwise Percy never again spoke of Quesnel's injury. He had
visited the sickroom and each time emerged looking thoughtful.
Rue wasn't certain if that was a good or a bad thing.

*If Percy is too much for me to have puzzled out in the space of twenty
years, that's not going to change anytime soon.*

"Take her down, please, Mr Tunstell. We could use some
water. Plus everyone would like a bath I'm sure. Take us far out
from shore so we have a clear view of possible attackers. Anitra,
please let our friends know."

Anitra waved her handkerchiefs while Percy de-puffed them
to hover over the lapping waves, nearly cutting the surface with
their propeller.

They spent a few hours sucking water into the boilers through
their large hydrological tube, while anyone who wished took a
dip. Percy wore his smalls, given that his striped bathing costume had been sacrificed for a flag.

Rue ensured a strict rotation so not everyone frolicked at
once. She set watch at the stern, focusing on the place where the
Nile fed out of the lake. She kept the portside Gatling manned
by two at all times. Just in case the enemy caught up to them.

Nothing approached.

By nightfall, Rue was wondering if they had lost the hunters.

They drifted back up, eyes searching below for signs of civilisation. Sekhmet's lost pride was not making itself easy to find. A few villages dotted the shoreline, but they were abandoned summer stations for pastoral nomads.

The sunset over the lake was a sight so beautiful that Rue considered having Quesnel carried up to see. They'd managed to get him abovedecks a few times so he might take a bit of air. But Rue decided that tonight they were pushing things, having lurked around the lake for most of the day. Besides, last she heard, Quesnel was in engineering. Able to sit up for longer periods of time, they'd improvised a couch for him on the viewing platform at the top of the spiral staircase. He wasn't allowed to be there too long, smoke and soot and all that. But he did love being back in his own element and his favourite place, singing out orders through a bullhorn.

Miss Sekhmet appeared next to Rue as soon as the last rays sunk below the horizon.

"So, here we are."

"No sign of your people. We've been circling a while. It's making me nervous."

"You have to know where to look. Ah. There." The werecat pointed to one of the papyrus islands, floating some distance offshore relatively near the mouth of the Nile.

Rue put her glassicals on and stared hard. "It's empty."

"Just go at it."

So they did, taking a slow downward approach. It became gradually clear that the papyrus was not, as with the other islands, floating directly atop the water. Instead it had grown to form an arched roof, beneath which were structures, woven into the reeds. It was a massive barge.

"A fake floating island. That's amazing."

Tasherit looked smug. "It's all engineered. You think a people who built the pyramids could not handle such a task?"

"I don't know what to think."

They de-puffed. Percy took his time to better narrow in on the target. *The Spotted Custard* was considered extremely manoeuvrable for an airship, but she was having a rough time of it. Rue would never admit it to him, but they were lucky to have Percy at the helm.

The Drifter balloons stayed clustered above, like a curious bouquet of bubbles. They lowered a little, then netted together but showed no interest in landing. Rue liked them there above her on the lookout. It felt safe.

The closer the *Custard* got, the less it looked like an island. It was several storeys up out of the water, much higher than Rue realised at first. Strands of papyrus and other vegetation trailed out from the sides, tent-like, which made it look both bigger and more connected to the water. The rounded nature of the reed roof seemed more rounded, as if made of inflated canvas in a massive bubble.

Rue began to wonder how long they would be allowed an uncontested approach. Did the residents intend to entirely ignore a landing dirigible? Or was the place abandoned? Quite apart from all that, what could they moor to? The island seemed to have no protrusions whatsoever.

A flare of light and the sound of air compression came from the island. Followed by a loud, damp *thunk*.

The *Custard* rocked at impact.

"They've fired something at us," said Rue. "Something, uh, squishy? Any damage?"

"Looks like they hurled a big clump of mud at us. Warning shot? No damage." Willard leaned over the main deck railing. "Pain to clean off, though."

They were about three storeys above the island now. Miss Sekhmet, with one of her feral smiles, shifted herself to lioness shape and leapt over the railings, leaving a pile of silken robes behind.

Primrose, who'd been taking tea near the helm on the poop

deck, gave a squeak of alarm and rushed over to look down. Rue flipped her glassicals down from her hat and followed the leap with interest.

The lioness landed, undamaged, and bounced, rather higher and with more enthusiasm than squishy papyrus ought to allow. She came to an ungainly stop, closer to the edge of the island than she likely intended.

"What on earth?" said Rue.

"Not earth, I don't think," Primrose said from the poop deck.

"Agreed."

"Bouncy." Spoo joined them.

"No, Spoo, you can't go after." Rue didn't even need to look at her.

"Spoilsport." Spoo made a face.

Rue laughed. "Back to your station, and watch the horizon, Spoo, not the island. I'll tell you if we need to fire on *them*. But right now, we're assuming they aren't hostile. I don't think bullets would be healthy for that island. It's clearly inflated."

Miss Sekhmet disappeared over the edge of said island, under the tent-like vegetation, presumably heading to where the occupants actually lived.

Primrose jumped down to cross the quarterdeck. "It occurs to me that such a pontoon – or whatever that thing happens to be called – is a very odd place for a load of immortal cats to live. You know, in the middle of a lake."

"Truer words," agreed Rue. "Hold position, Percy."

Primrose hopped off the quarterdeck. "Do you think they'll all look like her?"

"Goodness, I hope not. Can you imagine?" Rue bumped shoulders with her friend as she leaned next to her.

"Rather well, actually." Prim flushed.

"The world is not ready for that kind of excess."

"No wonder the ancients thought they were goddesses."

"I suspect," said Rue, "that the part where they could change into massive lionesses probably did the trick."

"Beauty always helps."

"You should know."

"Flatterer," said Prim.

Miss Sekhmet reappeared in human form. She hoisted herself up and walked back across the papyrus. She was draped in a white robe and followed by two other women. While similarly dressed, neither, thank goodness for Prim's peace of mind, was as beautiful as Tasherit.

"Come on down," the werecat yelled up.

Rue signalled for Willard to bung over the rope ladder. "Right, I'm going. Who else?"

She considered. Circumstances being different, she would have taken Quesnel with her. She looked over her crew. Percy must stay at the helm, in case of attack. Spoo and Willard were needed to marshal troops. Virgil had to keep Percy calm. Aggie must stay in engineering; besides, she'd cock up any diplomatic mission. Floote was standing to one side, looking interested but inconspicuous. Frail as he was, he likely couldn't handle the climb. Anitra was on Quesnel duty down in engineering. Rue didn't mind. She and Quesnel had talked little over the past week; serious matters remained unresolved. But Rue had decided to trust that his intentions towards her were mostly honourable, and his attentions towards Anitra were mostly platonic. Still, that really left only one person.

"Primrose, would you like to accompany me?" It seemed to be a good idea to take a female into this situation. And Prim had many skills, one of which was diplomacy.

Primrose didn't look excited by the rope ladder, but she kilted up her skirts and gave it her best effort. Rue was as graceless as ever but didn't fall off. At the bottom, she pressed her feet down cautiously. The surface appeared to be layers of vegetation mounded up to disguise stretched canvas. They bounced as they walked. Rue suppressed the urge to giggle.

Miss Sekhmet's two companions were of a similar complexion to her with strong features, heavy brows, and unconscionably long eyelashes. They stood tall and graceful with her lean edgy build and catlike grace. But they were not the same family. Their faces were too different. One was fierce and long with sharp cheekbones, and the other was round with a pointed chin and a mulish mouth. *She looks like she gets her own way.*

Tasherit made introductions. "My fur sisters, Queen Henuttawy and Miw-Sher, Lost Pride of the Desert Wind, meet my sisters-who-float, Primrose, and the skin-stalker, Prudence, Pride of *The Spotted Custard.*"

The queen – the one with the pert chin – spoke first. This was correct, given her rank. "A skin-stalker, rare indeed. What bloodline?"

"Roman," said Miss Sekhmet.

They must be asking about my preternatural ancestry. Preternaturals always bred true, so Rue's mother's family, the Tarabottis, stretched very far back.

"We say Italian now, not Roman, yes?" That was the other werelioness, Miw-Sher. At least Rue assumed they were both werecats; hard to know without touching one of them.

Miss Sekhmet nodded, surprised. "You keep congress with the outside world?"

"You are not the only one to have left us and returned, sister," answered Miw-Sher.

"Although, they were sent away willingly and welcomed back with open arms. You are not." Queen Henuttawy's tone was cool.

Rue had always suspected bad blood between Tasherit and her pride; apparently it was very bad indeed.

"Is this skin-stalker your excuse? While interesting, of course, she is not enough to allow you to return." The queen evaluated Rue from down her nose, as if Rue were some kind of question-able pork sausage at a market stand.

Tasherit's face twisted. "I am not interested in returning to you or your pride. I merely visit as a courtesy. I have become known to the outside world and there is no way to stopper up that knowledge. The Daughters of Sekhmet will not be able to remain lost any longer. The British are coming."

"So you led them to us?" Miw-Sher pounced.

"They would have found you regardless. Just as they found the Source of the Nile. Just as they will find the secret you guard. It is a most desirable resource. The British prefer other people's resources."

"Traitor," hissed Miw-Sher.

"Don't be ridiculous, sister. You have been prepared for this a hundred years or more. It was only the Sudd that kept the first explorers at bay. Now there are ships in the aether. Barriers of water are no longer barriers in truth. I'm surprise you have not already been discovered."

The queen looked more annoyed than angry. "Who is to say we have not? And dealt with the threat as we shall deal with this one."

"Well, so. I have delivered my warning and I have brought you a proof."

"You tell us she is a skin-stalker, but there has been no proof." Queen Henuttawy raised one hand. Her attention had never shifted off Rue.

Watching these immortals circle each other verbally was not unlike watching ally cats fight.

"You want me to touch one of you?" Rue asked.

Queen Henuttawy moved forward, barely bouncing. *She must have very relaxed knees*, thought Rue.

One might have expected Miw-Sher to protest the danger to her queen, but apparently this was not that kind of monarchy. Rue supposed that one simply did not question the decision of a cat.

Rue put out her hand, and after a moment's hesitation, Queen Henuttawy touched fingertips.

Rue's bones began their painful fracturing and re-forming, her muscles shifted, her skin stretched and slid about, and her hair crawled over her body to form fur.

She stood on four legs, panting among her clothes, pleased in her choice of attire for once. She had not destroyed her robe. Primrose would be proud.

"There, you see," said Tasherit proudly.

The queen wore a look of profound discomfort. "Mortality feels odd, after so long."

"You wear it well enough," said Miw-Sher.

Queen Henuttawy shrugged, an awkward jerky movement as if she would rather lash a tail. She took a slow measured walk around Rue.

Rue sat under her regard, whiskers twitching. This cat form felt no different than when she stole it from Tasherit. This was no surprise, for that was how it worked with werewolves. Rue stole their immorality, but the animal shape was her own.

"So it is true, a skin-stalker is among us. Is this the end of nights?" Miw-Sher spoke into the silence.

Tasherit rolled her eyes. "Don't be ridiculous. No one believes that old nonsense."

The queen's eyes narrowed. "Still so dismissive. You have not changed."

Tasherit inclined her head. "I have not." She angled her body away from the queen and towards Primrose, a sway of intent like of a compass needle towards true north.

"Ah," said Miw-Sher. The queen flinched.

Tasherit continued. "I have done as I see fit. Heed my warning or not. We will leave you to it."

Queen Henuttawy shifted towards her, fingers reaching to touch Tasherit's infinitely beautiful face. "You could come back to us. Back to me."

Tasherit angled her head in as if scenting the other woman's flesh. "Too late. I've changed too much."

"You look the same."

"And you look mortal. Let us put some distance between you and the skin-stalker, for your own safety."

The queen turned to Miw-Sher, dismissing all the others.

"Well, I'm glad I came," said Primrose, who hadn't said a word until that moment.

"You were necessary nevertheless," assured Tasherit.

"I was?"

"She needed to know I wasn't hers to command any more."

"And how would I help with that?"

"Because now she knows I am yours to command."

Primrose ducked her head, hugely embarrassed. "Preposterous! Whoever heard of commanding a cat to do anything?"

Tasherit laughed. "It is a euphemism. Now, come along." She was smart not to press her advantage. "We should get back aboard."

Rue looked at the swaying ladder in confusion. How on earth was a lioness supposed to climb a rope? But the decklings had already thought of that. They lowered the blasted basket carrier. Rue sighed and leapt into it. They hoisted her up.

Rue stayed a cat once aboard. They were not far enough away yet; her tether to the queen remained.

Primrose, polite to the end, turned back once she had climbed on deck to wave goodbye. The two werecats were already gone.

"They spoke English," said Primrose on a sudden realisation.

"Did you know that housecats, like Footnote, developed a whole set of meows simply to communicate with humans?" Tasherit hoisted up the rope ladder, coiling it back into its proper place.

"What does that have to do with anything?"

The werecat laughed. "We felines have a reputation for always going sideways to get to the point. Put plainly? Cats are good at languages. One of your early explorers, looking for the Source of the Nile, found the Daughters of Sekhmet as well and never left the lake. How do you think I learned the language before I met you?"

"How long have you been gone?" Primrose prodded.

"Long enough to no longer wish to return. But then I was always a wanderer. Rue, should I give the order to lift?"

Rue nodded.

"Take us up, please, Mr Tunstell," said Tasherit.

Rue thought that if Tasherit had decided they were her new pride, perhaps she should make it official and take the werelioness on as first mate. It'd be a good idea to establish a chain of command. Tasherit was clearly up to the job.

Above them, one of the Drifter balloons lit up a lantern and waved it back and forth. Then another. A bell sounded, ringing faintly into the night.

From the crow's nest came a cry. "Enemy coming in fast, Captain. Three, no, four dirigibles. Possible ornithopters strapped to deploy."

Tasherit instantly began yelling orders. "Ready the Gatling gun. Primrose, run and fetch the captain's special parasol and a robe, please. She'll need both once she's human again. Percy, tell engineering we're under attack. Decklings, to your stations, crossbows at the ready. Spoo, Willard, Gatling aimed?"

"Yes, sir!"

"Percy, puff us up."

Rue, still a cat, took her station on the forecastle at the very front near the bowsprit, first line of defence. The enemy dirigibles were moving swiftly in over the lake, coming from the north over the Nile. They weren't firing. Whatever else their intent, they apparently didn't want to destroy *The Spotted Custard* outright. Rue supposed that was a kind of mercy. She, however, didn't feel as magnanimous. Soon as the hunters were in range, she wanted Spoo to shoot.

Percy brought the ship around using the flapper, presenting a smaller target but angled enough so the Gatling could still fire off port side.

They did have a duty to protect the Daughters of Sekhmet and their island. It was time to make a stand.

We don't have a petticoat's chance in hell, thought Rue.

The four coming in towards them were well armed and expertly crewed, no doubt by mercenary types accustomed to battle.

Let's hope they really don't want to shoot us out of the sky.

Tasherit seemed to feel the same. "Spoo, aim for their balloons. If we can tip their ballast enough, either way, we send them up to aether or down to water. They're likely intent on landing on the island. Let's make certain they can't."

The Drifters were doing their best to help. They'd moved to engage, or at least to try to block the path of the oncoming floatillah. But they were nothing more than augmented hot air balloons with little manoeuvrability.

The attackers clearly did not feel compelled to take precautions with Drifter safety. They shot at the Drifters. One balloon ripped asunder, the gondola falling down in a spinning flutter to splash into the lake. It bobbed. Rue hoped fervently that the Drifters could float on water as well as they did on air.

"Floote, can you speak with the scarves, like your granddaughter?"

Floote shuffled forward, nodding.

"Please tell our friends to stay out of it. We bargained for escort, not defence. They're no good in this fight."

Floote nodded, producing two red handkerchiefs that were more like actual handkerchiefs than Anitra's scarves. He could not raise his hands as high, nor were his movements as graceful, but communication occurred.

He put his arms down. "It's no good. Anitra's family agreed to leave, but Ay insists his people stay. He says that the sacred war cats of the ancestors must be protected."

Tasherit rolled her eyes. "And what have the Daughters ever done for Drifters?"

Floote looked at her, startled. "Did you forget? It was your people who gave the Drifters their freedom. They sing a legend of Sekhmet-on-Earth who returned after the others had fled, to free their ancestors from bondage. She led them out into the sands, where her hot breath inflated the first balloon. Hyperbolic, I grant you, but it is their origin story."

"Don't be ridiculous. It was the French who brought balloons to Egypt. We were long gone by then."

Rue yowled at the both of them. Now was not the time for a history argument.

"Quite right," said Tasherit. "Apologies, Mr Floote. If they insist on staying, I can't stop them. Just ask them to keep out of our line of fire."

Floote nodded, looking exhausted, but began waving his handkerchiefs.

Tasherit resumed battle preparations. "Spoo, are they in range?"

"No, sir."

"Hold your fire until they are. We haven't the ammunition for anything more than a few passes. Concentrate on the balloons of the closest ship. Take down one at a time. Keep in mind that bullets go through things – someone we like may be on the other side. Got it?"

"Yes, sir." Spoo's eyes were narrowed and intent. Next to her, Willard manned the crank. No doubt he would be ready to change positions the moment Spoo realised it was too much gun for her small frame. But he wasn't dumb enough to argue with her ahead of time. Spoo's pride took careful handling. It was best to let her figure these things out for herself.

The first dirigible came within range.

Something tore through their own spotted balloon. A carefully aimed shot, not rapid fire but a single very loud bang from an elephant gun. Helium began to outgas.

"Patcher to the balloon!" Willard's voice had already gone to squeak. The leak was directly overhead.

"We've lost puff!" squeaked Percy.

Rue could feel it, too. Her tether, stretching as they rose away from the island, was now back in full as they sank down.

"Meower!" Rue's cat voice was also high. She sounded like an excited kitten.

Rue considered running to engineering for a dip in the tank. She ought to give Queen Henuttawy back her form, for her protection.

But then their attackers deployed ornithopters.

Four short-range airships flapped down and out from their respective mooring. These were similar to the ones they'd encountered in Khartoom, two-man craft designed for nimbleness.

"They're trying to board us!" squeak-yelled Tasherit. "They want to take the ship!"

Rue risked a glance up where two decklings worked furiously to patch the leak. Not fast enough, they continued to sink. And squeak.

Primrose reappeared on deck, carrying the Parasol-of-Another-Colour. She took in the crisis at a glance and instead of hiding as per normal, ran up the quarterdeck to take position on the poop deck near her brother. Rue couldn't order her to safety, but it wasn't a bad decision. Percy could use the support of his level-minded sister. And Primrose did, in theory, know how to use the parasol.

The enemy was approaching them front and port. The Gatling was closer to the rear of the ship, so Spoo was still unable to fire without risk to the *Custard*.

Tasherit strode across the main deck and leapt to the fore-castle. She was now higher up and visible to most of the crew. This also put her away from the helium leak, the better to issue orders. She would stay in human form as long as necessary, but that didn't mean she couldn't fight. She was still an immortal either way, stronger, quicker, and self-healing. One of the deckhands passed her a wicked-looking curved knife, likely purchased at one of the Egyptian bazaars.

Rue joined Tasherit on the forecastle, deciding not to go to engineering. It was more important to have her fighting strong as an immortal than any courtesy to the tribe below.

The ornithopters closed in on *The Spotted Custard*.

Crossbow bolts flew.

"Spoo, Willard, fire a volley," Tasherit ordered.

"Yes, sir!" The voices, in unison, sounded normal. The leak

was fixed, but the *Custard* had lost a considerable amount of helium. And helium was a great deal more challenging to replace than water or coal.

The Gatling gun put a neat line of holes in the lower part of the balloon of an enemy dirigible. That must be their helium chamber as well, for they instantly began to sink, much faster than *The Spotted Custard*. They hit Lake Victoria, not too far from the fallen Drifter balloon.

"One down!"

Rue's supernatural eyesight could make out Percy tugging madly at the puffer, but *The Spotted Custard* was barely maintaining what little height she had. Rue figured they couldn't outgas enough air at this juncture to rise and still keep the balloon from collapsing. They hadn't enough helium left to get them up into the aetherosphere. They were trapped, unless they shed a lot of weight.

The decklings, meanwhile, managed to eliminate one of the ornithopters with bolts. However, the three others made it through their defences, gliding in to land – or more properly crash – one after another on the main deck.

"Gatling, fire at those dirigibles as you like! Decklings, crossbows inwards, watch for flames, and clean that codswattle off our decks!" yelled Tasherit. "Mind your aim. We can't take another hit to the helium. And I'd like to keep my skinny hide intact." With which the werecat gave an animal roar and jumped off the forecastle into the fray.

All was chaos. The three invading ornithopters took up most of the main deck. They'd splintered a good deal of wood, both Rue's beloved ship and their own. The ornithopters were light beasties, practically paperweight, but carried enough speed to do superficial damage. The decklings dashed in and about, clearing the deck, putting out fires, and tossing excess weight over the side.

The six men who'd been inside the ornithopters were now on Rue's ship. They'd jumped clear and were, mostly, ignoring the decklings. Two of the men carried weapons Rue knew all too well, a particular kind of gun that her father had once carried. A particular kind of gun that was pointed at Rue and at Tasherit, to the exclusion of all others.

Sundowner pistols.

"Nobody move," said one of the men.

Everyone stopped and turned.

The six were dressed in the white robes of Egyptian natives but there was no mistaking the leader's origin. He spoke English well enough, but he had an accent and it certainly wasn't Arabic.

It was Italian.

"We've your cat and your captain in our sights. These are silver cage bullets and we don't miss."

Everyone froze.

Rue gave a screeching hiss of annoyance at her inability to speak.

Out of the corner of her eye, she saw Spoo twitch. Fortunately, the Gatling was mounted in such a way that it did not swing around and could only shoot outwards. She didn't think Spoo foolish enough to shoot towards the *Custard*, but she also didn't want to find out if that was wishful thinking.

The Italian eased towards the starboard side.

Rue placed herself between him and Spoo.

He kept his gun on Rue.

He pushed the white robe back from his head, revealing dark hair, thick and black. The moon was now up, and while only a sliver, it was enough to see by. He was extraordinarily handsome. Not uncommon among the Italians, Rue had heard. He was tan with an aquiline nose, like her mother. Both looked better on a man. Come to think on it, there was something of her mother about his eyes as well, large and liquid dark. No one had ever said anything negative about Lady Maccon's eyes. In fact, they were much admired in certain circles. Rue always wished she had got them instead of the Maccon yellow. *Why on earth am I fixated on eye colour at a time like this?*

Rue lashed her tail. She was fixated because he looked familiar. Yet not.

He kept advancing towards her. Which was fine by Rue. There would come a point when he'd be close enough for her supernatural reflexes to be faster than his trigger finger, or so she hoped.

He was focused, intent on her, leaving his fellows to guard Miss Sekhmet and the restless deck crew. Maybe he thought Rue was the real werecat and Miss Sekhmet the captain. That might work out for them. Rue could let them capture her instead. Then soon as they were far enough away, snap. Rue licked her whiskers, imagining the surprise when these collectors suddenly had a mortal in their cage. Tasherit would be left with *The Spotted Custard*, safe and unstuffed.

It wasn't a bad plan, she reasoned with herself. It did, unfortunately, put her in the hands of the enemy. Fine, then, it was a reasonable *backup* plan, if nothing else worked out.

Rue tried to understand the Italian's intent. Did he think to shoot her with a silver bullet in a non-fatal spot and then drag her away? Where to? How would they get off the *Custard*? She didn't see a net. What was his goal in all this?

A voice said, "Don't let him touch you!"

It was an elderly voice.

One of the men not armed with a sundowner shot his pistol.

Floote, at the top of the main stairs, fell with a sickening series of thuds.

Someone belowdecks screamed.

"I said no one move!" The Italian still didn't look away from Rue.

Rue lunged.

He lunged at the same time, wrapping her tightly in both arms.

Rue was shifting, fur becoming hair, paws becoming hands, and tail shrinking upwards. She knew that sensation. Of course she knew it. She'd experienced it on and off most of her life.

The touch of a soulless. The sucking nullification feeling of a preternatural. Her mother's touch.

"Hello, little cousin." The Italian held her, vise-like, from behind. Together they faced an audience of startled *Spotted Custard* crew.

Oh dear, thought Rue, *they were after me all along.*

For why else send a preternatural, unless you had a metanatural to catch?

CHAPTER
EIGHTEEN

Killing Cousins

"I am such an idiot." Rue's voice was sharp in the ensuing silence. "You're not hunting werecats. You're hunting me."

The Italian brought his cheek down to hers. She could feel him smile. "Never doubt we'll kill the monster where she stands. We've no interest in taking her alive. We've no interest in taking any of them alive. But if you come along quietly, we'll leave them be. Promise. For you, my pretty little cousin, are unique."

Rue gritted her teeth and squirmed, trying to break his grasp. Unfortunately, he was a lot bigger and stronger. He was only mortal strong, but that was plenty good enough. Rue rolled her head away from skin contact and caught sight of the Gatling gun to her left. *A gift. From Dama. On my twenty-first birthday.*

"My *majority*. I gained my majority." Dama had tried to warn her. *Without government protection, or us vampires looking out for you, there are people who may want you dead.* So had Mother, in her awkward way, handing over that mysterious secret parasol club. So had Paw, always harping on about safety, always urging her to learn to fight.

"In India, as I understand it. Fair game at last. We started tracking you at once. Took us a while to catch up and, by that time you'd returned to London. It's never easy to get into London these days. And, of course, you've many friends there, don't you, cousin? Not to mention family. But not all the vampires in England, not any more."

Rue could grow to hate this man. "And Queen Victoria cut me loose, too. Withdrew the Crown's protection."

"You've no sundowner weapon, have you, cousin?" He pressed his own sundowner against her side, a cold hard reminder.

Rue had known that Lord Akeldama was her guardian as well as her adopted father, and she'd known it was some sort of deal her parents struck to keep the vampires from killing her. She hadn't realised that it incurred an obligation of protection from all vampires. Now that she was legally an adult, that protection was gone. And then she'd cocked up her legal standing with the Crown as well.

What had Dama said? "Just a little token, Puggle, because, you're all grown up and a fully-fledged independent now, and knowing your family propensities, you're going to need a ruddy big gun." She'd dismissed her parents' concern, thought they were just being overprotective and worried.

Family propensities come wrapped in Italian silk. "Cousin, hmm? I take it Grandfather Alessandro enjoyed dropping his breeches overmuch?"

"Bit of a cad, to be honest with you. Your mother never knew she had an older half-brother, did she? Poor old Dad. Took me in for Templar training, just like him, just like all us daemons get in Italy." His mouth curled against her skin. "It's an honour to be Templar trained. We do God's work. We are weapons of His justice. Doomed to burn in hell because we've no soul to get into heaven. But we work for God while we're here. And that's what counts."

"You trying to convince me or yourself?" Rue kept him talking while her mind whirled. There had to be a way to turn the tables on this man.

"Oh, the little soul-stealer has teeth."

"Who, me?"

"An original, you are. I imagine they want to study you. Maybe cut you up a bit. See how you tick."

"Charming."

"Don't worry, cousin. I won't let them hurt you. Much."

He was focused on her and she was naked. She wondered if he carried any of their shared grandfather's propensities. She wriggled a bit, testing – not a *get free* wiggle, but an *introducing my bottom* wiggle. *Wouldn't you know? It appears he likes curvy young ladies.*

"Stop that."

There came a solid hiss and a wet *thunk*. The Italian jerked against Rue and then slid to the deck, arms loosening about her, although he stayed mostly coiled about her body until he lay slack at her feet. It was an unpleasant experience.

Rue stepped free.

At the same time, she saw the other man with the sundowner gun collapse.

Both men had darts sticking out of their backs. Lefoux-made numbing darts, Rue was pretty darn certain. But who had fired them? Even if Quesnel made it out of bed, he couldn't make it up the stair from engineering.

Rue twisted to look behind her to the poop deck, and there – all forgotten – stood the twins. Percy was wearing Quesnel's wrist emitter, looking frightened but also fierce and set. Primrose was holding the Parasol-of-Another-Colour steady in the firing position. She had it aimed now at one of the other invaders. There was a look of both possession and anger on her pretty face. Rue swallowed a smile. The man she'd shot had been threatening Tasherit.

"Told you that parasol would go with some outfit of yours eventually." Rue grinned at her.

Prim didn't take her eyes off her next target. "I concede the point. Sometimes it is better to be practical than pretty."

"Very nice shooting, both of you." Rue believed in giving praise when due.

"We Tunstells can be practical *as well as* pretty." Now Primrose was grinning.

Percy joined in the game. "I hope you'll excuse us interfering in your little family spat?"

"By all means, carry on, my dears." Rue nodded to her two oldest friends.

Percy gave Rue a most un-Percy like wink and returned to steadying the airship, which was still holding position over the floating island. He seemed to think, and Rue concurred, that if they needed to abandon ship, or crash-land, a bouncy papyrus bubble was a better option than Lake Victoria.

Rue returned her attention to the standoff around her. The odds were now in their favour. Certainly the four remaining men were armed, but not with sundowner guns. And they knew it. They were looking nervous and kept waving their pistols about, trying to decide on targets.

Rue said, without malice, to her crew, "Didn't I hear Miss Sekhmet ask you all to clear the trash off the deck? Well, I fully concur, my dears, and frankly I'm rather peckish. If we could conclude our business with these gentlemen?" The decklings relaxed at her ridiculousness. This was the Lady Captain they were accustomed to. They were even accustomed to her being naked.

A pause.

"And . . . fire!" Rue relished the order.

The decklings and Primrose fired on the four remaining invaders. Spoo and Willard also took the order as an excuse to let loose a Gatling barrage at the enemy dirigibles. Rue hoped they weren't wasting bullets but didn't turn to find out.

Two of the invaders fell, one bloodied and screaming. The other incapacitated by Prim's numbing dart. That was one powerful parasol, and Primrose was an inordinately good shot.

Bork charged one of the two invaders left standing, biffing him on the nose with excellent boxer's form. Tasherit, in a whirl of silk and angled legs, lashed out, turning the last one into unrecognisable pulp with a combination of kicks and punches. She looked like some exotic urn of fine wine, but she fought like an old tankard full off beer, rough and mean and likely to curdle one's innards.

"Tie them up! As tight as you can." Rue thought quickly. "Get them downstairs and locked in the stateroom. Leave a guard with a crossbow and barricade the door. Do we know how long those numbing darts last?"

She looked to the twins.

"I just shoot them." Prim took the opportunity to dial down the parasol and holster it at her side.

"And beautifully, too. Thank you for my part," Tasherit, helping to truss up the miscreants, practically purred at her.

Primrose blushed.

Percy was focused on his navigation. "Ask Quesnel. They're Lefoux make. He should know the expected incapacitation duration for each susceptible species."

Someone tossed Rue a robe. They kept them stashed around the deck these days. Everyone was learning that with both Rue and Tasherit on board, it was better for everyone's peace of mind if robes were handy. And meat snacks. Although in the heat, meat snacks went to pong easily.

Now that the immediate danger was eliminated, everyone ran to other defences. They were low on crossbow bolts and the Gatling was out of bullets, but the enemy didn't know that. The remaining attack dirigibles had drifted away, presumably to recoup.

"Oh dear Floote!" Rue tied her robe and remembered. "Tasherit, are you good up here for a moment?"

"Better than. They're out of range and they've no way to board. Ay looks to be moving into position over them. Might be able to drop a couple hot braziers onto those oiled balloons of theirs. Could use Anitra to ask . . . Oh, I suppose she's with her grandfather?"

"I'm going to see." Rue made her way down the main stairs,

dreading the inevitable sight of Floote's old crumpled body. She hadn't known him long but he'd seemed a decent sort. Knowledgeable. Useful. Agreeable. Loyal even.

There was no crumpled body. There was a smear of blood on the bottom step.

Rue glanced around, confused, and then took two steps to the open hatch that led to the boiler room. She stuck her head in, looking down the spiral staircase.

The muzzle of something deadly stuffed itself into her face.

"Only me." Rue pushed it aside.

The weapon lowered to show the very white face of a sickly Quesnel, who was propped up against his chaise on the observation platform in such a way as to have a clear shot out the hatch.

"What are you doing out of bed?" Rue was instantly worried. He was practically grey and shaking slightly.

"Rue, you're alive! What's going on up there?"

"We were boarded by my cousin and some cronies and it looks like they've been after me all along, not Tasherit. The twins came to the rescue with those darts of yours. Thank you for that."

"What?"

"Quesnel, darling, love of my life, I am in a bit of a hurry. *Things* are happening. I'll explain all the details later. Mruuffph!"

Quesnel grabbed her with shaky arms and kissed her fiercely. She wouldn't have thought he had the strength. And frankly, he didn't really. He was leaning against her for support. It was absolutely glorious.

"I want details on the *love of my life* part, too." He pulled back, still greyish but grinning like a fool.

"If you insist. But later, please? Now, where was I?"

He kissed her again.

"True I *was* there, but . . . oh, yes. Any idea how long they hold? Those darts of yours?"

Quesnel looked like he very much wanted to kiss her again, and while Rue thought that was a splendid idea, she couldn't afford to get further derailed.

"On normal humans, about an hour."

Rue helped her lover back into his makeshift bed. "And on a soulless?"

Quesnel blinked.

"The aforementioned cousin of mine is a Tarabotti." Rue fluffed Quesnel's pillows, fussing about him because what she wanted to do was pounce on top of him and kiss him senseless. Given his weakened state, if she did pounce, he would likely indeed lose consciousness.

"Oh. Oh! Um, should be the same. Preternaturals have normal mortal human chemistry, you know, apart from the lack of soul."

"Excellent. And now Floote. Is he okay? Did . . . ?"

Quesnel's face fell. "Anitra brought him down. It wasn't a direct shot but it's pretty bad. He's too old for that kind of thing. Even older than you might think. The shock likely did it. Heart attack or something. I'm afraid he's dead."

Rue bit her lip in sympathy. "Oh, poor Anitra. Did he . . . was there . . . a remnant?" Rue had never witnessed an unbirth. As with normal births, they were not something an unmarried lady ought to observe.

"Yes."

Rue pressed a glass of barley water on him. "Does he wish for the ghost holder or should I provide transitive services?"

Quesnel sipped, making a face, but his colour improved. "What do you mean . . . ? Oh, I forgot. Metanaturals can perform exorcisms."

"I've never done it, but I understand that's the theory."

"Go down. Talk to them. See what they say. It should be his choice. He has given your family many years of service, in one form or another. Perhaps he wants to rest now."

Rue made certain Quesnel had his bullhorn within reach, so if he wanted to yell instructions at Aggie he could, and climbed down the spiral stairs.

The boiler room was a hive of activity as sooties, greasers, and firemen worked to keep the ship steady despite the loss of helium and the low altitude. Aggie was busy barking orders and ignoring Rue, which suited them both. They were still in the air and that was saying something. Rue felt no need to interfere.

In the far corner, near Quesnel's tank, Anitra was on her knees next to her dead grandfather. Or adopted grandfather. Not that the particulars mattered. Rue always felt as if Dama were her blood relation, adopted or no, and she knew how awful she would feel if he died.

Floote's wrinkled face was as impassive in death as it had been in life. Up from his body, in a silver wispy thread, came a long faint shimmering mist. It was struggling to coalesce into a proper ghostly form. It was amorphous. Floote needed to remember what he looked like in life.

Then, as if being dead were a momentary lapse, like forgetting how to spell a word, Formerly Floote popped into non-existence. He looked, Rue figured, as he might have appeared when he was valet to her grandfather, younger, old-fashioned clothing. Obviously, his clearest memory of himself was from that point in his life.

The ghost looked around. He took in Anitra's crumpled form and then glanced thoughtfully at Rue. She kept herself well away, not wanting to risk contact with his body lest she sever his tether and with it his last connection to the mortal plane.

"Odd sensation." His voice had a new breathy component, which was weird considering there was no breath at all behind it.

He seemed more animated as a ghost, but still nondescript, wearing the ghostly representation of valet clothing from sixty years ago. Rue wondered if he had been less reserved back then and sobered over the years, or if he simply conceived himself as more lively than he actually was.

"Formerly Floote." Rue gave him the honour of his new title. "You are not bound to stay if you do not wish it. I can see you released."

Formerly Floote sighed. Wisps of himself shifted with an

imagined breath. "There is much still unfinished. I believe I should like to stay a little longer. But not to poltergeist. That is too undignified an end."

Rue was relieved. "We have the tank for you. You could keep preserved quite a long time in that, if you like. Otherwise, the moment we hit aether, you would, uh, cease."

Formerly Floote rotated slowly in the air, to look at the tank behind him. "Ah. Was this Madame Lefoux's idea, or Lady Maccon's, or your young man's?"

"Lord Akeldama's."

"I should have known. It was meant for me all along?"

"He thinks I need you."

He drifted a bit from side to side. "And do you?"

He had known, back on the deck, of her cousin's soullessness. He had known, with the Drifters, how to negotiate for help. He had told her some of her mother's history. He had more to tell about her grandfather's. And, quite frankly, Rue liked him. He was calming. Not a lot of people in her life were. He seemed like the kind of man who needed to be needed, even if he was dead.

"Yes." Rue raised her chin. "I rather suspect I do need you."

"Then I'll stay." There was no hesitation in Formerly Floote's voice. His posture was perfectly straight. He was already focused on stopping a propensity to waft.

With Rue unable to touch the body, they had to get Aggie to help load it into the tank. She wasn't as awful as she could have been, for Anitra's sake. Even Aggie had sympathies for the bereaved.

"I don't know about leaving him to haunt us all down here," she did grumble at Rue.

"We'll figure out a better spot," Rue assured her calmly. "I'll want to make certain his tether stretches to most of the ship, so he has freedom of movement. It'll probably involve moving the tank."

Aggie frowned. "We going to have some floaty wafting into our private quarters of an evening?"

"I'm sure Formerly Floote will respect everyone's privacy. Miss Phinkerlington, do you think you might save your ire, just this once, for a later date? Say, tomorrow afternoon? I promise I will come back and you can rail at me all you like."

"Promise?"

Rue nodded.

"Oh very well, then, puff off."

Rue puffed.

Abovedecks, not a great deal had changed. They were still at an impasse. The Italian was tied up and locked in the stateroom with his best men, but no one else could really go anywhere, either. The remaining dirigibles were floating out of range, watching and waiting. They'd gone down to retrieve their fallen comrades. Decklings reported that the downed Drifter family had made their way to the werecat's island, where they had disappeared beneath, presumably into the reluctant care of the still hidden Daughters of Sekhmet.

Anitra followed Rue up the main stairs. Her pretty round face was soot-stained and tear-streaked. She managed some handkerchief communication, which informed them that the crashed Drifter ship changed matters. They now couldn't decide whether to stay and help or go and leave these foreigners to deal with their own mess.

Anitra rubbed at her face with one of the handkerchiefs. "They feel their agreement with you is concluded but they also feel a historical obligation to the Daughters."

Rue sighed. "We have a bigger problem. Even if we could get away, the *Custard* doesn't have enough helium to attain aether. I'd risk an uncharted current at this juncture, but we can't even try. We're pipped."

Tasherit squinted. "I might be able to help there but it'll take Queen Henuttawy's approval. She's difficult to persuade.

Especially by me. Anitra, you know much of the history of our people, and you are connected to Lady Prudence's history as well. Would you consider talking to her?"

Anitra's eyes shone. "Meet the lost pride? I would be honoured."

"Very well, then, Captain, if I may be excused?"

Rue inclined her head. If Tasherit really thought the werecats could help, Rue couldn't think of a better plan. "Very well. But please be careful and try not to get them any more angry with you."

Miss Sekhmet transformed into a lioness and Anitra, cautiously, took a seat astride her back.

Tasherit padded to the edge of the deck and leapt over the rail, coming to land, bouncing lightly, on the island below. The two disappeared beneath.

Rue wasn't sure what to expect. What would be the sign of a successful negotiation? Lioness warriors appearing atop the island? The deployment of a massive weapon of some ancient and exotic type?

Fifteen minutes later, what she got was the most remarkable thing she had ever seen in her life. And Rue had once witnessed a whole party of American tourists actually refuse to drink tea, in a London teahouse, so that's saying something.

The island below them took flight.

Percy swore and kicked up the propeller to get *The Spotted Custard* out of the way or the darn thing would have crashed into them.

Narrowly missing a collision, they puttered out of danger as the massive thing took to the skies. Whatever had fastened the island to the bottom of the lake not only held it floating on water, but had held it fast to the earth as well. Cut free, the island lifted up, dripping long strands of vegetation, and mud, and a few surprised guppies.

Thus the island revealed itself to be a massive airship, larger than any dirigible Rue had ever seen. Ten times as big as the biggest of Queen Victoria's troop transport floatillah. As big as a whole city block or a small hamlet. The island top bulged, not just one balloon, but multiples, rammed together, like a bouquet of marigolds. Only they were all brown and dirty. So it was more like a bouquet of cow muffins.

It rose up in majestic steadiness. It wasn't using heat like a hot air balloon; this airship was helium-filled – a very great deal of helium. Ropes kept the bouquet attached to what had once been underwater living accommodations. These dripped and stretched and held until the whole thing plucked itself out of the water, like a water lily. It was amazing. No less so for the reality of the fact now facing them – a pride of lionesses had lived underwater for decades and were now taking to the skies.

Rue grabbed a spyglass to look in wonder at the amazing craft.

The upper deck – which had likely rested directly above water level, hidden by the trailing vines – was occupied by a pack of people. Strong-looking women in filmy draped gowns strode about manning the airship, Olympian goddesses acting the part of decklings. That must be the pride. There were others with them – Chosen Ones, Tasherit had called them – the werecat version of clavigers. The mortals who hitched their lives to the Daughters of Sekhmet, sink or fly. Rue spotted the fallen Drifter family helping to crew the massive airship.

Rue saw Tasherit, pacing the deck nearest to them, waiting for the opportunity to leap. Anitra was riding her. The Drifter girl had a long tube tucked under one arm. It stretched up to one of the massive balloons above, like a sipping straw.

"Percy, bring us about and nudge towards them. We have friends who want to return home. I think they bring a gift."

From the crow's nest, Rue heard the call. One of her decklings was still doing his duty – keeping eyes to the enemy and not focusing on the behemoth next to them.

"Hostile dirigibles are fleeing, Lady Captain. They don't fancy going up against that beauty."

Rue put down the glass. "I don't blame them." She couldn't

see any weapons on the werecat's ship, but that didn't mean there were none. Immortals were usually prepared for combat. Even her Dama, who mostly fought with words, was a dab hand with a war scythe when he was in the mood.

Rue moved to the forecastle to confirm. The enemy was indeed speeding away, puffing up as fast as possible, until they were mere specks. Eventually they blinked out, jumping into the aetherosphere and damn the consequences of uncharted currents.

Rue let out a low whistle. "Guess we now have prisoners rather than hostages in our stateroom."

Percy held them steady as the cumbersome former island nudged in close.

Rue strode the length of her ship, across the main deck, avoiding the scampering decklings; those who weren't transfixed by the monstrosity next to them were still clearing away crashed ornithopter guts.

Rue jumped up to the quarterdeck and from there to the poop deck, coming to stop next to Percy, Primrose, and the helm.

"They don't have flapper rudders or propellers." She handed Percy a spyglass but they were too close for him to really confirm her assessment.

Percy waved the looker away. "Big and unwieldy, I understand."

"Bring us in as near as possible."

Percy bit his lip, sweating slightly, but did as instructed.

Primrose flipped her glassicals up. "She can't really be considering what I think she's considering." She looked to Rue for support.

Rue gave one of her maniacal grins. "Cats can jump pretty far."

"That's insane." Prim let out a little shriek of awe and fear as Tasherit took a running start and then leapt with a gloriously amazing flex of muscles from the long low deck of that ancient watery craft to the new, if damaged, main deck of *The Spotted Custard*.

The lioness slid quite a bit on landing, almost skidding right over the opposite side, where the railing no longer existed due to crashing ornithopters.

Anitra, much to everyone's amazement, managed to keep hold of the tube from the bigger ship, as well as her own seat on the werecat's back. When Rue ran to meet them, however, it was less impressive. She'd been strapped on.

"Here." Anitra handed Rue the tube. It was capped off and very light, seeming to want to float away.

Rue wrapped both arms around it lovingly. *Helium!*

"Helium," Anitra explained unnecessarily, on a gasp of breath. She was drawn with fear, tear tracks still visible on her face, brown eyes wide with awe at her own daring. "They have plenty. Turns out they've been mining vast parts of Africa for years. Then hoarding the helium here."

She untied herself while Rue issued orders to deckhands, and deckhands to decklings to get their squeaker straw hooked into the helium port above.

"Make certain those patches hold." Rue wasn't about to outgas such a precious resource again.

The crew hopped to with renewed energy. It had been a long night. Everyone was starting to flag a bit, but this was beyond exciting, and resources were resources.

While they refilled, Anitra explained that the Daughters of Sekhmet had been arguing about coming to their aid when the Drifters sought refuge. When Ay's balloon bobbed down to collect them, a dialogue had ensued. The cats agreed to help, not for the sake of Rue and her crew, but for the sake of reuniting with the Drifters. "It's a romantic notion, lost tribe, lost pride, returning to a nomad's life. Leaving the lake for the desert. They are ready to rejoin the world, I think. Ay can be most persuasive. He didn't become a leader solely through skill in trade."

Miss Sekhmet grunted out a cat sound of disgust.

"Whether or not they are really ready for the world, they are excited to be part of a culture that reveres cats once more."

Primrose raised both eyebrows nearly into her hat. "Those poor Drifters."

Tasherit twitched her whiskers.

"Well, you do get rather superior, you shape-shifter types." Primrose verbally twitched her whiskers right back. "Yes, I include you, Rue. I *like* the Drifters. They seem a decent sort."

Anitra smiled. "I think my people will do fine. There will be growing pains, but watch this."

The Spotted Custard finished the helium refuel and let the tube go. It floated back and was gathered in by the werecat crew.

While Percy checked to make certain everything was in decent working order aboard *The Spotted Custard*, the massive airship floated away from them. The Drifters circled in around it, looking very small next to such a great lumbering thing.

The Drifters netted out, one after another, arranging themselves so they seemed to orbit the werecat's craft, colourful bumblebees to one tumescent muddy flower.

Together they caught a breeze and began drifting northwards towards the Sudd and the desert beyond. Homeward for all of them.

CHAPTER

NINETEEN

Affairs and Affaires in Order

"Well, that was fun." Miss Sekhmet broke the ensuing reverent silence by returning to her human form.

"They look good together." Primrose sounded as if she were observing a newly married couple. She turned to Anitra. "You're staying with us?"

Anitra turned to Rue. "You don't mind?"

"Course not!" Rue grinned at her. "Stay as long as you like. I'm sure Formerly Floote will love that."

"I won't be a burden?"

"Goodness no! You're handy with your medical herbs, fluent in various languages, and accustomed to floating. We're lucky to have you. Primrose will put you on the roster. Won't you, Prim? Assign permanent quarters and whatnot? Oh, and we have a resident ghost now. You'll need to decide where to install his tank so that he has the most shipboard access. Quesnel will help with that."

Prim held up a hand. "We need food, Rue."

"And fuel," Percy said. For some reason he was looking particularly pleased about something. He was letting the *Custard* drift and not running the propeller any more.

"How long do we have before both are exhausted?" Rue snapped to business.

"Two days." Prim knew without having to check her ledger.

"Four with minimal use. One and a half at full power." Percy didn't call the boiler room; no doubt he, too, had already checked.

It's like we're a proper dirigible crew at last! Rue was secretly delighted, but she did give their situation some thought.

She came to a decision. "We make for the aetherosphere."

"Rue, it's uncharted," Percy protested, but his hand was already hovering over the puff button.

"So we chart it. Find something that takes us, what, east-wards? Where do you think the nearest major city is?"

"Zanzibar," said Percy promptly. "But that's the other side of Kilimanjaro."

"Zanzibar it is."

Naturally, he found them a current. Percy may be a pill of par-ticularly fine vintage, but he was awfully good at navigation. He was ridiculously pleased with himself as a result, making murmurs about reporting *his* new current to the Royal Geologic Society and whether he could convince them to name it the Tunstell Thoroughfare.

Nearly everyone who could be spared went to bed the moment they hit the grey, leaving Percy and a skeleton crew up top in case anything more went wrong. Miss Sekhmet, of course, was dead to the world regardless. Formerly Floote stayed trapped in the ghost holder while they were in the aetherosphere. Everyone else went willingly to their respective beds.

Except Rue. Rue went to Quesnel's bed.

They'd moved him back from engineering to his improvised sickroom, much to his disgust. Rue promised he could go back to his platform in the boiler room once he got some sleep.

They were both beyond exhausted.

Rue insisted Quesnel take a little more laudanum because he

was back to looking positively awful. He agreed to a dram *only* after she settled on the bed next to him, trying not to jostle him.

"Where are we off to now?" He snaked his good arm around her, tugging her close against his side, and began stroking her tangled hair in a meditative way.

"Zanzibar, we hope. We'll catch a restock and a refuel there."

"And then?"

"Got us a stateroom full of prisoners. I'll turn them over to the German authorities as poachers. Except my dear cousin. He's staying with us."

"Oh yes?"

"What, shouldn't I get to know my family better?" Rue gave a vicious smile.

"And by *get to know* I'm assuming you mean with a few sharp objects? Try not to cut off anything important."

"I don't like being hunted. I thought I might take the time to instruct him as to how *much* I don't like it."

"That's my sweet gentle girl. And then?"

"Exploring. If there are werelionesses and weremonkeys, what else might there be out there?"

"Other kinds of vampires, like the Rakshasa." He wasn't trying to put a dampener on her enthusiasm – just trying to keep her realistic.

"Eww. Yes, but also new and amazing creatures we haven't even dreamed of! Immortals lost to myth and history and ... Oh, it will be *such fun.*" Rue's zeal was arrested by a sudden fear. She turned against his side and leaned up on an elbow to look into those amazing violet eyes.

"You'll stay?"

When Rue had first pulled together a crew, she promised the officers it would only be temporary.

"Do you want me to stay?"

"You'll have to fix this kefuffle with Percy."

"He's staying?"

"He likes this life. Won't ever admit it, but he *does*. Secretly always had a flair for drama and adventure, despite his hermit tendencies."

"And Primrose?" The poppy was starting to slur his speech. "What a silly question. Of course she is staying."

"She still claims to be engaged. We'll have to settle that when we return to England. But for now, yes."

"Which means Tasherit is staying." Quesnel smiled at her.

"And Anitra." Rue smoothed back his hair, the strands soft against her fingertips. "And Formerly Floote."

"About Percy. We've come to an agreement."

"Anything to do with his wearing your wrist emitter? You know he saved my life with that thing."

"As he should. We've agreed to co-publish. Of course, we can't decide on who gets to be first in the byline, but . . . "

Rue laughed.

"So you *do* want me to stay, *chérie*?"

"For as long as you're willing."

He smiled. His eyelids were beginning to close whether he willed it or not. The robins and their feathers were pressing in. "I have a great deal more to teach you. Years and years worth."

"Should we marry, do you think?"

"That'd likely make it easier. With the lessons, I mean."

"I do love your lessons."

"And me?" His pansy eyes opened wide and winning; perhaps the laudanum hadn't quite taken him yet.

"Yes. I very much love you, too."

"Thank goodness." The poor boy was shaking ever so slightly. "I really thought you'd never take me seriously."

"I wouldn't go overboard if I were you." Rue bent and peppered his neck with little kisses, careful to avoid the bandages. He squirmed a bit. "Hold still."

"Don't tease, *chérie*."

"Don't you want to know how well I remember said lessons?"

"More than you could possibly imagine. But I'm not exactly capable of a full assessment at the moment."

Rue chuckled and relaxed down next to him. She did want to do more. But he was right: he was still recovering, and apparently, they would have the rest of their lives to pursue this particular line of study.

He was drifting off. The lines of pain pulling on his face eased. The happiness remained.

"You'll sleep here?" He pulled her as close as he could with his good arm.

Rue felt a spike of giddy joy. So he *did* want to sleep next to her. "All night?"

"I promise not to snore if you promise not to turn into a wolf, or a lioness, or a mongoose, or any other odd supernatural thing next to me."

"Agreed," said Rue.

Author's Note

Place and street names in this book (when not entirely fictitious) are based on those listed in Amelia B. Edward's *A Thousand Miles Up the Nile* (published in 1877) and written on maps of Africa from the 1890s. Spelling is authentic to the time period, e.g. Assûan, Wady Halfeh, Abu Hammed, and Khartoom.

Acknowledgements

This one is for my fans, with particular love to all who have taken time to reach out and connect with me over the years. You know who you are. You who started fan groups and helped moderate them; who wrote reviews and asked for interviews; who created costumes, artwork, and delicious baked goods – Skye, Ty, Ris, Katie, Stephen, Nicole, Dick, Jami, Clinton, Veronica, Angelica, Hannah, Claire, Christine, Amanda, Bethany, Miss K and the St Louis Parasol Girls, and so many more! Your support means everything. I feel like I have enjoyed life's greatest gifts: to be blessed with many friends.

You see, I have always written, but without you (yes, you with the eyeballs reading this now) I'm only a writer, not an author. When a reader takes time to reach out to me the circle completes and I know I'm not sending words out into an empty void.

Thank you.